FARSHORE CHRONICLES

BOOKS 1-3

JUSTIN FIKE

FALLBRANDT PRESS

BOOKS BY JUSTIN FIKE

Farshore Chronicles

Shadows of the Past: Companion novella

* * *

A Thief in Farshore
Into the Shattered City
Crown of a Mad King
Vaults of the Undergloom
Flowers of Belhame
Siege of Farshore

* * *

Farshore Chronicles Box Set: Books 1-3

For all the misfits, friends, and rogues
who walked this journey with me.

FOREWORD

The Farshore Chronicles Was Born Out Of A "What If?"

What if the discovery of the New World had also included the re-discovery of myth and magic?

What if those hearty pioneers who stepped off the first ships had discovered elves ranging through the forests, dwarf pirates prowling the waves, feral halflings haunting the southern jungles, and all the horrible monsters and wild magic that had shaped their folklore and ancient legends hiding within every cave, hollow, and lost ruins within a hundred miles?

I used that idea as the starting point for a tabletop RPG campaign I created for a group of friends years ago, and it stayed with me long after the game ended. Many years, one Masters Degree in Creative Writing, and more cups of coffee than I care to admit have come and gone since then, but A Thief In Farshore finally made it from my brain to the page. Inspired by the colorful, swashbuckling action of D&D and 90's fantasy greats like R.A. Salvatore, Mercedes Lackey, and Raymond Fiest, the Farshore Chronicles are basically the kind of books that I combed my library shelves trying to find more of as a kid. Magic, monsters, epic duels, cursed cities, romance, betrayal, ghost armies, demon hordes, lost gods, and quite possibly the end of the world await!

I release a new Farshore Chronicles story every month, and will keep right on doing that until I've released all 12 books by late 2020. As an avid reader myself, I know there's not much worse than finding characters and a world that you love, and then learning you'll have to wait months or years for the next release. Thankfully, you can read this book safe in the knowledge that the next installment of Charity's adventures is right around the corner if it isn't available already.

The Farshore Chronicles Books:
1. A Thief In Farshore
2. Into The Shattered City
3. Crown Of The Mad King
4. Vaults Of The Undergloom

So, thanks for choosing to spend some of your valuable time with Charity and her friends, and Happy Reading!

A THIEF IN FARSHORE

FARSHORE CHRONICLES BOOK 1

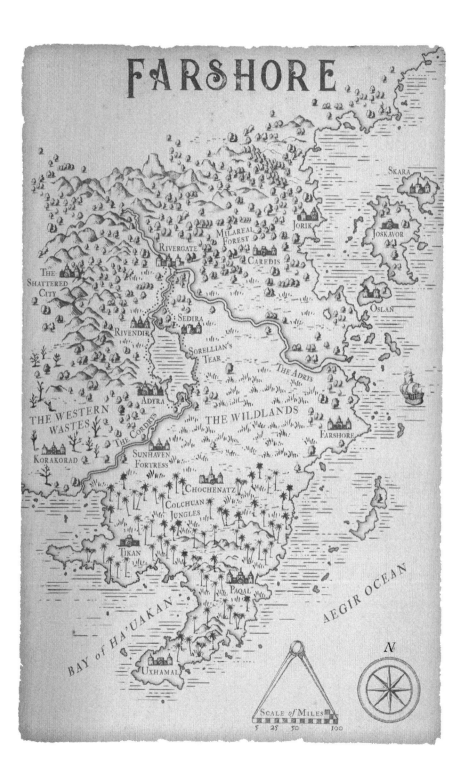

FARSHORE

SKARA

JORIK

JOSKAVOR

MILAREAL
FOREST

RIVERGATE

CAREDIS

THE
SHATTERED
CITY

OSLAN

SEDIRA

RIVENDIR

SORELLIAN'S
TEAR

THE ADRYS

ADYRA

THE WESTERN
WASTES

THE WILDLANDS

THE CORDRYS

FARSHORE

KORAKORAD

SUNHAVEN
FORTRESS

CHOCHENATZ

COLCHUAN
JUNGLES

TIKAN

PAQAL

BAY of HA'UAKAN

AEGIR OCEAN

N

UXHAMAL

SCALE of MILES
5   25   50   100

JOURNAL ENTRY

The Farshore Chronicles
    From the quill of Charity The Godslayer
    Penned by her own hand this 1576th year of Jovian's Wise Rule

Legends always outgrow the truth.

Just because I became one doesn't mean I'm ok with that.

Sure, my story has it's share of swordfights, wild magic, new love, horrible monsters, vengeful gods, and last-ditch heroics. But there was also more mud, blood, fear, pain, and loss along the way than any of the tellings I've heard have ever acknowledged.

Saving the world takes a toll on a person, and I'm sick and tired of hearing scholars and temple cantors tell our tale like we glided from victory to glorious victory on the gods' own wings while skipping over the price we all paid along the way.

That's why I finally decided to pick up a quill and write it myself. I'm going to tell you about all of it; good and bad, ugly and glorious. But in order to do that, we have to go all the way back to the beginning, to the day when a girl who didn't know half as much about the world as she thought she did first stepped off of a prison ship on the shores of a strange new world.

1

I'd only been breathing the air of the New World for a few minutes and I already hated it. No rot of open sewage, no horse's sweat, or dust clouds stirred up by ten thousand pairs of feet on market day. Just air so clean and cold it burned the back of your throat, full of salt from the sea and pine sap from the forest just beyond the docks.

"State your name, prisoner."

"It's Charity."

Three months at sea and he hadn't bothered to learn my name. To be fair, I hadn't cared to learn his either, or the names of the other legion soldiers who'd been sent to make sure our chains stayed locked tight during the voyage. Each one looked just like the rest; black hair that had long since outgrown regulation close-crop as days turned to weeks, noses beaked sharper than the bow of our ship, and brown Byzantian skin that had only browned further beneath the fierce sun that beat down on the upper decks each day.

The soldiers had spent the entire trip complaining about the ill fortune that had posted them to a ship sailing to the ass end of the world and taking their bad temper out on those of us chained below decks. The whole journey had been miserable, but the pointless chains they fastened to our ankles every evening had been the worst indignity of all. Where did they think we would escape to, with nothing but rolling sea waves stretching to the horizon in every direction?

He stared at me for a moment, waiting for a family name to go along with my given one, but I had none to add. The Daughters of Vesta had only given me the one when they'd swept me up off the streets, and it was all I'd taken with me again when they'd thrown me out.

"Fair enough, girl."

He marked it down in his ledger, then gestured down the gangplank. I wobbled my way down the length of wood as best my sore and sea-worn legs could manage and turned to look back at the hulk of timber that had been my prison cell for three long months. The *Typhon* was a sturdy, ocean-going vessel. Even a street rat like me could see it was nothing like the sleek galleys which glided through the calm waters of the Mare Nostri back home.

Home. The word still sent a twist through my guts. If you'd asked me back before the magister had sentenced me to slavery and servitude here in their new world, I would have told you that I had no home. Only Byzantia's cobbled streets and twisting alleyways, and the crawlspace above the ovens of the bakery on the Plaza Chrisari in winter. Now that Byzantia and all the other cities of the Imperium were lost to me forever, I found that I'd had enough home to miss after all.

I shuffled down the dock with the other prisoners, linked together as we were by the heavy chain that the ship's crew had retrieved from the stowage hold when we'd first sighted land. The dock led from the deep water where the *Typhon* sat at anchor to a forested shoreline broken by a collection of rough-hewn buildings and dirt tracks that ran along the waterfront. Two of the buildings were large enough to serve as warehouses, and one even had a small canal with a winch dock for punts to pull in and unload cargo, though for now it sat idle. I saw the Consortium's sign hanging over the door of a merchant and lending exchange, a small tavern that was far too quiet for this late hour, and a collection of houses whose walls and beams still bore the white scars and loose splinters of the axe that had planed them.

A few souls had gathered at the end of the docks to stare at the ship, and at us, in undisguised glee. I had no doubt that our arrival was the most exciting event these docks had seen in a long, long time.

"This is Farshore?"

The man chained in front of me kept scanning up and down the coast as though he expected the rest of the city to emerge from the trees at any moment. The despair in his voice would have been comical if I hadn't been feeling the same way myself. I'd known the colony was young, but I'd at least expected something that a country peasant might be tempted to call a town. All I could see above the small collection of rooftops were trees, rocks, and endless sky ahead of us. All I could hear was a looming green silence broken only by the harsh calls of birds I didn't recognize, and the unbroken rumble of the ocean surf at our backs.

"Don't be daft," one of the *Typhon's* sailors snorted as he walked beside us down the dock. "This is just Shoreside. The governor's keen on turning it into a proper port town. Wasn't long ago this was just a dock and a stretch of dry beach. The city lies inland a ways."

A half-dozen soldiers wearing the same legion breastplates and short blades as the one who'd taken my name on the ship waited at the end of the dock. They looked bored, but they unlocked our chains, sorted us into groups, and loaded us into the three wagons that stood waiting with a tired kind of efficiency. The driver snapped his whip, my wagon jolted, and we were off.

"Divines preserve us," whispered the stocky blacksmith on the seat beside me as he made the sign of Jovian's Wise Eye with his shackled hand. His failing business had left him unable to pay his debts, and then in irons aboard a prison ship, which he'd spent the better part of the passage complaining about to anyone who would lend him an ear.

"They've done a shit job of it so far," I said. "Don't see a reason we should expect that to change now."

"Hold your tongue, girl," said the pudgy seamstress seated across from me. I had no idea why she was here, but she hadn't offered her story during the trip, and I hadn't cared to ask. "Or if you must tempt ill fate, at least wait until I'm not seated so close to you."

"Who's to say the gods can even see us from across the waves, or stretch their oh-so-exalted and glorious hands far enough to reach us if they could?" I snapped at her.

"The Divines see all, know all, and are in all."

She spoke the familiar words with reverence, as if they offered the ultimate answer, though they still sounded as hollow as ever to my ears. "We are alive, are we not? What greater sign of their favor do you require?"

I spat over the side of the wagon in answer but decided to waste no more words on her. The passage had taken its toll, true enough. Seven of the forty-one souls who'd begun the trip had perished before we made landfall, but I saw no great Divine hand in my survival. I'd lived because I was too damn stubborn to do otherwise. I had no great hopes for my future here in Farshore, but I'd be damned if I was going to meet my end retching out my guts in the dark, and that was all there was to it.

I rubbed at the chafed and swollen band where the heavy chains had worn into my ankles during the voyage, and thought about how easy it would be to dive over the side of the wagon and disappear into the tree-line before anyone could stop me now that they were gone. Easy though it might have been, I knew it was just an idle thought, a way to pass the time as our wagon lurched and jolted along the rough dirt trail. I'd heard enough stories about our new home on the passage over that I would have sooner tried my luck at swimming back to Byzantia than brave those woods alone.

The magister who'd sentenced me had expected me to be grateful for his great mercy in sparing me from the headsman's block. As we rode beneath the shadow of trees taller than a temple spire that stretched out their branches like they meant to pluck me from the wagon and devour me, I thought again that it would have been an even greater mercy to just take my head and be done with it. Before Tiberius the Wanderer had made landfall in this accursed place they would have done just that, but the First Colony of the Byzantian Imperium was badly in need of bodies to work her fields and various labors if the mother city wished to continue receiving the wealth it had come to rely on.

When Tiberius' ships had returned with holds filled with riches and word of a new world ripe with fresh opportunities and land for the taking, volunteers had rushed to the docks in the thousands, but the next fleet of ships to return from Farshore brought the whole truth with them, inconceivable though it might have been.

Mythics. Creatures from the ancient legends had swarmed out of the shadows to kill and raid. The sailors spoke of Elves in the forests and Dwarven raiders prowling the seas in great warships, of bestial Orcs roaming the western plains, and feral Halflings who swarmed through the jungles of the south in search of victims for their strange blood rites. Worse monsters still were said to prowl through forests and lurk within caves, ready to pounce on the soft, foolish creatures who had come to their shores so unaware of its dangers.

Every child knew the old stories of brave heroes sent by the Divines to battle the inhuman menace that had once plagued humankind and kept us trembling within our walls at night in the distant past. One of the first lessons Sister Gizella taught me was of the Grand Crusade, when the legions of First Emperor Alexius had swept the last of the mythic creatures into the sea, but I had always assumed that her lessons were no more real than the tales of Chressus and Partho.

Some claimed the sailors' tales were nothing more than sun-addled madness, but the death rolls posted in the marketplace soon had others thinking twice. It wasn't long before the supply of volunteers dried up. It had begun to look like Farshore colony would have to be abandoned, no matter how rich her forests and mines might be, until some genius in the imperial court hit on the idea of sending those convicted of less serious crimes in their stead.

Farshore had already celebrated its sixtieth year by the time I came of age, and the passage of sailing ships leaving Byzantia's docks loaded with prisoners or returning with holds filled with fresh timber, gold and silver ore, furs, and other goods had become a regular occurrence. Now here I sat, rolling along in a wagon like a sow led to slaughter, and trying hard not to jump at every cry and rustle from beyond the forest's edge.

We endured the rest of the ride in silence. Our wagons made poor time, and by my guess the minutes had stretched to nearly an hour. Just as I'd begun to wonder if Farshore colony was as much a drunken sailor's tale as the mythics I'd yet to catch sight of our wagon crested the hill we'd been climbing and broke through the trees to give me my first good look at the city filling the valley below.

It wasn't much to look at. You could have tucked the whole lot of it into Byzantia's east end with room left over. But the sight of straight walls, sloping rooftops, and other evidence of human habitation in this strange and wild land sent a warm comfort through my bones.

Our wagon wound down the dusty road, and as the city grew closer, I saw that even though it was somewhat smaller than I'd expected, it was well built. Buildings of wood and stone, some boasting three stories and more, crowded together behind a sturdy wooden wall lined with watch towers.

The flag of the Imperium, five golden stars on a field of red, snapped in the breeze atop each of the towers, a defiant spot of color within the endless expanse of muted greens and browns that surrounded it. The sun was beginning to set behind the mountains to the west, and as we wound our way through the valley the glow of lanterns, candles, and tavern fires flickered to life throughout the city.

As we approached the wall, the driver of the lead wagon shouted up at the soldiers standing watch atop the gate, and soon the heavy wooden doors rolled open to allow us to enter. We rumbled through the yawning doorway, and then the gate crashed shut behind me like a portal to the eight hells.

My first sight of Farshore's streets felt oddly familiar. With rooftops and awnings to block the view of the wild lands beyond the walls you could almost believe you rode through any other Byzantian city of moderate size and means. Bakeries and taverns, clothing shops and houses of exchange all lined the streets, with the windows of the homes and apartments above them standing open to let in the fresh air and sunlight. Buckets were thrust out to dump the evening's wash water and stronger waste into the street below. Men and women went about their evening business, most giving our wagon only a brief passing glance. I even spotted a few street urchins and stray dogs, though far fewer of both than I was used to seeing in a city.

But in many ways those similarities only made the differences stand out even stronger. For one thing, the clothing here was a strange sight. It was heavier and more practical than the light, colorful garments that filled Byzantia's hot streets. The voices that I heard calling to one another from shop windows and across plazas all rang with a strange accent as well. They all spoke Byzantian, but their tones were short and guttural one minute, fluid and musical the next, and I heard a number of unfamiliar words mixed into their speech.

We rode past one shop whose sign I didn't recognize, a rounded glass beaker filled with a bubbling green liquid. I glanced through the door and caught sight of jars filled with eyes, tails, teeth, and worse lining the shelves within, and the strange odor that flooded my nose as we rolled past nearly sent my lunch up into my throat.

Then we took a turn down a new street and things got truly strange.

A smaller wall cut through the city, tracing a straight line from one side of the outer defensive wall to the other to separate one pocket of the city from the rest. Our wagon rumbled past a small gate guarded by two soldiers. The dusk had grown heavier now, but I could still make out shapes moving amongst the streets and buildings beyond the gate, and few of them looked human. Some were no larger than children, but walked alone or in pairs as though they had business to attend to. Some were far, far too large, with hulking shoulders and long, thick legs. One of those shapes stepped into the light that spilled from a window. Its skin was gray, its black hair was long and matted, and I swear I caught sight of a row of pointed yellow teeth curling up over its lips before our wagon rolled past the gate.

The more I saw of Farshore, the more I realized how far from home I truly was. Finally, our rolling tour came to a stop before the steps of the largest building I had seen yet, the local Temple of the Five Divines. Its twin stone spires soared into the air above me, casting their shadows over the nearby rooftops like the wings of a falcon ready to pounce on its prey. The soldiers ushered us out of the wagons and formed us into two lines at the base of the steps.

"Time to see what new life the Divines have in store for us, eh?" The blacksmith who'd ridden next to me in the cart tried to sound jovial, but fear and tension weighed down his words. The others shuffled their feet, looked up at the buildings around them, and made pointless conversation as they awaited their fate. I kept my mouth shut and my eyes on the ground. They could all accept the hand they'd been dealt without protest if they wished, but not me. I had a plan. Escape at the first chance I got, then beg, borrow, or steal what I needed to book passage on a ship back to the real world. No matter what it took, no matter how long I had to bide my time, I was going to find my way back home.

"Catella Lascari, seamstress, step forward."

As the guard captain called her name, the woman who'd lectured me during our wagon ride walked around the altar to stand before the temple nave, while those of us who remained stood beneath the feet of the statues of the Five Divines that loomed large on the wall behind us.

Farshore's Patriari, the legion officers, nobles, and principle citizens of the colony, walked among us with an uncomfortably keen interest. They'd been drawn by the promise of fresh labor for their various enterprises like city dogs circling a butcher's wagon.

"Thirty-three years of age and convicted of adultery. Sentenced to four years good service. Notable skills include the sewing and mending of garments."

So much for your lofty piety, madam.

By the way the woman squirmed and kept her eyes fixed on her feet you'd think they'd hauled her out there naked, but holding these proceedings within the temple walls instead of the market square was another one of those mercies the magister had spoken of back in Byzantia. Once our debt was paid, we would become honest citizens once more, and then we might be glad that only two-score others knew of our various sins.

After a short round of bidding, the seamstress was claimed for the barracks by Knight Captain Alexius, a stern-faced man with salt and pepper hair. No doubt his soldiers would thank him for it when they greeted the winter months dressed in new uniforms. Each of those gathered here had been granted a certain degree of credit, determined by their station and the importance of their duties and businesses to the colony, with which to bid for the contracts of the newly arrived convicts.

"Charity of Byzantia, step forward."

I swallowed hard and moved to stand in the space that the seamstress had just vacated. The Five Divines stared down at my back, while Farshore's gentry circled around me, and I couldn't decide which of the two left me more uncomfortable.

"Twenty-one years of age, and convicted of thievery, public drunkenness, resisting of arrest, assault on representatives of the law, licentious and indecent behavior, and blasphemy." I saw more than a few eyebrows raise as my list of crimes rolled on.

It would have saved us some time if you'd just said "convicted of trying to survive."

"Sentenced to ten years good service. No known skills or abilities."

Well, that won't do.

My list of various offenses already did me no favors, but if the good lords and ladies of Farshore colony thought I had nothing to offer, I'd surely be bound for the fields or a mining outpost before the sun had set.

"That's not true! I can read and write."

One of the requirements of continuing to reside with the Daughters of Vesta after they'd taken me in off the streets had been that I attend well to my studies. Their patron was the goddess of wisdom and learning, after all. Every so often each Vestan cloister adopted an unschooled orphan in her honor, and set about filling their head with every random fact and course of study they'd collected throughout humanity's long and surprisingly boring history. I'd given them hell for it, of course, but in the end I'd learned what they'd wished to teach me in exchange for continuing to eat their food and sleep within their warm walls. Truth be told I'd even come to enjoy their lessons, but if you ever breathe a word of that to Mother Shanti I swear I'll gut you like a carp.

"I'm familiar with history and the classics, and I've a decent head for figures if you don't rush me overmuch."

Even in my wildest dreams I doubted that anyone would risk taking on someone with a history like mine as a clerk or bookkeeper, but there was always a slim chance that one of those present was desperate. Very, very desperate.

"A lady thief who reads Porathus and Scytho? Now I have seen everything."

The gathering chuckled at the joke as a man walked up to give me a more thorough inspection. He was several inches taller than me, heavy set but not exactly fat, and kept his hair and beard well-trimmed to match his fine clothes.

"Governor Caligus," the guard captain said as he saluted.

So, this is the man himself.

I'd heard of the governor back in Byzantia even before I got nicked. The emperor had sent him to take command of Farshore after the previous governor died of a fever, and he'd done enough to improve the colony's fortunes and reputation in that time to lead some of the Imperium's more optimistic citizens to volunteer for the ocean crossing once more. I gritted my teeth and offered him a proper curtsy as he circled around behind me.

"It seems a shame to waste such a delicate young creature on hard labor. Perhaps we can find a better use for your many talents, eh?"

He came to a stop in front of me once again with a smile on his face and a light in his eye that was anything but fatherly.

Oh shit.

I've never held to any pretense of beauty. My jaw is too square and my hands too rough. I crop my soot-black hair with a dull knife when it's grown too long, and the one time I got my hands on a box of rouge and blush I sold it to the first corner doxy I could find for a pouch of coppers and a decent meal. But although I wasn't born beautiful, neither was I blessed with enough ugliness to keep men's eyes away from me completely. I have legs, breasts, and breath in my lungs, and I've found that for most men that's more than enough to attract their unwanted attentions.

"What say you, girl? Wouldn't you like to come work for me? I assure you that employment in my household comes with all manner of…benefits."

I knew how this worked. Now that he'd shown interest none of the others would dare to bid for me even if they'd wanted to. I felt a cold chill crawl its way up my spine, but I gave him my best smile to show him that I still had all my teeth. He leaned forward for a closer look.

As soon as he'd come close enough, I drove my knee between his legs as hard as I could.

I may be many things, but I'm nobody's whore.

The governor collapsed to his knees, clutching his privates and gasping for air as the gathered gentry erupted in a mixture of startled gasps and hearty laughter.

"Come near me again and I'll take your bits clean off, you shit eating bastard."

I went for his face, but the guard captain caught my wrists and pinned my arms behind my back.

"Aaaaaagh!" The governor finally found his voice, sounding for all the world like a zitar with its strings stretched to breaking. I knew I was about to pay for my moment of defiance, but I would rather endure a whole lifetime of digging in a mine than ten years as a bed slave. "Take this demon to the arena pits!"

Double shit. I didn't think of that.

Despite Farshore's strangeness, it seemed that a fondness for arena games was one of the few legacies of the old world that had survived the time and distance intact. In Byzantia the crowds loved few things more than a contest of arms to honor the Divines, especially one that ended in blood.

I was rather partial to the arena myself. Its crowded stands had always proved a ready source of unguarded pockets to pick, but the thought of being the one to stand out there on the arena sand while the crowd screamed for my death drained all the strength from my legs.

The guard captain hauled me away, twisting my shoulder in its socket with a shock of pain as he marched me towards the door. I saw no pity in the faces of those who watched my departure, only varying degrees of anger, disgust, and cold calculation, as those with a fondness for gambling tried to decide their wagers on how long I'd last. I doubted many of them felt inclined to wager in my favor, and at that moment neither did I.

2

The guard captain passed me off to two soldiers who'd been standing watch at the temple door and ordered them to hand me over to the Master of the Games without delay. We set off at a brisk pace, each one with a hand clasped tight to one of my elbows. Neither man seemed inclined to conversation, which suited me just fine. My head was still reeling from the speed of the day. I'd awoken this morning in the same corner of the prison ship that I'd slept in every night for the past three months, and now I was being marched to my eventual but certain death before the sun had finished its dive behind the city walls.

It seemed that my sour luck had managed to follow me across the waves. I thought briefly of the seamstress' warning against tempting the Divines' ire. It hardly seemed fair that the gods, who as far as I could tell had never lifted a finger in my aid or defense, should be so quick to condemn me for speaking my mind. But now that I considered it, that seemed like exactly the sort of petty horse shit they would find entertaining.

In truth, I remember little of that forced march through Farshore's streets. I recall faces turned towards me, a good deal of pointing and whispered words, but little else. At one point we wove through a series of market stalls whose vendors had begun packing away their goods for the evening. Sometime later we marched through the pools of light that spilled out the door of a tavern ringing with voices, laughter, and the clatter of plates and mugs on wooden tables. I'm not sure how long our trek lasted, only that the fog that clouded my thoughts abruptly cleared as our journey through the streets came to a stop before the arena's walls.

Farshore's arena was nowhere near as grand as Byzantia's Hippodrome, but it still towered over me as I craned my neck to look up at the imposing bulk of its high wall crowned with the fiery glow of the sunset beyond it. The arena curved outward, molding the street that ran in front of it into a half circle. From the wooden guard tower that rose up behind it I guessed that the structure had been built up against the city wall itself. The entrance was a wide archway designed to let the crowds pour in all at once, and I could see the open arena floor and rows of benches within.

The guards ignored the entrance, however, and led me around the wall to the left until we stood facing a smaller, iron-banded door watched over by a large, muscular man in a loose shirt and pants. He sported a black mustache whose tips draped down to frame his mouth and swayed in the breeze as he leaned his chair back against the arena walls. I spotted a wicked-looking cudgel set with iron bands leaning against the wall next to him.

At first I thought he was napping on the job, but he cracked one eye open as we approached. As we came to a stop in front of him the man yawned, then let his chair fall forward to sit upright once again as he stared up at my two traveling companions with obvious boredom.

"Got a prisoner for the pits," said Left Guard.

"Get gone," said the man, his words rolling out in the lilting accent of the Gaellean tribes from the forests north of Byzantia.

"This is the arena, not a boarding house for children."

"Governor gave the order himself, so shut it and take her to the Master," said Right Guard. He gave me a little shove forward to emphasize his point.

The man sighed and stood to his feet. He was a full head taller than all three of us, and I had to fight the urge to take a step backward as he loomed over me.

"You came in on the prison ship this afternoon?"

I nodded.

"And you couldn't manage a single night without getting yourself sentenced to the arena?"

"I'm good at making friends."

I was surprised to see him smile in return, and I realized that he was younger than I'd first thought. A few years older than me at most.

"I can see that." He turned and lifted the heavy iron bar from the door with one hand, then pushed it open. A set of stairs led down into darkness, lit only by a torch that stood in a wall sconce just inside the door. Left Guard shoved me forward again, then turned and marched off with Right Guard close on his heels.

I scanned the street, judging the distance between me and the closest building. It wasn't far, but to reach shelter I'd have to get past the Mustache Giant, and my instinct told me that for all his size the man could move quick when he wanted to. Besides, where would I go? Unlike Byzantia, I had no bolt holes or hideaways to lay low in. No, for now the safest way for me was forward, which was a rather depressing thought considering that "forward" meant "down into the arena pit where men wait their turn to fight to the death." I sighed, took one last look at the rays of the sun spread across the open sky, then stepped through the door.

Mustache Giant followed me in and pulled the door shut with a thud behind him as he retrieved the torch and gestured for me to lead the way. I realized that he didn't want me at his back, even if I was only half his size, which meant that he was taking me at least a little bit seriously. I decided that I liked him.

"You got a name, Mustache?"

We walked down a dozen steps in silence, until I thought he wasn't going to answer.

"Cael," his voice rumbled at my back and bounced off the walls.

"I'm Charity."

We reached the bottom of the staircase to find another heavy wooden door waiting for us. Cael reached around me and used a key I hadn't spotted before to unlock it, then slipped the key inside his shirt. He caught my eyes following it, and grinned.

"Somehow, I doubt that." He pulled the door open, gesturing again for me to step through first.

I found myself standing in a hallway of carved stone. The floor was level, and the ceiling was short enough that Cael had to tilt his head just a bit to avoid bumping into it, but it was dry, and more torches lined both walls to fill the space with light. There was a door set into the wall just a few paces ahead on our right. Cael led me up to it and knocked twice.

"Enter," called a thin voice from inside. Cael opened the door and we both stepped through.

The room turned out to be an office, not richly furnished, but comfortable. Shelves loaded with books and scrolls lined one wall, a tapestry of green fabric with beautiful, spiraling patterns in silver thread hung on the other, and a large desk stood between them. A table stood in the corner covered with bottles filled with strange colored liquids, half-burnt candles and various stones, leaves, animal bones, and bowls of powder. Lanterns gave the room a brighter light than the hallway outside, and a fireplace was dug into the back wall. It held a few burning logs which cracked and sizzled as they fought to keep the underground room warm, and a man sat at the desk with his back to the fire. He looked up as we entered, and frowned.

"What's this, then?"

"A new prisoner for the games," Cael answered. "Sent by the governor himself, I'm told."

The man's frown deepened, but he stood and circled around the desk. He was as noticeably short as Cael was noticeably tall, with a thin face, beaked nose, and thinning black hair. He regarded me with a long, appraising look before he spoke, looking for all the world like an ill-fed bird in winter.

"I am Trebonious Leucator, Master of the Games here in the arena, and now the right hand of the Divines themselves as far as you're concerned."

I considered making a comment about exactly what he could do with his right hand, but even I have my limits of unnecessary stupidity. Instead I just nodded and waited for him to continue.

"This is your world now. You live for the crowds, and will most likely die for them."

He tilted his head to one side and studied me as though he sought to fix the exact worth of my life in coin and found the answer somewhat disappointing.

"Fight well, and you will enjoy glory and some measure of comfort, perhaps even freedom and riches. Fight poorly, and, well…," he shrugged.

"But most important of all is this: do not cause trouble, attempt to escape, or inconvenience me in any way. If you're smart, this conversation is the last that we shall have together. If you force me to turn my attention to you again you will find me far less pleasant. Am I understood?"

I nodded again. I could already tell that this Trebonious did not suffer from an abundance of good humor, and with the way this day was going I thought it best not to trust my mouth overmuch.

"Excellent. Now, while I assure you that I take you and all the other criminal garbage who wash ashore here entirely at your word, common sense dictates that I not rely solely on your good intentions to ensure your behavior."

He turned and walked to the table covered in strange items, then retrieved a wooden box and began unpacking its contents. He placed a small pair of silver scissors, a spool of silver thread, and a knife with a blade of clear glass side by side on his desk.

"Now, hold still."

He picked up the scissors and stepped towards me. I don't know about you, but I have never in my life known a time when someone ordering me to hold still and then advancing on me with a sharp object worked out in my favor. I tried to jump back, but instead of opening some distance between us all I managed to do was collide with six plus feet of muscle and mustache. Cael had moved to stand behind me while I was distracted.

"Relax," he said, although he had a pretty firm grip on my arms as he said it. "He's not going to hurt you."

If the man wasn't so damnably tall I might have tried putting my heel in his groin and telling him to relax, but I wasn't sure I could reach high enough to do any real damage, and I didn't see much sense in angering him without getting results. As I was thinking all that through Trebonious stepped forward and snipped off a good-sized lock of my hair.

"That's it?" I asked, feeling equal parts confused and relieved.

"Almost." He grabbed my hand in a surprisingly strong grip for a man his size and made a quick, shallow cut across my palm with the glass knife. He muttered some strange words under his breath, then smeared the ends of the lock of hair in the blood that had welled up from the cut.

"There, now I have what I need."

He returned to the desk and began to wrap the silver thread around the lock of hair.

"Having just arrived from Byzantia I'm sure you are filled with all manner of skepticism regarding the magical arts, but I have neither the time nor the inclination to attempt to change your mind. I will say this only once, and I advise you to suspend your disbelief if you would prefer for your insides to remain on the inside."

He held the loop of hair in front of my face. A single drop of my blood clung to the bottom for a moment, then plunged to the floor. Just looking at the thing set my teeth on edge.

"When I finish the incantation this evening, this will become an effigy. Your effigy, specifically. I'll spare you the technical details and simply say that with this I can bring you to such a gruesomely painful end that being eviscerated in the arena would seem a mercy in comparison. I trust you will not force me to use it?"

"Not planning on it, no."

I kept my voice and expression neutral. He clearly believed in what he said even if I didn't. The gullible and foolish wasted many an evening back home with whispered talk of strange forces and magic spells that could charm a lover, curse an enemy, or worse. Those rumors had grown a hundred-fold since the first ships returned from Farshore carrying word of terrible monsters and mythical races who wielded strange magics, but so far I'd seen no sign of any such thing. Whatever I'd seen through the gate we'd ridden past earlier had probably just been a trick of the dim light and an anxious mind.

In fact, I was beginning to suspect that all the talk of wild magic and wizards had been nothing more than eager imagination and exaggerated reports spun by sailors looking to impress their friends into buying them drinks. The clerics of the Divines made dire proclamations every day about the ill fortune that would befall those who defied the will of the gods, but little ever came of it. Was this really any different?

But, magic or no, this man had the power to make my life miserable, short, or both, so I thought it best to avoid offending another powerful official in the city unless I absolutely had to. The only thing I wanted now was to get out of his sight and hope he forgot all about me by dinner time.

"Good. Cael, show her the facilities and see her settled in her quarters." Trebonious turned back to his desk in dismissal as Cael led me out into the hallway and shut the door behind him.

We continued down the hall for several paces in silence.

"Kitchens," Cael said as we passed by a door. "And the guard barracks," he said with a nod towards another door further down.

"Not that it matters. You won't be passing by this way again."

His voice remained light and pleasant, but the complete certainty with which he spoke those words did more to dampen my spirits than any of Trebonious' threats had managed.

Soon the hallway ended in another heavy door with an iron crossbar that slid into the stone of the wall itself. I heard a muted hum of voices on the far side, which rose to a full-pitched roar as Cael drew back the crossbar and pushed the door open.

The room beyond was far larger and wider than any I had seen thus far. Oil lamps hung from a ceiling that was twice the height of the hallway, and the floor was set with a dozen long tables that currently hosted an evening meal in full swing. More than fifty men of all sizes and colors sat on benches or stood against the walls as they ate, and their shouts, curses, and laughter echoed through the hall. I counted six guards with swords at their hips and cudgels like Cael's in their hands, but they seemed content to leave the men to their meal as long as no one was causing trouble.

My look around the room ended on the table nearest me. Two men sat on one side, cheering for a third. Their champion was nearly a match for Cael in size, and was locked in the middle of an arm-wrestling contest with a fellow who sat across the table. He was as thick as an ale barrel, with arms and legs like fallen logs, and was short enough that he had to kneel on the bench to get good leverage on the table. His head was crowned with a shock of fiery red hair that flowed down into one of the most impressive beards I had ever seen. His opponent strained and heaved at his arm so hard that his face had turned red, but the short man mostly just looked bored.

Finally, the bearded one seemed to tire of their game. He slammed the other man's hand down on the table as if he was swatting a fly, then jumped up onto the table and spread his arms wide.

"Ha! This be no sport at all! Are there none here fit to challenge Magnus Ironprow?" He leaned down, snatched up the man's mug, and drained its contents in three large gulps.

"Who be next to donate their beer to a more worthy stomach?"

The rest of the room mostly ignored his taunts and jeers, but I couldn't pull my eyes away from him. He looked like no man I'd ever seen before. In fact, I was starting to realize that he didn't look much like a man at all.

"Is..is that a...?" I seemed to have trouble forming words.

"The dwarf? What of him?"

Cael sounded like I'd just asked him why the sky was blue. I hadn't really known what to make of the strange tales of mythic races in the new world, but I certainly had never expected to see one standing on top of a table shouting for another round of arm wrestling.

"You have a mythic in here?"

"Oh right, I forgot that you just arrived. We've more than one, actually."

Cael pointed to another table, where a slender man with flowing blonde hair was playing at cards with a half dozen others. I'd overlooked him before, but now that Cael pointed him out I noticed that his features were far more delicate and graceful than any human face I'd seen before, and I spotted two pointed ear tips peeking through his hair.

"Elf." Cael shifted his hand to point towards the shadows in the far corner of the room.

At first glance I thought he pointed at thin air. Then a pair of yellow eyes flashed in the lamplight, and I realized that the shadows concealed someone even smaller than the dwarf. The eyes shifted back and forth, constantly scanning the room. As they swung back again, they fixed on mine with the sudden attention of a hunting bird. As the figure leaned forward into the light I realized that it was a small woman, with a heart-shaped face framed beneath short, brown hair.

"Halfling. Wouldn't recommend trying to make friends."

The halfling clearly knew we were speaking of her. She grinned at me like a cat sighting prey, and ran the tip of her tongue across her small, white teeth.

Cael's finger moved towards another table, where a hulking brute with wiry black hair that had been braided in tight rows across its scalp to fall like a bundle of cords down its back sat scooping great spoonfuls of stew into its mouth. I saw now that its skin was more of a grey-green than the black I had mistaken it for in the lamp light, and that the mouth making short work of the food was lined with round, pointed teeth.

"What is that?" I whispered.

"*She* is an orc. Nataka."

My face must have gone a bit pale, because when Cael turned back towards me he burst into a fit of laughter.

"Cuernos' balls, girl, she's not going to eat you. Not unless you give her a reason to. Although I might suggest a bit less staring."

I realized my jaw had dropped open a bit, so I shut it and fixed my eyes on Cael's smiling and comfortingly human face.

"But what are they doing here?"

Cael just shrugged.

"Pissed off the wrong person or broke the law in the city, same as you. Magnus broke every table in a tavern on the Breezeway during a brawl, Nataka beat three men senseless for offending the spirits or some such, and we found Sheska chewing her way through a merchant's ribcage."

I glanced up to see if he was having one over on me. He wasn't smiling.

"Claims he earned his death. From what I knew of the merchant she may have been right. Now the elf just walked up and knocked on the door one day asking if he could join the arena. Strangest damn thing I've ever seen, but his kind is always strange. It's more mythics than we usually have at one time, I suppose, but that just means bigger crowds."

"Won't their kin come for them? You know, be angry that we've thrown them in here to fight or die?"

"Mmm, those that visit Farshore or choose to take up residence here are told of our laws and what comes of breaking them. If anything, their folk think we're a bit soft. A chance to fight your way to freedom is a damned sight better than most of them would give a criminal. Come on, let's get you settled."

Cael led me down the center aisle that ran between the tables towards an open doorway on the far wall. I felt the eyes of everyone in the room turn towards me and heard the raised voices fade into whispers and muttered speculation as we walked through the crowded hall. He led me to an empty table at the far end of the room and gestured towards the bench.

"Have a seat. The guards will bring you food, and you're granted one half-mug of beer with each meal."

"You don't get many women here, I take it?"

Cael turned around, and the volume of noise returned to normal as he glared about the room before turning back to me.

"Not many, no. Not human ones, anyways. You might stand out a bit until they get used to you, but you don't need to worry about anyone bothering you. Stay within sight of a guard and you'll be safer than if you went walking the streets alone."

Great. Inhuman monsters straight out of a bedtime story, but I'm the strange one in the room?

"Go ahead and eat," Cael continued. "I need to speak to the quartermaster about your room. I'll be back." He turned and left without waiting for a reply.

I kept my head down until a guard passed by and left a bowl of stew and a mug of beer on the table. I tucked in, and was surprised to find that the food was actually pretty good. Nothing fancy, but better than a lot of meals I'd eaten back home, and a damn sight better than the ship's biscuits and water they'd fed us during the crossing. Being consigned to the arena was basically just a drawn out death sentence, but at least I'd eat well while I waited for my inevitable end.

A shadow fell across my table, and I looked up to find a pure-bred Byzantian alley bruiser blocking my lamplight. His hair was shaved down to his scalp and his nose had been broken at least once before, but it was his eyes that gave him away. They were the eyes of a man who'd grown used to taking whatever he wanted whenever he damn well pleased.

"You're in my seat," he growled.

I'd seen his type a thousand times. They were common as paving stones in my part of town, and suddenly I felt right at home. Mythical creatures on the far side of the world were one thing, but this was a good old-fashioned shake down, and that was something I understood. I hadn't expected the testing to start quite so soon, but if this thug and his friends were that eager to find out where I was going to stand around here, who was I to say no? Even as adrenaline flooded through my veins I couldn't help but smile.

"Thanks," I said, keeping his attention on my face while my hand inched towards my mug. "It's been a hell of a day. I think I needed this."

"Don't thank me yet, puppet. We haven't discussed how you'll be making it up to me."

"Well, how bout we start with a drink?"

I flung my mug at his head before he could answer. I hated to waste good beer, but the opening it bought me was well worth it. I screamed and launched myself at him, ramming my knee into his gut with all the force I could manage, then smashing my soup bowl over his head as he doubled over. He dropped to all fours as the clay bowl shattered and sent hot soup into his eyes. I'd hoped the blow would put him down for keeps, but he just shook his head, sending beer foam and cooked vegetables flying in all directions. He fixed me with a look of pure murder and started to launch himself at me.

A knee struck his back and drove him to the floor with a thud, and an iron-banded cudgel smacked the stone an inch from his nose.

"Saying hello to the new blood, Borus?" Cael asked.

For a minute I thought Borus would try to fight back. Then he seemed to think better of it.

"Aye," he growled, "I was just offering a friendly greeting when this *bruta* jumped me."

"Hmm. I'll tell the guard to keep you safe from her from now on."

Laughter echoed through the room, and Borus flushed red all across his shaved head. Cael looked up at me.

"I take it you've finished your meal?"

"Quite, and I enjoyed every minute of it."

Cael just shook his head and pointed me towards the open doorway that I assumed led back to the fighters' rooms.

"Let's get you settled, then." He took my arm and marched me out of the mess hall without another word.

The corridor we entered branched to the left and right, and the walls of both passages were lined with narrow wooden doors set into the stone wall. We turned left and walked for a while in silence. I could tell that he was upset, but I figured if he was bothered enough to say something then he'd speak up, and if he wasn't then there was no need for me to do it for him.

"I guess you really are good at making friends," he finally said into the silence.

"I was only defending myself," I protested. "If I'd backed down the first time some two-copper thug bared his teeth at me, everyone else would know I was easy pickings."

"But that wasn't just some two-copper thug. Borus is the arena champion."

26

Cael might as well have just dumped a bucket of ice-cold water over my head.

"What?"

"Going on four years now, the longest anyone I know of has held the title. He's won so many bouts that we've stopped counting. Trebonious granted him his freedom last year, believe it or not. Borus told him the arena was his home now, and he had no intention of ever leaving."

And some twig of a girl just broke a soup bowl over his head in front of all his friends. Wonderful.

We came to a stop in front of one of the last doors on the wall before the hallway ended in another heavy, locked gate. Cael pushed the cell door open to reveal a simple, bare room. Four stone walls were lit by a small lantern. A straw pallet, a chamber pot, and a stool were all that waited for me inside.

"This is mine?"

"It's not much, but the door locks from the inside, and you can't beat the view."

"It's perfect," I said, and I meant it. A room of my own. It was nicer than anything I'd seen since the Daughters of Vesta had tossed me out and closed the temple doors behind me.

"So what happens now? Do I have to report for inspection or something?"

"Ha, no, nothing like that. In fact, you're free to mind your own business during the day unless there's a fight scheduled."

"When's the next one?"

"Tomorrow," he answered, then chuckled at my involuntary gasp. "Don't worry, I'm sure the Master won't send you out onto the sand that fast. And don't worry about Borus, either. Just keep your head down for a few days. Another win in the arena should do wonders for his pride, and he'll forget all about you."

"I'll try."

He nodded, and turned to leave.

"And Cael?" He stopped and looked back at me.

"Thank you."

He seemed surprised at first, then a pleased grin spread across his face. He nodded, then walked back down the corridor.

I stepped inside my new home and closed the door. I drew the bolt home, paused for a minute, then checked again to make sure it was as locked as it could get. I wasn't sure what time it was, but with no way to see the sun I supposed it didn't really matter, and I was exhausted. I blew out the lantern, stretched out on the pallet, and fell asleep before I'd finished my third breath.

3

I woke up to the sound of muffled voices in the hallway outside my door. I still had no sense of what time it was, but after smashing the better part of my last meal over Borus' head I was hungry enough that I didn't much care. As I opened the door and stepped into the hall the two bruisers who'd been chatting it up a few cells down caught sight of me and went quiet. They stared at me as I walked past, but didn't make a move or speak to me. Apparently word of my run in with the arena champion had already made the rounds.

First day here and I'm already famous. Lucky me.

The common room was mostly empty when I wandered in. A few men sat alone or in pairs around the room, and I spotted the blonde elf-man cleaning off his plate at a nearby table. I felt their eyes follow me as I moved to sit at the same table that Borus had tried to roust me from yesterday. I glared around the room, daring someone to say something about it, but they all just turned back to their meals as the quiet hum of morning conversation picked back up again.

A few minutes later a guard set a bowl of porridge and a hunk of dark bread in front of me. I tucked in and tried to think of some way to keep myself alive and un-maimed through the end of the week.

I'd never been to prison before, a fact which I'd taken a great deal of pride in until recently, but I'd talked to enough of those who had to understand the way of it well enough. I'd made the biggest man here look stupid, so it was sure as shit he was looking to make an example of me to keep others from trying to do the same. Now every man here who wanted to be on better terms with him had a good reason to rough me up, or worse, and it didn't take a Vestan Sister to deduce how long that list would be.

The arena guards couldn't watch every nook and hallway at once, which meant someone would get to me sooner or later. It wasn't a happy thought, but trying to fool myself into thinking otherwise wouldn't change the facts. That meant my only hope of keeping my skin in one piece was either to make nice with Borus somehow, or find enough folks willing to watch my back to make the risk of trying something too much trouble to bother with. Either way, that meant making friends, and making friends fell right above "growing daisies out of my ass" on the list of things that I was good at.

I let out a sigh as I chewed my breakfast. How did I keep managing to turn a bad thing worse? First the senator whose purse I'd snatched back in Byzantia to get myself sentenced to this shithole in the first place, then the governor and Borus once I'd arrived. After years of doing a reasonably good job of keeping my head down and my stomach filled, it seemed I'd suddenly developed a stunning capacity for pissing off exactly the wrong person at exactly the wrong time.

Still, thinking back over the chain of events that had led me here, I couldn't honestly say I'd do things any different if I was given the chance.

Nothing about life is fair. Never has been, and never will be. The strong and the rich hold all the cards, and they know exactly how to play them. The only thing a street rat like me has going is that they don't ever expect you to fight back, so when life backs you into a corner your only play is to hit first as hard as you can and hope it buys you enough time to run. It had worked for me well enough so far, but somehow I didn't think that either fighting or running were going to save me now.

"I'd offer you a copper for your thoughts, but from the look on your face I'm not sure they'd be worth the coin."

I looked up and found the elf man standing over me with a smile on his face. It took me a moment to realize that the words I'd heard had been his.

"You can talk?"

Surprise had loosened my tongue, and those words were the first that tumbled out.

So much for making friends, but the smile on his face just spread into a grin.

"I should certainly hope so, or else my dear parents would be even more disappointed in me than they already are."

I felt the blood rising to my cheeks as I shook my head. He might be an inhuman monster, but he wasn't half bad to look at, and here I was babbling like a sun-addled idiot.

"I just didn't expect you to speak Byzantian, is all. Don't your people have their own language?"

"Indeed we do, but I've taken a liking to yours."

He sat down on the opposite bench without waiting for an invitation.

"It's so colorful. I don't know how you'd begin to call someone a shit eating cock-for-brains in elvish, but I'm certain it wouldn't have half the same spice. Besides, your Byzantian is a rather simple tongue to master, truth be told. Nothing like trying to get your mouth around a dwarven syllable, that's for certain. I suppose that's why many here in Danan have adopted your speech as a sort of common language. Makes it a far sight easier to communicate, given that most would rather chop off their own hand than be heard speaking their enemies' native tongue. So, thank you for that I suppose."

"Danan? I thought this city was called Farshore?"

"Your city is, but I'm speaking of the continent you built it on, love. Goodness, haven't they even bothered to tell you its name? Oh, and speaking of names, mine is Alleron. At your service, to be sure."

"Charity," I mumbled as I shoveled the last of the porridge into my mouth. It didn't seem like this Alleron planned anything that might force me to break my bowl over his head, but I wanted to get all the food out of it this time, just in case.

"So I've heard. In fact, I'd wager there's not a man in here who hasn't. You made quite an entrance."

"That bad, huh? Does Borus have a lot of friends?"

"Lanari's tits, I should think not. He's a shit eating cock-for-brains."

He paused, and his eyes drifted towards the ceiling as though they chased after some important thought that had nearly escaped him.

"On the other hand, I've never before seen an individual who was quite so adept at killing people, so most go out of their way to remain in his good graces. It did my heart a world of good to see you go after him the way you did."

"Glad I could brighten your day."

I'm normally fairly good at reading people. You have to be to stay alive on the streets, but I had no idea what to make of this one. His smile was friendly enough, but something about the grace in his movements or the way he kept a casual watch on the room told me that he could take care of himself if he needed to.

"So, Alleron, what are you doing down here in the pits, anyway? Did you eat someone you weren't supposed to?"

Most of the Farshore stories I'd heard either started or ended with someone being eaten by a mythic, but my question mostly just seemed to confuse him.

"I volunteered, actually."

"You can do that?"

"I wasn't entirely certain myself until I tried, but that Trebonious fellow seemed happy enough to have a 'sharp ear' in his arena when I asked him about it."

"But why would you want to risk your life down here by choice? You get tired of breathing?"

"Nothing of the sort. In fact, I'm waiting to meet someone here."

"Oh? Friend of yours?"

"Not yet, but I'm hoping she will be one day."

"Wait, then how do you know the person you're waiting for will end up here if you haven't met them yet?"

He leaned forward as though he wanted to swap secrets, so I leaned forward too.

"I have *foreseen* it."

His voice was full of cheap theatrics, and he wiggled his fingers in front of his face as though he were playing with invisible puppets. He grinned and raised one eyebrow as he waited for me to laugh at his joke. The only problem being that I had no bleeding idea what he was going on about. All I could do was stare back at him in confusion as his smile wilted away.

"Um, you know…magic, that is."

Just then I was glad that I'd already finished my food. I'm sure I would have choked on it otherwise.

"Say what now?"

Alleron laughed and shook his head.

"Ah yes, you're fresh off that boat of yours. Are there truly no wizards or sorceresses where you come from? Not even a hedge witch or two? Life must be exceedingly dull there."

I only half heard what he said after that. A good night's sleep had put Trebonious' threatening talk of magic out of my mind. At the time I'd dismissed it as nothing more than the eccentric ramblings of a man who'd been away from Byzantia a little too long; just one more strange part of a strange day. Yet now an elf (and I had only just begun to make my peace with using that word as it was) sat across the table from me, prattling on about magic like we were discussing suits of clothing or possible breakfast options.

"...not as flashy as Evocation magic of course, though I dare say it's a damned sight more practical indoors. Most laugh when they hear that I've devoted the better part of the past century to mastering the nuances of Divination, but I wouldn't trade it for all the stone golems or pillars of bale-fire in the Emerald Magus' spell tome."

I knew that some of the Divines' clerics had shoved the stick of holy righteousness so far up their asses that they'd been able to channel the gods' power into miraculous signs and wonders, but none would ever have been mad enough to claim that the power was their own. The old legends were filled with enchantments; fire from the sky, hundred year sleeps, conjured beasts and the like, but everyone knew they were just stories.

Yesterday I'd have sooner believed a man offering to sell me a gilded mansion in the Silk District on the cheap than one claiming to weave spells and incantations, but I was having a harder and harder time ignoring the fact that everyone around here seemed to take the idea as a given. I realized that Alleron had paused and seemed to be waiting to hear my thoughts on the matter.

"Well...good for you, I suppose. Most people are idiots anyway."

His face brightened.

"And here I thought I was the only one who'd noticed that. Come on, Trebonious will be posting the matches for today's games any minute now.

Care to join me in a round of pointing and laughing at the unlucky sods who'll be risking life and limb today?"

In truth I didn't much care who would be fighting in the games now that I knew my name wouldn't be on the list. Alleron seemed eager to go, however, and as I'd somehow managed to avoid offending him so far, I decided to at least make some effort to keep it that way. I nodded, grabbed the last of the bread off my plate, and stood to follow him.

Alleron threaded between tables as he headed toward the door on what I had come to think of as the west wall. A guard stood next to it, cudgel in hand and a scowl on his face, but he made no move to stop us as Alleron reached forward and swung the door open, so I followed him into the hallway. It was a short corridor of blank stone that ended in another door. I could hear the muted sound of a crowd of voices through its thick wooden planks, and when Alleron opened it and stepped through I saw that most of those who'd been gathered in the common room when I arrived now milled around the room inside.

The first thing I noticed about the large room was the glorious morning sunlight that flooded into it through the open grates in the ceiling. The sudden brilliance sent a shock of pain through my eyes, but I drank it in all the same. Even though I'd only spent a day or so underground, I was surprised at how much a spot of real sunlight did to lift my spirits.

As my eyes adjusted, I scanned the rest of the large, circular room and realized that it was mostly devoted to training and general exercise. Boulders of various sizes were lined up against the far wall just waiting for the next muscle ox to lift or roll them about. They stood next to racks filled with wooden or blunted practice weapons, while battered straw dummies and sand pits for wrestling or sparring were spread around the room.

None of the men around us were training, however. They stood alone or in small groups, filling the room with the hum of conversation. I scanned their faces and let out a small sigh of relief when I saw that Borus was not among them. Still, I knew better than to let down my guard. Just because the big dog wasn't here didn't mean another one of his pack wouldn't try to take a swipe at me if I gave them the chance. I caught sight of the orc Cael had called Nataka exchanging quiet words with a large bearded man and the dwarf Magnus on the far side of the room, but I saw no sign of the halfling.

No one paid either Alleron or myself much notice as we entered. Probably because they all kept one eye on the only other door I could see. Its heavy frame, iron bands, and lack of a handle all told me that it led out to the guards' quarters and offices I'd passed through on my way into the pits yesterday.

Then the room echoed with the rasp of an iron bar being drawn back and the squeak of protesting hinges as the door swung open to reveal Cael's tall form standing on the other side. The shadow of a smile that had played at the corners of his mouth yesterday was nowhere to be seen. In fact, if I didn't know better, it looked to me like he wanted to hit someone, and he didn't much care who it was.

He walked into the room without acknowledging anyone. I noticed that he carried a sheet of paper in one hand and a small hammer and spike in the other. He crossed to the large wooden column that supported the ceiling in the center of the room, pressed the paper to it, and drove the spike into it with one solid strike of the hammer.

Everyone crowded forward to get a look at the page he had nailed to the column as Cael turned and marched back the way he had come. I kept my eyes on Cael's back as he shoved his way to the door. He seemed in a hurry to leave, but he paused as he reached the door to look back over the crowd. I was surprised when his gaze found mine and stopped there. He stared at me for a moment, his face so still and cold that I couldn't begin to guess at what he was thinking. Then he frowned, shook his head, and turned to leave, drawing the heavy door closed behind him with a crash. The look on his face as he'd turned away left a cold, queasy feeling in the pit of my stomach. It was the kind of look a man wears to a friend's funeral.

The crowd was pressed in tight around the column, but one by one they pushed their way free and headed out of the room after they'd had their chance to look at the page, so Alleron and I just waited at the back for things to thin out a bit. I noticed that more than a few of those who left cast glances of their own in my direction as they passed by. None of them were friendly.

"Nervous?" Alleron asked as a little half-smile tugged at the corners of his mouth.

"Of course not," I lied. "Are you?"

"Hardly. I won my last match, after all. There's no reason for you to worry, either. Trebonious always gives winners and new blood alike a break from the games to get their feet back under them."

That might have made me feel better if I'd had a chance to take it in, but Alleron spotted a gap in the crowd and dove into it, pulling me along behind him. After a short scuffle he managed to force his way to the front and stopped to read the page, blocking my view with a curtain of golden hair.

"Oh my...well, this is unexpected."

"Damn it, Alleron. Let me through!"

I managed to elbow him aside far enough to get a look at the page. As I'd expected, it was a list of names paired together; the schedule of who would be facing off against each other in today's games. I scanned the list, picking my way through a lot of names I didn't recognize until I found one that I did.

My own, right beside Borus the Kinslayer in the final match of the day.

4

I spent the rest of the day tucked away in my cell listening to men die. The roar of the crowd mingled with the screams of the defeated and dismembered to soak down through my ceiling like cold water. All I could do was huddle on my pallet and try to keep the rising panic in my gut from spreading out to the rest of me, but it was better than enduring the constant staring and whispering I'd been getting in the mess hall. It seemed word had gotten around. I didn't have much appetite for lunch, but I tried to keep my head down and eat a meal just to keep my strength up.

Even Alleron had seemed far less cheerful. He kept muttering about how "it wasn't supposed to happen this way" and "how could I have missed this?" until I finally snapped and told him to stow the chatter before I stuffed my bowl in his mouth. My anger seemed to snap him out of whatever fog he'd been in. He stared at me for a moment, then shrugged and broke out the glowing smile he normally kept firmly lodged on his face.

"You're right of course. When faced with the unexpected we must simply find a way to make the best of things until events resolve themselves onto a clear path once more."

He nodded as though he'd arrived at some important decision, then began shouting over the mess hall's noise that he was now taking wagers on my chances. Soon he had more toughs lined up to place bets than you'd find beggars outside a Vestan temple on festival day. I took the opportunity to slip off to my room. At least there I could have a proper nervous breakdown in private.

I'm not sure exactly how long I waited, but it was long enough that I actually felt relieved when a loud knock on my door announced that my turn in the arena had arrived. As I stood to unlock the door I wondered if anyone had ever tried to just sit tight and pretend no one was home. The bolt would hold them back for a while, but I knew Cael carried a master key, and the other guards would not take kindly to being forced to call him. I undid the latch and found to my surprise that it was Cael himself who waited for me on the other side.

He nodded a greeting, but didn't speak as he turned and walked to the nearby door that formed the end of the hallway. Now it stood open, and I saw that the floor beyond slanted upwards towards sunlight and echoed with the shouts, cheers, and screams I'd been hearing all day long. Once we stepped through the door, I saw that a room stood to my right and left at the base of the ramp. The room to my right reeked of blood and fear, and I caught a glimpse of men writhing on tables as a harried medicus and his assistants tried to save those they could. I turned away before my stomach got the better of me, and was relieved when Cael turned and stepped into the room on my left.

That feeling of relief faded fast once I had a chance to look around. The room was filled with more implements of death than I'd ever seen in one place before. Swords, spears, axes, shields, and a whole host of weapons whose name and purpose I couldn't begin to guess at stood in shining rows on tables and filled racks on the wall.

"Take your pick," Cael said as he gestured around the room. "You can use whatever you can carry."

As I looked around the room the last bit of hope I'd clung to drained out of me in a hurry. I knew how to handle myself well enough. You don't survive Byzantia's streets without becoming at least passingly acquainted with violence. I'd busted a few heads and broken a few noses, even knifed a guy once when he decided he'd rather kill me than share our haul, though I'd let him live to tell about it.

But for the most part I'd kept my skin in one piece by avoiding the kinds of situations that called for weapons like these. They can't kill what they can't catch. One of the few perks of life as a nameless street waif is that you're not burdened by any honor worth defending in the first place, so turning tail at the first sign of trouble is usually the best way to stay alive. With gods only knew how much earth, stone, and locked doors standing between me and freedom running wasn't exactly an option. Soon I'd be fighting for my life against a very motivated bruiser with a taste for blood and more practice with blades like these than I could hope to match even if they'd given me a year to train.

"Don't suppose you have time for a quick lesson?" I asked Cael with a weak smile. I'd meant it as a joke, but he nodded like he'd been hoping I'd ask all along and led me over to a table loaded with rows of gleaming swords and daggers.

"Forget about the heavy stuff," he said as he picked up a longsword, tested its balance, then returned it to the table. "That's what Borus will bring, but he's got more strength, skill, and instinct than you can ever hope to match."

"Thanks for the encouraging words."

"It's only the plain truth. Hiding from it won't save you, but heeding it might. He's strong, but you're fast. He's got experience, but he'll think you an easy victory, which means he'll try to make a show of killing you to please the crowd."

He selected a short legion gladius and handed it to me. I gave it a quick twirl and had to admit that the balance felt better than I'd expected.

"What about something longer, like those spears over there?"

As soon as Cael turned towards where I was pointing I slipped a dagger off the table and tucked it into my boot. I was grateful for his help, I truly was, but I hadn't forgotten that he was Trebonious' right hand man. I didn't think he was likely to go reporting on my preparations, but it was my life on the line, so I saw no sense in finding out the hard way.

"I understand the instinct, but in close is where you want to be," he said as he turned back to me. "He's a cocky sod, so he might just give you an opening. If he does, strike hard and make it count, because he won't give you a second one."

I nodded, but I doubted any of his advice would do me much good. It sounded nice in theory, but I'd seen enough of fighting to know that all the planning in the world is worth less than a bent Drangian copper when your heart is pounding in your ears and someone is after your blood. Once the fighting started I was going to give it everything I had, but that didn't mean I was feeling optimistic about my chances.

Cael must have sensed some of what I was feeling, because he put his hand on my shoulder and opened his mouth to say something else.

"Fighters, to your stations!" the baritone voice of the fight announcer rumbled down the ramp and echoed through the room.

Cael closed his mouth, thought for a moment, then nodded as if he'd made some sort of decision.

"Grass rise up to meet you. Sky reach down to hold you. Stand tall, fight well, die with honor."

His words sent a small shiver through my bones, and I could tell they held a special meaning to him. Just then the urge to cry hit me harder than any time I could remember since I'd been a girl of six hiding from Mother Shanti's temper beneath the cloister stairs. I stuffed the feeling down into my gut before it reached my eyes, smiled up at him, then turned and walked towards the door.

I'll be damned if your last memory of me is nothing but tear stains and snot.

I got a hold of myself again by the time I reached the door and paused to look back over my shoulder.

"Can I ask a favor of you?"

"You can ask. Can't promise I'll grant it."

"If Borus kills me, take a piss in his beer for me."

Cael's laughter echoed from the cold stone walls and followed me up the ramp as I marched my way towards the arena sands.

"You know his name, you know his deeds. Good sirs and dames, I give you Borus the Kinslayer, Farshore's Arena Champion!"

The center of the arena floor was occupied by a circle of tall stone pillars that blocked my view of its far side, but the steady din of shouts and cheers that filled the stands rose to a deafening roar as Borus entered. Alleron had said the man had earned the title Kinslayer after he killed both of his brothers over a woman back in Byzantia. Trebonious had claimed him for the arena before he'd taken two steps off the dock. Since then Borus had won so many victories that Trebonious rarely scheduled matches for him anymore, so the crowd had learned to expect a great show when they heard his name ring out.

"And now, fresh from the old world, Charity of Byzantia stands ready to fight for your entertainment!"

The announcer's voice was amplified by the clever acoustics of the box he stood in. It swept up his words and flung them around the circular walls, but I still almost missed my cue over the roar of the crowd in the stands. The guard nudged me with his elbow, I took a deep breath, and stepped out from the shade of the tunnel onto the arena sands.

The heat of the sun and the crash of sound all around hit me like a blow to the head. I'd seen fighters back home cheer, wave, or salute their fans as they entered the arena, but it was all I could do to put one foot in front of the other without falling over. As I walked forward the crowd's cheers began to die away, until all I heard was the quiet buzz of confused questions and muttered disappointment. I couldn't make out one voice from the next, but I could guess what they were saying all the same.

"What's that slip of a girl doing on the sand with our champion?"

"Has Trebonious lost his mind?"

"We waited all day for this?"

Nothing about this match made sense, and the crowd knew it. They paid good coin to watch a contest worthy of the Divines, and even I wasn't stupid or hopeful enough to think they were about to get one.

I looked up into the glare of the sun and saw Governor Caligus sitting in the shade of his private box, cradling a cup of wine in his hand and grinning down at me like a desert jackal.

Well, at least now I know who I have to thank for all this.

I should have realized what was going on the moment I saw my name besides Borus' on the list. I'd embarrassed the governor in front of Farshore's most influential citizens. He couldn't just let that pass without losing face, and it seemed he was willing to anger the arena crowd in order to make a very painful and public example of me to his lords and ladies.

I scowled up at him and spat on the ground, then turned back to the arena floor and put the governor out of my mind. He might be the reason I was standing here, but he wasn't the one who was about to try and kill me.

That honor went to the muscle-bound brute who had just stepped around a pillar and started walking towards me across the open sand.

Borus was clad in a pair of linen breeches, naked from the waist up and carrying a wicked-looking battle axe in each hand. I'd seen several suits of leather and metal armor in the armory. I'd ignored them because they were either too big or too heavy to be worth the trouble, but Borus could easily have worn any of them. The fact that he chose to face me with his scarred and tattooed chest exposed was the clearest sign I'd seen yet of just how bad my chances truly were.

As he drew closer I could tell from the look on his face that Borus was no more pleased to be here than I was, though for very different reasons. The crowd's muttering had grown louder, and I even heard a few boos ripple through the stands. Borus scowled, twirled his axes a few times, and settled into a fighting stance, clearly eager to get this over with and put it behind him.

"Warriors!" the announcer's voice boomed across the sands. "In the name of the Five Divines, fight with honor, die with courage, live on in glory. Begin!"

Borus came for me before the words had faded from the air, swinging his axes in a crescent swipe meant to take my head clean off my shoulders.

Thankfully, I ducked.

He turned his strike into a flurry of wild blows, swinging and chopping in a frenzy of muscles and rage. I spun, twisted, and dodged on pure instinct. I knew better than to try to block his wild swings with my sword. The force he put behind each one would have crushed through my guard in an instant, but it also meant that the momentum of each swipe carried his arms out to the side for a moment before he could recover. I watched and waited, getting a feel for his rhythm as I kept one step ahead of death. Then he swung just a little too wide.

I ducked beneath his blade and struck out at his exposed rib cage. The wind from his axe tugged at my hair as I felt the shock of my sword striking flesh.

If my blade had been a few inches longer it would have been the end of the fight altogether. Instead it only left a long red gash across his right side. Painful, no doubt, but not fatal. Which meant I was almost certainly a dead woman standing.

"First blood! First blood to the Byzantian Battle Queen!"

I thought that was stretching things a bit far, but the crowd went wild, screaming and hollering at the sight of the arena champion humbled by a girl half his size. Borus touched two fingers to the wound and raised them in front of his face, now dripping red. He stared at them for a moment, as if his mind couldn't accept what had just happened. When he looked back at me his eyes were pure murder.

This time when he charged he kept his anger locked up tight, and I got a close up view of the cold, ruthless skill that had ended countless lives on this very spot. His blows were short, controlled, and powerful now, leaving nothing exposed and giving little warning before they struck home. It was all I could do to stay a hair's breadth away from the razor edges of his axes, and any thought of counter attacking quickly faded from my mind.

My breath started to burn in my lungs, and I realized that it was only a matter of time before one of his swings caught up with me. The only thing I had left to try was something so stupid he would never expect it. Fortunately, reckless and stupid is a Charity specialty.

When the next swipe came at my head, I threw myself into a backwards somersault to gain some distance. I took quick aim as I rolled to my feet, then threw my sword at his chest with all the strength I could muster. The blade spun end over end in a deadly spiral that sent his eyes wide with shock as it flashed towards him. It was a good throw. If I'd faced off against an average fighter then I'm sure the shock of my unexpected attack would have bought my sword the split second it needed to bury itself in his heart. But Borus was anything but an average fighter.

He twisted aside with impossible speed, and the tip of my sword only grazed a shallow cut across his shoulder as it flew by. As Borus stood straight again his face lit up with a wolfish grin.

Uh oh.

Without waiting for his next move I turned and ran as fast as my legs would carry me.

Before long I heard the scuffle of feet and heavy breathing behind me. A quick glance over my shoulder confirmed that he was now hot on my heels, his axes held out away from his body on both sides like the wings of some freakish bird of prey.

I spun left as I passed a stone pillar, putting its solid bulk between me and Borus as I started running around the outer edge of the circle. The crowd began to boo as I robbed them of their glorious contest, but I didn't give two shits what they thought. As far as I was concerned, the first one of them who wanted to come down here and fight Borus himself was welcome to all the glory he could eat in one sitting. I was more concerned with staying alive than staying popular.

Still, I knew that running away had only bought me a few more minutes. On the streets you could run until you found somewhere to hide, but here in the arena there was only sand, sun, and stone pillars. I felt a whoosh of air at the back of my neck, then another, and realized that Borus had gained enough ground to try and swipe at me again.

"Aaagh! Stand and fight me like a man!" Borus roared behind me.

"Do you realize…how stupid…that sounds?" I panted back at him as I dodged around a pillar to regain some ground.

I was as good as dead if I didn't find some way to change the game in the next few minutes. My lungs were screaming at me now, my legs felt like mud, and the knife that I'd hidden in my boot dug into my ankle every time I took a step.

The knife!

Borus thought I was unarmed and defenseless now, so he wasn't bothering to guard himself anymore. A plan began to take shape, and I launched into it before I had time to think of all the many and gruesome ways it would probably get me killed.

I ran flat out for a pillar on the opposite side of the circle, willing my legs to move just a little bit faster. I risked another quick glance over my shoulder and saw that Borus was about two arm lengths behind me now, sweating and red faced but barreling towards me all the same.

Come on, you stupid ox. Come and get me.

When I was two steps away from the pillar I leapt up and used my momentum to run up its surface like I was scaling the wall of a nobleman's estate. I shot up its side until I was a good six feet in the air. Just as I felt my momentum begin to bleed away I pushed off the stone into a backflip that carried me out into open air.

Time slowed as I soared. Borus stared up at me with his mouth hanging open in disbelief as I spun over his head.

I tucked into a ball, pulled the knife from my boot, and landed on the sand in a crouch behind him. Before he could recover I lashed out with two quick strikes.

The temple library of the Daughters of Vesta contains all the knowledge worth possessing, or so Mother Shanti was fond of saying. I'd taken a special interest in the lessons on anatomy. At first that was only because the illustrations were far more interesting than another dry lecture on the history of kings and states or complex mathematical formulae. Soon I realized that understanding the way the body moves and functions offered some pretty interesting advantages. For example, Borus' legs might have been thicker than the mast of the *Typhon*, but they were connected to his feet by the ever-vulnerable Acheron's tendon, just like everyone else's. When my knife sliced through those tendons, he collapsed to his knees in a crash of dust.

I jumped to my feet, reached around in front of him, and cut his throat before he could recover.

Blood sprayed out onto the sand in a crimson fan. As the fallen arena champion toppled forward every sound in the arena died away into silence. Ten thousand faces stared down at me in shock. I felt my limbs start to tremble as the adrenaline died away and the reality of what I'd just done settled over me, but I knew that these next few moments mattered almost as much as the fight itself. I needed the crowd on my side if I hoped to survive in here much longer, and nobody enjoyed watching a girl bawl her eyes out.

I stood to my feet, pointed the bloody knife straight at Caligus, then opened my hand to let it fall to the ground. As the knife hit the floor the stands erupted in a deafening chorus of shouts, cheers, and chants that made everything that had come before it sound like polite applause. The announcer had recovered his wits enough to finally say something about the unexpected conclusion, but I couldn't hear his words over the roar that thundered all around me.

That jackal smile was gone from Caligus' face now, replaced by a beautifully sour frown that did wonders to cheer my spirits. I raised both arms over my head to salute the crowd, then spun on my heel and marched back to the tunnel I'd emerged from what now felt like a lifetime ago.

I was rather pleased that I made it all the way back to the shelter of its cool shadows before I vomited up what little remained of my breakfast.

5

D inner passed without incident. The other fighters steered clear of me after I walked out of the arena with Borus' blood on my clothes, and that suited me just fine. I stuffed food in my mouth without noticing the taste, then walked straight back to my room. Cael was waiting with a few sets of fresh clothing, along with a small table and chair to round out the decor of my cell.

He'd called them "the victor's reward." As far as I was concerned I was still breathing, and that was reward enough.

I slept like shit that night.

I was exhausted, but as I lay on my pallet in the darkness my thoughts kept returning to the final moments of my fight in the arena. The look of surprise on Borus' face as his brain caught up to what was happening faster than his body could react. The grinding shock that had trembled up my arm as my knife cut through flesh and into bone. The spray of blood across the sand.

I told myself that I had no reason to feel guilt over taking his life. I hadn't asked for that fight, and he'd made it damned clear that he intended to kill me and enjoy himself in the process. No doubt if he'd been the one standing over my corpse he would have crowed about it to the skies, drank an extra beer that night, and forgotten my face by the morning. But all the logic in the world didn't calm my stomach or make sleep any easier.

I lost track of how many hours I'd lain there when I finally gave up, pulled my new linen shirt over my head, and stepped out into the hall.

Everything was quiet. By my guess it was still the small hours of the morning so I doubted that the kitchens would be serving breakfast yet. Still, since I had nowhere else to go I decided to go claim myself a bench so that I could be sure I'd get one of the first plates they sent out. Seemed better than laying awake in the dark trying to keep my hands from shaking.

Given the early hour I assumed the main hall would be empty. I was wrong. The big orc I'd seen around a few times before sat alone at a table by the wall. She had her back turned towards me, but turned to look over her shoulder as I walked into the room even though I was sure I hadn't made a sound. She frowned, but scooted over on the bench and nodded to the seat beside her.

"I like to come here early to enjoy the silence before things get too crowded, but you may join me if you feel inclined towards company."

Her voice was deep and soothing. She spoke Byzantian with a strange, clipped accent, but she spoke it better than many alleycats I'd heard jabbering on back home. I couldn't help but glance nervously at her pointed teeth as she spoke. The two longer tusks that rose up from her jaw looked like they could punch through steel if she tried hard enough, but even I knew that moving to sit somewhere else would have been incredibly rude after such a civil welcome. I swallowed hard, nodded, and moved to join her.

"Your name is Nataka, right?"

She nodded.

"I'm Charity."

"So I have heard."

I wasn't sure if I should be flattered or concerned by that as I slid onto the bench. No sooner had I sat down than she stood to her feet.

"The cook was kind enough to brew some tea while he waited for the ovens to heat up. I will bring you some."

She disappeared through the kitchen door, then returned a few minutes later carrying two steaming cups. She set one down in front of me as she returned to her seat, then took a careful sip from her own mug and let out a contented sigh.

"Fresh-brewed Skariam leaf. If there is a better way to begin the morning, then I have not found it."

I blew on my tea for a bit, then took a sip. It was surprisingly spicy, with a hint of citrus and honey, and damn if it didn't leave me feeling a little bit better. We sat in silence for a while, enjoying our drinks and not bothering each other. I sat on a bench beside a monster out of the legends, and it was by far the calmest and most pleasant ten minutes I'd experienced in a long, long time.

"My people tell stories of your kind."

I jumped a little as her rumbling voice broke the stillness, then looked up at her.

"Oh? I didn't think there were any humans here in Danan before Tiberius and his fleet arrived."

"There weren't. But I think that there must have been, once. Legends speak of a strange race who once lived along the shore. Slower than elves, weaker than dwarves, more timid than halflings, yet far more dangerous than any of them in large numbers."

I blinked. That was news to me.

"That might have been humans, I suppose. What happened to them?"

"The legends only say that they vanished long ago. Until your kind returned to our shores I'd thought them nothing more than strange stories for children."

"Ha. Yeah, that's pretty much what we think of you."

"Is it true that none but your own kind live in your homeland?"

She furrowed her brow as I nodded, appearing more thoughtful than angry.

"It must be a strange thing to know nothing but peace."

"What?"

She tilted her head to one side and gave me a strange look.

"Did I use your words incorrectly? If you live only among your own kind, then you have no war, correct?"

Somehow I managed to catch myself before I laughed out loud.

"Um, no. We humans can find an excuse for war faster than a dog can sniff out shit. If the kingdoms aren't fighting, then they're scheming about how to start a fight to their best advantage. Orcs don't fight amongst themselves?"

She shook her head.

"One orc may fight with another. Blood debts must always be settled and young blood will always seek to test itself, but that is not the same as war."

"A noble conflict is the greatest teacher, for it reveals the nature of man to himself."

"Wise words for one so young."

"Thanks," I grinned, "but they aren't mine. That was Epicus, a third era philosopher. He was big on instilling virtue, so Mother Shanti made me read his work twice."

From the way she stared at me you'd have thought I'd just said I like to eat babies for breakfast.

"You are *Gelerhtag*?"

"I'm sorry?"

"Ack, your words are too small for such a large thing. *Gelerhtag* is a vessel of knowledge, a keeper of the old wisdom and a teller of tales. They are the greatest and most respected among my kin."

"That's definitely not me then."

"But you can read your people's script?"

I nodded.

"And write it as well?"

"Yeah, although Mother Shanti always said my scribbles were so ugly that it was unfair to scribes to call them writing."

She grinned. Our conversation hadn't made her teeth any less unsettling.

"That is the second time you've mentioned her. She sounds like a wise woman."

"Sure," I said, not bothering to hide the bitterness in my voice. "She was a peach."

"She is dead, your mother?"

"She's not—" I paused, unsure of how to explain my strange relationship with the woman who had raised me, then abandoned me. Then I decided it wasn't worth trying. The old hag had been cold, distant, uncompromising, and ruthless. She had also been by far the closest thing I'd ever had to a real mother, and that sad truth was more than I could handle on an empty stomach.

"I honestly don't know if she's dead or not, but she might as well be as far as I'm concerned."

Nataka frowned, but seemed to know when to leave well enough alone. We sat in silence once again until the hall began to fill behind us. Finally, she finished the last of her tea and stood to her feet.

"I hope we are never matched against one another on the list, young Charity. It would sadden me to kill a *Gelerhtag* of your people. Even one with poor penmanship."

She dipped her head in a solemn bow, then turned and walked out the door before I could think of a proper response.

The common room continued to fill as the other fighters gathered for breakfast. A guard brought me a bowl of porridge and an apple. No one bothered to join me, which suited me just fine. I ate without giving the food much thought, focusing instead on the strange conversation I'd just had with an orc. She wasn't anything like what I'd expected, which I was beginning to think was going to be true of many things here in Farshore.

Her reaction to learning that I was literate had taken me especially by surprise. I suppose that reading and writing were rare enough skills to find in Byzantia's gutters. Most were too busy hunting down their next meal to make the time to learn, even if there'd been someone willing to teach. No doubt I'd have been the same if the Daughters of Vesta hadn't made consistent improvement in the academic sciences a condition of remaining within their walls and eating their food.

But Nataka had seemed more than just impressed. From the way she'd spoken of it you'd have thought that reading and writing was a sacred thing. I wonder how she'd have felt if she knew what else was rattling around in my brain?

Stories, poems, formulae, detailed medical recipes and more had been jostling and squabbling over headspace since the day I first walked through the temple gates. I often worried that I was becoming a modern day Archicus, the thief who managed to unlock the gates of Charydis to steal from the gods. He stole so much knowledge from Vesta's table that he forgot how to feed himself and starved to death once he returned home. Sister Jesra had been especially fond of that tale, and the moral that went along with it; a little knowledge can be a dangerous thing. Only a lifetime of rigorous study and discipline could prepare one's mind to sustain the weight of Vesta's glory.

I sighed, pushed away my empty bowl and stood to my feet. I hadn't thought about the temple in years, but my thoughts seemed inclined to return there often since I'd arrived in Farshore. It seemed that losing the sad excuse for a life that I'd built for myself was dragging up memories of the last time I'd been forced to start again with nothing but what I could carry in my head. Still, I had to admit that even the Daughters' endless rules and lectures were more pleasant to dwell on than the recent monopoly that blood and death had maintained on my thoughts, so that was something.

"Well, well. Here she is in the flesh."

I turned to find myself face to face with a pack of scowling thugs. I looked them over, instantly alert.

Four men. Their Byzantian short-cropped hair said "ex-legion," the fact that it had only just begun to grow out again said that they'd been tossed out recently, and the ugly in their eyes said they'd earned their discharge the hard way.

"You boys come here often?"

They grinned at my weak joke, but there was no laughter in their eyes. The one in the lead leaned in a little, close enough to give me a whiff of his sour breath as he growled an answer.

"Aye, that we do. Used to share a meal here every morning with the finest man I've ever known. His name was Borus, and a two-copper whore like you weren't fit to clean up his shit, let alone enter the ring with him."

I tossed a quick glance at the nearest guard. He was talking with two men seated at a table against the far wall. Even if I screamed it would be ten seconds or more before he caught up to what was happening and made it across the room to intervene, and I was well aware of just how much damage a few motivated bruisers could do in ten seconds.

"Funny you should mention whores," I said to keep their eyes on me as I reached around behind my back.

"Borus asked a favor of me before we faced off. Maybe you could help me honor his wishes?"

"Oh?" They looked at each other, unsure of how to respond. My fingers found the spoon I'd left in my empty bowl. I closed a fist over the round end to leave the metal handle sticking out through my knuckles. If I could take one down fast it might slow the others long enough for the guard to get involved. Or it might just make them mad enough to crack my skull open instead of just breaking my face a bit, but any chance seemed better than just standing still and waiting for the pain to start. I cleared my throat and spit on the lead basher's foot.

"Yep. Turns out he fucked your mother last night, but hadn't gotten around to paying her yet. You don't happen to have a coin to spare, do you?"

His eyes went wide, then lit with rage as he pulled back his fist.

Perfect.

I jumped toward the opening he'd given me and punched my makeshift dagger at his throat. Even the blunt end of a spoon handle can do some serious damage if you land it hard enough in the right spot. I have no doubt that it would have done just that if his head hadn't jerked out of the way just as I began my swing. He flew past me as I swiped at empty air. I caught the look of surprise on his face before it was slammed down onto the table behind me.

His friends and I stared at their fallen comrade. Our eyes looked from his bleeding face to his arm twisted tight in its socket, and finally to the dwarf who held his wrist in an iron grip and glared back up at us with fire in his eyes.

"Hey! Break that up!"

The dwarf looked over his shoulder at the approaching guard without letting go.

"We're just talking."

He didn't shout, but the warning in his voice was clear. The guard opened his mouth to snap a reply, then caught himself and glanced around the room. Two more were on their way. He pointed his club at the dwarf, but didn't move any closer.

"Let him go, Magnus."

"I just told the good soldier here that we're only having a friendly chat," Magnus growled as he twisted the thug's arm a little tighter. "Now, are we just talking? Or do you plan to make a liar out of me?"

"Aye!" the man yelped as he rose up onto his toes. "Just talking!"

"That's a good lad," Magnus said as he let go of the man's arm and patted his head like a puppy who'd just taken a shit outside for the first time. The bruiser stood to his feet, rolled his shoulder with a wince of pain, then shot a final glare at me before storming off towards the training hall with his friends trailing after him. The guard nodded and turned to walk back to his post by the door, but not before I caught the look of relief that flashed across his face.

"Thanks," I said as I turned to my unexpected rescuer, "but I could have handled—"

"Don't," he snapped as he held up a hand.

"Don't what?"

"Don't thank me. I wasn't helping you, so don't waste your words."

"Mind telling me what you were doing, then?"

"Just staking my claim."

"Pardon?" I didn't like the sound of that.

He sighed and shook his head.

"That Borus was a right bastard, but he was also the only halfway decent challenge in this rotten hole. The thought of facing him in honest combat was one of the last decent ways I had of passing the hours, until you got to him first. So now I'm forced to settle for killing you, instead. Your blood doesn't deserve to grace my axe, but if I'm going to be forced to make do then I'll be damned if I let some dog turd with a grudge leave you any weaker than you already are before we face off in the arena."

He looked me over from top to toe, then shook his head again and turned to march off to a different table.

"Nice to meet you too," I called after him. He took a seat, grabbed a bowl, and set about ignoring my existence.

I looked around the room. Everyone else was following his lead. Back when I ran Byzantia's streets I would have kissed a Novari yak for the power to turn invisible, but just then it was beginning to grow rather old. I scowled, turned my back on the room, and went in search of something to fill up the rest of what was starting to look like a very long day.

6

"**B**lood is spilled! Honor is given! Lords and dames, cheer for the victor!"
The announcer's voice boomed down the ramp as I stepped into the
armory once again to find Cael already waiting for me. My restlessness had
grown so bad over the past week that I actually felt a flood of relief when
he'd appeared in the training room that morning to post the list for the new
games and I'd found my name on it. I wasn't eager to risk my life again, but
at least it meant that something was happening. The strange bit was that
there was no opponent listed next to my name, just the word "challenge" in
bold letters. I had no idea what that meant, but I hoped that I might not have
to spill blood in order to survive for another day.

Now that I heard the dying screams of whoever had just lost that fight
mixed with the roar of the crowd overhead I was feeling decidedly less
excited.

"Now enjoy yourselves while the next combatant makes their final preparations. Eat, drink, and place your wagers, for the contest you are about to
witness will be unlike anything you have ever seen before."

I didn't love the sound of that, but my turn on the sands had come
whether I was ready or not. I smiled at Cael and offered him a nod in greeting. He didn't smile back. In fact, he looked like someone had snuck sawdust
into his breakfast when he wasn't looking.

"Choose your weapon," he said as he pointed to the many options around the room.

"Any suggestions? The list didn't name my opponent, so I don't know what I'm dealing with."

"I am not permitted to advise the combatants on their preparations." His face was as blank and cold as the stone walls.

Ah. Sounds like someone got a bit of a talking to after my last fight.

I guess it made sense that Trebonious had looked for a scapegoat to vent his frustrations on after a nameless girl had taken down his star fighter. He had no way of knowing that I'd kept the knife hidden from Cael, too. It wasn't fair that he'd gotten in trouble for it. Then again, it wasn't fair that I was being forced to fight for my life while he got to stay safe down here and sulk, so I wasn't feeling an abundance of sympathy just then.

"Right. My mistake."

I sighed and picked up the same gladius I'd carried when I fought Borus. Without any information to go on I didn't see any reason to choose something else. I gave the blade a quick once over, then turned for the door.

"Wait."

I turned to find Cael staring at the ground. He chewed at his lip for a moment, opened his mouth to say something, then seemed to think better of it. He looked up at me, and I saw genuine concern in his eyes.

"If you're going to wish me luck now would be a good time. Got an appointment to keep, and from the look on your face I think I'm going to need it."

That earned me a small smile. Then he nodded once and turned to look at a rack of polearms on the wall next to him. He reached up and took down a short spear. The shaft was only about four feet long, but the blade on the end added another foot of sharpened steel that looked more like the straight blade of a dagger than the leaf-shaped tips I'd seen on legion spears.

"This is called a *haska*. It's a Gallean weapon, though not one most warriors would choose to wield. Our women train with them. It gives good reach, and the blade lets you cut as well as thrust."

I smiled, then nodded like I used to when I sat through one of Sister Gizella's lectures.

"Very interesting. You know, I am struck by the sudden and completely unpredictable desire to try out this fascinating weapon for myself. In the interest of cultural exploration, you understand."

He smiled back and tossed the spear to me. I caught it out of the air and gave it a quick twirl. I could see what he meant. The center of balance made quick swipes and stabs much easier, even with my lighter frame.

"Of course, they always wield it with a shield," he said as he lifted one from a table and carried it over to me.

"If it's good enough for a Gallean housewife then it's good enough for me."

"Your arm goes here."

He took my hand and guided it through the leather straps. His fingers were callused from a lifetime of sword drills, but surprisingly gentle as he helped me fit the shield in place. It was made of sturdy oak with an iron rim, an iron boss at the center, and was wrapped in cured leather. I was surprised to find that it was lighter than I'd expected once I had it secured onto my arm.

"Stay low, move fast, and keep your shield up," he said as he squeezed my shoulder.

"Always. And thank you."

He nodded as I headed for the door and marched up the ramp to see what Trebonious had in store for me this time.

I shielded my eyes from the sun's glare as I reached the top of the ramp and looked out into the arena. There was nothing there. The pillars that had stood there previously were gone, and all I saw now was empty sand.

"Now entering the arena for the second time, the slayer of champions and battle queen of Byzantia, Charity!"

I took my cue and stepped out into the sunlight. This time the crowd cheered my entrance. I had no doubt that the story of my fight with Borus had made its way round the city by now. I looked around, but still saw no sign of my opponent. But now that my eyes had adjusted I saw that the arena wasn't as empty as I'd first thought. A large wooden tub sat to my right, filled to the brim with water, while a decent sized stack of firewood stood on my left.

"My lords and dames, you are about to enjoy a contest unique in the history of the arena, a battle not of flesh against flesh, but one of strength and skill pitted against the fury of the elements themselves."

I still didn't have any clue what he was talking about, but I knew there was no way it could be good for my continued health. Before I had a chance to do much of anything a figure emerged from the shade of the governor's box. As I squinted up at it I realized that it was an elf, and a female at that. She wore flowing robes of black and red that matched her onyx hair, and I noticed an intricate pattern of tattooes spiraling up her neck to snake around her eyes.

She stared down at me for a moment, then smirked, knelt on the floor of the stand, and closed her eyes. The heavy door slammed shut behind me as I walked out to the center of the arena.

"Warrior!" The announcer's voice shattered the eager hush that had fallen over the crowd. "In the name of the Five Divines, fight with honor, die with courage, live on in glory. Begin!"

As his voice echoed across the sand an archer stepped up next to the woman. The tip of his arrow danced with a smoldering flame as he pulled back his bowstring, took aim, and fired. I raised my shield, but the flaming missile shot to my left to bury itself in the woodpile. The wood must have been treated with oil, because it roared into a full bonfire in an instant. The archer stepped back into the shadows, and I turned in a slow circle as I searched for whatever was coming to kill me.

Nothing moved. A breeze teased at my hair as the fire snapped and popped beside me. The crowd began to mutter and whisper as they waited for something to happen, but the elf still knelt with her eyes closed, and the door to the other arena entrance remained shut.

Then I felt it.

The hairs on my neck prickled to life as the breeze died away. A whisper tickled my ear, but when I spun around I found nothing there. My senses screamed that there was someone standing beside me even though my eyes were certain that I was alone. If there had been shadows I would have searched them for signs of someone hiding there, but the bright sun had long since burned them all away.

Then the fire exploded behind me. A wave of hot air sent me stumbling forward. I spun around to find pieces of smoldering firewood scattered across the sand, with only a bed of glowing coals where the bonfire had stood. Then a hand burst up out of the embers.

It was the same size and shape as a human hand but was formed of black rock shot through with veins of fire that pulsed an angry crimson. It slammed to the ground, dug its fingers into the sand, and pulled. A head pushed up through the coals, then a pair of shoulders and another hand like the first. The head had no face, only two eyes that glowed like embers at the heart of a forge as the creature gave one final heave and hauled itself up out of the earth. It pushed up onto its knees, then stood to its feet.

I heard a loud splash behind me and whirled around to find another man-sized figure standing where the tub of water had been. Broken planks and bits of bent hooping littered the sand around the shimmering, translucent body.

A woman screamed in the stands, and her voice broke the spell of silence that had gripped the crowd. People stood and began pushing their way towards the exits as they sought to escape the sudden and unexpected display of magic.

"Fear not, good citizens of Farshore!" the announcer shouted over the rising panic. "Rest assured that the magic you see before you is kept well in hand, and has been sanctioned by Jovian's prelate for your entertainment. Behold! A contest unlike any this arena has ever seen unfolds before you."

I saw some continue their flight, but for most their curiosity overcame their caution. The stands refilled and the good men and women of Farshore redoubled their frenzied cheers and screams. I cast a quick glance up at the elf woman. I had no idea how any of this was even possible, but I was sure she was responsible for it somehow. She opened her eyes and looked down at me as if she had felt my gaze on her. They were completely black. The sight of two bottomless pools of ink staring down at me where her eyes should have been unnerved me far more than her creatures had managed.

Then she screamed. It was a long, shrieking cry of fury and rage, and suddenly the two creatures echoed the cry and rushed at me.

"See how elemental beings respond to the enchantress' very will!"

I jumped backward to avoid being caught between them, but the elementals charged in on me with abandon. Fire swung a fist at my head while Water swept a low kick at my legs. I got my shield up and deflected the punch in a shower of sparks just as the column of water knocked my legs out from under me. I scrambled back as I hit the sand, rolling out of the way just as two fists struck the spot where I'd lain. Sand exploded in a shower of steam and the two elementals stumbled back from the blast, giving me enough time to scramble to my feet.

I was ready for their next attack. I put all the impossible magic shit out of my mind and focused on fighting as if they were just two humans with a skin condition. I dodged to the left as they charged at me, slashed my spear through Water's torso, then spun it around and drove the blade into Fire's chest.

The crowd gasped as Water clutched his chest and stumbled backward. The gash I'd opened with my spear flowed together like water poured into a bowl. The spear was ripped from my fingers, and I turned to see Fire toss it away from him. He'd pulled the blade from his chest like I'd just stuck him with a sewing needle. I'd just struck them each with what should have been a fatal hit, but I didn't see any sign that they'd even felt it.

This wasn't a battle. It was an execution.

For the second time in my arena career I turned around and ran like hell. This time the crowd screamed encouragements instead of booing me. Seemed that they'd taken my side against the inhuman monsters that were now chasing after me, but their support didn't do me a damned bit of good.

A flaming rock singed my ear as it shot by an inch from my head to explode against the arena wall. I looked back to see Fire conjure another missile and launch it straight at me. I spun around and got my shield up just before it hit me. Flames swept around me, burning my shins as the force of the blast sent me stumbling backward. Then Water burst through the cloud of smoke. His arms now ended in shimmering blades of ice where his hands had been, and he slashed them both at my head as he ran forward. I deflected one strike with my shield as I ducked beneath the second.

Suddenly a column of water flowed around my shield and struck me in the face. It surged into my nose and mouth and forced its way into my lungs. The shield was ripped from my arm as I flew up into the air. I looked down to see that Water held me in the air, his hand covering my face as my feet dangled above the sand. I couldn't breathe, and my efforts to do so only sucked more water down my throat. I clawed and scratched at his arm as my vision began to blur and blacken, but my fingers passed harmlessly through him.

I was three heartbeats away from Magren's door, and there wasn't a damned thing I could do about it.

Another explosion of steam threw me backwards to slam into the wall and fall to the ground. I'm sure it would have knocked all the air out of me if I'd had any left. I coughed up a bucketful of water and sucked down a huge gasping breath. Then I heard a long shriek of pain ring out through the arena and looked up to see Water standing there with his arm and most of his shoulder missing, then past him to where Fire stood with another flaming missile ready in his hands. He must have thrown one at me just as Water picked me up, and struck his friend instead of me.

The scream had belonged to a woman, though. I looked over their heads to where the elven woman knelt in the governor's box. She clutched her head in her hands as if she fought off the worst headache in the history of hang-overs. It seemed her little toys didn't play so well together, and she seemed to feel it when that happened. She shook her head and glared down at me, another wordless cry of rage tearing its way through her throat as she aimed a slender finger straight at my chest.

Fire and Water leapt back into action, racing towards me at her command. I still had no way to fight them, but I thought I saw a slim chance to strike at the bitch directly. It would probably still get me killed, but at least I'd give her a bloody nose on the way down.

I scrambled to my feet, but this time I ran towards the duo instead of away from them. The crowd cheered as I charged forward, then dove beneath Water's kick to scoop up my shield. I raised it just in time to block Fire's fist as it swept down at my head. The blow drove me down to one knee, and I rolled forward just as his second fist smashed the ground. I leapt up, squared my feet, and slammed my shield into Fire's back.

The heat that radiated off of him was incredible. The rim of my shield began to glow, and I knew that the treated leather was all that kept it from catching fire, although that wouldn't last much longer. I dug my toes into the sand, screamed out all the fear and anger that coursed through me, and slammed my shoulder against the shield.

Fire and I stumbled forward together and collided with Water as he ran towards me.

My world dissolved in a flash of white. I flew through the air for what felt like a lifetime, then hit the ground hard. I lay there gasping on the sand like a fresh-caught fish while I waited for the world to stop spinning. If my little gambit had failed then I knew the elementals would be coming to finish the job, but I was too tired to care or do much about it. The skin on my arms and legs throbbed with fire. Breathing hurt. Everything hurt, actually, but I finally forced myself up onto my elbows to take a look around.

Two black scorch marks in the sand were all that remained of Fire and Water. I looked up at the governor's stand. The elf lay slumped on the ground. Steam rose from her ears and open mouth. Her eyes had cleared, but now they just stared sightlessly ahead in shock.

The arena was so quiet that I could hear birds singing in the trees beyond the wall. No one moved. Now that the shock had worn off, the reality of what had just happened began to crash down on me. I'd just seen someone wield the kind of magic that was only supposed to exist in a children's tale, and she'd very nearly killed me with it. My hands began to tremble, but I stuffed it down and forced myself up to my feet. All I wanted in the world just then was to make it back to my cell and lock the door for a week.

"Unbelievable! The Byzantian Battle Queen has beaten the odds once more. Truly she is favored by the Divines themselves!"

The crowd erupted in a storm of shouting, waving, stamping, and screaming as the announcer finally recovered his wits. Men and women hugged one another, and I saw more than a few tear-stained faces as thousands of people made the sign of Jovian's Wise Eye in salute. Seemed the sight of a helpless human girl winning out over evil magic had really brightened their day.

I scowled and started limping towards the exit. The Divines didn't have two shits to do with it. I'd gotten lucky, and I knew exactly how close I'd come to never seeing another sunrise. The crowd chanted my name, but I didn't care. I had exactly one thought in my head as I stepped through the arena doors and began to shuffle down the ramp back to the arena pits.

Time to get the hells out of this madhouse.

7

———

A t first I hadn't really felt the cuts and burns I'd taken in that final blast, but damn if they weren't screaming at me by the time I'd reached the bottom of the ramp. The medicus who tended me said I'd been lucky. If the force of the explosion hadn't thrown me backwards before the steam had time to really do its work I would have been in far worse shape, but it was hard to feel grateful as he slathered stinging salve on my skin and wrapped a set of bandages around the burns. I tried to fight the blackness that pressed in on me. An alleycat's worst nightmare is to be laid out sleeping and helpless while a pack of men you don't know loom over you, but soon the pain grew so bad that it sent me spiraling down into unconsciousness.

I'm not sure how long I was out, but when I jolted awake from the nightmare I'd been having I found myself laying on the cot in my cell. I was tired, sore, angry, and really damned sick of the arena. My last thought as I'd walked off the arena sands had been getting the hells out while my limbs were still attached to my body. It seemed like my brain hadn't stopped thinking about it even as I lay there snoring, because by the time I woke up it already had a plan ready and waiting for me. I turned the details over in my mind as I lay still to keep from aggravating my wounds, then nodded once in the darkness.

My new escape plan had a better chance of working out than some of the half-baked schemes I'd run with in the past, but even if the odds had been slimmer than Drangian silk I would have given it a shot anyway. Gasping out my last breath with a guardsman's arrow in my back wasn't all that different than watching my guts spill onto the sand in the end, but at least this way the choice would be mine again. With the decision made I let out a long breath and closed my eyes. All I needed now was time, rest, and a few pieces of stolen silverware.

I gave myself a week to heal while I gathered what I needed. I made a mental note that if I ever had to go and get myself injured again, the arena pits was probably the best place to do it. I'd been hurt bad before, and finding a quiet hole to lick your wounds and heal was never easy when you still had to find food and keep a wary eye out for anyone looking to take you for a free ride at the same time. Trebonious had tried his best to kill me twice, but I had to admit that he did a damned fine job of patching me up afterward. He sent a medicus to check my burns for signs of rot and change out the bandage and salve each day. By the end of the week a few patches of itchy red skin were all I had left to show for my recent brush with death.

At first I just ate a lot and slept even more. Walking hurt like the fifth hell at first, but every day the pain faded a bit more, and by the end of the week I could even stand a short round of exercise in the training room without crying. I spent my time making sure my legs were back to being as strong and steady as I could get them, and that I could keep up a decent running pace for five minutes or more.

My body wasn't the only thing I prepared. I slipped a fork and spoon into my boot during the dinner bustle, and spent two evenings fashioning them into a tension wrench and a set of picks. I tore one of the two blankets that a guard had delivered to my room after my last win into strips, then braided the strips into a length of rope which I kept hidden beneath my cot. It made for a few cold nights, but that was a small price to pay for freedom.

Over the past two days I'd also hid an apple and a few pieces of bread up my sleeve to tuck away in my room. My room was chill enough to keep them edible until I was ready to move. I knew I would need to hit the streets running, and that would be a lot easier if I didn't have to go searching for a meal on my first night beyond the arena walls.

I'd assumed that Trebonious would follow the same pattern as before and take a few weeks off between games, but the clamor I heard coming from the training room one morning told me I'd been wrong. I scowled, palmed a piece of dried fruit to add to my growing stash, and followed the crowd to go and see which unlucky sods would be next to fight and die for Farshore's amusement.

The packed room buzzed with idle speculation about why Trebonious had scheduled another contest so soon as Cael made his way through the throng and posted the list on the wooden pillar. I had thought that I'd have a bit more time to prepare before I had to make my move, but I decided as I pushed through the crowd that if I saw my name on that damned list again I'd take my chances and try to leg it that afternoon before the work crews arrived to start setting up for the games. I'd planned on slipping out during the small hours of the night and doubted that an escape could even work during the daytime, but I liked my odds of surviving whatever Trebonious had in store for me one more time even less.

My guts were tied up in so many knots as I elbowed my way through the crowd that it would have taken a gray-haired sailor half a day to untie them, but to my surprise my name wasn't on the list. I scanned the parchment one more time to be sure, then stumbled back to my room in a haze of relief. After my nerves settled and I had a chance to think it over I realized that these unexpected games presented me an opportunity. Trebonious always ordered more and better food served the night after games had been held. And, more importantly, an extra mug of ale for prisoners and guardsmen alike.

By the end of the day everyone would be spent from celebrating the end of the games or distracted with tending the wounded or burying the fallen, which meant that tonight would afford me a better chance than most to make my escape. Even if I had been inclined to wait, the shouts and screams that echoed through my room all evening would have pushed me over the edge for sure.

I listened and waited as the announcer's voice ushered the crowd back to their homes, then the tromp of boots and jovial shouts moving towards the mess hall marked the start of the celebrations. I counted the stones in my cell wall as the merriment dragged on. My nerves wound tighter by the hour, but every good thief learns how to keep their muscles loose and their mind clear during the long wait for all the pieces to fall into place at the beginning of a job.

Hours later even the most determined revelers had begun to make their way back to their cells. Once I heard the last door slam shut down the hallway I counted to one hundred, then gathered up my supplies, drew the latch, and slipped outside. I'd already confirmed that they didn't post a guard in the hall after the fighters had turned in for the night. A guard stayed by the exit that connected the common room to the hallway leading up past Trebonious' office to the streets above, but why bother putting a man on the door to the arena itself when it was already locked and only led up to an empty space surrounded by twenty foot walls?

I gave the door a quick once-over, and was surprised to find that the lock barely deserved the name. I'd expected something far worse, but what I found was only a simple keyhole that turned a latch on the far side.

Am I seriously the only person who has ever tried this before?

I had the door unlocked before I'd finished that thought. I slipped through, pulled it close, and locked it again from the other side before turning to look around. The hallway was shrouded in darkness, without even the faintest bit of moonlight shining down from the top of the ramp. The doors to the armory and infirmary were both locked. I had no doubt they would have been just as easy to get into, but I already had everything I needed, and every second I lingered increased the odds that someone might happen by at exactly the wrong moment.

I headed up the ramp at a thief's pace; not a run, but more than a walk, with each step taken heel to toe to keep from making any noise. I reached the top and checked the door. This one wasn't even locked. I shook my head at the sudden run of luck and pushed it open just wide enough to slip through, then flattened myself against the wall and scanned the arena floor.

I couldn't have asked for better conditions if Vesta herself had appeared before me and offered me her aid. A light rain fell from thick clouds that hid the moon and sky overhead. The city lights beyond the wall lit the scene just well enough for me to see where I was going, but the long shadows were thick enough to swim through. Still, I held tight for another dozen heartbeats as I swept my gaze back and forth along the top of the arena wall.

Only an idiot trusted in good luck over their own senses.

Nothing moved, but I figured if anyone was unfortunate enough to be posted to guard duty on a night like this then they were likely huddled up underneath something to avoid the rain. Didn't seem like they would have thought to post a watch on the walls when they hadn't bothered to guard the door that led there. Still, being cautious hurt nothing, while being hasty might end up hurting a whole hell of a lot. I let the drizzle trickle down my face as I watched and waited.

Finally, I decided that the way really was as open as it seemed and began to slide through the shadows along the base of the wall. I followed its curve until I'd reached the far side of the arena to stand beneath the governor's box. Its wooden railing reached several feet out from the wall above the arena floor. Plenty of railing up there for something to catch on.

I untied my makeshift rope from around my waist and knotted the spoon I'd pinched to one end as a counter-weight. I spun the rope in a circle at my side, faster and faster until the momentum felt right, then launched it skyward. It soared up over the railing to clatter to the wooden platform. A bit of careful jostling finally knocked the spoon loose to tumble back down to me. I held up a hand to catch it, but nothing reached me.

The rope was too short. I'd done my best to weave as much as I could manage from the material I had on hand while still making it strong enough to hold me, but it hadn't been enough. The spoon twirled in the air several feet above my head. I chewed on my bottom lip as I looked for a solution. Five minutes of thinking and I'd only come up with one idea, but in truth it wasn't very promising. Still, it couldn't hurt to try.

I backed away from the wall, pulling the rope with me until the spoon had risen all the way back to the edge of the platform, then launched myself toward the arena wall. I sprinted forward, kicked off the wall, and leapt up into the air as I reached for the spoon. I missed.

My hand closed on empty air as I tumbled back to the ground in a heap. I pushed up onto my knees, spit out a mouthful of sand, and glared at the spoon that now lay on the ground beside me. I could just imagine the stupid little shit taunting my feeble efforts. I was two inches away from freedom, but it might as well have been two hundred miles.

I gauged the distance again as I stood to my feet, and I could see why I hadn't gotten high enough. I'd been thinking about the ground when I'd jumped, and thinking about landing again had sapped some of the strength from my legs. I was pretty sure that I could make it if I gave that jump every-thing I had and then some. Probably. Of course, if I missed again I was in for a much harder landing than the last one. I'd covered bigger distances when

I'd leapt across Byzantia's rooftops, but it was easy to jump as hard as you could manage when the alternative was a broken neck. Still, risking a twisted ankle seemed like a better alternative than another round in the arena games.

I tossed the spoon back over the railing, took a few deep breaths, and threw myself forward. This time I used my momentum to take two good steps up the wall before I flung myself up and out. I spun around and reached out as I soared through the air, straining forward like a drowning man reaching for a life rope. My fingers brushed metal and grabbed hold.

The force of my swing carried me up and out over the sand. I tossed a dizzy glance down to the ground that spun beneath me as I began to fall backward, then scrambled up the rope and heaved myself up to grab the railing. The wood was slick with rain, but I held on tight and swung my other hand up to latch on as well. I hung there for a moment, dangling above the ground like an exhausted plum before harvest, then slowly began to pull myself up to safety.

"You could find easier exercise inside."

The voice came from just above my head. I looked up in shock to see a heart-shaped face, olive brown skin, and intense yellow eyes staring back into mine. I gasped as my grip slipped off the railing, and then I was falling.

My thoughts tumbled right along with me all the way to the ground as I tried to make sense of what had just happened. I hit the dirt before I had a good answer. The sand was softer that a cobbled street, but not by much. I bounced hard and landed in a tangle of limbs a few feet away. My vision danced with pops of color and swirls of black and I had to think really hard about breathing before my lungs finally remembered what to do. I coughed, then gasped, then forced myself to move.

Everything hurt, but at least it was the throbbing ache of deep bruises rather than the sharp stab of broken bones. I pushed myself up onto one elbow just in time to see a figure walking towards me through the rain.

It was the halfling woman I'd seen lurking in the shadows when I'd first arrived in the arena. She moved with the steady, deliberate grace of a cat hunting sparrows, and she carried a knife. Its blade was half the length of her leg and scattered stray shards of light off its razor edge as she moved. She stopped next to me and crouched down until her face was level with mine.

"Going somewhere?"

"I was until you showed up and scared a week's worth of shit out of me. What in the hells are you doing out here?"

"I would ask the same question of you."

I almost snapped back at her, but she had a knife and a hard look in her eye, so I decided to play it civil for as long as possible.

"I'm getting out of this death pit while I still can, and if you had half a brain in your skull you'd be coming with me instead of getting in my way."

What? I never said I was *good* at being civil.

"I think it is you who is missing their brain," she said with a shake of her head. "Unless you've found some way to deal with your effigy."

"My what?"

Then I remembered the strange little lecture Trebonious had given me as he dipped a lock of my hair in my own blood. He'd claimed he could use it to visit a nasty death upon me if I ever caused him trouble, or some such nonsense. I snorted a little spray of water from my nose.

"You don't actually believe that horseshit is real, do you?"

"I do, and it is. Did you not stop to wonder why it was so easy to leave in the first place?"

I'd noticed that very thing, in fact, but had just chalked it up to uncommon good luck. I had to admit that Farshore's arena was, without a doubt, the most poorly guarded prison I had ever seen. Almost as if they weren't terribly bothered by the idea of someone breaking out of it...

"If you run you will die."

She spoke the words with such casual certainty that for a moment I almost believed her. I'd been so busy trying to keep my skin in one piece that I'd forgotten all about the damned thing, so I hadn't bothered to factor it into my escape plans. Could that sour-faced little scarecrow really use a bloody chunk of hair to reach out and kill me?

Then I got a hold of myself. No doubt Trebonious was simply clever enough to use the locals' superstition against them by making them too scared to run for it. I gave him credit for a good con, but that didn't mean I had to fall for it too.

"Thanks, but I'll take my chances."

Sheska's knife was at my throat. I hadn't even seen her move, but suddenly her blade dug a painful line across my skin.

"You will not. If you insist on trying I will kill you myself."

68

I held very, very still. I'd seen bluffs before. This was not one of them.

"Why do you care? If you're right then Trebonious will kill me, if you're wrong then I get to enjoy my life in peace. What difference does my fate make to you?"

"None," she said with a shrug. I tried not to wince as her blade bit into my skin. "But if you go over that wall then the small man in black will reduce our rations to make an example. I am more fond of a full meal than I am of you. Now make your choice. I find this rain unpleasant."

For a moment I thought about flinging sand at her eyes and rolling away to make a run for it, but something told me that even a bit of dirty fighting wouldn't be enough to get the drop on her. The small woman gave me chills, and it wasn't just from the cold water that ran down the back of my shirt. I sighed and pushed her blade away.

"Fine, you win. Let's get back inside."

She nodded and watched me struggle to my feet without offering to help. Then she kept right on watching me, following a few steps behind as I hobbled my way across the sand, down the ramp, and back through the arena door. I pulled it shut behind us and dug out my makeshift picks to lock the door again.

"You know, if we worked together I think we could get our hands on the—"

She was gone by the time I turned around. I hadn't even heard the whisper of her boots on the stone floor, and that simple fact left me feeling far more nervous than even her wicked looking knife had managed. I thought about popping the door for a third time and making a break for it, but I couldn't shake the thought that she would know about it somehow, and probably wouldn't bother to stop and chat if I tried to scale the wall again.

I sighed and limped back to my cell. Planning my escape had kept me focused and effective, but I felt that sense of purpose drain out of me with each step. I walked into my room, pulled the door shut, and flopped down on my cot without even bothering to peel off my soggy clothes. An hour ago I'd been riding high on thoughts of freedom. Now all I had was wet clothes, an aching back, and a future full of fighting and pain until the odds finally caught up with me and put me in the ground for good.

8

"**D**amn it, Charity! Keep your guard up if you want to keep your head."

I bit back a stream of choice curses and crawled my way back onto my feet, ignoring the screams of protest from the muscles in my hips, thighs, shoulders, arms, and more as I bent to retrieve my wooden training swords and resumed a fighting stance in front of Cael.

The sad and sodden end to my hopes of escape had left me in one hell of a funk. I picked at my food, kept to myself, and snapped at Alleron when he'd asked what was bothering me even though he'd been the only one to notice or care enough to do so. A week went by without games being scheduled, and then another. I overheard two of the guards discussing the cotton harvest, so I gathered that a good portion of the city must have been too occupied with picking and bagging for it to have been worth scheduling new festivities. No point in forcing people to kill each other if no one bought tickets to come and watch.

As much as I'd come to dread seeing my name on the games' list again, a few weeks of drudgery were the last thing I needed just then. My sleep grew worse every night, and before long I felt worse than I can ever remember feeling without actually being sick or on the verge of starvation. I finally realized that I needed to find something to occupy myself with if I wanted to avoid going full on insane. Given that needlepoint wasn't an option, I eventually decided that if I couldn't escape another trip to the arena then I might as well spend my time improving my odds of surviving it.

It took me a full day to work up the courage to ask Cael for help, but to my surprise he'd been eager to do so. I thought he'd felt sorry for me. Turned out he was just a horrible sadist who enjoyed yelling at girls and whacking them on the head with a training sword whenever they let their guard slip. Bastard.

He'd been driving me harder than a Vera ngi slave master, and every time I paused or complained he just used the distraction to hit me again and tell me that I'd be dead right now if we'd been fighting for real.

After my first week of abuse I learned to save my breath for the training, and even though I'd fallen asleep cursing his name and thinking of exquisitely painful ways to kill him, I had to admit that Cael's methods were proving effective. I'd begun to notice the change in my body as my muscles hardened and absorbed his lessons, and some of the stances, parries, attacks, and evasions I had once thought impossible had begun to feel routine.

"Blood of the gods, are you swatting at flies? Stop waving those toothpicks around and perform the exchange like I've shown you."

Cael had started me out with a broadsword and shield, the proper weapons of a warrior, as he'd called them. He'd gone on and on about how a good shield provided both defense and offense in a trained warrior's hands. I gave it my best try seeing as the shield he'd given me had saved my life in the fight against the elementals, but I'd lacked the upper body strength to do much more than hide underneath it and wait for the beating to stop.

In the end it had been Alleron who'd suggested that I exchange both weapons for two sabers. Apparently it was a common fighting style among his people, who were lighter and shorter like me. The first time I'd fought with them had been a revelation. You don't have to be stronger than your opponent if you're fast enough to turn his guard with one blade and strike through it with the other. Cael had grumbled about it for days, but I'd taken to it immediately and refused to fight with anything else after that.

One evening over dinner I asked Alleron why he kept helping me out. I wasn't used to kindness that didn't come with a string attached or a dagger hidden inside it. He hadn't done anything to make me question his motives yet, and that was starting to make me very uncomfortable.

"Well, for one thing your unlikely win against Borus won me more beer and favors than I'll be able to enjoy in ten lifetimes, so I suppose I feel indebted to you."

"Wait, you wagered that I'd win?"

"Of course I did," he answered, seeming honestly confused by the question. I suppose I should have been flattered, but all I could think in the moment was that he'd just removed the last doubt I'd had as to whether or not he was completely crazy.

"In truth, however, I'm helping you because I have great hopes you'll do the same for me in the future."

Ah, now we were getting back into more familiar territory.

"Have anything specific in mind?" I asked cautiously.

"I do, indeed. Someday in the not too distant future you're going to help me save my people."

"Oh…is that all?"

I honestly didn't know how to respond to that. I would have assumed he was joking if his expression hadn't gone so serious all of a sudden.

"You sure you got the right Byzantian? Lot of girls with brown skin and black hair where I'm from."

"Quite certain. I had already seen your face many times before you arrived here."

Then a lopsided grin spread across his face like sun breaking through the clouds as he leaned back in his seat.

"Then again, perhaps my visions have finally pushed me over the edge and I don't even realize how mad I am. Who can say?"

I let out the breath I'd been holding and smiled back in relief as I shook my head at his poor joke. In truth, his words had sent a shiver through my gut, but I hid my unease beneath a laugh.

"I knew you were full of shit. Don't know how you'd expect me to save anyone from in here anyways."

"Oh, we won't remain in the arena much longer."

I sat up and looked around, suddenly nervous. Even with the noise in the dining hall his voice was pitched a tad too loud for comfort.

"Not so loud. You got a plan then?"

"Nothing like your little midnight escapade, if that's what you're asking."

"You know about that?"

He smirked and waggled his fingers at me.

"Wizard, remember? Diviner extraordinaire. I may be working off of old information without my equipment and reagents, but I knew you'd try to go over the wall. Would have stopped you myself if Sheska hadn't beaten me to it."

I scowled as he mentioned the halfling's name.

"I still have half a mind to find a quiet moment to resume our little conversation when she isn't looking. I would have been ten miles gone by now if that *bruta* hadn't stopped me."

"More like six feet under the ground," he chuckled. "Your arena master may be just a human, but he's learned quickly. The effigies he crafted are no jest, and neither is Sheska, so I'd recommend you leave her be if you enjoy breathing and having all your limbs fixed in place."

"Really? She's the only one in here who's smaller than me."

"Indeed, and she also holds the record for most kills in the arena now that Borus is no more."

He laughed at the look of shock that settled onto my face.

"Halflings are rather…feral, you see. Most have the good sense to leave them be. 'A halfling never goes hungry,' as the old saying goes."

"What does eating have to do with it?"

"Quite a lot, given that halflings eat what they kill."

"Oh." I felt another one of those shivers Sheska had given me trace its way down my spine. Seemed that the stories of horrible man-eating mythics in Farshore weren't entirely false, they were just shorter than I'd expected.

"In any case, now that your abortive venture is behind us it should only be a matter of days before we're on our way."

"On our way to what, exactly?"

"Why spoil the surprise?"

"I hate surprises."

"In that case, Charity my dear, I suggest you prepare yourself for a long string of disappointments. Oh, do you plan on finishing that loaf?"

My cycle of training, eating, and sleeping continued on, folding over on itself until the routine was all I knew. I have no idea how long my days might have gone on like that, if it all hadn't changed one morning without warning.

I awoke to the sound of hammering, sawing, and the muffled shouts of men hard at work filtering down through my stone ceiling from the arena floor overhead. I'd become accustomed to waking in my own good time, so the intruding noise had me in a foul mood by the time I'd dressed and made my way down to the mess hall. It was more crowded than usual, nearly as full as the evening I'd first arrived.

Looks like I'm not the only one who got turned out of their bed early by all this racket.

I spotted Alleron at a nearby table, and noticed that he'd somehow managed to keep a seat open. I wove through the crowd and plopped myself down in it with a grunt.

"What in the eight frozen hells is going on up there?" I asked as he slid me a plate of eggs and roasted potatoes.

"Today is Farshore's seventieth year of glorious existence, don't you know? Seems that the occasion calls for something extra special for today's games."

"Are they building us a fleet to hold naval battles?"

The hammering and banging could be heard even above the din of conversation in the crowded room.

Alleron just shrugged, but pointed towards my plate of food.

"Better eat hearty, just in case."

It was sound advice, so I set about following it. As I scraped the last of the food off my plate, a voice from across the room shouted that the pairings for today's games had just been posted, and the room echoed with the scrape of dozens of benches and chairs on the stone floor as everyone stood at once to go look for themselves.

"It finally begins," Alleron whispered to himself. Or, at least I thought that's what I heard him say. With all the racket it was hard to be sure. When I turned to ask him what he was on about this time I realized that he was already halfway to the door, so I scrambled to catch up with him.

The training room was more crowded than I'd ever seen it, but we managed to press our way through. The familiar sheet of paper was nailed to the central post, but this one had only a single list of names on it instead of the usual two columns of paired names that designated that day's matches. I elbowed my way closer, and saw the words "Battle of the Victors" in large script across the top, followed by a very short list of names. Mine was among them. So was Alleron's. In fact, the eight names on the list were the winners of the last three games.

"So, what then?" I asked a gray-haired man standing next to me. "Today's games will only have one match? Some sort of battle to the death?" The thought of the carnage that would ensue if they set us against each other all at once turned my blood to ice, but I tried to keep my expression calm and disinterested.

"One match, aye, but Cael made the announcement when he posted the sheet. You won't be fighting against each other. You'll be fighting as a team."

At first I wasn't sure I'd heard him right, but I soon realized that it was all that anyone else was talking about. Alleron beamed at me like a child who'd just learned he'd be allowed to eat his fill of sweet buns, but I could only offer a weak smile in return. I was relieved to learn I wouldn't have to cross swords with him, but that relief didn't have much room to grow next to the question that was taking up most of my thoughts.

If Trebonious intends for us to all fight together as a team…what in the name of Vesta's ample tits is he sending us up against?

9

———

"If anyone so much as touches my axe I swear I'll make a winter coat from their hide!"

Magnus shoved his way past me to be the first one into the weapon room. He raced across the room with surprising speed given the length of his legs, and lifted a huge double-sided war axe down from a rack.

"There's my girl. Have they treated you well? No nicks or scratches on you?"

The rest of us filed into the room while Magnus continued to whisper to his weapon as he checked its edge for signs of wear. I retrieved a pair of curved sabers from the sword table as the others spread out through the room to equip themselves as they saw fit. No one seemed inclined to talk, but the tension in the air was so thick you could have cut it with...well, just about anything in the room, actually. None of the victors had ever faced one another in the arena, obviously, but more than a few had lost a friend to the other's blade, and none were the trusting sort by nature.

In addition to Magnus and Alleron, the orc Nataka and Sheska herself had also been on the list. The remaining three were comfortingly human. Olney was a legionary veteran with a touch of white in his hair and an eyepatch covering his left eye, while Keegan was a bear of a man sporting a scraggly black beard and biceps the size of dinner plates. The third was a man named Cassus, a lean fellow with black hair that fell to his shoulders and eyes that never seemed to stop checking the shadows.

"Any of you have some sense of what we'll be facing up there?" I asked. I doubted anyone had much to offer, but a girl can only listen to the clatter of armor and the rasp of whetstones over blades for so long.

"Not I." Keegan's voice was muffled by the chainmail shirt he was attempting to squeeze over his head and shoulders. "Though I'll wager... unf, that it'll be something special. Why go to all this, aargh...trouble, otherwise?" He finally managed to get the chainmail settled onto his torso. Didn't look like he could breathe too well, but he seemed pleased.

"Well, shouldn't we discuss some tactics, then?" I asked the room. "You know, compare strengths and weaknesses and such. We'll stand a better chance against whatever they have planned if we work together."

"I hunt alone," said a voice by my ear. It took all the self-control I could muster not to jump five feet in the air. Instead I turned around to find Sheska crouched on top of the table behind me, staring at me with her strange yellow eyes. She carried a shortbow and a quiver full of arrows, and had painted a pair of black soot lines across her face.

"If you get in my way, you are dead. If you do not, you may do as you please."

"Right, um, that's more or less what I was talking about, I suppose. Thanks."

Sheska nodded once, but didn't take her eyes off me. Even though she was less than half my size, I started to think that now I had a better sense of how a dormouse feels when a cat prowls into the room. I didn't want to be the first one to look away. No sense in letting her know how badly she unnerved me, so I squared my jaw and glared back at her. Just when I was starting to think that getting into a staring contest with a halfling might be a losing proposition, the arena master's voice thundered down the passageway.

"Fighters, to your stations!"

Sheska blinked once, sniffed, then jumped down from the table and walked past me towards the door. I turned to find Alleron trying to hide a smile as he shook his head. I shot a glare in his direction and joined the others in heading for the door.

We all walked up the ramp together, and I found myself feeling a good deal more confident than any of the other times I'd made the journey before. I still had no idea what we'd be facing once we got up there, but thanks to Cael and Alleron I was significantly better prepared to deal with whatever Trebonious threw at us. Besides, I was now surrounded by a pack of battle-tested fighters who had fought and won before. I figured all I really needed to do was focus on keeping myself alive and in one piece, and they could take care of the rest.

As we approached the top of the ramp I realized that it was later in the day than I'd thought. It was dark, but the arena floor was lit by hundreds of blazing torches that ringed the top of the wall.

"What in the bloody hells is all this?" Olney grumbled from the front.

I had to wait for the rest of the group to shuffle through the entrance before I could see what he was talking about. The arena floor had been transformed. It was filled with an artificial forest of wooden trees that stretched from wall to wall. A platform that had been made to resemble a rocky cliff face rose above them in the center, and a path led towards it from the ramp entrance.

I guess now we know what was causing that racket all day. But why did they go to all this trouble?

One thing was certain; there was no way Trebonious had put all of this together just to throw us a celebration picnic. With the torchlight shining in my eyes I couldn't see the crowd in the stands, but I heard enough excited whispers and shuffling to know that every available seat was filled, though it seemed that for some reason they had been told to remain silent as we entered. What I could see in the shadows of the torchlight were dozens of men standing all along the top of the wall, each one holding a crossbow at the ready.

"My noble lords and dames, welcome to these special games," the arena master's voice echoed in the eerie silence.

"In the name of the Five Divines, and in honor of Farshore's seventieth glorious year, Governor Caligus bids you welcome! Tonight the finest champions ever to grace the arena sands will fight for your entertainment and the glory of the gods."

I looked around, but I still saw no sign of who they were expecting us to battle. Were other fighters hiding out there among the trees?

"Warriors! In the name of the Five Divines, fight with honor, die with courage, live on in glory. Begin!"

I'm not ashamed to admit that I jumped a bit when the heavy wooden doors of the passageway slammed closed behind us, but otherwise nothing moved as the echo faded away.

"Bah!" Keegan snorted in disgust as he frowned down at me, then turned and marched straight down the path that led towards the false cliff face at the center of the arena. I looked at Alleron, but he just shrugged and followed the others in Keegan's wake. The hairs on the back of my neck were prickling with unease, but I preferred staying with the group to hanging back on my own, so I hurried to catch up with them.

We drew closer to the platform, and I spotted a large opening towards the top. It looked like the entrance to a cave. As we stepped into the small clearing that surrounded the cliff, the squeal of rusty metal hinges echoed out of the cave. The sound cut off as abruptly as it had started, then a pair of orange eyes flared to life in the darkness.

More than ten thousand pairs of lungs drew in a startled gasp all at once as a shape emerged from the cave and began to climb down the platform. It looked a lot like a cat, but as it reached the ground and started stalking its way towards us I realized that it was easily twice the size of a horse. Its coat was as black as spilled ink, and it moved with the fluid grace of a hunter on the prowl.

"Kla ses ka'sani netak," I heard a shaking voice say beside me, and I looked down to see Sheska rooted in place, her eyes wide with shock and fear as she stared at the approaching monster. "Mother and Father save us, a Jauguai."

The huge creature crouched low to the ground, its tail lashing back and forth as its gaze darted to each one of us in turn.

"Keep your skirts on, little one," Keegan chuckled as he stepped forward. "It's a might bigger than most, but it's just a cat all the same. Should make a nice rug for my room." He clashed his sword against his shield as he rolled his shoulders and stepped forward.

"Come on, kitten. Let's see what you look like on the inside."

The beast snarled, and two black tendrils rose up from its shoulders to sway in the air above its head. They looked exactly like its tail, except that each was tipped in a curved, bone-white talon that looked wickedly sharp even from here.

"Well, that's different," Magnus muttered as he hefted his axe. He started to move towards Keegan, but Sheska grabbed his arm.

"Stop, you fool! Do not move. Do not even breathe."

"Let me go, you crazed she-devil," Magnus pulled his arm free.

"Raaaargh!" Keegan bellowed, and leaped forward.

The Jauguai roared in answer, a hungry, feral challenge that rattled my bones. Then it disappeared.

One moment the huge cat was standing there plain as porridge. The next its shape blurred and warped like smoke for an instant before it vanished completely. Keegan's charge turned into a stumbling halt.

"What in the eight frozen—"

The air in front of his face blurred black, then his head was torn from his shoulders. A crimson spray of blood shot into the air as his headless body stood motionless for a brief moment before it collapsed like a puppet whose strings had just been cut.

The crowd erupted in a chorus of shrieks and cheers. Before my brain had managed to wrap itself around what I'd just seen I heard a scream behind me, and spun around to see Olney kicking and flailing in the Jauguai's jaws. The beast crunched down hard and the flailing stopped. It dropped the limp body to the ground, licked the blood from its muzzle with a long, pink tongue, then disappeared again.

"Form up!" Nataka shouted. "Back to back. Now!"

Her gruff voice broke through my shock, and I jumped to take my place in the outward-facing circle we formed, my swords raised and ready. I scanned the open ground in front of me, starting at every flickering shadow cast by the torchlight, but saw nothing that would reveal the beast's presence.

"What in the bloody hells is that thing?" Cassus sounded even more terrified than I felt, which I hadn't thought was possible.

"Jauguai hunt the deep jungles of my home." Sheska stood beside me, an arrow drawn back on her bow and both eyes searching the trees. "I have never seen one before, but I know the stories. They are demons clothed in flesh."

"I could handle a demon if I could see it," Magnus grunted. "How does it keep disappearing like that?"

"He cloaks himself in shadow. We will not see him until it is too late."

"Then how do we kill it?" I asked.

"Kill it? Ha!" Sheska actually sounded amused. "You don't kill Jauguai. If they hunt you then you run, you hide, or you die."

"Not terribly fond of any of those options, personally," Alleron said behind me.

"Then why are we just standing out in the open waiting to be ripped to shreds?" Cassus' voice was laced with panic, and when I glanced back at him I saw that he was sweating like he'd just been jolted out of a nightmare.

"Because," I answered, careful to keep my voice calm and even, "if we stand together we can watch each other's backs. That's something, at least."

Another roar split the air from the trees in front of me, but when I spun around all I saw was the briefest hint of black gliding between the trees.

"No, no, no, no," Cassus stammered, "you sods can stand here and get eaten if you like, but I'm getting gone."

"Wait!" I shouted, but he was already racing down the path towards the closed doors of the ramp entrance.

He covered about half the distance in short order. Just when I started to think he might reach the doors one of the cat's strange shoulder-tails whipped out of the trees. The curved talon buried itself in his back, then pulled him off his feet to fly backwards. Cassus landed in a heap, and had just enough time for one horrible scream before the Jauguai blurred back into view and ripped him to pieces. Once the beast had reduced the man to bloody shreds it turned to look back at us, and I swear by the gods that it grinned at me before it faded from view once more.

Panic screamed through me and set my limbs trembling. Our group was down by three in just about as many minutes, and I expected more would follow soon. I knew I needed to think clearly now more than I ever had before, but one thought kept repeating itself in my mind over and over, leaving no room for anything else.

This can't be happening, this can't be real. This can't be happening, this can't be real.

Since arriving in Farshore I'd bounced from one immediate problem to the next so quickly that I hadn't had time to stop and really absorb everything that had happened. Life had been hard back in Byzantia, but at least the rules made sense and I knew how to handle each day as it came. Now I stood back to back with an elf, a dwarf, an orc, and a halfling while an invisible demon cat tried to decide what order it wanted to eat us in. It was like a bad children's story, except it was all real, and in a few minutes more it was going to be the death of me.

There is no problem that knowledge and sound reason cannot solve. Mother Shanti's oft-repeated words broke through the terrified chatter in my mind, and I felt like I could hear the impatient tapping of her shoe as she frowned down at me. Suddenly, I was a foolish girl again, whining and complaining when the solution was right in front of my nose if I would just bother to slow down enough to see it.

Alright, you blight-faced old nag. What would you say if you were here, eh? Her dry voice resumed its droning in my memory.

Every problem is composed of constituent parts. Cause to effect, Charity. Always cause to effect. Follow the chain until you reach the root cause of the problem, and you will find your answer.

My mind was finally working again, and a sudden growl that rumbled through the air behind me whipped it into full gallop like a frightened horse.

So what's the root problem? Several hundred pounds of bloodthirsty muscles and teeth. Except that's not really the problem, is it? That beast is scary, but together we could probably bring it down if we could see it coming. As long as it keeps disappearing like that, we're as good as dead.

We needed a way to force it into the open. I thought of one. The only problem was that I hated it almost as much as I hated shaking in my boots while death prowled around just out of sight. The only way I could think to draw the big cat out would require us all to work together, and that meant I'd be trusting my life to a bunch of strangers who weren't even human. If they decided to use me as bait to save their own skins there'd be nothing I could do to stop them. I knew, because in that moment I would have done exactly that to any one of them if it would have gotten me out of the arena alive. Still, I didn't see any other options.

"Alright, you lot," I said aloud. "I'm personally feeling thoroughly sick of being hunted by something I can't see. Shall we do something about it?"

"You have some magic that can break its cloak?" Nataka asked, sounding like she was ready to kill me herself for holding out on them.

"Not magic, but a plan. Or, something like a plan, at least."

"Let's hear it then, girlie," Magnus snapped, "Anything is better than standing here with my head up my ass waiting to be gutted."

"Well, we can't fight it if we can't see it, but it will just stay invisible until we give it an opening."

Sheska snorted. "Your words sound familiar. Perhaps because I said them myself not long ago?"

I gritted my teeth, but continued. "But it's not always invisible. It reappears every time it attacks. Why? I think it's because it can't keep up that cloaking trick while it's chewing on something."

"Hmmm, you may be right at that," Alleron said. "An illusion like that requires a great deal of effort."

"Right, so if we can lure it into attacking when we're ready for it, we can all strike at once and bring it down."

"Perhaps," said Sheska, though she did not sound convinced. "But will the creature not simply vanish again when we strike back?"

"I might be able to help with that, actually," said Alleron. "I think I have a sense of how it's managing to disappear. If we can force it to reveal itself for more than a few seconds I think I can keep it that way. Probably."

"If you're wrong then my axe will split you open before the beastie gets to you," grumbled Magnus.

"You can keep it visible? That's it?"

My heart sank into my stomach. My plan had pretty much boiled down to "lure the cat into attacking and keep it busy so that Alleron can melt it into a puddle." After all his ramblings about magic, I was hoping for something a little bit more...permanent.

"I thought you were a grand and glorious wizard? Can't you burn it to cinders or turn it to stone?"

"Oh yes, of course, why didn't I think of that?" Alleron snapped. "If you have scrolls detailing the spell you had in mind and a few quiet months for study and practice I'd be happy to oblige you. If you'd prefer something right now, however, then I'm afraid that 'visible' is the best I can do."

"If I can see it then I can root it in place and render it vulnerable," Nataka offered.

"Good, then Hilda can find out what color its brains are," Magnus said as he gave his axe a quick twirl, "but how do we draw it out?"

"We run."

Sheska spoke as though she were suggesting a summer picnic, but even though my mind followed the logic of her plan, my stomach threatened to rebel at the thought.

"This creature is a hunter. It will stalk and harass until we show weakness. The elf remains in the center while we four run in opposite directions. It will attack, and he will have his chance."

"But what about the one it picks as its next meal?" I asked over my shoulder.

"Would you rather stand here until the Deathstalker attacks on its own time?"

I hated to admit it, but she was right. So far the Jauguai had kept its distance from our little circle, but it was bound to grow restless sooner or later. Standing still was a death sentence in the end. At least if we acted first we'd have the element of surprise, and maybe some slight chance of surviving the night.

"Alright," I nodded. "So, do we count to three, or—"

"Yaaargh!" Magnus bellowed as he charged out into the night. "Come get some you flea-ridden hellspawn!"

"…just start running."

Sheska and Nataka were already racing in opposite directions. I drew in a deep breath, tried not to wonder if it was going to be my last, and began sprinting towards the fake trees in front of me.

Running is usually something I do very well, but that time my heartbeat was hammering in my ears before I'd taken ten steps, and my breath burned hot in my lungs. My eyes kept darting left, right, and up even though I knew they wouldn't see death coming for me anyway.

Every muscle in my back and shoulders was clenched tight as I waited to feel a set of razor-sharp claws tear into them at any moment. I'd been in a lot of bad scrapes before, but I had never felt as helpless and vulnerable as I did running exposed across the open ground, certain that two tons of hunting fury were watching my every step.

Then I saw it, a faint ripple in the air right in front of me like heat rising from a baker's oven on a cold day. Normally I doubt I would have even noticed it, but now my mind screamed a warning and I dove to the ground without a second thought. I felt a rush of wind as a heavy paw slashed through the air where my head had been a split second before. Then I hit the dirt and tucked into a ball. When I rolled to a stop I looked up to find the Jauguai staring right back at me.

Its head was enormous, nearly the size of one of the three-man tables in the arena pits. I was lying pinned between its two front legs, surprised to find I was still breathing. The big cat looked surprised too, but only for a moment. Then its glowing eyes narrowed to slits and its lips pulled back in a snarl that revealed a set of teeth the length of kitchen knives still stained with blood. It reared back and opened its jaws, and I knew I was about to die.

"Haaaiiii!" a shrill battle cry split the air, and a second later two arrows thudded into the Jauguai's neck. It stumbled back with a snarl of pain and surprise, giving me enough room to roll clear. I jumped to my feet and saw Sheska racing towards me with another arrow already drawn back, her small face alive with battle fury. Further behind her I saw that Alleron still stood where he'd been when I'd started running. It looked like he was just staring down at his hands and muttering to himself, and for a second I wondered if he'd lost his cool just like Cassus had.

As the Jauguai recovered from its shock, its form began to warp and blur once again.

"Now or never, Alleron!" I shouted. The elf looked up, and his eyes were glowing with an eerie green light.

He shouted out a string of strange words, and I felt a tingle ripple across my skin. Air pressed in against my ear drums like the feeling before a storm breaks loose, and then that same green light sprang to life around his hands. He flung them out with his fingers pointed at the Jauguai, and the light shot across the space between them to wrap itself around the huge cat just as it finished its vanishing act again.

The Jauguai was gone, it's massive black body invisible once again. But this time, a perfect green outline of its shape shimmered in the air. The glowing green cat shape turned and began moving towards the trees, and from the way it walked without turning towards us I knew that it didn't realize we could see it plain as day. For the first time since it had come stalking out of its cave I felt a surge of hope.

Nataka came running from my right. She twirled her spear above her head, but instead of using it to attack she skidded to a halt and slammed the butt into the earth.

"Legra and Sodek, Dwellers in the Deep Earth, wake your kin!" The Jauguai's head whipped around at the sound of her voice. It turned and crouched to leap at her, but a sudden rumble in the ground halted its attack. Then a tangle of thick roots burst up all around the cat and began to wrap themselves around its legs and body. The Jauguai howled and began to thrash in wild fury, but for every root it snapped three more whipped up around it. Soon it was bound tight to the earth.

"Your blood is mine, Deathstalker!" Sheska ran past me, an arrow aimed straight at the cat's eye. She was so focused on her target that she didn't see the Jauguai's shoulder-tails whipping towards her until it was too late. One tail coiled itself around her shoulders while the other wrapped around her leg, and with a heave they flung her up off the ground. She arced through the air, and I realized that she was sailing straight towards the monster's open jaws.

Dammit to all the hells. I leaped towards the cat before I could think better of it.

The halfling wasn't a friend. In fact, she'd made it clear that she'd rather gut me than share a meal. But she had just saved my life less than ten heart-beats ago, and that was the kind of debt I didn't like to leave unpaid. I ran up a thick cable of roots, keeping my balance just like I would if I'd been moving along a rope line between rooftops back home, then jumped up to land on its shoulders and struck out with my sabers.

I grinned as my blades drew another howl from the beast, and its two shoulder-tails thudded to the ground. Sheska tumbled to a stop a few feet from the Jauguai's snapping jaws. She sat up, scrambled free of the lifeless coils, and stared up at me with a look of total shock frozen on her face.

"Drazi kan Kahad!" Magnus bellowed. His war cry echoed in the air as he leaped over Sheska where she lay sprawled on the ground and brought his axe down on the Jauguai's forehead. The thwack that it made as it hit home would have done a timberman proud. The beast roared and heaved itself at Magnus, but the roots held it fast. For a moment I thought that the cat's rage would somehow keep it fighting on even with an axe buried in its skull. Then the yellow light faded from the monster's eyes and it slumped to the ground.

My breath came fast and heavy as I jumped down from its back. I heard a roaring, whistling sound in my ears. For a moment I wondered if the strange magic they'd been throwing around had played havoc with my ears, until I realized that what I heard was the frenzied cheering of the crowd in the arena stands.

"By all the gods! Truly we have witnessed a battle worthy of song and praise."

The arena master's voice thundered through the stands, bringing me back to reality. Despite his enthusiasm I sensed a note of true surprise in his words, and I guessed that none of us had been favored to survive the night. If we'd fought alone I had no doubt we'd each be lying in a pool of our own blood right now, but working together had turned out better than I'd dared hope.

"My lords and dames, I give you your champions!"

"Bah!" Magnus snorted as he yanked his axe out of the Jauguai's skull and slung it across his shoulder.

"Damned crazy human sacks of—" his voice trailed off as he turned and marched back towards the arena entrance.

Sheska was still staring at me, her face a mixture of confusion and murderous rage. It would have bothered me if I had enough energy left to worry about it. Now that the danger had passed all the adrenaline was quickly draining away from me. Suddenly I felt so tired that I started seriously considering a quick nap right there on the sand, and it left me in no mood for games.

"Problem?" I asked her.

The halfling opened her mouth, paused, then snapped it shut again and turned to follow after Magnus. I sighed and started making my own way towards the doors, not bothering to bow or salute the crowd. They could shower their empty praise on someone else, because just then the only reward I cared for was a bed and a good night's sleep.

10

The walk down the ramp felt longer than it ever had before. The only sound I heard was the clatter of five pairs of boots on stone, three pairs fewer than the number that had walked up to the arena just a few minutes ago. I'd faced death before — the looming threat of starvation on the streets or the glint of a knife in a back alley — but I had always faced it alone, which meant there was no one but myself and the empty sky to see me walk away. I didn't know these people that walked with me back down into the pits, but we'd just stood together against a nightmare, and for a moment I'd felt like we'd been more than strangers.

I wished that I could think of something to say that could capture that feeling and make it real, but the only words that came to me sounded hollow and foolish. In the end I resigned myself to silence as we all returned our borrowed armor and weapons and made our way back into the pits. As we reached the branching point in the hallway, I squared my shoulders and turned to walk alone towards my room without looking back.

This is how the world is. How it will always be. No sense in crying over something you can't change.

The words sounded nice, but I still planned on indulging in a good round of sulking once I got back to my room. And that's probably exactly how I would have spent my evening if Cael hadn't been waiting for me outside my door.

When I first saw him I felt an unexpected thrill run down my spine. I had to admit that he was the kind of man that a girl looked at twice. He'd been far kinder to me than I'd had any right to expect, and my heart was still beating a little faster in my chest from the battle in the arena.

But when I saw the look on his face I gathered that he hadn't come for a social call. He seemed tense and distracted, and only acknowledged that he'd seen me with the briefest of nods as I walked up to him.

"Trebonious sent me to fetch you to his office," he said without greeting. I didn't need to hear the grim tone in his voice to know that this was not a good thing.

"Why? Or let me guess, he's angry that we survived that little death trap of his and wants to tell me what my horrible punishment will be in person?"

I didn't think he'd actually punish us for winning in the games. It seemed like a bad sort of precedent to set, but it was the only reason I could think of for why he'd have me brought to him now.

Cael just shook his head and started leading me back down the hallway towards the common room.

"No. If anything he seemed...excited."

You wouldn't think that would be cause for concern, but something in the way that Cael said it left me unsettled as we wove our way through the common room.

He nodded to the two guards stationed by the door. They lifted the bar and swung it open for us, and I found myself standing in the same stone hallway he had led me down when I'd first arrived at the arena all those months ago. Some stairs and a few turns later we approached the door to Trebonious' office, and I saw that all four of my recent fighting companions were already waiting outside.

"What's this all about then, Cael?" Magnus grumbled. "I was just about to start in on my second pint."

"If I knew, Magnus, I still wouldn't tell you. Just hold tight until I return." Cael entered the office and closed the door behind him.

The others appeared relaxed, but I could sense that this unusual summons had them as much on edge as I was. Even Alleron seemed too caught up with his own thoughts for conversation, which was a first as far as

I could recall. The only one of them to pay me any attention was Sheska. She studied me with that same focused glare she had been giving me ever since we killed the Jauguai, except this time there was no mistaking the anger that burned in her eyes. It had been a long day, and what little patience the Divines had given me had just about reached its breaking point.

"Look," I snapped, returning her glare and then some, "you've been eying me up and down ever since we walked out of the arena. If you've got something to say then let's hear it, otherwise find something else to stare at and leave me the hells alone."

The halfling blinked in surprise. Then she growled at me. I mean, she actually growled like a dog on a tether, which was not a sound I was used to hearing coming from someone who was more or less a person. For a moment I wondered if she planned on biting me, but with a visible effort of will she got a hold of herself and took a deep breath as though she was bracing herself for something unpleasant.

"You will have to take my life, human girl, for I will never be your slave."

"I'm sorry...what?"

"I will never be a slave again!" she shouted, her hands closing into fists.

Just when I thought I was starting to understand Farshore.

"Whoa, slow down," I said, raising my hands and trying to keep my voice calm and even. "Who said anything about making you a slave?"

She paused, and her anger slowly gave way to confusion as she realized that I truly didn't know what she was talking about.

"You saved my life, so now you hold my debt," she said, talking slowly as if she were explaining to a child that water is wet. "The Mother and Father's Law demands that now I serve you until the end of my days. They sent their servant to claim me, but you turned him back and stole me from their court. Death is my only escape from the curse you have placed on me. All I can do now is ask that you release me. Please."

The word caught in her throat a little, and I got the sense that this was the closest she had ever come to begging, which made me feel a little sick inside.

I guess the Divines aren't the only gods around who make unreasonable demands that ruin peoples' lives. At least this time I can do something about it.

"Look Sheska, all I know is that if you hadn't come charging in when you did I'd be enjoying a lovely view of the inside of a cat's stomach right now.

You saved my life, I saved yours, and we both walked out of the arena on our own two feet. Can't we just shake hands and leave it at that?"

She startled back as if I'd just slapped her across the face, but she seemed more surprised than angry.

"You...you wish to declare Ko'koan?"

"Oh by Vesta's left ass cheek...sure, fine, why not?"

"Um, Charity..." Alleron whispered as he tugged at my sleeve, but I waved him off.

"If it will put all this to rest and keep you from throwing yourself off a bridge or cutting my throat while I sleep then I'll declare whatever the hells you want."

She studied me for a long moment, but just when I was starting to wonder if she'd dozed off or something her face lit up into one of the biggest grins I'd ever seen.

"Ha! You surprise me, young sister. In my wildest dreams I could never have imagined it, but your words feel right to me. We are both outcasts, both survivors, and you've proven your strength twice over. Stars know I would prefer a bondmate to a master...very well, from today we two will breathe as one."

"Uh...we will?"

I turned to find Alleron doing everything he could not to burst out laughing, and only partially succeeding.

"She doesn't mean that literally, right?"

After all the crazy magical things I'd seen since I got here that seemed like a question worth asking.

"Well, not literally, but close enough to count. In her tongue "Ko'koan" means "two who breathe as one." It's just about the strongest pledge the halflings make. Ko'koan share everything together. Food, danger...mates."

Sheska's grin grew even broader, which I hadn't thought possible.

"Now wait a minute, I didn't..."

The office door swung open. "The Master is ready for you now," Cael said as he waved us inside.

"Come sister," Sheska slapped my leg as she marched past me, "let's see what the pale human wants with us."

"Oh, this is too wonderful." Alleron still chuckled to himself as he followed after her. "I just love a good surprise, don't you? In my line of work they're far too rare."

"But I…"

"Move it, girly, you're blocking the door," Magnus said as he prodded my back. "If we hurry we might get through this damned interruption before those vultures pick the kitchens clean."

"No doubt the others give thanks to the spirits even now for the chance to eat a decent meal in peace, barrel belly," Nataka said under her breath as she stepped around us both to walk through the door.

"What's that, greyskin? It sounded like you were asking me what it feels like to be punched in the face by a dwarf."

By this time I was standing alone in the hallway, trying to make sense out of what had just happened.

"Are you just going to stand there?" Cael asked as he gestured for me to follow the others. I decided that sorting out the implications of whatever Sheska thought I'd just agreed to would have to wait, and stepped inside to find out what Trebonious had summoned us for in the first place.

The office hadn't changed since I stood in it last. Same shelves, same furniture, same table covered with strange items. Even the logs in the fireplace looked like the ones that had burned there before. Trebonious sat behind his desk, but he smiled and stood to his feet as I entered.

"And here is the young warrior queen herself, fresh from victory. I confess when you first came to us I didn't hold out much hope for your chances in the arena, but you've certainly proven me wrong on that account."

I heard the edge of frustration underneath his pleasant tone. No doubt I'd caused him a fair bit of grief and a great deal of lost coin when I'd beaten the odds and survived his death matches. I nodded to him in response but decided to hold my tongue until I had a better sense of his intentions. It turns out I actually can learn a thing or two eventually.

"In fact," he continued, "you've all shown yourselves to be quite formidable, not just individually, but as a team. Your victory over my little jungle curiosity was most impressive. Enough so that I've decided to extend a rare and generous offer to you."

"You could start with some decent blankets," Nataka interrupted. "Winter is coming and I'd rather not freeze to death in my cell."

Trebonious clearly did not enjoy being interrupted, but he managed to keep a thin smile on his face.

"I was thinking of something rather more substantial than linens."

"Such as?"

"Your freedom, for a start. Oh, and a great deal of gold as well."

No one spoke, but I could see that the others were just as surprised as I was, and just as eager to hear more.

"Ah, now I have your attention," Trebonious said as he reclaimed his seat and leaned back in his chair. "It is within my power as Master of the Arena to grant you each a full pardon, and I'm prepared to send you on your way with enough coin in hand to set yourselves up quite comfortably here in the city, or travel onwards to wherever you like."

"And I assume you want something from us in exchange, yes?" I asked. His offer was the stuff of dreams and children's stories, but even though I'd come to accept that life in Farshore involved a good deal more of both than I'd ever thought possible, I still recognized a baited hook when I saw one.

"Of course," he answered, "but nothing beyond your capabilities, as you've so recently demonstrated. I simply require that you retrieve something for me."

"And what would that be?"

"High King Tyrial's crown."

From the startled gasps and stunned looks that erupted around me you'd think he'd just asked us to raid the emperor's treasure vaults and kidnap his twin daughters. Even Cael looked surprised. In fact, Alleron and I seemed to be the only ones not showing much of a reaction, although in his case I suspected it was because he already knew what Trebonious would ask of us.

"Let's pretend that I only stepped off a ship from Byzantia a few months ago," I said, trying to keep the irritation I felt from creeping into my voice. I hated being the only one in the room who didn't know what was going on. Everyone turned to Alleron, clearly waiting for him to speak first.

"Tyrial was the last High King of the Elves." Alleron turned towards me with the same "looks like someone needs a history lesson" expression that Mother Shanti used to get right before she launched into a discourse on Grand Empress Jupricia's bowel movements or some such.

"It's been a long day, Alleron," I held up a hand before he could get started. "Any chance we could stick to the high points and save the details for later?"

"You want the high points?" Magnus grumbled. "How's this: the good king Tyrial managed to shove his head even further up his own ass than the rest of his elven kin. So much further, in fact, that he unleashed the greatest magical catastrophe Danan has ever seen on the rest of us."

I raised an eyebrow at Alleron, but he just shrugged.

"Our grizzled friend is correct, more or less. A little over five hundred years ago my people ruled all of Danan from our capital of Shirael Toris, the Shining City. Apparently Tyrial felt that death was an indignity he had no wish to suffer, and his search for alternatives seemed to have...gone wrong, somehow."

"Gone wrong?" Nataka scoffed. "That's a gentle way to speak of the Sundering. A decade of skyfire and drought, my people left homeless, your glorious city cursed for all eternity, and you call that 'gone wrong'?"

"I'm sorry," Alleron said through a thin smile, "I should have said that it seemed to have gone *very* wrong, somehow. The point is, the elves never truly recovered, and the western half of the continent is still a barren wasteland. Shirael Toris and everyone who lived there was destroyed in an instant, including Tyrial and his court."

"Which means you'll be spared a long and tedious search, as we know precisely where his crown can be found," Trebonious said from behind his desk.

"Are you mad, or just slow in the head?" Sheska asked. "Even in my jungles we know of the Shattered City. Anyone foolish enough to go within ten leagues of it is never seen again."

"Which is why I have waited so long to find such talented individuals as yourselves. I'm certain you'll have no trouble overcoming whatever minor difficulties might arise."

"Not bloody likely," said Magnus. "I'd sooner wrestle a hundred of your devil kittens than walk up to the gates of the Shattered City and knock. I fear no flesh and blood, but only a fool disturbs the restless dead."

"You can refuse, of course, and choose to remain here. I would be disappointed, but rest assured that would in no way affect your treatment here in the arena. I would redouble my efforts to present you with only the most glorious and challenging of contests to test yourselves against. I am certain you would all prove equal to the task."

I exchanged wary glances with the others, and saw that we all understood exactly what Trebonious was trying so hard not to say. If we refused he'd make sure we bled out in the arena within the week, and there wasn't a damned thing we could do about it.

"Let's assume for a moment that we do as you ask," I said. "What guarantee do we have that you'd hold to your end of the bargain?"

"I am both hurt and offended that you misjudge my character so badly, but as it so happens I suspected that you might require proof of my good intentions."

He opened a drawer in his desk, pulled out a small stack of papers, and spread them out in front of us. There were five of them, each with an intricate wax seal affixed to the bottom.

"These are your official pardons, signed and sealed," he said, tapping each one in turn. "When you return with the crown you can watch me dispatch them to the governor's villa yourselves, and Cael will join you on your mission to lend his aid and ensure that you remain focused on your task."

I snuck a sideways glance in Cael's direction. He looked surprised, but didn't offer any protest, which left me wondering what kind of hold Trebonious had over him.

"In addition, I have placed two hundred gold drachins on deposit at the Farshore Exchange in each of your names, which will await your successful return."

My mouth went dry. Ten drachins would keep a family fed for a year, and fifty would buy you a house on the banks of the Oxius.

As my brain struggled to wrap itself around the thought of me walking out of the exchange richer than a silk merchant, Trebonious opened a second drawer and withdrew a small wooden box.

"But just in case any of you might consider taking advantage of my generosity by escaping before retrieving the crown, I thought it only fair to remind you of the consequences that would entail."

He opened the box and removed its contents; five small loops of hair bound by silver thread, their ends crusted with dried blood. As he placed one on each of the pardons, I spotted my own curl of black hair among the red, brown, and golden blonde. Looking at it for just a few seconds sent a cramp through my gut and a shiver down my spine at the same time, and I could see that the others felt equally uncomfortable about theirs.

"I believe two months should be more than enough time for you to make the trip and return with the crown. Should you fail to do so within that time I would be forced to assume that you have broken faith with me, and that would leave me most displeased."

"So let me get this straight," I said, careful to look at Trebonious instead of my effigy. "You want us to march across the continent, find a lost city filled with unknown danger that will probably kill us, and retrieve a crown. If we say no, we're as good as dead. If we take longer than two months, we're dead for sure. But, if we somehow survive all of that and come back in one piece we'll gain our freedom and enough gold to keep Magnus swimming in ale until the day he dies?"

"You have a remarkable gift for summary, miss Charity," Trebonious said as he leaned back in his chair once more and awaited our answers.

I turned and looked at Alleron, Cael, Magnus, Nataka, and Sheska in turn. Each one gave me a grim but determined nod. I tried not to smile as I kept a lid on the surge of hope that flooded through me. I had just found my way home. I didn't like the sound of this Shattered City, but how bad could it be with a band of some of the toughest customers I'd ever met along for the ride? All I had to do was sit back, let them do most of the heavy lifting, and make my way back here in one piece to claim my freedom and more gold that I'd ever seen in one place. For a moment I could almost hear Byzantia's bells calling the hour and smell frying *kafta* on market day.

I turned back to Trebonious and added my own nod to theirs.

"Excellent!" he said as he stood to his feet. "I have horses and provisions standing by. You ride tonight, and may the Divines themselves attend your journey."

The story continues in *Into The Shattered City*,
the next installment in the Farshore Chronicles

INTO THE SHATTERED CITY

FARSHORE CHRONICLES BOOK 2

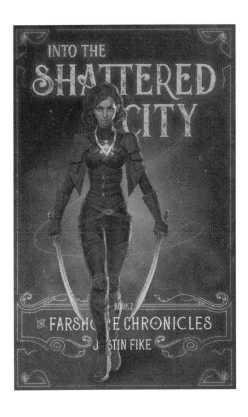

JOURNAL ENTRY

The Farshore Chronicles
   From the quill of Charity The Godslayer
Penned by her own hand this 1576th year of Jovian's Wise Rule

My story may have begun out on Farshore's arena sands, but it didn't really begin until I found myself treking across a new world with only a ragged band of misfits and outcasts for company.

I'd survived the worst that Trebonious, the master of Farshore's arena games, had thrown at me, but my reward was just a tall glass of blackmail with a stiff shot of impending doom to chase it down. Now Cael, Alleron, Magnus, Nataka, Sheska and I were all bound for the one place in Danaan that even the bravest warrior and hulking mosters knew better than to enter, the ruins of the elves lost capitol city in the heart of the western mountains.

"A human soldier, elven wizard, dwarven warrior, orcish shaman, halfling archer, and Byzantian thief-in-exile ride through Danaan's Wildlands" sounds like the start of a truly terrible joke, but I promise you that none of us were laughing about it. At the time, all I wanted was to survive the trip and make it back to Farshore to collect Trebonious' bounty and catch the first ship back to the real world. If you'd have told me then about everything that would happen as a result of that little adventure, I would have run the other way to avoid catching whatever disease had rotted your brain.

My new companions were all too eager to fill my ear with stories of the dangers that awaited in the Shattered City, but even they didn't really know what awaited us there. Their dire tales sent a shiver down my spine each night around our meager campfire, but it turned out that the truth behind the city's curse was far worse than we could have imagined...

1

Have you ever awoken next to a snoring dwarf with rocks and pine cones digging into your back and frost clinging to your eyelashes? Ridden a horse for so long your ass blisters and your legs go numb, then wake up before the sun rises to do it again? Lived on nothing but dry biscuits and cold water for weeks on end? If you answered no to any of the above, then count yourself blessed and lie, kill, or do whatever you have to do to keep it that way.

Our strange little group had been traveling westward for more than a month, and I'd been in a foul mood for most of that time. Alleron, Magnus, Nataka, and Sheska all seemed thrilled to no end to be outside Farshore's walls. Alleron wouldn't shut up about how good it was to smell trees and clean air again, while Magnus kept disappearing into the woods and returning with some prized mushroom or strange moss for that night's stew.

Nataka maintained a running conversation of whispered muttering with herself. At first I thought the sun had baked her brains to mush, but when I asked if she was alright she said she was "speaking with the spirits of the land," which is how I learned never to ask an orc why she is muttering to herself. I even caught Sheska smiling once. A genuine smile of happiness, mind you, not the "I'm thinking of many ways to kill you" smile she usually put on.

Cael was the only one out of the whole lot who didn't seem thrilled to be on this little adventure, and if I hadn't already respected the man, then the frown he'd worn under his mustache since Farshore's flags and rooftops had disappeared beneath the tree line would have done the trick. It's not that I have anything against nature, per se. I'm glad that trees, thorny bushes, screeching birds and all the rest exist, and I'm perfectly happy to leave them all the hells alone if they return the favor. But there's a reason our ancestors invented lanterns, blankets, fireplaces, regular meals, and buildings with roofs and thick walls. Anyone who actually enjoys leaving all that behind to sleep on the cold ground and wear themselves out swatting at a never-ending swarm of bugs has more things wrong with them than Vesta herself would know how to cure.

My only comfort lay in the fact that Alleron had announced as we made camp last night that, after five weeks on the road, we were only about one more day's ride from the mountains that surrounded the Shattered City. One more day of discomfort and we would arrive at the object of our long journey, although that thought raised an entirely new set of concerns as I tried to roll out from under my blanket without slicing my face on the blade of the axe that Magnus insisted on sleeping with. He'd flatly refused to leave town at all until Trebonious sent someone to fetch "Hilda" from the arena armory, and he hadn't let the thing out of his sight since.

Most of the others were sleeping soundly, although I couldn't tell you how they managed that given the circumstances. We'd camped in the lee of a large grove of fir trees that provided a small measure of shelter from the biting wind, but if there was more than three inches of ground free of knobby roots and pine cones then I hadn't been able to find it. Sheska's bedroll was the only one empty, but she was always slipping away on her own business, so I didn't think much of it.

I trekked away from our little camp in search of a tree large enough to afford me some morning privacy and tried to get my head around everything that had happened in the past month. The strange thing that my life had become still stole my breath away sometimes. Riding alongside an elf, a dwarf, an orc, and a halfling had become normal enough that I no longer jumped when I caught sight of one of them out of the corner of my eye, and the land we rode through was enough like the hills and forests outside

Byzantia that you could be forgiven for thinking that the countryside was normal too. But it wasn't.

We rode through the heart of Danan, a land filled with mythic races, strange magic, and countless other storybook wonders. If someone had walked up to me on Byzantia's streets and started telling me about half of the things I'd seen since I stepped off the prison ship, I would have run the other way to keep from catching whatever sickness had rotted their brain.

Not anymore. We'd fought things that writhed in the shadows of our campfire, stumbled into a field of flowers that moved about on their own and tried to put us to sleep with clouds of yellow pollen, and ridden three days out of our way to avoid a magical storm of chaotic energy that Alleron had casually theorized would polymorph the lot of us into rocks and trees if we entered it. After the first week I stopped asking questions and learned to look three times before I went into the woods to take a shit.

And it wasn't just the dangers of the wilderness. We'd spent several days riding through boggy marshland to avoid an elven city. I'd been all for stopping there the moment I heard of it, but Alleron assured me that our strange band would not be well received by the city's patrols. As we traveled Nataka told me of her people's huge roving caravans on the western plains, Sheska spoke of massive stone cities in the heart of the southern jungles, and Magnus spun stories of dwarven holds on the outer island that rang with ale song and the signal horns of departing longships.

The picture of a land rich in history, conflict, and mistrust began to take shape in my mind even though I saw little more than its wild and untamed reaches as we traveled. Apparently the Wildlands, as the others called the countryside we rode through, had once been claimed by the elven kingdom before the Sundering blasted most of it into ruin and left the remnants of a once proud people clinging to life in the few cities and outposts that had survived the catastrophe. Now it's hills, caves, and forests were haunted by all manner of wild beasts and monsters, which we'd spent the past month hiding from or fending off with depressing regularity.

I soon realized that Farshore colony was just a small and lonely outpost of humanity on the coast of a continent far larger than the lands Byzantia claimed as its empire, and possibly even those of the nations beyond its borders as well. Danan was enormous, untamed, and strange in more ways than I could count. The more I saw of it, the more determined I became to make my way back home again, assuming we survived this little adventure and made it back to Farshore to claim our promised reward.

I'd long since made my peace with the fact that many things I'd grown up believing were nothing more than fables were actually all too real. Some part of me kept expecting to wake up from the strangest dream I'd ever had and swear off late-night drinking for good. But even though they hardly noticed any of the dozens of unusual sights that had left me speechless on our journey, I could tell from the looks my companions shared when we spoke of it that this Shattered City we rode towards was dangerous. They hadn't seemed particularly impressed by any of the dangers we'd overcome so far, so I could only imagine what kind of trouble lay ahead.

"I have caught us breakfast."

I jumped halfway out of my skin, and only managed to avoid soiling my pant legs through some very deft footwork. When I regained my balance and turned around, I found Sheska perched on one of the lower limbs of the tree with her shortbow in one hand and an impressively plump rabbit in the other.

"*Chaso di bruta*! You just frightened ten years off of me."

"You are not happy? After all your complaining over trail rations, I thought you would be pleased to eat fresh meat." She looked hurt, and I realized she'd gotten up early to go hunting for my sake.

"Of course I am, and thank you. But maybe cough or snap a twig or two the next time you sneak up behind someone who's not wearing pants."

She stared down at me for a moment, sniffed, and disappeared into the trees in the direction of our camp without saying a word. I sighed, finished cleaning up, and followed after her. Of all the strange new things in my life that I was having trouble adjusting to, "playing well with others" was at the top of the list.

By the time I made it back to camp Magnus already had the rabbit sizzling on a spit over a crackling fire. Within the first few days of our journey I'd discovered to my surprise that the otherwise taciturn dwarf warrior hid a deep love of cooking within his oak-barrel chest. So far it had been the only subject that he'd been willing to give more than a grunt or a few short words to.

"I stuffed this beauty with those grangia roots I dug up yesterday, plus a few sprigs of green onion and wild parsley. In a few minutes you'll think you're dining in King Olenson's own mead hall."

"Shouldn't we start breaking camp?" Cael huffed. "I'd prefer to be on the move before high noon."

"Aye, you most certainly should, longshanks. And while you're about it I'll get breakfast roasted and ready. If you stop pestering me I might even give you some."

True to his word, Magnus had divvied up the meal before we'd packed away our things, and the wonderful smell easily banished any lingering complaints that might have been offered.

We gathered around the last embers of his cooking fire as he doled out a portion to each of us. I made a point of thanking Sheska again for providing our first decent meal all week, but she just shrugged my words away, and was still sulking by the time we broke camp.

We rode for the better part of the day without a rest. I would have given anything to get down off of that infernal torture device that everyone kept calling a horse, but I didn't want to be the first one to suggest it once again. Instead I just gritted my teeth and tried to keep up. I'd named my horse Shanti, because just like the good Vestan Mother, she really was a horrible nag. She would wander off the trail to graze or wet the ground the instant I let the reins fall slack. I couldn't decide whether the aching in my back and arms or the bruises on my ass bothered me more. Still, I kept her mostly in line behind the others, and since no one else had the good sense to suggest a break, we made rather good time throughout the day. By the time the sun had begun to droop down into our eyes along the far horizon even I could see how the land had changed since we'd started out that morning.

For most of our journey we'd ridden through thick forests and open fields, forded rivers and skirted around lakes so large you couldn't see the shore on the far side. Now the endless wall of green trees had given way to sparse pine and outcroppings of jagged gray stone as we rode along a gravelly ridge that wound up into the mountains. The trip had taken the better part of five weeks, more than half of the total time that Trebonious had named before he'd use the effigies he'd created to pull our guts out through our noses or something equally unpleasant. The others didn't seem concerned about it, though. Cael had said a few nights back that most of our time had been spent in charting a course through unfamiliar terrain. If we followed the same route back we could return in far less time.

Our horses had slowed to a crawl as we made our way up a particularly steep hillside, threading our way between a rocky cliff face that rose a good thirty feet overhead to our left, and boulders larger than a senator's carriage that lay strewn and jumbled down the slope to our right. The land rose steadily skyward in front of us, stretching up towards the blue sky overhead. We hadn't truly reached the mountains yet, but I could see that we were drawing close.

The sharp-witted among you will have realized by now that I was no great lover of the wild outdoors. Before coming to Farshore I'd only stepped outside Byzantia's walls a handful of times to assist Sister Hazera in gathering herbs. I didn't understand the sounds and rhythms of nature, so if you'd asked me at the time why the hairs on my neck had begun to prickle as my instincts started screaming at me to find a safe place to hide, I couldn't have told you why.

I didn't actually notice that all the birdsong had suddenly died away, leaving only an eerie stillness in its wake. I didn't notice that the logs and boulders that blocked our narrow path up ahead had no natural reason to fall where they were. All I knew was that every one of my senses was warning me of danger.

Most folk have felt that creeping sensation before, but most folk ignore it because they're stupid, and because the few among them who'd learned the hard way that they ought to trust their instincts had already bled out in a gutter somewhere before they could pass on the lesson. But if my life so far had taught me anything, it was that whenever you feel like someone is watching you from the shadows with ill intent, it's usually because they are. Better to do something and look foolish that keep quiet and die brave and stupid.

"Um, guys, I think something's wro--"

Something buzzed out of the shadows to my left before I could finish my sentence. I threw myself against my horse's neck on instinct, and the arrow shattered against the rock where my head had been just a moment before. Shrill, screaming voices filled the air as hundreds of little grey-green creatures carrying clubs, spears, bows, and rusted short swords swarmed over the rocks all around us.

"Scratch that, something is definitely wrong!"

"*Grodin ak'atz!*" Nataka snarled. "Filthy goblin spawn."

Our group scattered as everyone leapt into action on their own. Magnus snatched Hilda from his saddle and flung himself off of his horse and straight at the nearest group of goblins while Nataka spurred her horse and charged in the opposite direction with her spear leveled. Cael had the presence of mind to throw his horse's reins over a tree branch before hefting his shield and broadsword, and I'd already lost sight of Sheska. Within the space of a few quick breaths Alleron and I were the only ones still sitting on our horses on the narrow trail.

As Alleron shouted out a string of syllables a cascade of colored lights burst from his fingertips to leave a gang of screaming goblins stumbling and tripping blindly, but his spell managed to spook his horse at the same time. The beast reared back, dumping the wizard in a heap on the ground before bolting back down the trail the way we'd come. I drew the twin sabers that hung at my belt, but paused a moment to survey the scene rather than charging off in some random direction to start using them.

Everything was utter chaos. It looked like the goblins hadn't expected such a swift and fierce response, but they rallied and pressed forward in a never-ending wave of tiny little bodies with murder shining in their beady eyes. Even the tallest among them would have barely reached my waist. Their heads, hands, feet, and ears all seemed too large for their bodies.

If it had only been a few of them attacking us I would probably have just laughed as they scrambled down from the rocks and waved their tiny weapons above their heads. Given that there were several hundred of them, the only thing I was interested in doing was getting the hells out of there with my skin in one piece. As the goblin horde closed in on us, I had to admit that the odds of that happening were dropping by the second.

2

_____

I had to admit that the little terrors had picked a good spot for their ambush. With the cliffs to our left and nothing but broken, boulder-strewn hillside to our right, our only options were to advance up the path -- which the tiny bastards had blocked with debris -- or return back the way we had come. Either way, I could see that our only hope of survival lay in beating a hasty retreat before the goblin swarm completely surrounded us.

The only problem with my plan was that I seemed to be the only one who had thought about running away. Magnus was happily bellowing out the notes of what I would have assumed was some sort of drinking song if he hadn't punctuated each beat in the rhythm with a swipe of his axe. Cael pressed forward with his shield held high, but just before he could strike, an arrow zipped over his shoulder from behind, grazing his ear as it thudded into the back of his shield less than an inch from his hand.

"Move, big man!" Sheska's voice called down from a nearby boulder. "You keep standing where my arrows want to go."

Nataka screamed in incoherent fury from atop her horse. I'd never seen her do much more than frown before, but now she was wild with bloodlust.

"You thrice-cursed mud spawn!" She screamed. "My Kalidar will have his bloody vengeance!"

A moment later a cloud of small rocks rose up from the earth to hover for a moment in the air before exploding away from her in all directions, felling a score of goblins in a storm of screams and blood.

But it wasn't going to be enough. No matter how well we fought, six against five hundred was a fight that could only end one way. I spurred Shanti over to Alleron as he struggled to his feet, a hand pressed against a gash that had soaked his blonde hair with a thick smear of crimson red.

"Alleron, we have to get out of here!"

"We what?" he looked a little dizzy, but I couldn't wait for him to gather his wits in his own sweet time. I reached down and slapped his cheek hard enough to get his attention, then grabbed the front of his shirt and hauled him up over the back of my saddle.

Thank Vesta it was the elf who lost his horse. Wouldn't want to try that on Magnus.

"We need to run while we still have a chance," I shouted back at him as he struggled to sit up without falling off. "Can you do anything about their barricade?"

He finally gained his seat and looked up the path towards where I was pointing. The debris wasn't really a proper barricade, just loose boulders and tree stumps that the goblins had rolled into the narrow space where the path threaded between the cliff and a large jutting rock, but it was too big for our horses to jump, and that was big enough to keep us trapped.

"Mphh, probably," he groaned, "but not with a horde of goblins trying to chew on my liver."

"Right, then hang on tight."

I urged Shanti forward, charging up the trail as goblins dove out of the way of its hooves.

"Cael!" I screamed with all the air I could fit in my lungs. He batted a goblin into a boulder with his shield, then turned towards me.

"We have to go!" I pointed towards the barricade, then at Alleron seated behind me, hoping he would understand me. Relief flooded through me when I saw him nod, then snatch the goblin who had jumped up onto his back and fling it at Magnus to get his attention.

"We're moving, tree stump. Try to keep up."

"What? This was just getting fun," the dwarf shouted back, but they both ran to their horses and leapt into the saddle.

"Sheska!" I called, hoping she could hear me over the chorus of goblin screams, "keep them off of us!"

I listened for an answer, but heard none. Just when I was starting to worry that something had happened to her, an arrow breezed my cheek and felled a goblin who had been sneaking up behind us without my noticing. I raised a hand in thanks, then turned to find Nataka riding towards me. Her face and armor were spattered with blood and that crazed fury still haunted her eyes, but she'd gathered her wits enough to rejoin us, and that was good enough for me.

"Where is the halfling?" she asked as she reined in her mount next to mine.

Before I could answer, a scream like the cry of a diving falcon rang out over the din, and Sheska came pounding around a nearby boulder atop the shaggy pony that Trebonious had provided her with a gang of goblins close on her heels. She spun in the saddle as she rode to loose arrow after arrow behind her. By the time she reached us the only goblins behind her lay twitching on the ground.

"I thought we were leaving?" she asked as she joined our circle.

"Waiting on Alleron," I said, jerking a thumb over my shoulder.

"Unless you enjoy the thought of being accidentally disintegrated, I suggest you keep quiet and let me concentrate. Improvised magic is dangerous enough as it is."

I almost snapped a retort back at him, but managed to keep my mouth shut to give him room to do whatever it was he was doing. Now that all of us had regrouped, the goblins had paused their assault for the moment, but more of them kept appearing every second. Soon every rock, tree, and bush around us sported a small green body or three perched atop it brandishing their weapons and baring their tiny fangs like an army of armed and feral lapdogs. All it would take was one of the little creatures to gather just a little bit more courage than his fellows and we'd be buried under a stinking green avalanche of tiny death.

Then I felt it. Alleron still clung to the back of my horse, so as his spell took hold a rush of sharp, static energy flooded through my back and arms. Pressure built in my ears as though I'd suddenly dove to the bottom of a pond, and soon even the roots of my teeth started to ache.

It ended as suddenly as it had begun. One moment I was starting to worry that I might black out and tumble onto the little forest of goblin spear points that inched slowly towards us, the next I felt the power flow away from us like a river breaking through a dam. I heard a grinding, rumbling sound from the barrier behind me, then silence.

"Ride, you fools!" Alleron grunted, his voice straining as though he struggled to hold one of those boulders overhead himself. "I can't keep this up for long."

I wheeled my horse around to see a cloud of rocks, stumps, and fallen logs floating a dozen feet up in the air, leaving a clear path through the narrow gap. A few weeks ago I would have stared in slack-jawed disbelief at the sight, but I'd come to terms with magic well enough to manage just a single double take before I spurred Shanti towards the gap and the promise of safety on the other side. From the clatter of hooves that echoed through the canyon I knew that the others were following my lead. We'd barely ridden three strides past the floating barricade when Alleron slumped against my back with a sigh of relief and the sound of our galloping horses was drowned out by a deafening thunder as all the debris crashed back to earth.

I spun in my saddle to look behind me with my heart in my throat, certain that one of our group had been trapped beneath the rubble, but a quick head count confirmed that everyone had made it through safely. I was surprised by the feeling of relief that flooded through me. It wasn't that long ago that I wouldn't have much cared what happened to the person behind me as long as it wasn't happening to me too. I'd survived as long as I had largely because I never let anyone get close enough to stick a knife in my back, or lead me into doing something stupid to stop them from getting a knife stuck in theirs.

The realization that my guard might have begun to drop without me even noticing it after weeks on the road with this ragged band of misfits left me ten kinds of uncomfortable, but I didn't have much time to think on it just then. No sooner had I confirmed that my companions were alright than I caught sight of several hundred goblin heads appearing over the top of the barricade, followed closely by several hundred armed goblin bodies scrambling and tumbling down towards us.

"Keep moving!" I shouted as I turned and spurred my horse along the path that wound further up into the canyon. I might have just discovered that I actually cared whether my new-found friends lived to see the next sunrise, but I still had every intention of keeping them between me and the horde of pointy death chasing after us.

I kept Shanti moving faster than was safe on the rocky, winding path, but that was still only about half the speed I would have liked. I risked a quick glance over my shoulder and confirmed that the little green bastards didn't seem to have any trouble keeping up with us in this rough terrain. In fact, they seemed to be gaining ground on us little by little. The closest goblin was now only a few paces behind Sheska's pony, shrieking out what I'm sure he thought was a terrifying war cry and running as hard as his little legs would carry him. If any of us so much as stumbled on a loose rock the horde would cut them into tiny pieces before they hit the ground.

"I've got ten silver that says we don't make it out of this alive," Alleron said in my ear. It actually sounded like he was enjoying himself, and it took all the self-control I could muster not to reach back and punch him for it.

"Idiot," I called back. "What kind of a bet is that? If you win you can't collect, but if I win you owe me ten silver."

"Hmm, a good point. Five silver, then."

Up ahead I could see that the winding path crested a rise between two cliffs that towered to either side and seemed to disappear down the other side. If we could reach it, the narrow pass would force the teeming horde behind us to funnel down to just a few bodies at a time, and we might be able find some kind of defensive position where we could make enough of a stand to drive them off.

"You're on!"

It was a slim chance at survival, but it was also the only one I'd seen yet, and I leapt for it like a drowning sailor straining for a rope. Shanti was beginning to tire, but I had to give her credit for the valiant effort she'd made so far. Foam from her mouth flecked my boots as she struggled up the steep trail, but I leaned forward and urged her to give me everything she had left, for both our sakes.

The goblin shrieks sounded as close in my ear as Alleron's voice. I kept waiting to feel the sharp stab of a spear point in my back any minute, but I focused all my attention on guiding Shanti around the dangers in the trail. Just when I thought her legs might give out beneath me the sunlight overhead fell away into cool shadows as we thundered into the narrow pass.

The steep trail leveled out immediately, giving the poor horse a much-needed break, but I saw no sign of fallen rocks or other cover in the canyon ahead of me. The floor and the rock walls were completely smooth, as though a giant had simply cleaved the pass through the mountain rock with one stroke of his sword. My heart sank as I realized that the pass was wider than it had looked from farther down the trail. There was no way its entrance would offer enough of a barrier for just the six of us to keep the tide of goblins at bay. I couldn't think of anything other than to keep riding, but even as I tried to urge Shanti to run just a few minutes more I knew there was no chance we'd reach the far end of the strange passage alive.

"Charity!" Cael's voice broke through my dark thoughts, sounding more surprised than alarmed. Now that he'd caught my attention, I realized that the chorus of goblin screaming that had filled the air since they first sprang their ambush was gone, leaving only an eerie quiet in its wake. I pulled Shanti to a stop and turned to see the rest of our group behind me, and a crowd of goblins gathered behind them. Not one of the little beasts had stepped out of the sunlight into the shadow of the canyon. Sheska and Magnus sat on their horses only a few paces ahead of them, but the goblins just shuffled from foot to foot, jostling each other and muttering as they cast fearful glances in our direction.

Without warning they all turned around together and disappeared back down the trail.

"What in the eight hells just happened?" I asked as I rode back to rejoin the group.

"I've no idea," Cael answered. "Maybe they finally caught a good whiff of Magnus and decided that eating him just wasn't worth the trouble."

"No," Nataka said as she scowled and shook her head. Somehow I didn't think she'd understood Cael's joke.

"Goblins are weaklings and cowards, but in large numbers they will not stop until they bring down even the greatest warrior." She scowled at the last of the retreating goblin horde as though she contemplated chasing after them, and I got the sense that she wasn't referring to any of us.

"The only reason those *sckretchgazen* would turn back now is if they fear what lies beyond this canyon more than they fear death itself."

That sounded a lot like the Shattered City we'd ridden all this way to find, but hearing that we might have finally reached our goal didn't bring me much comfort considering the fact that everyone else who'd done that had never been heard from again. I wasn't any more excited about it now than I was when we'd first ridden through Farshore's gates, but finding it and the crown of its last king was what we'd come out here to do, and at the moment I preferred the thought of riding through a pile of ruined buildings than going another round with the goblins.

"Lovely," I said, "let's go ride straight towards it then, shall we?"

The rest of the group exchanged wary glances, but seeing as going back the way we'd come wasn't an option, we didn't really have much of a choice. Together we turned our horses and rode deeper into the cold shadows of the strange and empty canyon.

A fter a short, silent ride we reached the end of the canyon and pulled our horses to a stop just beyond its walls. We sat atop a high cliff that dropped away to a valley floor several hundred feet below. Mountain peaks like the one we'd just ridden through surrounded the valley on all sides, forming a natural bowl that was filled from end to end with the unmistakable straight lines of buildings and streets.

My first look at the Shattered City was a good bit less imposing than I'd been expecting. It was decently large. Not as big as Byzantia, of course, but easily three or four times the size of Farshore. I could tell even from this distance that this was no human city. The buildings were too pretty, for one thing, all graceful arches of white stone with glazed roof tiles of red, green, gold, and blue. The streets were wide and lined with trees that were impossibly well-tended, looking more like green sculptures than living things.

I had no idea how the foliage had maintained its perfect condition after five hundred years of neglect, but the rest of the ruined city seemed equally pristine. The city looked more like a piece of art than a place to live. I was beginning to suspect that I would have had trouble finding a decent tavern or shadow-soaked alleyway down there even if I'd come when the city was still alive.

It was dead now though, that much was certain. The only movement I could see within its sprawl was the gentle swaying of branches as the wind danced down tree-lined avenues. The whole valley was completely still, without even birdsong to break the silence. The longer I looked, the more the white spires and walls began to look like the bleached bones of some long-dead beast left to rot in the sun.

There was no way that the narrow canyon we'd ridden through was the primary entrance into the valley. I scanned the surrounding mountains and spotted a much larger break in the mountain ridge on the opposite side of the city from where we stood. It was flanked by statues so large that I could make out the rivets of their armor even from here, and I could just make out a large, paved avenue that cut through the pass and into the city. I was begin-ning to get a sense of the city's layout, and realized that the route we'd taken had led us to what must have been a rarely-used rear entrance to the valley. Perhaps there had once been a ramp, or even a system of moving platforms like you could find in some parts of Byzantia to carry travelers from below to the cliff where we now stood, but I saw no sign of anything like that now.

Just when I was about to ask if anyone had an idea of how we could make our way down the cliff without breaking our necks, Sheska discovered the remnants of a winding trail cut into the rock that traced a worn and treacherous path to the valley floor. I spent the whole ride torturing poor Shanti by digging my trembling knees into her ribs and grabbing at her mane in white-knuckled terror, but eventually we made it down without incident.

The path leveled out at the base of the cliff, becoming a small road of paved stones that ran straight towards the outline of the city's spires ahead. A two-story building, likely some sort of gatehouse, sat across the road. The road itself passed through an archway that divided the building into two halves. The archway was set with thick wooden gates that could be closed and locked to bar the road, but currently they sat open on their hinges. Not that it would have mattered greatly, as we could have simply ridden around the building to rejoin the road on the other side. It had clearly been meant to serve more as a tollhouse and guard barracks than any kind of defensive structure, but I suppose the elves who built it had seen little need for walls when their city was surrounded on all sides by the biggest damned cliffs I'd ever seen.

As we rode closer I got my first good look at the gatehouse, and as I did my casual once-over quickly turned into a wide-eyed stare. From a distance the building had appeared normal enough, but as we approached I realized that it was anything but. Its walls, windows, and roof were covered in ripples like the surface of a pond stirred by a gust of wind, as though the whole building had been melted and then reformed in the same breath. Its entire western corner flowed into a puddle that spread over the ground like a pool of melted wax.

"Mother of Mysteries," I whispered, "how is this even possible?"

"It isn't." I'd been so focused on what I was seeing that I hadn't even realized Cael had ridden his horse up next to mine. "Or, it shouldn't be, at least. And yet..." he tossed his chin towards the unmistakable proof that sat right in front of us.

The building's strange liquid appearance wasn't the only unnatural thing about it. As we rode closer I noticed strange shapes embedded in the walls. Some were round, while others were longer protrusions that looked a bit like small tree limbs sticking out at strange angles. It took me a moment to realize that the round shapes had eyes staring back at me in frozen horror, and the limbs sported fingers clawing at the air. The shapes were the stone outlines of people, elves in armor now preserved forever in their poses of terror and death within the building's walls.

"Alleron, please tell me that your people used to have a thing for carving horrible, disturbing sculptures into the sides of their buildings?"

I was having trouble breathing. The thought of being suddenly frozen inside a wall to die without even one final scream was not a pleasant one, and my elven friend didn't look like he was faring much better as he shook his head in answer to my question. The gate still lay open in front of us, but without a word we all turned our horses onto the grass and traced a wide circle around the gatehouse before rejoining the road on the far side to continue on towards the city.

We rode for nearly half an hour through the open land that separated the city proper from the mountain walls. The land around us was empty aside from a series of low stone walls which divided it up into fields that I guessed had once served as farmland or pastures. I could only imagine that the limited land within the caldera had been at quite a premium, which meant that farmland like this must have been preserved by law, probably in an effort to keep the city more self-sufficient. Given Byzantia's own history of starvations and food riots I had to admit that it wasn't a terrible idea.

The sun was sliding lower in the sky and the light breeze kept us cool. In other circumstances I would have been overjoyed to finally be riding towards civilization with the promise of a real bed and a proper dinner ahead of me, but my thoughts kept returning to the elves trapped within the gatehouse wall. Nataka's horse walked beside mine, and I found myself increasingly desperate to break the eerie silence of the valley.

"What's a *skretchgazen*?"

She started in her saddle at the sound of my voice.

"The word loses much in your tongue."

"Care to try anyway?"

She squinted up into the sky for a moment, then looked back at me.

"You have experienced the kind of shit that comes out after a particularly unpleasant meal?"

I blinked twice, then nodded.

"That is *sckretchgazen*."

I nodded again as I focused on keeping a straight face.

"Thank you for explaining."

She turned back to the road ahead and resumed her silence. My mind scrambled for something else to talk about and I landed on the first thought it offered.

"When we fought the goblins you shouted something about 'Kalidar's vengeance.' Is that an orc legend?"

I thought I might be able to draw a story out of her as we rode, but she turned on me with a cold and angry scowl. She opened her mouth, giving me a clear view of her pointed teeth, then caught herself with a visible effort of will before she said whatever had been on her tongue.

"No. Though if the world was a just place it would be by now. Khalidar was my son."

"Oh," I mumbled, aware that I had just stumbled into a sensitive topic and suddenly unsure of how to proceed.

"What happened to him?"

"Are all humans so fond of pointless questions?"

She spurred her horse further down the road before I could respond, leaving me wondering what steaming pile I'd just stuck my foot into this time.

No one else was in the mood for talking. The eerie silence of the place stretched on and on, broken only by the muted clatter of our horses' hooves on paving stones.

Finally the open countryside gave way to a proper city sprawl ahead. As we approached the first buildings that formed the outer ring of the city itself, my worst suspicion was confirmed. Every single one was melted and warped like the guardhouse. Every single one was "decorated" with the twisted shapes of its former occupants in various poses of panic and agony. Even the streets themselves were marred by the grasping hands and screaming faces of those who'd been out walking when the catastrophe struck. Soon I learned to just keep my eyes fixed between Shanti's ears as we carefully picked our way around their grasping hands and pleading eyes to ride ever deeper into the nightmare scene that the city had become.

Now that there was more than one building to observe it was clear that whatever force had done this had swept through the city in an expanding wave from a point near its center. The streets mostly ran inward in straight lines from the city's outer edge like the spokes of a great wheel, which I imagined was exactly what it would have looked like to a bird flying overhead, if any birds had ever gathered enough courage to do so. So far, the sky had been as empty as the streets themselves. Still, the layout was well planned and easy to follow, so at least we didn't need to worry about getting lost along the way.

Nothing in the city made any sense. After more than five hundred years I had expected collapsed roofs, crumbling walls, and forest life swarming through the ruins, but I didn't see so much as a moldy awning anywhere in sight. The city was perfect, its streets and buildings far cleaner than Byzantia's even on a good day. Sure, they were bent and melted in wholly unnatural ways, but they were otherwise in marvelous condition. If it weren't for that and the crowds of tortured and terrified statues stumbling through doorways and fleeing through the streets, I might have thought the entire population had simply decided to leave the city on holiday that morning.

Cael called a halt to water our horses as we rode through an open courtyard with a fountain at its center. The fountain looked to have once been adorned by an elegant statue at its center, but whatever its shape had once been was now warped into a twisted spiral that drooped to one side, looking for all the world like a pile of dog shit that had sat too long in the hot sun.

"That looks to be a smithy," he said as our horses drank their fill.

He pointed across the courtyard towards a building with an open roof built out from its side that covered a small forge with a stone furnace at its center and wooden racks along the walls that sported rows of spotless tools. It must have been a busy place in its day, because several hundred men, women, and children stood in various poses of panic and terror. Some fled in the general direction we'd just come from, out towards the edges of the city. Others were partially embedded in the flagstones and the walls of the buildings that ringed the square, as though they'd been wading through water that had instantly turned to stone.

Everywhere I looked I saw horror, panic, and pain so lifelike that it was easy to think they might pick right up where they left off if I just reached out and touched one. In my mind I kept hearing the chorus of screams that their stone mouths could no longer make, but the only sound my ears could hear was the gentle slurping sounds our horses made as they eased their thirst, and the pounding of my heart against my ribs.

"Seems as good a place as any to make camp for the night," Cael continued, drawing my attention back to the present.

"Did you take a few goblin clubs to the head while we were fighting?" I asked. "You want us to sleep here?"

"We'll not make it to the palace and back again before nightfall," he argued, his voice maddeningly calm as he pointed towards the western mountains now painted red and gold by the setting sun.

"He's right," Magnus said, though it sounded like the words caught in his throat a little. "Our horses need rest, and we need food. Better to proceed in the morning when we're fresh."

"I don't know what's wrong with you two, but I sure as shit won't be getting any sleep surrounded by all this," I snapped, waving my arms at the scene around us.

"You would rather ride amongst them in the dark?" Sheska asked.

"I--" that did put a different spin on things.

"Fine," I sighed. "Let's be about it then so we can put this damned place behind us."

No one seemed inclined to argue.

4

I'd already learned that nightfall comes on fast in the wilderness, but we had everything in order by the time the last of the sun's rays ducked below the mountain peaks. Nataka and Sheska got a nice fire blazing away in the forge while Alleron set out the bedrolls, Magnus prepared supper, and Cael and I refilled our waterskins and gathered more wood from other buildings around the square.

Thankfully, it looked like the blacksmith who'd owned the forge had been out when the city was turned into horrible stone gargoyles, because I saw no sign of his statue anywhere around the place as we settled down to eat. I sat close to the crackling fire and tried to let it warm the chill from my bones, but the moonlit shadows looming over the tortured shapes in the courtyard beyond our little circle of light kept putting a chill right back into them.

Supper was a quiet affair. Everyone finished their meal and retired to their bedroll to sharpen steel, oil leather, tighten straps, or whatever other mundane task they could find to occupy their attention before sleep. Even Alleron, who normally filled every resting moment with words, seemed content to study one of the scrolls he carried in his pack in silence. On most nights that would have suited me just fine, but without the usual hum of city life or even a nighttime chorus of crickets and animal calls to fill the silence, I found I wanted to at least hear someone else's voice.

"Can I ask you a question, Alleron?" I asked, plopping myself down beside his bedroll and leaning my back against the wall without waiting for an answer.

"Looks like you're about to either way," he answered, but he smiled as he said it, and I got the sense that he was grateful for the intrusion.

"What happened here?"

"You don't know?" His brow hunched down into a confused frown. "I could have sworn I'd told the story a dozen times by now. You see five hundred years or so ago our High King Tyrial enacted a great ritual of some sort that turned the--"

"Yes, I know the history," I cut him off before he could build up too much steam. "I guess I really should have asked how it happened. I mean, magic, obviously, but how?"

"No one is entirely certain, to be honest. Records from that era indicate that Tyrial was obsessed with the obscurities of chronomancy, the manipulation of time itself."

"Is that even possible?" Sooner or later I knew I'd get tired of asking that question, but it slipped past my lips before I could catch it.

"Possible, yes, but also highly unstable and dangerous. The flow of time is a weighty thing, and toying with it can have...unintended consequences," he said with a nod of his head towards the courtyard beyond the firelight.

"If this king of yours was so unhinged, why didn't someone try to stop him?"

"Well it's not as though Tyrial set out to destroy his city and condemn those of his people who survived to five centuries of slow decline and misery," he huffed, sounding more defensive than I was used to. "Most agree that he was attempting something else entirely, something extraordinary, but that his ritual got somewhat...out of hand."

"Too bad no one is offering a prize for the greatest understatement of the year. You'd have won for sure."

Alleron shot me a quick glare, but continued anyway.

"The point is, magic can be unpredictable even under the best of circumstances, and the greater the spell, the greater the potential for disaster. Working beyond the laws of our mortal sphere tends to warp the mind over time. Hence the need for rituals and focuses and such. Hells, every great Diviner who made a name in the art became a raving lunatic eventually."

"What? Then why do you practice it yourself? Aren't you worried the same will happen to you?"

"Isn't it obvious? I needed help with the ladies." He smiled as he said it, but his smile was brittle. I snorted, but didn't speak, waiting him out for a better answer. He looked down at his hands as though he might find that answer hidden beneath his fingers. As the silence stretched out, I began to wonder if I'd lost him, until he spoke in a whisper so quiet that I had to lean in to hear it.

"I could accept madness," he said, "if I found the path before it claimed me."

"What path?"

He looked up and met my gaze, his face far more serious than I'd thought possible for him.

"The path to a better future."

Then he smiled again, his dour mood dissolving like clouds after a rain.

"In the meantime, I play my little games to keep the crazy at bay."

"Little games? You mean your wagers?" In a flash the things he'd told me all clicked together, and I caught a glimpse behind his mask. "If you've seen the future, then the moments when you don't know what's about to happen become more important, don't they?"

He looked at me for a moment as though he was seeing me for the first time. "You know, you're the first person who's ever figured that out. Reveling in uncertainty helps me stay grounded. Well, as grounded as possible for a dashing master of the arcane such as myself."

"So if magic is so unpredictable and dangerous, why are so many able to practice it without disintegrating themselves or whatever?"

"Ah, well most wizards and whatnot stick to the well-worn paths. They work with tried and tested incantations or rituals that have been handed down by the braver pioneers who went before them rather than attempting to create something new."

"That's what you meant earlier when you said that improvised magic is dangerous?"

"Indeed. I was working from the starting point of an existing spell I'm already familiar with, so I had a reasonably solid handle on things. Even so, there was certainly a chance I might have simply hoisted the lot of us into the air instead of that barrier, or something even worse."

"But when I've seen Nataka work her magic it always looks like she's making it up as she goes along."

"That's because she is. Well, to some degree, anyway. She's a tribal shaman, so she communes with whatever spirits are present at the moment and draws on their power for her spells. The rules are a little different for her."

"I don't understand," I said, unable to keep the growing frustration from my voice. My time with the Daughters of Vesta had left me with an inescapable drive to analyze and understand when presented with a new problem, especially one that seemed to violate every law of nature that I'd ever learned. "How can two approaches to magic be so different and yet still work? Which one is right?"

"Two approaches? My dear, there are dozens. Blood magic, astromancy, runes and sigils; reading off a list of all the magic disciplines I know of would put an insomniac to sleep, and I'm quite certain there are many more that I've never even heard of. But why the sudden interest? I thought "close your eyes until it goes away" was your preferred stance on all things arcane and mystical."

I had to think about his question for a moment. I hadn't really considered what prompted my growing interest in understanding the strange things I'd seen and experienced since arriving in Danan, but the answer came to me soon enough.

"I suppose it boils down to survival, just like everything else. I may not like it, but it's pretty clear that magic is a regular part of life here, and if there's one thing I learned on the streets it's that knowing what to expect is the difference between living and taking a long dirt nap. Learning more about how magic operates here isn't that different than knowing where the city guard patrol or which merchants pay the local Ghazi boss for protection and which ones don't."

Alleron chuckled as he shook his head. "Leave it to you to find a way to be utterly pragmatic about the mysteries of the arcane. Very well then, if it's a lesson in magical theory you're after, you shall have it." He cleared his throat and sat up straighter, and as I watched a growing enthusiasm light up his eyes I began to wonder what I'd just gotten myself into.

"It might help if you think of magic a little bit like water," he began. "All water is essentially the same, but your experience of it depends very much on when and where you interact with it. Is water a raging river or a gentle rain? The vast ocean or a tiny pond? Is it ice, a warm bath, or rolling clouds of fog?"

He paused and stared at me, awaiting my answer.

"All of them, I suppose."

"Indeed, and yet you could have said that it is none of them and still have been correct. Water is itself. Its true essence does not change despite the many forms it takes, and magic is much the same. The various traditions focus on different aspects or expressions of magic, but in the end, it is simply a force for change that can be channeled and harnessed by those with the will and ability to do so."

"That...actually makes a lot of sense," I admitted as my mind worked to absorb the implications of everything he'd just said.

"Of course it does!" Alleron gave his knee an excited slap, looking immensely pleased with himself. "It really is an excellent metaphor. I'm surprised I've not heard it used before. I shall have to write it down before I forget it."

"So if magic is like water, can anyone learn to work with it?" I asked, following the track of my thoughts as I tried to keep him focused.

"Hmm, well that's something of a debated subject, actually. Most agree that while all sentient creatures have some innate connection or sensitivity towards the flow of magic, most lack the strength or ability to manipulate it directly. Amongst my own people the young are tested at a certain age, and only those who display the proper aptitude are accepted for study by the Chromatis Arcani. I know of similar traditions amongst many of the other races. Philosophy aside, it's certainly true that some are born with an innate facility for magic which others lack."

I let his words roll around in my mind for a moment. Ever since I was forced to accept the evidence of my own senses when I'd first encountered magic in Danan I'd felt cast adrift from everything I thought I'd known. Before I stepped off the boat in Farshore life had made sense. It could be a real shit show for people like me, but at least I'd known the rules and had a chance to use my wits and instincts to help me turn them to my advantage.

The discovery that for all its initial mystery, magic might simply be one vast system whose structure I just didn't comprehend yet came as an immense relief. The Daughters of Vesta had shown me that even the most complex of subjects could be broken down and understood given enough time and determination. I drew in a deep breath, feeling better than I had in weeks, and decided that that was exactly what I was going to do.

"Thanks, Alleron, that was actually very helpful. I think I'll have more questions for you in the future if you don't mind answering them, but that's probably enough for one night."

"Anytime," he said with another one of his brilliant grins. "My bedroll is always open."

I managed to keep my reaction to a few rapid blinks even though his words felt like a splash of cold water in my face. Had he meant that the way it sounded? His eyes stayed locked on mine, but I couldn't read them well enough to be certain either way.

"Right...um, well...I'd better go get set up for first watch. Thanks again," I mumbled as I stood and retreated to the front of the forge.

We'd all agreed that posting a watch was prudent despite the fact that we hadn't seen the slightest sign of life since we entered the city, and now I was doubly glad that I'd volunteered to go first. I snatched a blanket from my pack, wrapped it around my shoulders, and sat down with my back against a wooden post as I stared out into the courtyard and tried to put Alleron's unreadable smile out of my mind.

The others settled into sleep one by one as the hours rolled by, until all I heard behind me was the snap and pop of the wood Cael had banked up in the forge punctuated by Sheska and Magnus' dueling snores. I let my thoughts wander where they willed, and soon found myself wondering what life in the strange and silent city had been like before King Tyrial had destroyed it.

Did elves gather on market days to exchange gossip and watch executions like the citizens of Byzantia? Had they needed to guard their money-belts from pick pockets, or were they above such things? If you'd asked me to guess not that long ago I would have assumed that the sylvan folk went about their days held aloft by quiet dignity and majestic poise, but weeks of traveling with Alleron had shown me that he at least was just as mortal as the rest of us, with all of the attendant vices and quirks that went along with it.

Take that elven girl who had just entered the square with her basket held ready for whatever she'd come in search of. She looked close to my own age, and if you took away the tall, pointed ears and the shimmering blue light that surrounded her she would hardly have drawn a second glance among the stalls of the Concordium.

I bolted upright as the reality of what I was seeing startled me fully awake. A quick rub of my eyes confirmed that I wasn't dreaming -- the glowing figure of a young elven woman was gliding across the open stones of the square towards the fountain at its center. She wore an elegant dress that trailed into tattered flickers of light that drifted away on the breeze behind her. As I watched she paused and waved at a spot of empty air on the far side of the fountain as a smile spread across her face.

Or it had been empty air, at least. When I looked again I saw the brilliant outline of another woman waving back. She was older than the first, but might otherwise have been her twin, and as the two moved to meet up by the fountain a swirling ball of blue light blossomed into the shape of a tall man holding a young boy by the hand as they walked in the opposite direction. That sight was followed by a dozen more like it, then a hundred, until in a span of a few rapid breaths the entire square teemed with the ghostly motions of a crowd on market day.

"Um, guys...I think you should see this," I whispered over my shoulder as I reached back to give the toe of Nataka's boot a good shake.

"No mice..." she muttered as she kicked at my hand.

"Mother's grace," a small voice whispered in my ear. I turned to find Sheska crouched beside me, shortbow in hand as she stared out at the scene that filled the courtyard. As she turned back to me I saw fear written plain across her face, and that did more to unnerve me than all those ghostly whatever they weres had managed on their own. If Sheska was afraid enough to let it break through that mask she called a face, then I knew for sure we were in a very bad spot. She turned and slipped back into the forge without making a sound, and soon I heard rustling fabric and whispered words as she woke the others with the news that we were not as alone in the Shattered City as we had thought.

Alright, Charity, just keep calm and hold still. The ghosts of everyone who was horribly murdered here are floating around a stone's throw from where you're sitting, but maybe they're the friendly sort. This is definitely not the reason that everyone who's ever come here was never heard from again. Everything is going to be fine.

No matter how hard I tried to convince myself that things might not be as bad as they seemed, every danger sense I possessed -- from the tingling in my scalp to the itch in my palms -- was screaming at me to burrow into the deepest hole I could manage and stay there until the sun came out.

At least they don't seem to have noticed us. Maybe if we just sit tight and quiet until morning then--

"Unhand me, Rhadgar! You'll pay for your treachery!" Magnus' voice thundered through the still night air as Sheska shook him from his sleep. I heard muffled curses as the others rushed to clamp hands over his mouth, but it was too late. Every one of the ghostly silhouettes outside snapped their heads in our direction at once, their pantomime shattered by the foreign sound.

The girl whom I'd first seen enter the square raised her arm and extended a slender finger to point straight at my heart. I watched in frozen terror as her mouth fell open to unleash a terrible scream. Her jaw dropped lower and lower, until it draped past her chest like some grotesque wax shape that had melted and run in the heat of a fire as the sound that blasted out from her grew louder. The piercing wail of horror, fury, and pain scraped across my ears and continued on and on long past the point when breath would have failed in living lungs.

The figures all around her raised shimmering arms and shrill screams as their faces warped to match hers, then as one body they surged towards us in a rolling wave of blue light, wild eyes, and gaping mouths.

I scrambled backwards into the forge. The only thing my mind could manage in response was pure, animal terror that drove me to run, hide, escape. I collided hard with Magnus and went tumbling to the floor as he pushed past me, his axe Hilda held overhead and a scream of blind fury on his lips. From the crazed look in his eyes I doubted he was even fully awake, just driven by instinct and the rage that haunted his dreams to throw himself at the new threat without hesitation.

"Wait!" I screamed as I dove for his boot, but he barreled past me and charged out into the courtyard alone.

He met the onrushing swarm of ghostly figures with a lateral swipe of his axe that cleaved through the first four in a single blow. Their shimmering outlines parted at the waist, swirling like fog teased by the wind for a brief moment before flowing back to their original form. Before he could recover for another swing the ghosts fell on him in a mass of flailing limbs and piercing screams.

A brilliant flash of light burst outward as they made contact with him. I buried my head in my elbow to shield my eyes. When I looked up again a half second later Magnus had vanished. Some detached part of my brain observed that the ghost of the elven matron who had greeted the girl I'd first seen had also disappeared. The rest of my brain focused on the fact that there were more than enough ghosts to take her place, and that they had all just turned their attention on me.

I scrambled to my feet and ran further back into the forge. If Magnus' axe hadn't stopped them, I didn't see what good my swords would do, even if I'd had time to retrieve them from the pile next to my bedroll. I saw Alleron gesturing as the air around him began to crackle with energy. Cael stood in front of him with his sword and shield held ready. He shouted something as I ran past, but I couldn't make out his words over the endless chorus of screams that followed on my heels. As I dove over a barrel and rolled to my feet on the other side, two more bursts of light flared over my shoulder. A backward glance confirmed that now there were more ghosts surging towards me where the two men had stood a moment before.

I kept running, my mind frantically searching for an escape, but finding none. Three more steps carried me to the back of the forge where its cold stone wall rose impassive and immovable to block my path. Another flash of light, and when I spun round with my back pressed against the wall, I saw that only Sheska and I were left standing. She must have been just a half-step behind me the whole way, but she could see the wall that blocked our escape as well as I.

Sheska took one look at my face, saw the wild terror written plain across it and the wet line of tears that had made their own way down my cheeks, and turned to plant herself in between me and the horde of iridescent blue figures that chased after us. She tossed her shortbow aside, drew the long skinning knife she kept on her belt, and dug in her heels as the wailing phantoms surged towards us.

The fear that had gripped me and driven me near to madness since the ghosts had first sighted us broke apart at the sight of my tiny halfling friend placing herself square in their path to save me. She was barely half my size, yet even as I cowered like a frightened puppy, she stood determined to do what she could, ready to fight to the last. I had never taken her talk of becoming "Ko'koan" very seriously.

Tying your life so closely with another's seemed like the height of madness to a street waif like me, but in that space between heartbeats I realized that Sheska had just put her life on the line for my sake without thinking twice because of that bond.

For the first time since the sound had begun, I found myself feeling grateful for the ghost's horrible wailing, because it meant that Sheska couldn't hear the half-sob that caught in my throat as I realized that for the first time in my life I wasn't standing nose to eyeball with danger on my own. I grabbed the leg of a wooden stool and brandished it like a club as I leaped forward to stand side by side with my Ko'koan.

If the ghosts were moved by our futile show of defiance, they gave no sign of it. They just flowed through or around whatever solid objects stood in their way as they surged towards us with crooked fingers clawing at the air. I found myself staring into the eyes of the girl that I'd first seen enter the square as she reached for me.

She held her basket clutched to her chest with one hand as the other stretched towards my face. As I met her gaze, I realized that her eyes were filled with the wild, unreasoning panic of a drowning man in the instant before he was claimed by the waves. A terror greater than anything I could imagine drove her flight, and even as she reached for me, I felt a strange sympathy for her rising up beneath my own fear.

As her fingers brushed my face an electric shock flowed through my skin to crash down into my bones. My world dissolved in a flash of brilliant blue, and then I felt nothing at all.

5

I awoke with a smile on my lips and a song in my heart, threw back the covers and leaped across the floor to my wardrobe like a meadowlark riding a spring breeze. I let my hand rest on the handle for a moment, savoring the last of the delicious anticipation that had kept me from sleep all night long, before throwing the doors open to reveal my beautiful new dress in all its satin glory.

It was the kindest, most thoughtful gift mother had ever given me. No doubt that harpy Cressida would positively die of envy when she saw me turning heads at the Solstice Gala tonight, especially if its low-cut back and off the shoulder grace drew Adarian's eye to me like I hoped it would. Perhaps it would finally spur the gorgeous lout to offer his arm and claim the first dance. I dressed in a flurry of white lace and daydreams, and before long I stood before my dressing mirror to assess the results.

"Acceptably adequate," I said to my reflection. I'd done up my blonde tresses in high court fashion, pinned in place with a silver comb to empha-size the slender peak of my ears.

A wave of dizziness struck me without warning. I caught myself against the mirror's wooden frame for support, and for a moment my vision blurred so badly that I saw another figure altogether staring back out of the mirror. Rough cropped black hair hung to her shoulders, framing a face with skin the color of mother's morning cha set with a pair of emerald green eyes. Everything about that face felt both familiar and foreign in equal measure. The dizziness grew stronger, until I squeezed my eyes shut and focused on drawing in a few deep, calming breaths to steady my wild nerves.

When I finally dared open my eyes again, I saw my own true reflection looking back at me; confused, frightened, but the correct shape, size, and color once more. The feeling of something being out of place still lingered in my mind like the sensation of opening your mouth to speak only to find that the words you were searching for have run just out of reach of your tongue. It was unsettling, but I shook my head, squared my shoulders, and decided to attribute it to an excess of nerves and a poor night's sleep before turning for the door.

I picked up a bread roll from the table and a basket from its hook by the front door before stepping out into the street. I was greeted by the sun's warm glow and the symphony of birdsong that always graced the city's streets. I had taken less than ten steps when the rolling chorus of silver bells called the hour in a rippling wave of music that flowed from the palace at the city's center to lift my heart and clear away the last of the uncertainty from the morning's strange episode.

I loved my city. Shirael Toris, the Shining City, earned its name anew each and every day. Its colors and majestic vistas, music and cultured grace were known and admired the world over. Today promised to be even more glorious than most, for the King had made it known that he intended to grace his subjects with a wonderful gift in honor of the city's one thousandth year. It seemed that the city had done nothing but speculate and gossip as to the nature of that gift since King Tyrial had made the proclamation, but the only clue he had offered was that it was a greater gift than any in the long history of elvenkind, and would light the way to a truly glorious future for our people.

As I rounded the corner onto the Avenue of Green Branches, I was struck by another episode of disorientation. My head exploded with wave after wave of stabbing pain that sent me stumbling like a drunkard for the shade of one of the trees that gave the street its name. I leaned against the rough bark and dug the heel of my palms into my eyes as I waited for the spell to pass. After what felt like an eternity, the pain faded into a dull ache that was at least somewhat bearable. I raised my head again, careful not to move too quickly, but what I saw when I opened my eyes ripped a scream of terror from my throat.

Dark clouds rolled overhead where the sun had shone just a moment before. The buildings that lined the avenue, shops and houses I knew well, had been warped into unnatural shapes like the surface of a lake frozen an instant after it was struck by a stone. As disturbing as those sights were, my scream had been caused by something closer to hand and far more horrifying. Less than an arm's length in front of my face stood the stone shape of a man frozen in mid-step as he ran towards me, his face a mask of wild panic as his hands clawed the air between us.

I turned in a slow, dazed circle as I looked at hundreds more just like him scattered across the street and among the trees all around me. Men and women of all ages and classes, their faces contorted in silent terror as they fled together from something further up the street, although I saw nothing but more statues when I looked in that direction.

I stumbled backward, only to trip over a park bench and tumble to the ground in my haste to escape the visions of horror that surrounded me. How could this have happened? The Shining City and everyone in it had been swallowed by death in the few brief moments I'd closed my eyes. Was I the only one left? I wrapped my arms around my head, curled into a ball, and fought the nausea that threatened to bring up the meager contents of my stomach at any moment.

"Are you all right, miss?"

An uneasy voice above my head broke through my fear. I looked up to find the sun shining in the sky once more, and the same man I'd seen standing as a tortured statue a moment before looking down at me with a mixture of pity and wary concern on his face. Others stood staring behind him, drawn by my outburst.

"I...yes, thank you, I can't think what came over me." I allowed him to help me to my feet and retrieve my basket from beside the park bench I'd tripped over.

"Would you like to see a doctor?" he asked, speaking like a man trying to soothe a crazed horse with calm words. "I know an excellent one in the Adrinoth Heights I could take you to."

"Oh no, that's hardly necessary," I answered as I stepped past him, "it was probably just the summer heat. Please excuse me."

I hurried through the crowd that had gathered and moved up the street as fast as I could manage without breaking into an outright run, my cheeks burning with every step. I had no true excuse or explanation for what had happened, at least not one that I wished to share with a crowd of strangers.

In truth, I was beginning to wonder if speaking to someone about these strange visions wouldn't be such a bad idea. With the beautiful day now in full force all around me it was difficult to believe in the things I'd just seen, but the memory lingered with me, sharp and heavy with the sense of impending danger. Those few moments had felt just as real to me as anything I'd ever experienced, and I found that I could not simply dismiss them as the product of an overwrought imagination no matter how badly I wanted to. By the time I'd reached the entrance to Veridian Square I had made up my mind to tell mother about the two strange episodes and ask for her counsel.

Simply stepping onto the flagstones of the square did a great deal to calm my nerves. I'd spent many days here since my childhood, playing among the alleyways and shop awnings that circled around it, and even splashing happily in the waters of the fountain at its center on hot summer days. My uncle Joriel ran his smithy here, and his reputation drew customers from all across Danan, while my mother's apothecary shop stood nearby. If any place in the Shining City could offer relief from the dark visions that seemed determined to haunt my day, it was here.

"Spare a coin in honor of the day, child?" An old woman sat on a ragged blanket with her back against the stone wall and a cup lying eager and ready at her feet.

"I'm sorry, Granny, but I'm in a hurry today."

"Have you no time for charity, dear?"

Her words struck me like a slap to the face. Images and memories crashed down on me; Mother Shanti's pinched and disapproving face, the same look on the face of the magister who sentenced me to a life of service in exile to Farshore colony. I remembered the cramped hold of the ship that carried me across the ocean, the first sight of Farshore's peaked rooftops and wooden wall. I remembered Cael's mustache twitching as he tried to hold back a laugh, Magnus standing on a table and challenging all comers to another round of arm wrestling, Alleron's smile, Sheska's scowl, and Nataka's quiet dignity. As the memories fell atop one another like stones in a wall, I remembered myself.

"Charity. We...I am Charity."

"Not from where I'm sitting you aren't," the beggar woman huffed before turning to look for more promising targets as I tried to make sense of what I was experiencing.

The sensation of being two minds in one body was almost too much to bear. Hearing my own name spoken out loud seemed to have been the shock that I needed to recall myself, but the elven girl's thoughts and feelings crowded in all around me, fighting against my will to regain control of her own body. I gritted my teeth and pushed her aside by focusing on what I should do next to put an end to whatever strange magic had landed me here in the first place.

As I looked around, I realized that I was standing on the edge of the square where we'd been camped when the horde of screaming spirits had swept in on us. The fountain in the center splashed with clear, fresh water. At its center stood three elven figures wielding bows that fired water in graceful arcs to splash down into the basin below. The fountain's statue and the buildings around the square all stood comfortingly straight and solid, but it was the same place all right.

As I stood on my tiptoes to get a look at the smithy where we'd made camp it occurred to me that if I'd come here in the body of the girl who'd gotten her ghost claws into me then maybe the others would be around here as well, buried in the minds of the spirits that had taken them. It was a complete and total guess, but it seemed reasonable enough, and seeing as how I couldn't think of anything better, I set off to try and find my friends.

The determination I'd first felt as I merged with the crowd soon faded into hopeless frustration. Everyone looked and acted like a normal elf on a normal day, and I quickly realized that I had no idea what signs I might look for to tell me which ones out of that milling throng held my friends trapped inside them, assuming my guess was even correct to begin with.

After nearly an hour of aimless wandering I threw myself down on the low stone wall of the fountain. The elf girl's thoughts of confusion and irritation buzzed at me like a swarm of flies, which made it hard to maintain focus. I decided to allow myself a few minutes to rest and splash some water on the back of my neck to give myself something else to think about besides the growing fear that I might be trapped here alone and half-mad forever.

"And then we'll eat cake!" squealed a small voice behind me.

"Yes, my boy," laughed a man's voice in answer. "All the cake we can squeeze into that growing stomach of yours."

As I turned to look over my shoulder, I recognized the speakers. It was the father and son I had last seen as ghostly blue figures holding hands and drifting across the square in the moonlight. As I stared harder at them a stab of pain lanced through my brain, and for a moment it was as if I looked at two people standing in the same space. The elven father walked by me, and so did Alleron looking frantic and confused. The boy held tight to his father's hand, but his face also sported a thick mustache and Cael's angry eyes searching for escape.

"Excuse me," I called as I leaped from my seat by the fountain and ran up to them.

"Yes? May I help you miss?"

"I was wondering if...that is, have you felt anything...odd lately?"

"Odd, you say? Why, I can't say that I have. Now if you'll please excuse us."

The man's tone and expression as he turned to leave made it clear that I was the only odd thing he'd had to deal with so far today, and that he was quite eager to get as far away from me as possible. I racked my brains for something even remotely rational to say to keep him with me until I figured out how to shake my friends loose, but came up empty.

"Oh, sod it. Snap out of it, Alleron!" I shouted at his back.

The man froze in mid-step, his every muscle rigid with tension.

"Papa?" his son said as he tugged on his arm.

"You too, Cael. You have to fight!"

The boy's eyes went wide. A few heartbeats passed, then a few more as the crowd moved around us casting irritated glances our way. Just when I began to worry that something had gone wrong the man turned around to face me, and I saw a familiar amused smile tugging at the corner of his mouth.

"Well, that was a first."

"Alleron?"

"In the flesh," he answered, then looked down at his hands. "Well, more or less."

A feeling of immense relief flooded through me. True, we were still just as trapped as we had been a moment before, but at least I wouldn't have to face it on my own.

"What's going on?" the boy asked. His voice was still young and chirpy, but any trace of youthful innocence had been replaced by Cael's serious tone. The effect would have been rather funny if the whole thing wasn't so damned unnerving.

"We're in the Shattered City the way it was before whatever happened actually happened," I said, then explained everything I'd seen and felt since I woke up in the elven girl's room.

"So we're in the past, then?" Cael asked. I could only offer a shrug in answer, as his guess was as good as mine. We both turned to Alleron to find him staring at the spires and arches of the surrounding buildings in undisguised wonder, clearly deaf to Cael's question.

"It's even more wonderful than I could have dreamed," he whispered as he turned a small circle. "To think that once we soared to such heights..."

"Hey," I reached out and shook his shoulder. "You can play tourist later. Right now we need to figure out what's going on."

"What?" He turned to look at me, but it took a moment before his attention followed. "Sorry, it's just...never mind. What were you saying?"

"Cael asked if we've been transported to the past somehow."

"Unlikely," Alleron answered as he looked down at his host's unfamiliar hands. "Chronomancy does seem to be involved, but if we'd merely been transported in time, we would still be resident in our own bodies. Being trapped in the minds of the spirits who attacked us speaks of something more at play."

"Could this all be some sort of illusion?" I asked. "Like a dream we just need to wake up from or something?"

"I don't think so." Alleron steepled his fingers and tapped them against his lips in a gesture I'd come to think of as his 'don't rush me, I'm thinking' face.

"The world around us is far too solid and consistent for that. It seems that we truly are *here*, wherever here is, and I suspect that whatever happens to us in this place would have very real consequences for us."

"Lovely."

"It gets worse, I'm afraid. From what you've told us and the thoughts that keep popping into my head as well, I can only conclude that we're in Shirael Toris on the exact day of its destruction."

A cold chill swept through me.

"What does that mean?"

"It means that if we can't figure out what magic placed us here and undo it before the sun sets on the city's last day, we're going to get a very up close and personal view of the catastrophe that melted the city and turned everyone here into stone."

"Wonderful. That's great," I snapped. Even I could hear the raw edge of panic in my voice. "So what do we do about it?"

"First we find the others," Cael said, standing on the tips of his toes as he tried and failed to get a better view through the crowd. "I'm guessing they're around here somewhere just like we were."

"Brilliant plan, oh tiny one. That way, when the end comes, we can all hold hands and die together."

The thought of spending the rest of eternity as a stone statue in a haunted city was driving me to the edge of my nerves. I knew I wasn't handling it well, and the more panicked I became the more I felt the elf girl's conscious-ness pressing against mine, fighting for control. I pressed a hand to my head as the pain started building again. Her thoughts and feelings grew louder with every pounding beat of my heart. Thankfully, the solid weight of a hand on my shoulder pulled my attention back again, and I opened my eyes to see a familiar grin on an unfamiliar face.

"He's right, Charity," Not-Alleron said. "Nataka understands spirits better than any of us, and I think that their involvement is a key part of what happened to us. Besides, once we figure out how to get home again, we may not have much time to do it. We'll need to all be together to seize the moment."

Not-Cael reached out a small hand and awkwardly patted my knee. "We have a plan, and it will work."

"Right," I nodded, drawing in a deep breath and releasing it slowly as I took refuge in their reassurance. "We have a plan and it will work. Let's get to it."

6

We decided that splitting up would be the quickest way to search the square, so I explained what signs they should look for to spot our friends trapped in someone else's body and what to do about it when they did. We agreed to meet back by the fountain as soon as we'd found one of our companions or in thirty minutes, whichever came first.

It took nearly all of those thirty minutes, but I finally found Sheska trapped in the body of the blacksmith who owned the forge where we'd made camp. He was returning from some errand, but happily stopped to give me a smile and a warm hug when he caught sight of me wandering the square and staring hard at everyone I passed. At first I tried to excuse myself and get away from him as quickly as I could. I was so busy worrying that he would realize there was something very wrong with his niece that I almost missed the flickering double vision moments of yellow eyes and a small round face hovering across his features.

"Wake up, Ko'koan." I pitched my voice just loud enough for her to hear me without drawing attention from those around us, leaning in and staring hard into the eyes of the taller elf. He reeled back as if I'd just struck him in the face, shook his head, and opened his mouth to speak. All that came out was an odd gurgling sound, then silence. He stared over the top of my head into the crowd for what seemed like ages, but just as I began to worry that I'd broken the man somehow he shook his head again like a dog flinging water from its fur, and turned back to meet my gaze with a frown.

"Mother's grace," the blacksmith said, "that was a thing."

I threw my arms around her and squeezed hard, not bothering to hide my relief that she had been able to break free of the fog. The memory of my little friend standing with her knife between me and a horde of screeching ghosts sprang to mind, and I squeezed harder.

"Oof, I think you just bruised a rib," she grumbled as she pulled herself free, but she couldn't completely hide her pleased smile. Sheska turned to look out over the crowd, turning a quick circle as she took in her surroundings.

"So this is what it feels like to be a giant?"

I realized that the added factor of waking up inside a body several times bigger than your own must be making this even stranger for her than it was for the rest of us. Well, except maybe Cael.

"How does it feel?"

She finished her circle and looked down at her feet, then back at me.

"The ground is too far away," she said. "How do you manage not to break your head open on the ground?"

"We take it one step at a time," I chuckled as I took her hand and led her towards the fountain. "Come on, let's go find the others."

I gave her a brief explanation of our situation as we made our way through the crowd, and had just finished by the time we reached the fountain's edge, to find the rest of our group waiting for us. Cael and Alleron stood with a plump elven housewife in a green and white dress, and a reed-thin elven man dressed in the patchwork colors and jangling bells of a festival juggler. I assumed that their bodies held Magnus and Nataka but wasn't sure which one was which.

"That's a lovely dress," Sheska smirked as we approached. The house-wife's face flushed crimson.

"The next one who comments on my clothing gets a fist through their teeth," she grumbled, her hands clenched tight at her side.

Guess that answers that.

"Alleron has explained our situation," the juggler said in Nataka's slow and steady tone, "and I believe the picture is becoming clearer. In our world the souls of these people are trapped, unable to pass to their rest beyond.

They are bound to this place by a strange magic, neither truly dead nor truly alive. At night when the boundaries of magic weaken, their consciousness roams the streets as they did in life. When they sense the warmth of the living they reach out for aid, but the power that holds them is too strong. It pulls the souls of whomever they touch here into this place, and I suspect those souls are utterly destroyed when the catastrophe overtakes them each night."

We all took a minute to absorb Nataka's words. I mostly focused on the "utterly destroyed" part.

"So you're saying the specters that attacked us weren't ghosts?" Cael asked.

"Not in the traditional sense, no. More like the manifestations of a waking nightmare, an expression of their pain and fear." She looked at the people milling around us, her eyes filled with sorrow and pity. "These folk have suffered as no soul ever should. What was done to them is a crime greater than I can comprehend."

"And it's one I'd just as soon not share with them," I said, trying to keep my growing impatience from my voice as I steered the conversation back to the only subject that really mattered. "So what are we going to do about it?"

"If Nataka is correct, we are dealing with magic unlike anything I've ever heard of, but certain principles should still apply." Alleron had been staring hard at the flagstones beneath his feet while Nataka spoke, but looked up at her now with excitement growing in his eyes. "If you can weaken the hold these spirits have on us, I believe I can create a portal to shift us back to our own reality, and our own bodies."

"Combine our magic?" She frowned. "I do not even know if such a thing is possible, but I suppose it is worth the effort. We'll need somewhere quieter than this, though."

"I think I have just the place," Sheska said as she pointed over the heads of the crowd toward the forge owned by her host, the same place we'd made camp the night before.

The crowd in the square had grown thicker as evening approached. The business of the market had slowly given way to revelry and festival lights, and we made slow progress at first as Cael's small body struggled to keep pace without being knocked to the ground. Finally, Magnus scooped him up with a grunt and held the boy tight against his host's ample bossom as Cael squirmed and cursed like a sailor on the docks. His colorful language drew a number of shocked and disapproving glances our way, but together we pushed our way through the crowd until we tumbled into the forge.

Alleron and Nataka moved to stand by the back wall, their discussion growing ever more heated as they argued magical theory.

"But without a proper focus the conduit could unravel and..."

"No! The spirits of this place must be respected, however warped they have become. We must..."

"Did they teach you nothing of temporal resonance in that backwater village of yours? When we move the..."

Listening to the two of them hash out the details of their combined spell was a lot like listening to a sculptor and a blacksmith trying to bake a cake together for the first time. I kept one ear on their efforts, and one eye on the people milling about the square, alert for any unexpected changes. The stress of knowing that something terrible was about to happen, but not knowing the what or the when of it, was taking its toll on my nerves. A danger I could see and plan for was bad enough, but whatever had been unleashed on this city had apparently happened fast enough to catch all of its citizens unaware and unprepared. No matter how hard I tried to keep my mind clear and calm as Mother Shanti had taught me, I kept picturing myself frozen forever as one more terrified statue among thousands.

An hour passed, then two. Every time Nataka and Alleron resolved one issue to their satisfaction, two more were raised. I understood in a loose sense that what they were about to attempt was difficult, but from the way they spoke of it you'd think they were attempting to invent a new language and then use it to write an epic saga, all while racing the sun towards the horizon.

I kept myself occupied by keeping an eye on the people in the square. We didn't have any idea what to expect, so I decided I should just watch for anything and everything out of the ordinary. By the time dusk began to spread its shadowed fingers over the thinning crowd I'd only learned that watching Elven festivals was about as exciting as staring at paint as it dried. I began to wonder if Alleron had been wrong about the city's impending doom. Maybe this was just a normal day like any other? My stomach at least was convinced that our time would be better spent in search of a meal than standing around waiting for Alleron and Nataka to finish arguing.

Then the world turned inside out.

I was falling up into the sky and plummeting down into a fathomless ocean at the same time, my senses completely overwhelmed in an instant. My mind and body were melted into a puddle that spun wildly round a drain, disappearing into a yawning void. The assault was immediate and overpowering.

It stopped just as suddenly as it began. I stood trembling and confused in the same spot I'd been in when the chaos had claimed me, apparently unharmed but barely conscious. Everyone and everything around me stood as still and silent as I did, and it took only the briefest of glances to confirm that my friends and everyone else in the square must have experienced the same effects.

"Look!"

A woman stood by the fountain, eyes wide and mouth hanging open in shock as she pointed towards the center of the city. I followed her finger to see a thick cloud billowing up into the sky. At first I thought it was smoke from a fire, but I soon saw crackling bolts of blue and purple light flashing within the darkness. It rose several dozen feet in the air, but then seemed to gather in on itself rather than drifting away as smoke would have. It coiled tight for a moment, a swirling maelstrom that blocked out the light of the sun, then shot out in all directions like a breaking wave.

As the cloud raced towards me, I felt a surge of fear crash through my mind. Every instinct screamed at me that within that rolling fog lay a doom far, far worse than death. It called to me, whispering promises in my mind just beyond my understanding, but I knew that I had to flee in the same way the deer knows to run when lightning sparks a forest fire.

I had already taken three steps towards the square before I caught hold of myself. The busy chatter of the crowd had turned to shouts and screams as people ran, tripping and shoving past each other in their panicked haste to escape. It took all of my willpower to overcome a lifetime of instinct and keep myself from joining them. I was alive today because I'd learned long ago that when trouble kicked in your front door you didn't pause to think or check on your mates. You ran, plain and simple, and it was up to every rat to find their own hole.

But I knew well enough that trying to outrun that cloud would only buy me a few extra minutes at most. Strange as it felt to admit it, my only hope of survival lay with my friends now. I still didn't really understand what they were doing, but I knew that Alleron and Nataka wouldn't bother trying if there wasn't at least a slim hope of success. I took in a deep breath, held it for a moment as I watched the angry death cloud warp and twist the buildings in its path as it swept over them to reach us, then turned and walked back into the forge.

Alleron stood with his eyes closed in concentration, his hands outstretched towards the back wall of the smithy. Nataka knelt by the wall, the bells on her jester's outfit jingling wildly as she finished tracing a pattern onto the blank stone with a piece of chalk. It was the outline of a circle larger than a tavern door, with a series of strange shapes and symbols drawn around it at even intervals. From her slow and graceful movements you might have thought the orc shaman was preparing a table for tea.

"Anyone but me notice the giant, angry doom cloud headed this way?" I asked.

Sheska glared at me and placed a finger over her lips. The gesture was much more effective when delivered by a brawny elven face several inches above my own, but I stuck my tongue out at her and ignored her stern gaze as always.

"I'm just saying it wouldn't hurt to pick up the pace a bit if we don't want to find out what it's like to be a thousand-year-old statue."

"Anyone ever tell you that you're good at helping?" Cael asked in his boy voice as he elbowed my thigh. "Because if they did, you'd know for certain they're a natural born liar."

He smiled as he said it, but I could see the same tension in his eyes that was busy twisting my back muscles into knots.

Before I could think of a good retort, Alleron's voice rang out within the cramped forge. He spoke in a language I didn't understand, if it was a language at all, but I felt the power in his words all the same. Light flared on the wall and a wave of force cracked out and sent me stumbling back a step as I shielded my eyes with my arm.

When I looked up, the circle they had drawn on the stone had fallen away into a swirling void of spiraling green light. The sigils Nataka had drawn around its edge pulsed and crackled, and I had the sense that they were straining to hold back an immense force.

After a few seconds the swirling vortex inside the circle resolved itself into an image. I saw the same forge we stood in now, only this one had already been warped and twisted by angry, crackling cloud that swept through the city behind us. I don't think I'd ever seen anything more beautiful in my entire life.

"What are we waiting for?" The portly housewife that Magnus was riding in stepped towards the portal, but Alleron reached out and grabbed her shoulder.

"Wait! We must wait for the portal to fully solidify. If we enter while the magic is still raw the results could be devastating."

"There's no time!" I shouted, grabbing Alleron and spinning him around to point at the square behind us just as the cloud exploded over and through the buildings on the far side of the square and swept across the empty flagstones towards us. Dust and debris rode the shockwave before it, and as it reached the fountain statue the solid stone carving melted like glass, its form dissolving into a suspended pool of liquid white marble that was spun out and reformed as if the invisible hand of an angry child pulled and twisted it like wet clay. Then the cloud swept over it and surged towards us.

Alleron's eyes widened for a moment, then he shoved me towards the portal.

"Go now!"

The screaming panic in my mind had become deafening, and I realized as I stepped to the portal that it was the voice of the elf girl whose body I had shared since arriving here. The cloud was affecting her even worse than it was me, driving her beyond reason into pure animal terror. I felt a surge of pity for her, somehow hating the thought of simply abandoning her to her fate even though I knew that fate had been sealed centuries before I was even born.

I paused by the portal as the others piled through, each one disappearing in a flash of green. Being the last one through felt like a small gesture I could offer her, like sitting by a dying man's bed until the end. Sheska was the last of the group besides me, but she stopped in front of the portal rather than leaping into it.

"Get through!" She barked at me.

"I'll go la--" She grabbed me before I'd finished my protest, sweeping me into her arms like a child, which I supposed for the moment I was.

"Size does hold some advantages after all," she said, and tossed me into the portal.

Time stopped and sped up all at once. I felt myself stretched out across the weave of the infinite stars until my awareness was torn free from the body it had shared like a pit torn out of a plum. Lacking form, I spun and tumbled like a twig in a waterfall, reaching out for something solid and finding nothing but the void.

Without warning I crashed back into reality. I stood shaking and trembling in the ruined forge. The others stood around me in a group, looking various shades of green around the gills, but generally in one piece. I was relieved to see Sheska standing behind me, looking both immensely pleased with herself and gut-sick at the same time.

I drew in a breath, opened my mouth to say something witty and casual about our near-death experience, and promptly passed out.

7

"I didn't know you humans could snore like that."

"Most of us can't. Charity is special."

I cracked one eye open to see Magnus' red beard and Cael's thick mustache about an inch from my face.

"Vesta's bones, give a girl some space," I grumbled as I shoved them away and sat up.

"You had us worried for a moment," Cael said as he offered me a hand. I brushed it aside and struggled to my feet on my own. My head swam for a moment as I looked around the forge. I wasn't sure how long I'd been out, but it had apparently been long enough for the others to pack up our things even though the sky outside was only just beginning to show signs of the coming dawn.

We just stared at each other for a moment. My memories of what had happened were vague and fragmented. I remembered seeing the ghosts form in the square, remembered them swarming over us, and then it was all just a blur of odd scenes and feelings; a beautiful dress, the sun shining as I walked down the street, and one moment of crystal clarity when I heard my name spoken by a beggar woman and returned to myself. I guessed from the various looks on their faces that the others struggled with equally jumbled thoughts.

"So," I said, shaking off the pensive silence as I moved to check on my bag. "Anyone care to tell me what in the eight frozen hells just happened?"

"That's what we've been discussing," Cael replied.

"And?"

His only answer was a shrug and a frown.

"Really? You're the Danan natives here. You're telling me you've never heard of ghosts pulling people into a strange alternate realm where their minds are trapped inside someone's body until they're destroyed by a horrible cloud of magical doom that actually happened centuries ago? Nataka?"

"I do not know where we were taken." She frowned a toothy frown, obviously troubled. "It was like the spirit realm, and yet...very different. It smelled funny."

"Everything about this damned city smells funny," said Magnus. "The buildings look like they've been stood next to Garadin's forge all day, yet they're solid as stone should be. And even though it's been abandoned for more years than I care to count it hasn't been claimed by woods nor beasts like you'd expect. Gives me the itch."

I noticed that Alleron's eyes had hardly left the toes of his boots during our conversation.

"You're awfully quiet, Alleron. Have anything to add?"

He looked up with a start as though hearing his name spoken had snapped him out of a daydream.

"Pardon?"

"What gives with this place?" I asked again, pointing in a circle at the forge and the city beyond.

He opened his mouth to answer, paused to wrestle with his thoughts, then seemed to think better of whatever he'd been about to say.

"I have a theory," he finally said, "but it requires further consideration. I would not care to simply hazard a guess when so much rests on the answer."

Somehow I got the feeling that he wasn't just talking about whether we all went on breathing, but I was in no mood to tease it out of him now.

"Fine, do you think you can consider it on the move?" I asked as I shouldered my pack. "If we set out now, we should reach the palace before we lose too much daylight. If the gods are in a good mood, we might find that blasted crown and be out of the city before the ghosts come out to play tonight."

We were mounted up and riding by the time the sun had cracked the horizon.

The rest of the city continued on largely the same. The houses and buildings we rode past grew increasingly larger and more opulent, with walled and gated courtyards, private gardens, and spiraling towers all proudly on display, yet each had been twisted and warped into a strange parody of a building by the thundering cloud of wild magic I had seen through the elven girl's eyes. The frozen statues wore increasingly fine robes and jewelry, but each one looked just as terrified in their flight as the poor folk we'd seen on the city's outskirts.

Riding through their silent, open air tomb was all the more disturbing now that I had experienced a glimpse of their normal lives before disaster claimed them. Odd memories and sensations flashed through me as we rode, leaving me with a constant sense of recognizing a place or person even though you know you've never seen them before. I did observe a gradual change in the statues. The closer we drew to the palace the more the stone figures seemed to be caught standing in surprise rather than fleeing in terror. Some even faced toward the palace rather than running towards the city's outskirts, their mouths open and fingers pointed at the sky in awe.

We rode in silence, the ruined shell of a once proud people all around us leaving little room for banter, and ate a light meal of trail rations as we moved. After nearly two hours the street we rode down led us to a tall arched gate flanked by the statues of two armored sentries who had only just dropped their spears and begun to run when the cloud took them.

We rode through, and the way beyond opened up into a wide avenue of white marble. Silver barked trees with pale, slender leaves lined the road on either side, and the road itself was big enough to drive three wagons side by side without letting their wheels touch. The closest buildings were a good distance away from the road on either side, and partially hidden by a white stone wall that created an air of serene privacy all around us. With nothing left to block the view, I got my first look at the palace of the elven king waiting for us at the end of the road.

The clatter of our horses' hooves echoed in the still air as we made our way down the avenue and into the open courtyard in front of the palace. In some ways it was everything I had come to expect. It towered over us and spread out to curve around us on both sides, easily the size of the Grand Basilica in Byzantium, which was the largest building I'd ever seen up to that point. The palace was the first building I'd seen in the city that wasn't twisted or drooping like an old candle. Its rooftops sloped in straight, precise angles, and its walls stood tall and proud.

The beauty of its spires and long galleries was obvious, but to my eyes the whole complex whispered the hidden warning of everything built by the rich and powerful. This was where the king and his court made the laws that nobles used to fatten themselves at the expense of real people like me, and where the soldiers who enforced those laws liked to spend their time when they weren't busy chasing thieves through back alleys. Even though I knew that all of those things had been frozen into melted stone here in the Shattered City a long time ago, I couldn't help but hunch a little lower in my saddle.

"Well, this is different," Cael said behind me. I turned to see him pointing around the courtyard at the statues I'd been trying so hard to avoid looking at.

The statues here weren't like those we'd seen all around us since we entered the city, stumbling and falling in a blind panic to escape what loomed behind them. These people looked calm as they went about their daily court business. Some even looked bored. A group of five elven men in some of the finest clothes I'd yet seen had been caught in the middle of some heated debate. Musicians sat together on stools beneath the shade of an ivy trellis, their fingers hovering over stone strings. A young woman played coy as she sat on a bench beside her suitor, her smile hidden behind a fan that had hovered just an inch from her face for the last five hundred years.

The whole scene was so lifelike that my mind kept expecting everyone to begin moving again at any moment. The cloud had swept over them so fast that they'd had no time to react. Which could only mean one thing.

"That's where it all started," I said, my voice hushed to preserve the stillness as I pointed up the grand staircase towards the main palace entrance.

"Then that's where we need to go," said Alleron. He stepped down from his horse, tied its reins to a nearby bench, and began walking towards the stairs without waiting to see if the rest of us followed after him.

We did, of course, although I'll admit that I didn't mind letting the wizard go in first.

Each of the stairs was wide enough to hold a four-poster bed, meant to remind us of our own insignificance as we climbed towards the looming palace overhead. All it really did was put a cramp in my legs. When we finally reached the top Alleron stopped in front of the vast doorway for a moment, then reached out and pressed his hand to its surface.

"It's everything I dreamed and more," he whispered, although he was so quiet that I couldn't be sure I'd heard him right. He marveled up at the closed door that towered above him for another minute, then pushed. I hadn't expected his wiry arms to accomplish much of anything, but the doors opened inward as if gliding on a gentle breeze.

"Counterweights," he said when he caught my surprised look. Then he stepped inside.

We followed after him. The doorway was more than wide enough for us to enter as a group, which meant our eyes adjusted from the daylight at the same time. We all gasped at the same time.

Everything sparkled. The domed ceiling high overhead was set with cut glass mosaics in spiraling patterns that sent light swirling about the room. The light that flashed off of them was brighter than starlight, but softer than anything I'd ever seen reflected off of a mirror before. Then I realized that was because the mosaics weren't made of glass after all. They were made of diamonds.

Delicate crystal chandeliers hung from the ceiling overhead. I realized with a jolt that each one still held a live flame at its center, the source of most of the light that danced through the hall.

"How is that even possible after all this time?" I asked. No one had an answer to offer.

A thundering crash shook the room. I spun around to see that the doorway now stood shut tight behind us.

"Counterweights?" I asked Alleron. He shook his head. Cael and Magnus each stepped up to one of the huge, curved handles and pulled, straining backward with all the strength they could muster. The doors didn't shift an inch. Finally, they gave up and rejoined us, breathing hard.

"Perhaps we should leave this problem for a later time," Nataka said as she turned to peer down a hallway. "Inside is where we wished to be, after all."

"She's right," Sheska said. "Let's find what we came for before we worry about how to leave. Besides, I can always climb out that window if I must."

The window she pointed to was a thin strip of gilded glass. There was no way that anyone but a halfling could squeeze through it. I decided she was attempting a joke, even though her face remained as impassive as always. We turned and proceeded down the hallway.

It was no less grand than the ceiling above. The floor looked like one single piece of white marble. I didn't see even the faintest hint of a seam or tile edge anywhere. It flowed from the door where we stood like a river of pure snow to spill out into the open floor of a large, round atrium, beckoning us forward. The walls we walked past were filled with painted murals so lifelike that my eyes expected them to step down and join us any minute now. I saw scenes of festival banquets, soaring mountains, and great battles featuring elves in golden armor riding white horses with strange spiraling horns sprouting from their foreheads. The elven riders trampled bleeding orcs, dwarves, and other creatures I didn't recognize beneath their hooves as they surged forward.

"Hmph. Typical elven bullshit," Magnus snorted.

Guards stood frozen at attention at intervals along the hallway. The details of their faces and armor would have sent the greatest sculptor in the world into a fit of jealous depression if he thought that these statues had been created by an artist's hammer and chisel instead of an explosion of wild magic. We wove our way between other elves who stood locked in various poses of coming and going, feet standing in mid-step as they ferried written reports and messages to or from the King's throne room somewhere further inside the palace. Courtiers stood conversing in small groups, and all around us the evidence of daily life in the greatest center of power on the continent was unmistakable.

"All this, lost in an instant," I marveled out loud. During our time on the road I had gathered from comments and context that although the elves had once ruled undisputed over all of Danan, they had not fared well in the years since the fall of the Shining City.

How could so much power, wealth, and culture have been destroyed so suddenly?

My mind could barely process the sudden and utter destruction of an entire people. Somehow seeing this perfectly preserved moment from that long-lost world made the scale of the disaster even greater and more unnerving. I tried to imagine Byzantia in this state; its streets, wharfs, and markets left to stand for eternity in some grotesque parody of the bustling life it had once enjoyed, its people's souls doomed to relive their terror and torment every night without end. What would happen to the rest of the empire if her capitol were destroyed in a single day?

"Was this the only elven city on Danan?"

"Not remotely," Alleron answered, his brow knit tight in a cloud of repressed emotion as he stared at a young page bearing a tray as he marched towards a man seated on a bench. "But this was the heart of our culture and our empire. With the crown lost, and so much else beside it, my people fractured into separate states who squabbled and fought over the scraps that remained rather than join together to rebuild."

Bitterness and anger were plain in his voice.

"You blame your ancestors?"

"I do. So much more might have been saved if they'd just pulled their heads from their asses long enough to come to terms with reality. Of course the decades of rebellion and war that followed the cataclysm didn't help matters." He cast a sideways glance at Magnus and Nataka walking beside him. Magnus grinned beneath his beard as he kept walking, but Nataka turned and met Alleron's look with a steady gaze.

"If your people had been slaves for a thousand years, I think you would have seized your freedom as well." The orc didn't sound angry or defensive. It was simply a statement of fact, and a reasonable one at that.

"No doubt you're right," Alleron sighed. "I won't argue that my people owed a debt to Danan, but surely by now it has been paid in full. We lost our families, our home, our culture and history. I won't accept that we lost any hope of a future along with it."

He increased his pace, his boots sending a determined drumbeat echoing through the hallway as the rest of us lengthened our steps to keep up.

Our brisk walk soon brought us to a stop at the center of the atrium. The domed ceiling overhead was a riot of colored glass displaying images of ancient kings, powerful wizards, and beautiful queens all lit by the rising sun outside. Twin staircases spiraled up in front of us, looking as delicate as spun sugar as they disappeared into the ceiling. Doors lined the walls to our right and left, each marking a different route further into the palace.

"Where to now?" I asked the group. "This place is massive. There's no way we'll find the crown before nightfall if we just search doors at random, and I'd rather eat Magnus' beard than try to sleep in here."

"The girl be right," Magnus said, one hand stroking his thick red beard like a protective parent. "We'd best separate to cover more territory."

"Wait, what? That's not what I meant."

The thought of wandering alone through the palace halls with only some ghostly statues for company made my skin crawl.

"You'd rather we make our camp here and wait for the sunrise?" Sheska asked, and that thought made my skin want to crawl off altogether and hide in a hole somewhere. I shook my head.

"Right then," Cael said, taking charge. "We each take a direction and search. If you find the crown or anything significant shout it out and hopefully someone will be close enough to hear you. We meet back in this atrium in two hours to compare our findings. With any luck we'll have enough daylight remaining to leave the city before nightfall."

I couldn't think of a reason to argue with his plan, though I sure as hells tried. The others nodded agreement as well.

"I'll take the stairs, then," I sighed. "Stay safe, everyone."

And with that we all turned in a different direction to go in search of the mad king's crown.

8

It should come as no great shock to you to learn that I had never been inside of a palace before. Emperor Quintus wasn't in the habit of handing out luncheon invitations to street waifs, but I still guessed that this place had once been something rather special even as far as palaces went. Huge arched windows and vaulted ceiling domes let the outside light come streaming in to illuminate the endless train of artwork, fine carpets, and gleaming suits of armor that stood at intervals along the walls.

The style of the armor was different from anything I'd ever seen in Byzantia, or even read about in one of Sister Gizella's history tomes. They were beautiful for one thing, all graceful lines and polished metal plates embellished with spiraling designs. They were larger than normal suits of armor, too, at least seven feet tall and broader at the shoulder than a tavern window. I hadn't seen a single stone elf anywhere in the city who could have possibly worn one of the monstrous things, but even so the sense that the elven warriors of old must have been unstoppable giants was hard to shake, so I guess they did their job well enough.

The helmets sported a pair of wings on either side that swept up and back to form a sort of crest. The various pieces of the armor hung suspended on a concealed frame so that the suit itself appeared to be floating in the air.

Unlike the steel gray of every other piece of armor I'd ever seen, these suits were a rich, honeyed yellow color that glowed in the sunlight. *Some kind of bronze alloy, maybe?* I took a closer look as I walked by one, tapping at the metal and testing it with a fingernail. Not bronze. Gold. Every single one of these damned metal bathrobes was made of gold. The left boot of the suit I was looking at would have fed a family in the East End for a month.

I knew we were racing the sunset, but I couldn't help but try to pry a glove from the suit. It never hurt to have an insurance policy in case that weasel of an arena master stiffed us out of our reward when we returned to Farshore. After a round of heaving, twisting, and cursing, however, I was forced to accept that the armor had been welded to the frame inside. I'll confess that I considered running back to the blacksmith's forge for a hacksaw, but finally left the damned thing behind to resume my search.

It appeared that ancient High Elven royals were no different than those in Byzantia, and the discovery left me in a rotten mood as I walked through empty hallways and poked my head inside dusty bedrooms and dining halls with painted ceilings taller than pine trees. To hear Alleron talk of them you'd think that his ancestors had been nothing but noble sages who wrote poetry for breakfast, dispensed perfect justice for lunch, and shat golden roses after dinner, but everywhere I looked I saw the same message that Byzantian nobles had been perfecting for three thousand years: we have everything and we're not sharing.

That flaunting was what I hated most about their kind. I can understand the desire to use what you have to get more, but it seemed that most nobles couldn't enjoy what they had until they'd rubbed someone else's nose in the mud for the day. What right did they have to crow about their wealth and power? It's not like they'd ever done anything to earn it. The all-knowing Divines had seen fit to send them down a noblewoman's birth pipe rather than a washing maid's, and everything from that point forward more or less took care of itself.

I hadn't felt that kind of gnawing anger in a long time. Not since the first few weeks on the open ocean had washed the details of daily life in Byzantia from my mind. Now it was back in force. It hadn't been so bad before the Daughters of Vesta took me in. Sure, I'd hated the royals as much as all my friends when we'd run the streets and scrapped for a moldy crust of bread, but I hadn't understood how impossibly far their world was from mine.

Then the Daughters had taught me nearly everything worth learning.

History and literature, mathematics and geography, classics, poetry, political and military theory, rhetoric, medicine and anatomy, and a dozen other subjects beside. Once they had finished with me, I understood how beautiful the world could be for people with the means to savor it. I suppose a part of me has always hated them for opening my eyes to a world I could never have.

A loud clanging sound echoed down the corridor behind me, freezing me in mid-step. I turned to look, slow and steady, no sudden movements. The suit of armor I'd examined earlier now stood in the middle of the hallway. We stared at one another for a moment. The metal frame that had supported it stood against the wall like a bare tree in winter, but the parts and pieces of the suit still hung suspended in the air, imitating the shape of the elf who would have worn it even though I could see the hall behind it through each gap and joint. Then the armor took a step towards me.

The metallic echo of its footstep knocked me loose from my shock. I drew my twin sabers and settled into a guard stance, one sword high and forward, the other low and ready. As the armor took another ponderous step forward, the tip of the enormous greatsword it carried ripped a jagged scar in the red velvet carpet as it scraped across the stone floor. A pair of flickering blue flames lit the sockets of its helmet. Some detached part of my brain noted that the color was exactly the same as the ghosts who'd attacked us the night before. Then the armor swung the sword up above its head like it weighed less than nothing and lunged at me.

I almost lost my head in the first exchange. The armor moved with terrifying speed and precision, sweeping its sword in a wide arc aimed at my neck. I twisted backward, deflecting the angle of the blade with my own just far enough out of line. The wind from the cut pulled my hair down into my eyes. On instinct I turned my backward dodge into a roll to gain some distance. The sword slammed to the floor in the spot where I'd stood a moment before. The armor pressed forward, leaving me no room to breathe or think.

The weeks of harsh training Cael had forced on me back in the arena was the only thing that kept me alive. Any mortal arms would have needed at least a split second to halt the momentum of the first swing and begin the second, but the armor slashed, thrust, and cut without pause or hesitation. I reacted without thought or planning, deflecting the blows that I sensed I could handle and dodging the ones I could not. Each parry jarred my arms with a painful shock, and I realized that the suit's terrifying strength could crash through my guard and cleave me in half if I misjudged an angle by even a small amount.

The blue flames that burned where its eyes should have been never blinked or wavered. They bore into me with a wild hatred that grew stronger with each passing second. I sensed a cunning intelligence measuring and observing me as it sought to spill my blood, but I had little time to consider whether that made any sense at all.

Then I saw an opening. The armor cut at me with a fierce upswing, and its exposed armpit flared across my vision like a signal fire. I struck, and my blade slashed through the leather straps to bury itself in the hollow cavity of its chest. The thing looked down at me, and I felt a ripple of amused surprise brush against my awareness. Then it struck me across the face with the back of its gauntlet.

The force of the blow snapped my head to the side and sent me sliding across the floor. A chorus of bells louder than the Grand Basilica's echoed in my skull as blood pooled around my tongue and teeth. I clenched my jaw, forced myself to my knees, and realized that one of my swords was still buried in the suit of armor. It looked down at the blade, then straight back at me, and I swear by Magren's frosted tits that I heard a mocking laughter in my mind.

I risked a quick glance over my shoulder at the hallway I'd been following. I had no idea where it led, but I would have chanced it in a heartbeat if I thought I had a real chance of outrunning the thing. I'd seen it move though, and even if I managed to stay ahead of it, I would tire with every step while it would not. No, running would do little more than prolong the inevitable, while my best attempt at fighting back had proved fruitless, which left me with no good options. I spat an angry red smear onto the carpet to clear the blood from my mouth as I struggled to my feet and prepared myself for death.

Idiot.

Mother Shanti's favorite word filled my mind from across the years and miles since I'd seen her last.

So quick to surrender to frustration when the world does not conform to your expectations.

I'd lost count of how many times I'd heard that phrase within my first week of living in the temple. But how was I supposed to fight something that wasn't alive and couldn't be killed?

When an obstacle blocks your inquiry it is only because you have failed to see the alternate path.

Sister Gizella's voice this time, a shade kinder but no less strict.

Question your certainty. Discard your blind assumptions. Instead of looking for what you think you need, step back and see what is actually there.

The nagging voices of the women who had trained and abandoned me drew me back to the moment. I scanned the hallway, my mind darting from one thing to the next like a caged bird in search of escape.

Paintings and rich tapestries every six feet.

Wrap him in cloth? He's too strong.

A railing guarded the edge of a balcony that looked down onto the lower floor on my left.

Jump for it? Too far to the ground.

Huge chandeliers of bronze and crystal hung from the ceiling overhead.

I smiled and gathered myself to move before I'd had a chance to reconsider the crazed plan that had leapt into my head. If it failed, I'd be dead for sure, but that already looked like the likely outcome of this little ambush, and for the first time in my life I found that I preferred to go down fighting than to die as I ran. I snarled a wordless challenge, brandished my remaining saber, and lunged towards the monster.

My attack caught it by surprise for a moment, but it recovered and thrust its sword at my chest to skewer me where I stood. Except I wasn't standing there anymore. I dove forward beneath its blade, tucking into a somersault to roll past it. I'd leaped as hard and as far as my weary legs could manage, so my roll ended in an ungainly sprawl on the cold floor. The armor spun around and came for me, its sword raised high for the killing blow.

Two more steps you gilded bastard.

The suit planted its feet and begun to chop down. I threw my sword at its head with all my strength and rolled to the side. The greatsword crashed to the ground half an inch from my face as I looked up into its raging blue eyes. My blade had sailed over its helmet, completely missing the armor as it flashed upward in a razor spiral to strike the ceiling and clatter back to the ground. Thankfully, I'd been aiming at the rope that supported the chande-lier overhead.

I kept rolling, scrambled to my feet, and dove for the wall. The crash behind me was deafening, a tortured chorus of twisted metal and shattered crystal. I stood to my feet, my chest heaving as I watched the rubble for signs of movement. None came. With a sigh of relief, I stepped forward and looked down into the ruined heap. Pieces of the armor lay scattered beneath the wreckage, the light now gone from its eyes. I pushed and shoved my way through the debris, heaved for the last half inch I needed, and felt my fingers wrap around the hilt of the sword I'd rammed into the armor's chestpiece. I retrieved the blade, then walked over to the far wall to collect its twin and sheathed them both.

I was about to go and continue my search for King Tyrial's throne room when I noticed something moving within the heap of rubble. A flicker of blue light.

The flicker quickly grew into a blinding glow, then poured out of the armor like smoke to form the vague shape of a man floating in the air. He had no discernible features, only roiling flame and swirling images trapped within his form. He raised one hand and twitched a finger back and forth as though I were a child he'd caught stealing cookies. Then he dissolved into a cloud and swept back down the hallway. The cloud split into two, and each part flowed into a lifeless suit of armor. Blue fire kindled in their helmets as they stepped down from their racks and raised their weapons.

Well shit.

I turned and ran without a backwards glance.

I raced down the hallway, willing my legs to move faster. The steady crash of their metal footsteps filled the air and seemed to grow steadily closer, though I didn't dare risk a backward glance. I sped past more rooms, but none offered refuge or escape. Then I rounded a corner and found that the hallway ended in a flight of stairs. Their entrance was narrow enough that the large armor suits might not be able to follow, or would at least be slowed down as they did. Each gasping breath burned in my lungs and I felt like someone had begun to fill my legs with sand, but I took the stairs two at a time, scrambling on my hands and knees over the last few steps.

I stood at the entrance to a kitchen. Two large stoves filled the wall next to me, while three tables stood ready for chopping, mixing, and plating with knives, pots and pans, and other utensils hung on wall racks. Five stone statues stood frozen in various kitchen tasks, wielding carving knives or stirring pots whose contents had long since rotted away to nothing. A door stood open on the far wall, marking the only exit I could see. I listened for a moment, but didn't hear the clatter of metal that the suits would have made as they struggled up the stairs. I leaned back against the wall in relief.

A cloud of blue fire billowed through the door. It split into a dozen small balls of flame and spread throughout the room. Each one touched down on a knife or iron pan. They lifted into the air and swung around towards me.

"Oh that is just not fair."

I ducked as the first missile shot towards me, diving beneath one of the tables and crawling towards the door. Then a half-dozen knives and cleavers filled my vision as they floated down beneath the edge of the table. I shrieked and rolled to my left as the blades shot forward like arrows fired from a bow to bury themselves in the wall behind me. One of them caught my shoulder, leaving a throbbing line of pain in its wake, but the cut didn't feel too deep.

I stood to my feet only to duck down again as a frying pan swung for my face. I snatched a metal serving tray off the table just in time to deflect its second blow and send the pan spinning away with a loud clang.

An iron poker from the fireplace hurtled towards me like a spear. I managed to get the serving tray in between it and my chest, but the force of the blow ripped it from my hands and sent me staggering backwards. I turned and ran for the door. A streak of blue fire swirled around the iron handle and began to pull it closed. I knew that I was dead for sure if I let it trap me in the room. I took two more steps and dove forward to sail through the narrowing gap a split second before the door slammed shut. The door shook with a dozen crashes and thuds as the knives and pots that had been aimed at my exposed back struck home.

I stood gasping for air as I took a quick look around. A dining hall this time. A long table set with crystal glasses and golden dinnerware filled the room. Antique weapons were displayed along the walls, and the vaulted ceiling was painted with a hunting scene in a forest brought to life with brilliant colors and exquisite detail.

The cloud of fire poured beneath the gap in the door and swept around my ankles to reform into the man-shape I had seen before. He stared at me, his featureless face radiating an intense and unreasoning hatred that I felt in the pit of my stomach. He reached towards the wall, his arm stretching out impossibly long to retrieve a sword. I drew my sabers as I scanned the room. There were two doors besides the one I'd come in through, but both were on the other side of the room, and it looked like he didn't intend to let me by without a fight.

I leaped at him, stabbing high and slicing low. He didn't even bother to block my strikes. My blades passed through him, leaving swirling ripples in their wake but otherwise having no affect. Then he struck like a coiled snake, stabbing his sword at my stomach. I tried to twist aside, but we were too close and he moved far too fast. I managed to keep him from impaling me outright, but I felt the wicked edge of his sword bite deep to score a long gash across my guts. I twisted past him and rolled up onto the table, but the movement pulled the cut open even more and I screamed in pain as my vision blurred with tears.

I sheathed my swords as I struggled to my feet. They did me little good, and I needed my hands free to clamp down on the wound. Blood seeped through my fingers as I ran along the table, scattering priceless dinnerware in all directions. I felt the breeze from his wild slashes on my neck and drove myself to run faster even as the cut on my stomach and my exhausted legs competed to see who could protest the loudest.

I reached the end of the table and leaped over the back of the high chair that stood between me and the doors. I chose the left one at random and ran through it. The fire man and his damned sword were so close that I didn't even have time to pull it shut behind me. I didn't have a plan anymore. I ran on because stopping meant death, but I knew that I didn't have much running left in me.

Then I realized that I'd hit a dead end. The short hallway ended in a large door decorated with silver filigree in the shape of a tree with large, spreading limbs, but it had no handle that I could see. There was only the door in front of me, cold stone walls to my left and right, and one very angry fire ghost behind me. I kept running towards the door out of sheer stubbornness. Maybe I could kick it open and keep going?

Then the door swung open on its own. The warm glow of candlelight shone on the other side. With all of the crazy I'd just survived I was fully aware that this might be a trap of some kind, but I was past caring. The open door offered refuge, and even if it was only an illusion it was better than anything I had out here.

The fire ghost screamed behind me, a mind-numbing wail of rage and frustration. Part of my mind went liquid on the spot, unraveled by the horrible, unnatural sound. The other part realized that if my running for the door made the ghost that angry, there was a slim chance that I might somehow be safe on the other side of it.

My legs had begun to cramp. I could feel them begin to buckle, but I threw every last shred of energy I had into covering the twenty steps. I wasn't really running anymore, just scrambling forward on panic and sheer stubborn grit, but it was enough. I stumbled through the door and collapsed to the floor, then twisted around to kick it closed behind me, only to find that the heavy portal was already shut tight.

I'm sure that those of you sitting safe and comfortable as you read this are well aware that doors don't normally open and close themselves, but I was so shattered by exhaustion and the flood of adrenaline coursing through my veins just then that I didn't really think about it, and likely wouldn't have mustered the energy to worry much about it even if I had.

All I wanted in the entire world was to lie there on the carpet and bleed in peace while I caught my breath, but Sister Gerda had taught me enough medical lore in my first week at the temple to know exactly how that little indulgence would end. I struggled to my feet, cursing each of the Divines in turn in the most colorful terms I could muster as I drove myself to go looking for something to tend to my injuries.

Then I got my first real look at the room, and the words dried up on my tongue.

After a long moment of awe-struck gawking there was only one thing I could think to say that could do the sight any justice.

"Wow..."

9

There's a story told around every seedy tavern fire and thieves' squat in Byzantium; the legend of a man named Altrin. The story goes that he was so handsome the emperor's favored wife took one look at him in the market square and fell head-over-stupid in love. She had him smuggled into her chambers where they remained for an entire week of passion. Finally, while the empress snored in her sleep and drooled on her pillow (that part is very important and must never be skipped over) Altrin looted her room of every last gemstone and gold-plated bauble he could squeeze into two sacks and escaped out the window with enough wealth to buy himself a minor dukedom on the river Nila and live out his days in fabulous luxury. "I made out like Altrin," is the ultimate boast among thieves to this day.

I had never believed in the tale. No one really did. It was just a nice story that lightfingers and alley bruisers told each other over a thin ale when they'd had a dry run and wanted to dream of something better. How much wealth could someone really scrounge from a bedroom, anyway? Now I knew for a fact that even if Altrin's tale wasn't true, it absolutely could have been.

I stood inside a piece of jewelry disguised as a room. A huge four-poster bed anchored the space, draped in blue silk, white linen, and strings of diamonds. A large vanity made of white birch stood beside the bed. The handle of every drawer was a sapphire the size of a swallow's egg, and the mirror itself was so perfectly clear that every noblewoman in Byzantium would have murdered her husband to possess it.

The ceiling was set with a mosaic of sapphire, green jade, opal, and topaz in intricate spiraling patterns. The carpet was a spotless white so rich and thick that I actually felt bad for walking on it with my road-worn boots. It was woven through with silver thread that traced out the same design of the great tree I'd seen on the door. I caught sight of a row of tall dressers made of dark ebony and diamond inlaid inside a closet to my left, although it felt strange to call it a closet when it was three times the size of my room in the temple.

Jewels, precious metals, and rich fabrics sparkled on every surface, and yet as much as I hated the very idea of a room like this existing anywhere in the world, I honestly couldn't call its design anything but perfect. The colors, angles, fabrics, and textures all complimented and contrasted one another so precisely that it might as well have been designed by Kressida Bright-Weaver herself. Even the candles burned merrily in wall sconces set with diamonds and sapphires that caught their warm glow and spread it to every corner of the room.

And that's when I got a grip and started feeling nervous. The room was lit by several dozen candles, none of which had begun to show so much as a single drip of wax. They were the first sign of life or habitation I'd seen in this gilded tomb of a palace, and I didn't believe for a second that the explanation was as cozy and comfortable as this room was meant to appear.

And yet, comfortable was exactly how I felt. Comfortable, peaceful, and safe in a way I don't ever remember feeling before or since. It seemed ridiculous to think that anything in a space this calm and perfect could hurt anyone, especially me. I could stay here. Stay as long as I wanted, have everything I wanted, lie down on that beautiful bed and truly rest for the first time in my life. I took a step towards the bed, fully intending to give in to that urge when the cut on my side sent a bolt of white-hot pain shooting through my skull.

I shook my head and wiped the water that had welled up in my eyes with my sleeve.

"Really, Charity?" I muttered to myself. "You're going to stand around like a mooncalf while you bleed to death? There's work to do, *baka*. Best get to it."

I pulled a blue silk scarf from a rack of outerwear by the door, doubled it over, and wrapped it around the gash. I let myself scream a little as I cinched it down as tight as I could manage, but once it was done I was relieved to see that my makeshift bandage held the bleeding in check for the most part. This time I did walk to the bed, but only to retrieve one of the thick goose-down pillows from the headboard. I slashed a wide cut along one side, emptied its feathery contents on the ground, and got to work looting the room.

What? The baubles in that room hadn't been touched by living hands in the gods only knew how long, and even a small collection was worth more than every single score I'd managed in my entire lifetime put together. If you honestly thought I was just going to sigh and slip out empty handed then you must be crazier than a Shakri dervish fresh of a month of fasting in the desert.

At least I didn't stoop to prying gems loose from their settings on the furniture or walls. There were plenty of rings, tiaras, jeweled combs, and other small items just lying about.

The big pieces were tempting, but I stayed smart and kept to things that I could easily stash until I found a decent fence back in Farshore. The colonial city was founded more than five minutes ago, so I knew there had to be at least one working the shadows. By Nestor's bare ass cheeks, I was going to make their day when I got back.

Soon enough my makeshift treasure sack was full. I turned back to the vanity to check through the drawers for a few last small items to tuck into my boots before I left.

Then I saw the necklace. I don't know how I'd missed it before. It rested on a white neck-stand in the center of the desk. Its design was simple compared to the other jewelry and decoration in the room, and that made it all the more perfect. Silver links formed the chain, shaped with cunning precision to spiral from one to the next without revealing the joint. The chain ended in the largest gemstone I'd ever seen, a sapphire rich with the haunting dark blue of the ocean just after a storm. Its facets seemed to draw in the light rather than scatter it away, because the gem glowed with a faint blue light.

I had never been impressed by jewelry or fine clothing. Tying up your wealth in something that didn't improve your actual experience of daily life, and that could be easily stolen, of all things, had always seemed the height of stupidity. But I wanted to keep the sapphire necklace from the moment I saw it. It was so perfect, confidence and elegance given form. Even though I could never wear it openly I was certain that just knowing it was mine would add a small spark of joy to each day after this one.

I lifted the necklace from its stand and slipped it over my head. As the cold weight of the silver chain settled onto my skin a blizzard of white frost and piercing cold engulfed my mind.

I was standing in an open field buried waist deep in snow. My thin clothing was worse than useless. The driving snow had already soaked into the cloth and turned it into a frozen torture jacket. My hair cracked and broke away like icicles when I turned my head. There was nothing in sight, just an endless expanse of drifting white death, but I began to press forward through the snow because moving anywhere seemed a better idea than standing still.

Rest. Lie down and rest.

The wind howled with a woman's voice, shifting from a soothing whisper to a shriek of fury and back again.

So tired. You're so tired. The world is so cold. Just rest.

The torrent of wind and sleet drove me to my knees. Why was I walking? I needed to be somewhere, needed to keep moving, but I couldn't remember why. I tipped forward and the drifting snow rose up to catch me. It was softer than any bed I'd ever lain on.

Yeeeeeeeeees.

The voice in the wind purred like a cat who'd finally pinned its prey to the floor. That's when I got angry.

The realization that I was being hunted, that someone or something was savoring my helplessness, set my blood boiling. I clenched my jaw, buried my hands in the snow, and struggled back to my feet.

The wind screamed in protest. I looked down and saw steam curling up from two perfect handprints melted into the thick white carpet. I felt warmer than I had before. My anger smoldered in my stomach like a live coal, and I fed it everything I had. I was no one's prey. I would die someday just like everyone else, but I'd be damned if death would find me so easy to claim. I took another step forward.

You cannot resist!

The wind screamed louder than any gale I'd ever seen blow in off the Mare Nostri, but this time I heard panic amid the blustering anger.

"Watch me, *bruta!*"

I'd been helpless once, spent most of my life running, hiding, and hoping that I'd slip beneath everyone's notice for one more day. Never again. Maybe I couldn't win, but I could fight, and that was enough. I let my anger grow hotter still, holding it in front of me like a shield. The snow melted before me, leaving a clear path forward.

I looked up and saw a tree standing where there had only been emptiness before. It was the same tree I'd seen engraved on the door and woven into the carpet of the room where I'd found the necklace. As I recognized it more memories flooded back to me. I still didn't know where I was or what was going on, but at least now I knew that it wasn't real.

I pressed forward, walking at first, and then running as the path widened before me. The air around me shimmered with heat now, and I no longer felt the wind. Flames kindled in the palms of my hands and danced across my fingers as I ran towards the tree.

No! Stay back!

When I'd first heard the voice, it had sounded like it came from all around me. Now I knew that it came from within the tree. The wind grew into a whirlwind of power, shoving against me like a solid wall. My forward run ground down to a desperate stumble just to keep from being swept backwards. I lowered my head, gritted my teeth, and took a step forward. Then another. Every inch I gained was measured in sheer will, my determination against the force of panic and anger pushing back on me.

I took one more step, and it carried me to stand by the tree. I lunged forward and shoved my hands against the smooth white bark.

The fire caught hold in an instant, searing a blackened circle into the wood that spread outward from my touch. The tree screamed like a pine log tossed into a winter hearth.

Enough!

A force exploded from the tree. It caught me like a leaf and sent me tumbling legs over ears through the air. After five or six good spins I realized that I still hadn't hit the ground. I looked around and saw only an inky blackness lit with occasional flashes of rippling color. I looked down and saw the empty field and the tree far below me, growing smaller by the second as I hurtled up through the air. A brilliant glow overhead caught my attention, and I looked up to see myself sprawled on the bedroom floor.

My body raced closer. I was moving too fast. I screamed as I flew faster and faster, then my world exploded in a flash of white.

I bolted up from the floor in a panic, a half-remembered scream still on my lips, then caught hold of myself and just stood there for a moment, my chest heaving as I took stock. The room hadn't changed, and I could see now that I had never really left it, even though that snowy field had felt more than real. I patted myself down, still struggling to reconcile what I'd just experienced with what my senses told me was true and solid. Without thinking I pressed a hand to the gash in my side. It didn't hurt.

I hesitated for a moment, then peeled back my makeshift bandage. The skin underneath it was smooth and whole. The cloth itself was still crusted with blood, but there wasn't so much as a scar underneath.

"*Chaso di bruta,*" I whispered as I poked hard at my side for good measure.

How long had I lain on the floor? Long enough for my wound to heal on its own? Or had whatever I'd just gone through somehow healed me in the process? I had no way of knowing. I turned to look in the vanity mirror. My own face gaped back at me unchanged. The only thing I noticed that hadn't been there before was a faint bulge beneath my shirt. I pulled the neckline out to check and, sure enough, the sapphire necklace lay coiled on my chest. Now that I thought about it the thing felt heavier than it should have, as though someone were trying to pull it off my neck without my noticing.

I ripped off the necklace and threw it against the wall.

Or I meant to, at least. But when I bent to retrieve my sack of treasure the necklace thumped against my chest. I frowned and concentrated on grabbing hold of the chain with both hands to lift it over my head. My hands didn't move. I was sweating now, straining to do this simple yet impossible thing. It was like the part of my brain that should have sent the command to my arms just went numb whenever I thought about removing the necklace.

I closed my eyes and felt the same presence I'd heard within the tree watching me from the shadows of my mind. It crouched in the darkness like a wary cat, licking its wounds and tending to its wounded pride, but still watchful and ready to pounce. I opened my eyes, my hands trembling. I still didn't understand what had happened, but it was clear that I was no longer the master of my own mind, and that filled me with a deep and twisting dread.

I hadn't the faintest idea what to do, so my mind defaulted back to the simplest thoughts that it could process. No point in hiding in this room any longer. I still had no idea how long I'd been here, but the only way to find out was to go outside and rejoin my friends. Assuming I could even find my way back through the maze of rooms and corridors I'd run through to get here.

The path that I needed to take filled my mind as soon as I'd finished that thought. It wasn't the route I'd taken to get here. It was shorter and far safer as it moved through parts of the palace that he rarely visited. I didn't know where the knowledge came from, but the layout of the entire complex was now as familiar to me as the back alleys of the East End had ever been. I knew every twist and turn, and more than a few hidden passages, as though I'd planned the palace's construction myself. Which meant I knew now which room I stood in: High Queen Sapphery's private chambers.

I knew nothing else besides her name and the fact that this room and the rest of this wing had once been a private kingdom unto itself, but that left me with a rather clear guess as to who it was that had just staked a claim to some space in my brain. It didn't make much difference now, so I filed the information away for later use and got back to the problem at hand.

That's when I realized that as I concentrated on my newfound sense of direction, I could also sense the location of each of my companions elsewhere in the palace. They glowed across my awareness like a candle flame in the darkness, and I breathed a sigh of relief when I counted five of them moving about the building.

I still didn't understand how any of this was possible, but I decided to stop asking questions I couldn't answer and start doing something useful.

What was that old Sahkri proverb? When a friend gifts you a camel you should take it home before you search it for lice? Something to that effect.

I shrugged, decided not to think too hard about my sudden insight into ancient elven floorplans, and pushed the bedroom door open.

10

The hallway was quiet. No fire ghosts or floating cutlery in sight. I walked back down the short hallway to what I now knew had been Queen Sapphery's private dining hall, took the door I'd ignored previously, and continued to follow the map in my head. I stopped back in the atrium just long enough to stash my makeshift treasure sack by the still-locked front doors, then went in search of the others.

I found Sheska first, crouched behind a thick armchair in a dusty library. She seemed genuinely offended that I'd been able to find her hiding place, but her story of a shimmering blue figure bringing various things to life in a relentless attempt to crush her like a small bug was painfully familiar.

We found Nataka barricaded in a guest bedroom, Alleron locked inside a cupboard, Cael moving down a long hallway crouched and wary behind his shield, and Magnus standing in a huge pile of splintered wood and shredded foliage in the middle of a huge open-air garden enclosed within the palace grounds.

Each one told the same tale. Animated objects tried to kill them, then just when it had begun to look grim it all stopped. As near as I could determine the timeline, that had happened for everyone the moment I set foot in the queen's bedroom.

"So, what do we do now?" Cael grumbled through his mustache as he kept watch on the shadows. "We're running short on time." He didn't need to point up to the first fingers of the red sunset overhead to make his point clear, but he did it anyway.

"I found no indication of where Tyrial stood when the cataclysm occurred." Alleron frowned, studying the ripped sleeve of his robe as he spoke. "I even attempted a quick scry, but found nothing. I'm beginning to wonder if he was even in the palace when--"

"He was in his *alteriam*," I said, the words leaving my mouth before the thought had fully formed in my head. I didn't even know what an *alteriam* was, but I was completely certain now that if we found it, we'd find Tyrial's crown.

"What is an alteriam?" Sheska asked as she shot me a sideways glance.

"An elven wizard's private sanctum and laboratory," Alleron answered as he stared at me, clearly suspicious of how I, of all people, could possibly know that. I knew where the information had come from, but I wasn't the least bit comfortable telling the group about what had happened to me in the queen's chambers. I didn't understand any of it so I had no sense of how they would react, but in my experience letting others know how vulnerable you are is a great way to wind up with your throat cut as someone else walks off with your things. Until I had a better sense of how deep the shithole I'd stepped in really was and had some sense of how to climb out of it, I planned to keep my dice hidden in their cup.

"I found an...archive," I said, waving my hand vaguely. "Clerk's notes, that sort of thing. Tyrial had a hidden *alteriam*, and that's where he was when the shit went down. That's where we'll find the crown."

"It stands to reason," Nataka nodded, "but wizards are notorious for their secrecy. How will we find a hidden chamber in time to--"

"It's this way."

I turned and marched off without looking back. I heard five pairs of boots follow me after a moment of hesitation. I kept a fast pace, in part because we were racing the last light of the sun and in part to keep the group from asking more questions. The garden path led through a small atrium, and then into a large chamber that echoed with the crash of falling water. Concealed pipes along the ceiling sent water cascading down artfully constructed cliffs of dark rock. The water roiled and tumbled from all directions until it gathered into a single course and formed a waterfall that spilled down into a large pond occupying most of the room.

Grassy hillocks and water plants ringed the edge of the room, and a graceful wooden bridge led out to a small island in the center of the pond. A small open-air pavilion furnished with cushions and a low table waited on the island, peaceful and inviting despite centuries of neglect. I stepped out onto the bridge.

"Doesn't look like much of a workshop," Magnus said as he followed behind me.

"It isn't," Alleron replied. "A beautiful sanctuary to be sure, but this is no alteriam."

I ignored the doubt in his voice and stepped into the pavilion. I was certain that the chamber we needed to find was here somewhere. Now I just needed to find it. I looked around, but saw nothing out of place. Water surrounded the little island, its waves lapping gently against the shore. The air rumbled with just enough noise from the waterfall to fill the silence, but not so much as to make it hard to think. It really was a lovely place, but the nagging sense that I was missing something vital made it hard to appreciate the tranquility. I started tossing cushions left and right, searching for some sign of where to go next.

"Maybe we should go back and try a different path?" Nataka asked.

"No!" I snapped. "It's here, and we don't have time to waste. Just help me look for--"

I froze as my gaze swept over the table in the center of the pavilion. Its surface was decorated with an inlay of the same design I'd seen repeated countless times throughout the palace, three golden apples clustered beneath a laurel crown on a field of blue, the royal crest of the elven High King. But it wasn't the crest that had gripped my attention.

"That shouldn't be here," I said, pointing at the silver teapot and the small silver teacup that sat on the table.

"You don't like tea?" Sheska asked.

"No, it's not..." I concentrated, trying to put my intuition into words. Then it hit me. "This is a summer room," I said, pointing at the water lilies, river reeds, and thick moss around the edge of the chamber before turning back to the table. "But tea is a winter drink. It's not...proper." I couldn't believe I'd just said those words out loud, but I knew they were correct.

"She's right," Alleron said, now paying the table more interest. "Seasonal alignment was very important to the elven court. This would have been considered quite boorish." Then he turned his gaze back to me. "But how did you know that? More wisdom gleaned from that archive you found?"

"Not important." I waved him off and crouched down for a closer look. "What is important is that these are only here because Tyrial enjoyed hot tea more than he cared about court gossip. Which means we're in the right place."

I reached out and touched the teapot with two fingers, but snatched them back a heartbeat later.

"Still hot. Might as well have just been brewed."

I looked from the tea service to the inlaid crest and back again. Something tickled at my mind. It felt as though I were struggling to remember the details of an old story, except it was a story I'd never heard before. Something about the apples in the crest, and what each one represented.

"I wonder..." I placed the tea cup on top of the center apple in the bunch, then took the teapot by its elegant handle and poured a dark stream of tea into the cup. I waited as steam curled up around my hand, but nothing else happened.

"Should I fetch some biscuits for your tea, my lady?" Alleron asked. I shot him a glare, then sighed and set the teapot down. It had been worth a try at least.

Then the golden apple began to glow as the heat from the cup spread down into it. As the faint light grew brighter, a hum filled the air. I almost didn't hear it at first over the sound of the falls, but it grew stronger and stronger until even the crash of the water faded away. The surface of the pond began to bubble and froth, and the room itself began to shake.

"Is this...good?" Sheska asked as she grabbed hold of the pavilion railing for balance.

Before I could answer, the water between the island and the waterfall erupted with four geysers that shot up to the ceiling. When the spouts crashed back to the pond, I saw that four large, flat stones now stood where none had been before. They led directly from the island to the waterfall, and as my gaze followed the path, I saw that the curtain of water now parted to flow around a yawning black opening in the rock. The first two steps of a flight of stairs were visible at the entrance, but the rest disappeared down into the darkness.

"Remind me not to pour myself a drink here," Cael said as the room returned to silence.

"Come on," I said as I stood to my feet. "That's where we need to go."

I climbed over the low pavilion railing and hopped across the rocks until I reached the newly revealed entrance. Even as I stood on the top step, I couldn't see more than a few feet further down the staircase. Then a blue sphere of light floated over my shoulder and began to drift down the stairs. I looked behind me to see Alleron's lopsided smile. He gestured down the stairs with one hand while he held the other in a cramped pose in front of his chest.

"After you."

I sighed, and turned to follow the glowing ball.

Thankfully the staircase wasn't as long as I'd feared. After a few minutes of walking, it leveled out into a polished stone floor that ended in a solid wooden door. I scanned the frame and hinges but didn't see anything that indicated traps or danger, so I shrugged and tried the handle. The door swung open without a sound, revealing a room beyond that quickly disappeared in darkness. The light from Alleron's floating orb was swallowed up long before it could show me anything of the room. The others gathered around me as they finished descending the stairs.

"Can you make about a hundred more of those?" I pointed to the orb as we all stepped through the doorway and into the room.

"Sadly, I cannot, although that would make for a spectacular party trick. I don't think we'll need them, though."

He was studying the wall to the left of the staircase. A strange shape was painted on it in gold. Alleron reached out and traced his fingers along its curves as he whispered something. As he finished, the shape flared with golden light and the same hum we'd heard in the waterfall room filled the air. Light flooded the room as crystals set into the ceiling flared a warm golden yellow, and I got my first look at a wizard's alteriam.

The room was far more boring than I'd expected. The ceiling rose high overhead, supported by thick stone pillars that ran along both walls. The pillars turned each wall into a series of alcoves lined with bookshelves that were filled to bursting with scrolls, volumes, and tomes. Mother Shanti would have lost her girdle over it, no doubt, but I saw no sign of heads in wine jars or the bones of strange beasts hung from the ceiling.

The back of the room held a small, simple bed, a basin of water, smaller shelves that looked like they held various personal items, and a few large chests that stood against the wall. A large table stood in the center of the room, covered in loose paper, crystals and gemstones of various colors, strips of cloth, small bundles of fur, little piles of what looked like teeth, and countless small pots, jars and boxes that might have held all sorts of oddities.

Then I saw a crown suspended in the air above the table. It hovered around the height of someone's head, but I saw no sign of a body supporting it. I tensed, expecting to see the blue fire man appear out of thin air to bring the room to murderous life, but the crown didn't move.

After a moment of tense silence, we spread out to search the room. Cael, Magnus, and Sheska wandered off to browse the shelves or search through the sleeping space at the back of the room, while Alleron and Nataka went to examine the contents of the table. It looked like random junk to me, but they pointed and chattered back and forth like starving children who'd just discovered a picnic basket. I left them to it and walked over for a closer look at the crown.

As I stepped closer, I saw that the air around the crown shimmered like steam wafting from a cooking pot. The crown itself was beautiful. It was simpler than I'd expected, and far less ostentatious than the golden monstrosity I'd seen atop the Byzantine emperor's head in paintings and murals. The band of the crown was a simple circlet of white gold set with an alternating pattern of diamonds and emeralds.

The metal rose to a sloping peak at the center, which was set with a spiraling pattern of gemstones that drew your eyes to them as they played with the light. This was the thing we'd ridden halfway across the world to retrieve, and I had to admit that I could understand why Trebonious was so keen to get his hands on it. Giving it to him would earn me my life back. The pardon he'd signed would secure my freedom, and the money he'd promised would be enough to buy my own ship to sail wherever I damn well pleased.

I took a breath, then reached up to take the crown. As my fingers brushed the cold metal a burst of rage struck my mind and sent me stumbling backward. It was the same white-hot anger that I'd felt when I fought the suit of armor. The crown might as well have been encased in stone; my touch hadn't shifted it even a hair out of position.

"Are you well, Charity?" Nataka looked at me with concern. I nodded as I shook the tingling from my fingers.

"Any luck deciphering all of that?"

"Yes, actually. I've had my suspicions for some time, but I'm certain now. Can you imagine the sheer brilliance of it all? To even conceive of it, let alone attempt it and come so close to success?" Alleron pointed at the table, at the floating crown, and just about everything else in the room as he turned in a dizzying circle.

"It's staggering, it's monumental, it's...I can't even..."

"Did he finally break?" Magnus asked as he and the others joined us at the table, drawn by Alleron's excited voice.

"Seems that way." Cael folded his arms across his chest.

"Should I kill him?" Sheska had a dagger in her hand before she'd finished speaking. I shot her a look. She shrugged, but put the knife away.

"See if you're still feeling charitable after he turns us into frogs."

I caught the elf by his shoulders and gave him a good shake.

"Alleron, please try using words again, ok? What did Tyrial do?"

The mage's smile just grew bigger.

"He changed the shape of time."

The room fell silent as we all tried to understand what he'd just said.

"Well, those were words at least," Cael shrugged. "Not very useful words, but still."

"Here," Alleron sighed as he turned towards the table. "Let me show you." He cleared a space, and then began arranging various items in a straight line.

"Normally we mortals experience time as a progression from one point to another. Yesterday into tomorrow, now into later, that sort of thing."

Then he separated the items into two lines that curved above and below an empty space in the middle.

"But time doesn't always flow like that. It can be split and redirected by someone with enough knowledge and the power to put it into practice. A chronomancer."

"I definitely did not understand that," I said, pinching the bridge of my nose as I tried to follow his explanation. "But let's pretend that I did. Why would someone even want to do that?"

"Aha! A sound question." Alleron plucked a spiral seashell from the table and held it up for us to see, then placed it in the space between the two lines he'd formed. "Because anything you put in the space between time will then exist both within and without it equally, and that can lead to some very interesting results."

"Such as?"

"Well, immortality, for a start."

"Horseshit," Magnus huffed as he stared at Alleron's makeshift diagram. "Everything dies."

"Sooner or later, yes," Alleron nodded. "Unless one is removed from time. Then there is no later or sooner. Throughout history those who've sought immortality tried to prolong their life. Tyrial discovered how to stop the advance of time itself."

Suddenly everything we'd seen fit itself together in my mind. The stone statues throughout the city, the perfectly preserved food, clothes, and buildings, it all made sense.

"He tried to move the elves outside of time." I looked at Alleron, my mind spinning as the truth hit home. "Every single one of them."

He nodded. "Marvelous, isn't it?"

"It might have been, but he failed," Nataka replied, her voice a rough growl as she reached out and scattered the neat lines of his diagram across the table. "And the price of his folly was paid by many."

"My people still speak of the day the sky turned to ash and fire," Sheska whispered.

"For mine it was the sea itself that turned against." Magnus clenched his hands to fists. "Whole islands were lost to the waves."

"The orcs were scattered to the four winds as our homeland shattered and burned. To this day we do not even know where the bones of our ancestors lie."

Alleron's smile faded as the others turned their angry gazes on him.

"It's not as though King Tyrial intended for any of that to happen," he said, his voice sullen. "He was trying to give his people a gift, to make them as great as he knew they could be."

"He was chasing the light of his own pride," Nataka snapped. "To attempt what you have described on even a single creature is close to impossible. To work such magic on an entire race spread across the continent? No one sane would have dared such madness."

"And the elves have bled for it ever since!" Alleron yelled back at her, his face a mask of anger and pain. "Those who lived within the city were the fortunate ones. Countless more died outside the Shining City's walls that day. The Waygates failed, children starved and men fell to diseases we had long thought conquered." His voice grew distance as he looked down at his hands. "There is so little left of us now, and more is lost every day."

"Mayhap that's exactly what your kind deserved." Magnus still stood with clenched fists and a fighting light in his eyes.

"I think perhaps my ears are still ringing from the waterfall," Alleron said, his voice cold as he raised his gaze to meet the dwarf's. "Would you please repeat that?" Small flames began to dance in the palms of his hands. The others kept silent, but I saw that Cael's hand rested on the hilt of his sword, and Sheska had taken two small steps towards the door.

"I said, mayhap--"

"It doesn't matter!" I shouted, moving between them as Magnus took a step forward.

"Right now the only thing the six of us need to worry about is getting that crown and legging it back to Farshore before Trebonious decides we've skipped out on him and does something nasty. Everything else is just a history lesson."

I looked from Magnus to Alleron and held my breath.

"Bah!" the dwarf finally said as he waved a hand and turned away. "The sooner it's done the sooner I'm rid of the lot of ye." I sighed and turned back to Alleron.

"When I touched the crown I felt something...angry. It was the same energy I felt when I fought the fire ghost in the palace. Could that have been Tyrial?"

"It's possible," he said as he turned to study the crown. "He's not really dead, after all. Only trapped, along with every soul in this city."

"So the place the ghosts dragged us to..."

"Is here," he nodded. "The here that's not here anymore. The Shining City that now exists beyond time."

"That's fascinating," Cael said in the same voice one might use to discuss different colors of dirt. "You can write a treatise when we get home, but for now let's just take the crown and ride out before all those angry elven not-quite-ghosts wake up again."

"We can't."

Alleron was staring at the crown now, has hands clasped behind his back and his head tilted slightly to one side. Cael pushed past him and grabbed the crown. I didn't see any sign that he'd felt the same anger that had forced me back when I'd touched it. He pulled, but the crown didn't budge. Cael squared his shoulders, planted his feet, and heaved at the crown with all of his considerable strength. Nothing happened. Just when I thought one of the veins that stood out on his neck might burst open, he stumbled backwards, his chest heaving.

"I told you," Alleron said, "the crown isn't really here. Nothing you see is. Think of it all as the shell left behind after you crack an egg and remove the yolk. It's real, but the essence of what it was before is gone."

"Then how are we to recover what we came for?" Sheska asked as she pointed up to the crown that floated above her head.

"A delightful puzzle, is it not?"

My head had begun to throb as I tried to follow Alleron's explanation. It made a certain kind of sense until I tried to really get my head around the details, then it all dissolved into an impossible tangle. So I decided to stop trying to understand the magic of it all, and start thinking like a thief with a job to do. From that perspective things were far simpler. We'd found the vault, but the treasure wasn't here, at least not 'here' enough for us to take it. Which left only one option; we had to go where the treasure was.

"We have to go back to the ghost city," I said.

"Not a damned chance," Magnus grunted as he tried and failed to conceal a shiver. "If you think I'm going to let one of those blue bastards get their chill claws in me again you're crazier than the elf."

"Everything that's here is mirrored there," I said, growing more confident as I talked it through. "They're repeating their final day over and over again, which means that Tyrial is standing right here completing his ritual with that crown on his head. If that's where it really is, then that's where we have to go to get our hands on it."

Alleron grinned at me. "The Chromatis Arcana would just love you. Remind me to present you to them one day." He turned to Nataka. "It's unorthodox, but I believe she may be right. Going to the source may be our only chance to affect change here."

Nataka nodded, but she wore an unhappy frown. "I do not like the thought of disturbing those conflicted souls any further, but I fear we may have little choice."

"We barely escaped alive last time," Sheska reminded us. "I didn't even know that I was myself until my Ko'koan found me. How would this time be any different?"

"I believe I can do something about that, but not here." Alleron was already walking towards the staircase, forcing the rest of us to scramble to keep up.

"Don't tell me," I said to his back, "you need some incredibly rare ritual ingredients and we all need to separate to find them in time."

"Don't be silly, Charity," he said over his shoulder. "We just need to find a bloody big mirror."

11

"Any final questions before we begin?"

We stood together in front of a mirror larger than a senator's carriage, a strange and bedraggled group of misfits if ever I'd seen one. The wear and fatigue of the past weeks on the road, and especially the last two days, showed plain in every stain of dirt, sweat, and blood on our clothes and faces.

Sheska had remembered seeing the mirror in an antechamber adjacent to the throne room, and set a fast pace as she led us to it. She didn't have to explain why, and no one complained as we kept up with her. The sun was down by the time we'd emerged from the *alteriam*. I couldn't remember exactly how much time had passed from sundown the night before to the time the ghosts emerged, but I knew we didn't have long.

"Aye, I've a question for you. Who gets to gut you if this doesn't work?"

Magnus had complained about the plan with hardly a pause for breath since we'd left Tyrial's chamber, but he hadn't been able to offer an alternative. He tried to hide it, but I heard genuine fear beneath his angry bravado. I might have felt sorry for him if he'd stopped his grumbling long enough for me to think two thoughts.

"If my spell fails then I will be lost right along with you, so you'll just have to content yourself with that." Alleron maintained his usual smile, but the strain in his voice was clear.

"It will work." I held up my hands to forestall further argument before it began. I didn't know how I'd managed to become the peacemaker of the group. If we'd been seated at a tavern, I probably would have sipped my ale and watched them knock each other's teeth out, but I knew that the only way any of us made it home was to keep working together until we got there. If I'd learned one thing in my brief time here it was that there was little love lost between the mythic races of Danan. If they needed a human without all that baggage to tell them to shut up, then I supposed I would just have to keep volunteering until we were in the clear.

"We survived last time without any planning or preparation. This time we know what's coming, and we'll be ready."

I turned to Alleron and nodded. "Do it."

He returned my nod as a brief look of gratitude flashed across his face. Then he turned his attention to the mirror.

"Everyone focus your gaze on your own reflection. Ignore everything but the lines of your face. Contemplate every hair, every blemish, the smallest detail, as though you were seeing it for the first time."

I followed his instructions as he began to chant in a low voice. I was surprised to discover that the face of the girl in the mirror seemed foreign to me at first. She had the features I had come to know as mine; brown skin, green eyes, nose with a bridge sharp enough to cut glass. But the face was different in most of the ways that mattered. My eyes were calm and focused straight ahead, not darting from side to side in search of danger. My skin was weathered from weeks in the sun and open air, but it had a healthy glow to it that I'd not noticed before. All in all, she looked like someone who could handle herself. If I'd caught a glimpse of my face in a crowd I would have gone in search of a different mark.

I'd spent three months in the dark hold of a prison ship dreading my first day in Farshore. It certainly hadn't gone the way I'd expected, but since arriving here I'd eaten better, slept better, and spent more time in good company than I had in whole years back in Byzantia. I'd faced down monsters, witnessed more magic than I'd ever believed possible, and come out the other side still breathing. I still had every intention of legging it back home the first chance I got, but perhaps being exiled to the far side of the world hadn't been quite the disaster I'd feared.

A wave of green light filled my vision as Alleron finished his spell. My skin tingled as I fought a wave of dizziness, but it cleared as quickly as it had come on, leaving me looking at my reflection once more.

"That's it?" Magnus poked at his cheek with one finger.

"What were you expecting?" Alleron shrugged. "I've placed a small glamour deep within our minds. It should travel with you to the other city. Probably. In theory."

"Not helping," I whispered as I dug an elbow into his ribs.

"Oof...yes, well, the point is that once you see your reflection in that place the glamour will awaken you fully in the mind of your host as before."

"And what happens if we don't pass by a mirror at all ?" Cael asked.

"Then you'll have to recollect yourself on your own." Alleron held up a hand to forestall further protest. "You have some agency within your host, even if it isn't full control. Set your mind now on the importance of viewing your reflection, and direct all your energy towards it once we've crossed over."

I saw a flicker of blue light in the mirror behind us.

"I think planning time is over."

I turned and saw a shimmering blue courtesan float through the antechamber and pass through the closed doors into the throne room. Moments later two guards in gleaming armor appeared out of thin air to flank the door. None of us moved. They kept their eyes fixed straight ahead and their spears held at attention, but I knew it was only a matter of time until someone coughed and the ghosts turned their centuries of anger, fear, and psychic trauma on us like they had before. I looked around the group, meeting everyone's eyes in turn and exchanging firm nods. We were as ready as we'd ever be.

"Gather in the garden once you've gained control. We'll go for the crown from there."

I was already off and running before the words had left my mouth. The horrible screams and flashes of light behind me confirmed that the sound of my voice had shattered the fragile calm, and two of my friends were already on their way to the other city. I'd be close behind them, but if I was going to be trapped inside some ancient elf's mind again, I wanted to have a little more say in where I ended up this time. Someone with a bit of rank, who would have an easier time moving around the palace, and I had a guess on where I might find what I was looking for.

I ran back the way we'd come, ducking under outstretched arms and dodging ghostly fingers as I went. The chorus of soul-withering shrieks and wails behind me grew louder with every step, but I wasn't stupid enough to turn around and see how many phantoms trailed in my wake. I skidded around a corner and caught sight of the open door which led back to the waterfall pavilion that concealed the entrance to Tyrial's private sanctum.

Just as I'd expected there were now guards standing watch outside the door. As I stepped into view their mouths fell open in the horrible, gaping scream I'd come to know so well, but I was more interested in what I saw just beyond the door. An elf stood watch inside the room. He was somewhat taller than most others I'd seen.

His armor was ornate, and he wore an elegant cape that draped down to his calves. He stared at the ground beneath his feet, his brow furrowed in deep thought and a frown twisting at the edges of his mouth as he grasped the hilt of the sword at his side in a tight grip. Everything about him said, "I'm in charge of many things."

I ran down the corridor towards the door. As the two guards lunged for me, I dropped into a slide that carried me beneath their arms, then pushed back up to my feet and kept running. The tall elf turned towards me as my footsteps echoed in the chamber. He didn't start screaming, and his face didn't warp into a crazed and twisted mask like the others. He just looked surprised for a brief moment. Then he drew his sword, set his feet, and moved his lips as he shouted something at me. He didn't make a sound, and I probably wouldn't have understood him anyway, but the general sentiment of "stop or die" is rather universal.

I kept running towards him. He gathered himself, then lunged forward in a lightning fast thrust. Instead of dodging I threw myself at him. The tip of his sword passed through my chest with a burst of static shock that I felt down in my bones. Then everything went black.

Something was wrong.

It made little sense, and in truth I knew I had no reason for concern. Today was to be a glorious occasion even before King Tyrial proclaimed his intent to grant the city a great gift to honor its millennial anniversary. The citizens had talked of little else for weeks as they planned, prepared, and decorated. Even the usual quiet scheming of the court had settled into a kind of distracted contentment of late. I had reviewed every detail, walked every inch of the parade route myself, spoken to my spies, and even to agents of the ministry, in search of the faintest whisper of ill intent, and found nothing amiss.

But three hundred years of service as the captain of the palace guard had honed my instinct for danger to an edge far sharper than my sword's, and that instinct continued to scream at me that something was very wrong.

I tried to dismiss my concern as the product of weeks of vigilant preparation now in search of a focus, but each time I did, the memory of the look in Tyrial's eyes as he'd given me my orders this morning returned in full force. The whole city awaited his appearance, yet I was to let no one disturb him, not even the queen herself.

We'd been friends since we were boys. We'd grown to manhood together, fought orc rebels, troll raiders, and far worse side by side. I'd stood by him as he fought for the throne, protected him as shadowy foes sought his life, and followed his orders without hesitation for centuries. Yet I had never seen his eyes shine with the kind of wildfire that burned in them as he descended the steps to his alteriam.

"Today is the last day, Garridin." He'd gripped my shoulder with the strength of a drowning man, and his gaze cut through me in search of a future only he could see. "The last day, and the first. I will make our people something greater than even Sorellian Lightbringer himself could have imagined when he shaped us from the morning fog." The chill that passed through me at his words had not yet lifted.

I shook my head to clear my troubled thoughts and resumed my restless pacing before the locked and guarded door. The men who stood watch outside were utterly reliable, yet I trusted no one but myself to stand watch over the entrance to the king's chamber, which left me with little else to do but pace and wait.

I took in a deep, calming breath, then turned to walk down toward the still water of the pond. Everything that could be planned or prepared in advance had already been attended to, but as I waited in silence for the festivities to begin, I could at least take a moment to ensure that my own appearance did justice to the occasion. I rarely gave such trivial concerns much thought, but today was different. I had slept less than usual of late, and while my servants were quite diligent in preparing my clothes and armor, I was suddenly gripped with a deep concern that something in my face or attire might be horribly amiss. It would not do to bring shame on my office on a day such as this.

I reached the water's edge and leaned forward to check my reflection.

A girl stared back at me. Her skin was the color of corku bark, and her face carried an expression of such extreme irritation that I might have laughed if I had not been so entranced. It was as though I looked upon my own true face for the first time in my life. I leaned closer, but my body betrayed my commands and I pitched headlong into the water.

I jolted back from the shock of wet and cold as water streamed from my obnoxiously long hair. My fingers searched over my strange body as I gasped for breath. Bronze armor, pointed ears, thin cheeks. Everything was wrong, but at least this time I understood why.

"Charity." I said my name aloud, finding comfort in the familiar sound spoken by an unfamiliar voice. "Yeah, that doesn't get any easier."

I stood to my feet, squeezed water from my long auburn tresses, and headed for the door. I had no real sense of how time played itself out here. For all I knew the others might all be waiting and worrying in the garden already.

I pulled the door open and saw the two guards outside jump at the unexpected sound. They glanced backward, then turned and saluted as they saw me.

"Captain."

"Ah, yes...hello."

They shared a quick, uncertain glance.

"Do you have new orders, sir?"

"No, no. Just keep on doing...what I told you to do before. I'll be back shortly."

I stepped past them and continued down the hall before they could ask any more questions. Just as before, the people in this place all behaved normally, but knowing that it was all just a vast illusion that would repeat itself again tomorrow left me deeply uneasy. My stomach turned as I made my way through bustling rooms and passageways filled with souls busy at the same tasks that had occupied them for five hundred years. I hated the thought of all these people trapped in an endless nightmare without even an awareness of their fate, but there was little I could do about it.

Thankfully the walk wasn't far, and soon enough I stepped through the arched doorway into the palace gardens. I stood there, tense and uneasy, as I looked over graveled paths, flowering trees, and perfectly trimmed shrub bushes for some sign of my companions. I had little sense of what I was even looking for other than something out of place or unusual. Unfortunately, everything seemed perfect and serene. The closest thing to unusual I could see was a group of three elves standing together beside a small water feature. For lack of any better idea I set out across the trimmed grass in their direction.

I was focused on the task at hand. Find my friends, get to the king, take his crown, go home. I was so busy thinking about all the things that could go wrong in the next few minutes that I let down my guard to the present dangers in this place; namely, the confused and very angry elf whose body I had just conscripted.

He came at me hard and fast, striking with the precision and focus of a master swordsman. My vision blurred as he sought to overwhelm my aware-ness and regain control. It took every bit of mental discipline I could muster just to stay rooted in my sense of self. The elf captain's thoughts, memories, and emotions crowded in on me, building one atop the other as it became harder and harder to remember where he stopped and I began. Garridin had almost recalled his name. I felt him reaching for it as my grip on reality slipped away, and I began to fade back into the deep places of his mind.

In a panic I rallied my own memories around me like a shield. Good moments and bad, slow days, sadness, betrayals, and more than one close brush with death all formed a shelter from his assault. I held tight to each fragment of memory, especially the painful ones. The sharp sting of their jagged edges helped me stand my ground against the disorientation of expe-riencing another life that was both foreign and intimately familiar in equal measure. After a time, the howling gale of his onslaught began to fade. Once I had my feet firmly planted, I pressed forward again, and his will began to unravel into a tangle of confusion and dismay.

That's when Queen Sapphery joined the fight.

She chose her moment perfectly. I was tired from the contest with the elf captain, but had not yet regained full control. She swept down on me like an avalanche, bitter and irresistible. Her will struck my memory shield with terrible force and sent me tumbling backwards. She pressed forward, crushing me beneath the weight of her presence. The elf captain had fought to regain himself, but she sought to grind me to pieces until there was nothing left. A deep, numbing cold settled into me. Pain and fear gave way to fatigue, then fatigue became a cold nothingness, until I began to forget why I struggled at all.

It was Garridin who saved me. The space we battled in echoed with the shock of recognition, then flared red with his outrage and anger.

Is this your doing, witch?

He threw himself at her with abandon, striking and tearing like a hawk driving an intruder from its nest. At first it was difficult for me to notice or care, but as Queen Sapphery turned her attention on him the weight bearing down on me eased somewhat. She screamed as she threw herself on Garridin, and the sound was a storm of rage and thunder. He disappeared in a flurry of driving white and slashing ice, but his effort gave me space to gather myself again.

I could breathe. Then I could think. Then I got very, very angry.

The elf had saved me, and she'd hurt him for it. I knew that saving my life hadn't been his motive, but he'd just done it nonetheless, which meant that I owed him a debt I couldn't repay. That's one thing I really hate. Royals who bully, threaten, and take whatever they want was something I hated on an entirely different level. I had the measure of this queen now. She might be an ancient being of terrible power, but I'd seen her kind a hundred times before scowling from carriages that rumbled through Byzantia's streets or standing as distant outlines on inapproachable balconies safe and secure within their villa walls. She stamped and screamed because she'd been denied something, and she lashed out to make the world around her suffer for the slightest affront.

I exploded. There was no slow gathering of will this time, just a firestorm of righteous fury.

"Ok *bruta*. You want to dance? Let's fucking dance."

I threw myself at her like one of Jovian's own arrows. We tangled together in a riot of ice, fire, and steam. She screamed, but in pain this time as my blistering heat divided her essence and drove her back. She tried to fight me, to quench my fire beneath her cold fury, but I gave her no space or time to regroup. With a final shriek, she gathered the tatters of her presence and retreated into the depths of my mind once more.

"That's twice now!" I called after her, sending the thought ringing through the darkness. "Come at me again and see what happens."

I was showing my teeth, but in truth I was exhausted beyond belief. I didn't understand this mental battle I'd fought twice now. I'd acted on instinct, and thankfully that had been enough so far, because the same instinct told me that the consequences of losing to her would be very bad, and very permanent . Once we were free of this place and found ourselves a moment to breathe I knew I needed to ask for help. I hated the thought of admitting I'd done something wrong, and even worse, something very stupid, to land myself in this mess. But I hated the thought of having my mind destroyed from the inside by a disembodied spirit looking for a new home even more.

A thin flicker of light in the dark stillness of my mind drew my attention. I moved towards it, and found the elf captain, or what was left of him. His essence was almost gone. Only the strongest and brightest of his memories remained, flashing like a gemstone on a pedestal. I gathered him to me, sending calm, comforting thoughts to him as I tried to lend strength where I could.

"I'm sorry," I whispered.

When we'd first wrestled for control, he had been so certain of himself, full of pride and purpose. Now there was little more than simple awareness left. My throat squeezed tight, sending water to my eyes and making each breath a struggle. I didn't know if it was possible for him to recover himself with time, or if the very essence of his soul would now fade into oblivion. That seemed a fate far worse than simple death, and it would be on my hands. Queen Sapphery was the one who had hurt him, but I'd been the one who'd dove headfirst into his consciousness, bringing trouble with me.

I sighed and stood to my feet. Perhaps he'd awaken tomorrow morning to repeat his day once more without the nuisance of a stupid girl invading his mind for her own ends, but I feared that the damage he'd suffered was too great for that. Either way, I knew that all I could do now was get back to the task at hand whether I liked it or not.

I tucked him in between two of my gentlest, warmest memories and turned to find my way back to consciousness.

"Captain?"

The voice came from outside my mind this time, an anchor to the real world. I rushed up to meet it.

"Sir, are you well?"

My vision resolved back onto the palace garden once again. A guard stood in front of me, shifting from foot to foot as he looked at his commander with concern.

"I--" my voice was cracked and dry. I cleared my throat and tried again. "Yes, of course. I was just...thinking."

It was a poor answer, but my thoughts felt like they had to wade through a river of mud to reach my tongue. The guard leaned in close, staring hard at my face for a moment before relaxing into a smile.

"Charity?"

Hearing my own name out loud was like a drink of cool water on a hot day. I blinked, and this time I saw the hazy outline of another face, one with blue eyes, a strong jaw, and a rather large mustache.

"Cael!" I almost hugged him in relief, but managed to remember my surroundings in time to turn the gesture into a more soldierly arm clasp of greeting. "You've no idea how glad I am to see a friendly face. Well, more or less."

He nodded, then his grin faded back to his usual serious expression.

"Are you alright? You were staring at the ground so hard I thought you might wear a hole in it."

"I'm fine," I said, brushing his concern aside. "It just took a bit of extra work to get back to myself this time. Where are the others?"

"Close by." He turned and led the way towards a footbridge that spanned a small brook. "They were beginning to worry."

He said the words as though he hadn't cared much one way or the other, but it hadn't escaped my notice that he was the one who'd come to find me. As we crossed the bridge, I saw that it connected a small island of sorts to the rest of the garden. Four other elves stood beneath the shade of a tree. I had no doubt they were the strangest assortment of servants, soldiers, and gentry to stand together in that spot in a thousand years.

"It took you far too long to regain control," snapped an elf in kitchen clothes whose ample stomach revealed that he took great pains to sample all of his wares before he sent them to the table. "I expected better of you." Despite his soft appearance I recognized Sheska's voice immediately.

"Aww, you were worried about me."

The chef's glare could have curdled milk.

"I was no such thing."

"I'm truly touched, Ko'koan," I said, dipping my head in a small bow to hide my grin. "I'll do my best not to concern you in the future."

The chef's cheeks flared crimson, and then Sheska seemed to notice how easily her current body betrayed her feelings.

"We're wasting time." She marched past me and over the bridge without looking back. The rest of us shared a quick smile before we followed after her.

A tall, thin elven woman in an elegant gown gave my shoulder a squeeze as she walked by.

"I am glad you are well, Charity," she said in Nataka's sombre tones.

"Aye," said a guard who might have been Cael's twin. "We'll need all hands to fight our way clear of this mess. Even stick-thin humans who can barely fight can soak an arrow or two."

Maybe it was because of my recent brush with nothingness, but as I followed my friends towards the elf king's sanctum, I found that the lump in my throat had returned in full force.

12

"I thought you said that his ritual will hold his attention? Let's stop chattering about it and get down there so we can get ourselves home."

Magnus snorted with impatience as he cast another look down the dark staircase.

We stood at the entrance to the alteriam, but Alleron refused to allow us to proceed until he had finished explaining just how dangerous a foe Tyrial would be.

"True, but even so his power and skill were greater than any mage my people had produced in generations, and that was back when the High Elves were the greatest practitioners of magic in Danan."

"According to the High Elves," Nataka said under her breath. It did seem like Alleron might have been inflating the awesome power of his hero king a bit, but it didn't seem like a point worth arguing over.

"So he's dangerous," I said before Alleron could snap back at her. "How do we deal with him?"

Alleron shot a glare at the orc hidden within the body of an elven courtesan, then turned to answer my question.

"We spread out and divide his attention. We'll have the element of surprise on our side, and we need to make the most of it. Press the assault and don't give him room to focus on any one of us for too long. If you can occupy him sufficiently, I believe I can freeze him in place long enough for someone to take the crown, then it's back through a portal to our own world."

"Far simpler to just bury a blade in his skull." Magnus' hand had dropped to the hilt of the sword at his side.

"No doubt. But Tyrial is the focal anchor of this reality. There's no telling what might happen if he died here, but I doubt we would enjoy it much."

"And what happens if he kills us?" I asked. The question had been nagging at me since we first decided to return. "What happens to us if we're hurt or killed here in this place?"

"You know...I'm honestly not sure. I suppose it depends on the nature of our connection to the host body we're in. It's possible we might simply awaken in our own forms and time, but it's just as possible we might not awaken at all. On the other hand--"

"You think too much." Sheska cut him off with a wave of her hand, then gave me a comforting pat on the shoulder. "It's simple. Just don't let him kill you."

"Right," I sighed. "Why didn't I think of that?"

"We have a plan then, of a sort," Cael said as he moved towards the stairs. "Let's move."

It seemed like the right time for an encouraging word or two, but I couldn't think of anything to add, and no one else volunteered. Without a word we all followed Cael into the darkness.

The short flight of stairs was the same as the real set we'd walked down back in our own time, and ended at the same doorway.

Cael checked to make sure we were all ready. I gave him a tight smile and a nod when he looked my way. Then he kicked the door open and we charged inside.

The others had already begun to fan out through the room before I got a good look inside. Tyrial stood on the far side of the ritual table. He wasn't chanting or waving his arms. He just beamed a broad smile as he watched us enter his sanctum.

"Wonderful!" His voice was the rich purr of a cat eyeing dinner. "You've finally arrived. I've been waiting for you."

"Of course, your majesty," I said, trying to cover my surprise while I figured out what in the hells was going on. "I...thought I heard screaming. We came to investigate."

"I'm not speaking to that shade you're wearing," Tyrial said with a sneer. "I've been waiting for *you*." His gaze locked on mine as he spoke, and I knew without a doubt that he saw the real me within the elf captain's body.

"And your fine friends, of course. When I saw how my darling wife lured you into her gilded cage it occurred to me that I might do the same."

He waved one hand and the door slammed shut behind me. As the crash echoed through the room, six elves in full armor stepped out from the shadows. They each carried a drawn sword and a shield, and their grim faces left little doubt as to what they intended to do with them. Tyrial closed his eyes and whispered a few words as he bent his fingers into a strange pose, then flung his hands outward.

A wave of blue light pulsed out from them. Cael had been the first to charge into the room and so he now stood closest to Tyrial. As the wave of light swept through him the image of the elven guardsman warped and shifted for a moment. Then the elf collapsed to the floor like a sack of flour, and Cael himself stood in his place.

The same thing happened to each of my friends in turn. Then the light reached me. I was struck by a dizzy, spinning, pulling sensation, as though I was on the end of a rope being hauled through the ocean at great speed. Then it stopped as abruptly as it had started, and I looked down to see my own body standing over the elf captain's still form.

"And now, here you are. Quite the assortment of rogues and chattel," Tyrial said, sounding disappointed as he looked at each one of us in turn. "But at least there are a few viable options amongst you, if only until I find something more suitable. Restrain them," he called over his shoulder, "but injure no one until I've decided which vessel I will claim as my own."

The guards advanced in a line, then spread out as each of them stalked towards one of us. I looked around but the room offered no escape. There were few places to hide, and I knew better than to waste my time trying to open the door behind me. I drew my swords, and the room echoed with the hiss of steel as my friends readied their weapons. Then the guards all shouted in unison and charged.

The first exchange of cuts and parries was the worst. The elf was lightning fast. He used his shield to deflect my strikes, bind my blade, and conceal his own attacks with fluid grace. But after the first few seconds, I had the measure of him. His style reminded me of Alleron's movements when we'd trained together beneath the arena, with one very significant difference. The guardsman wasn't trying for a lethal strike. He aimed his cuts at my arms and legs, and clashed his blade against mine with sharp twisting motions in an effort to pull the sword from my hands.

Which left him at a rather severe disadvantage, because I had absolutely no qualms about ramming my sword through his chest if he gave me half a chance.

"Magnus, form up!" Cael's voice echoed through the room. I snuck in a glance to my left and saw Cael and Magnus moving to stand together. Our mage had kept his guardsman occupied with a flurry of small blue and white missiles that crashed against his shield and battered his armor, but it required all of his concentration to sustain the spell. The dwarf and the Gallean warrior shifted to stand in front of Alleron, drawing their opponents in and threatening Alleron's foe at the same time.

"Just do your job and leave these fools to us," Magnus yelled as he swept Hilda in a wide arc that forced the guardsmen back a step.

Alleron let his spell fade away, took a moment to catch his breath, then turned to face the elven king.

"*Sa sanien lores, Tyrial'tai,*" he called out over the clash of steel. "We come to you with a noble purpose. Your people have suffered terribly since the cataclysm, and even darker days lie ahead. We have need of your strength and wisdom now more than ever. You must return with us to restore what has been lost."

"He must what now?" I shouted. Bringing the king back into our world wasn't part of the plan, but Alleron ignored me.

Instead he crossed his arms over his chest and raised his face to the ceiling as he chanted a string of clipped syllables. The air around his hands glowed green, growing brighter and brighter as his voice rose in volume. Then he snapped his gaze back to the king and flung his arms towards him, fingers extended. A beam of brilliant green shot out and engulfed Tyrial. The king had just begun to turn towards our mage, but his movement slowed, then stopped entirely as the light washed over him. Small clusters of green crystal began to form across his body. Alleron's arms dropped to his side, and the light faded away. The room fell silent as the guardsmen all ceased their assault and stared in horror at the crystalline statue of their king.

Then Tyrial began to laugh.

He remained frozen in place down to the smallest muscle of his face, yet somehow a shrill, mocking cackle rang out from his body. Then he exploded. Crystal fragments flew out in all directions. Tyrial rolled his shoulders, stretched his arms, then wagged a finger at Alleron as a grin spread across his face, the exact same gesture he'd aimed at me after I defeated his animated armor.

"How disappointing."

Tyrial flicked one finger in Alleron's direction, quite obviously bored. A beam of light the exact same hue of green as the one Alleron had summoned shot out from it and struck the mage in the chest. Half a heartbeat later the air around the elf exploded in a brilliant flash of white and emerald, and I was forced to look away. When I turned back a pillar of green crystal stretched from floor to ceiling, with Alleron trapped inside like a fly in amber.

"Aaagh!"

One of the elves facing Magnus and Cael recovered his wits before anyone else, and had seized on the opening. His sword dripped with blood, and Cael's sword arm hung limp at his side as he squeezed a hand over the large gash in his shoulder.

"No!" Tyrial screamed as he turned on his soldier, his face twisted with rage. "I was beginning to like that one, and now you've ruined him!"

He raised both hands in front of his face, fingers cupped as though they held an invisible ball. The unfortunate guardsman flew into the air and hung suspended above the floor for a moment. Tyrial screamed, sounding for all the world like a child who'd just been denied a sweet, then flung his arms out wide. The elf exploded in a shower of blood and innards, bits of him sailing off in every direction.

I stared in shock at the gory remnants of what the mad king had just done to one of his own men. Tyrial sighed, wiped a speck of blood from his cheek with a slender finger, and shook his head.

"After centuries of boredom I had hoped this would prove more entertaining, but I suppose there will be time enough for amusements once I'm free."

He turned back towards us. His fingers danced and his lips moved as he whispered arcane words. As I saw the look in his eyes every instinct I possessed shouted a warning in unison.

"Run!" I screamed as I raced towards one of the stone pillars.

The room erupted in chaos. Stone spikes rose from the floor and flew at Sheska. The elf she'd been dueling was cut to shreds instantly, but the halfling reacted with the speed of a jungle cat. She twisted and dodged, then stopped in her tracks and looked down in surprise at the jagged shard embedded in her chest. As she fell to the floor, a bolt of lightning arced down from the ceiling. It coursed through Nataka and the elf beside her, blasting them both into the wall. The orc slid to the ground, smoke curling from her hair, eyes, and ears. A chorus of screams rang out behind me, then cut off abruptly. I was too busy running to turn and look.

A white-hot ball of fire flew at my head. If I hadn't already been moving I wouldn't have stood a chance, but the instant of warning had given me just enough time. The fire exploded where I'd stood, engulfing my opponent and singing the back of my legs as I leapt away. I rolled to my feet and kept running, sliding to a stop behind the solid bulk of one of the stone pillars the lined one side of the chamber as I gasped for breath.

I tried to fight my rising panic as my mind struggled to absorb what had just happened. He'd killed everyone in the span of a few heartbeats.

The pillar shuddered as something struck the far side of it.

"Are you going to force me to chase you, little girl?" The pillar shook again. "How very tedious. If you stand still I promise you won't feel a thing."

I looked left, right, even up, searching for anything that might offer an escape or some means to fight back, but finding nothing. I didn't even know what I was looking for. My friends had known what they were doing. I was just along for the ride. They had experience and power of their own. They belonged here. I was just a street waif from a world where at least the monsters looked like me and used men with swords to bully and kill instead of bolts of fire and death from the sky.

"So what's your plan, Tyrial?" I called, my chest heaving. Maybe if I could get him talking I'd be able to catch my breath and find a hole to bolt through.

"If you kill me won't you just stay trapped in this place forever?"

"Your lack of respect is most troubling," he huffed from the other side of the pillar. So far it didn't sound like he'd moved. "Do you think me a fool?

The young wizard is merely paralyzed, and I fully intend to travel back to Danan in his rather drab frame before your corpse has cooled and stiffened. A great relief, I can assure you. I've no idea what manner of creature you are, but judging from your appearance I've no doubt that you are positively riddled with all manner of vermin."

That explained why he clearly had no interest in keeping me alive, not that the alternative of having my body claimed as his personal meat carriage was much better. My mind raced in search of something else to keep him talking. As long as his lips were being used for normal words instead of casting horrible spells I'd be relatively safe.

"I wouldn't be so quick to fling insults around, asshole. I may need a bath, but at least I didn't destroy my entire civilization in one afternoon."

"How *dare* you!" He screamed. "I would have made them perfect, but they weren't pure enough to accept my gift. But rest assured that as soon as I am free of this cage I will raise a new empire from the ashes of the old, an immortal, unchanging beacon of perfection to bring order to this troubled world."

His voice shook with mad passion. Five hundred years trapped as the only self-aware being in and endless repetition of the day of his greatest failure had clearly not done wonders for his sanity.

"But first I need to deal with the little thief who stuck her nose where it didn't belong."

The menace in his voice sent a shiver down my spine, and I knew then that I was going to die here. My bones would lie cold and unseen in this empty chamber forever. I would never see Byzantia's twisting streets again.

I clenched my teeth, holding back the sob that shook my chest. I would have cut my own throat before I let him hear me cry. I might have been about to die, but I wouldn't give him that satisfaction.

Let me help you.

The words echoed in my mind. I'd heard that voice before. At least she'd spoken to me this time instead of launching a surprise assault, but I suspected that Queen Sapphery had simply decided to try a different approach towards the same end.

So you can break my mind and steal my body when I let my guard down? I'd rather let your delightful husband roast me like a goose, thank you.

The floor beneath me grew hot. I dove to the side just as the stone where

I'd stood turned into a pool of molten rock. I was still breathing, but had been forced out from behind the relative safety of the stone pillar. I looked to my left to see Tyrial in the same place where he'd stood since we entered the room, his face lit with a crazed smile. I knew it was hopeless, but I started running for the next pillar anyway.

You won't survive without magic. I can give you that!

And why should I trust you?

An arrow of silver light streaked past my face an inch from my nose to bury itself in the bookshelf beside me. I glanced back at Tyrial without breaking stride. A hundred more just like it hovered in the air around him. The *alteriam* echoed with his wild laughter once again, then two more arrows shot towards my chest. I leapt into the air and spun sideways. The bolts flew past on either side, but I had too much momentum from my sudden dodge to regain my balance. I landed in a half-run, then lost my footing entirely. A jolt of pain shot through me as I tumbled to the stone floor.

"Marvelous!" Tyrial called out as he began to clap for my display of acrobatics. "You should be proud you've lived this long." Then his smile vanished. "Now please die."

He raised both hands into the air, and the cloud of arrows drifted up along with them.

Fool! If you die I perish with you.

The image of the white tree filled my mind. A branch extended out towards me, crackling with energy.

Tyrial dropped his hands and a hundred arrows screamed through the air.

Please!

I reached out and took hold of the branch.

Mother Shanti once made me stand to my neck in a frozen stream for over an hour. Claimed it was to teach me that my mind controlled my body, but I think she was just in a shitty mood that day and felt like watching someone suffer. The pain I had felt as the cold pried its way into my veins nearly drove me insane. What I felt when I took hold of the branch was a thousand times worse.

Ice tore through my skin and shattered my bones. My blood became a river of glacial cold so fierce it burned. I died. Then I died again, over and over until something inside of me broke open.

And then it stopped. The cold was still there, flowing in and through me like the breath in my lungs, but it didn't hurt anymore. It was mine now.

I opened my eyes, then blinked in surprise. Tyrial's form and the rest of the room were warped and hazy. Then I realized the distortion was caused by the wall of ice that now stood beside me. Hundreds of silver arrows had buried themselves in the far side, leaving a spiderweb of chips and cracks spread across its surface. Then the arrows faded away, and the wall of ice crumbled to the floor. I stood to my feet, brushed the dust from my knees, and turned to face the mad king.

"Nice try, asshole."

His head tilted to one side and his brow furrowed as he studied me as though seeing me for the first time.

"How did--" His eyes went wide as he pointed at my chest. My eyes followed the line of his finger to find the sapphire necklace shining like a star in the darkness.

"Impossible! I made certain she could never leave that room."

Please give my beloved my warmest regards. Sapphery's tone could have frozen a blacksmith's forge solid.

"Your wife says hello."

I raised my hands as tendrils of ice snaked down from my shoulders to curl around my fingers. I had no idea what I was doing, yet somehow I knew exactly what to do. I thrust my arms forward, palms facing out, and two spears of ice flew towards him like ballista bolts.

Tyrial cried out and threw up his hands as he stumbled backwards. A dome of shimmering blue light flared around him. The first spear shattered against the dome, but the force of its impact tore a hole in its surface. The light of the dome wavered, then began to reform, but the second spear shot through the gap before it closed. I had done it.

Or, at least I thought I had. Tyrial's hands snapped up and caught the spike an inch from his chest. The force of the spear slid him backward a few inches, but he dug in his heels and ground to a stop. Blood dripped from his hands, but as the light of his protective dome died away, he tossed the ice aside to shatter on the floor.

"You were always so predictable, darling," he said as he wiped two bloody smears on his robe. "You could never best me in a duel. What makes you think--"

I drove a fist into his stomach and smashed the other across his jaw with all the force I could muster.

I'd started running at him as soon as I saw him snatch the ice spear out of the air. Sapphery's magic had saved my life, but it was up to me to make something of it. Of course, that didn't stop me from sheathing my fists in two blocks of solid ice before I'd hit him. Tyrial's power was unbelievable, but I had a hunch that even the greatest wizard in the universe would find it hard to magic me to death with no air in his lungs and a broken jaw.

The elf made a sound that fell somewhere between a raven's caw and the squeal of a pine log tossed on a bonfire as he dropped to the floor. I drew my knife, dropped a knee into his chest, and pressed the blade against his throat. Given that he was unconscious he didn't offer much resistance, but I wasn't taking any chances. My chest heaved as sweat traced its way down my forehead, but I tightened my grip on the knife and waited.

He recovered faster than I would have expected. He blinked his eyes back into focus and drew in a rasping breath around the blood in his mouth and the pressure of my knee on his chest as he glanced down at the knife. Then the bastard looked up at me and smiled.

"What now, little girl? Are you going to kill me?"

I realized that I didn't have an answer. The past few minutes had been one mad scramble to stay alive. Now that I had the upper hand, I wasn't sure what to do with it. Alleron would have known what to demand, but Alleron was gone. I fought to keep my face cold even as my heart ached. My mind ran in circles chasing an answer, but all it found was the memory of my fallen comrades. I was alone again.

Nothing in this place lasts forever.

Sapphery's voice shook me out of my despair. In all the chaos I'd forgotten that this place wasn't even real. I still didn't understand it, but I remembered that what happened here wasn't necessarily for keeps. I didn't need to understand its rules to work around them.

"Here's what's going to happen," I said, my voice growing steadier as my thoughts took shape. "You're going to turn back the clock. You'll put my friends back in one piece and send us all home, then we'll take your crown and be on our merry way, or I'll paint a second smile below your chin."

He blinked twice, then burst into fits of laughter.

"You...you went through all this...for my crown?" he gasped as he finally got a hold of himself. When he said it like that I had to admit it sounded rather stupid, but I just shrugged.

"A job's a job."

His eyes narrowed, and I could see the thoughts spinning in his head.

"How interesting. Very well, little girl, you have yourself a bargain. I don't suppose you'd be willing to remove the knife?"

"Not a chance," I dug the edge of the knife a bit deeper. He gulped.

"It was worth a try."

He closed his eyes, and I felt the shift of power as he focused his will. The room began to spin around me. The image of each of my friends' final moments began to unravel in my memory, leaving a blank space where they'd once stood. Tyrial opened his eyes, and their wild blue light burned into my soul. The sound of his voice was the last thing I remembered as I began to fall up into oblivion.

"I hope you know how to run, little girl."

13

I bolted up off the floor.

It took me a moment to realize where I was. I stood in Tyrial's alteriam, but everything had changed. The stone pillars where all shattered, their stumps standing up like broken teeth. The ritual table and bookshelves were nothing but piles of rotten wood and scraps of moldering parchment. Even the walls and ceiling of the room were riddled with long cracks and jagged gaps where stones had fallen loose.

I held something cool and solid in my hands. I looked down and saw a crown made of white gold and gemstones.

"Ugghhn."

Nataka groaned at my feet and tried to sit up. The others lay nearby, and they began to stir as I moved to help her to her feet. As I leaned forward Sapphery's necklace swung into view. I scrambled to tuck it back beneath my shirt, then blew out a breath when I realized no one had seen it.

"What happened?" Nataka asked as I helped her stand up.

"You don't remember?"

She shook her head, then winced and pressed a hand to her temple.

"We fought Tyrial and his minions," Sheska said as she stumbled over to join us. "And then..." her words trailed away in confusion.

"He was so focused on you all that I was able to take him by surprise," I told her, thinking fast. If they hadn't seen me wielding magic, then that meant I had a lot less explaining to do.

"But how could you--"

A grinding rumble shook the chamber. Dust trickled down onto our heads.

"Well this is different," Alleron said as he took notice of the changes in the room. "Looks a lot more like what you'd expect from centuries of wear and neglect."

The floor trembled as the sound of shifting stone and crumbling earth grew louder. As a ceiling stone the size of a dinner table crashed to the ground at the back of the room, I remembered Tyrial's parting words.

"Run now, talk later!" I shoved Nataka towards the door and made sure everyone was up and moving before I started running too.

We made it halfway up the stairs before things really started to fall apart.

The ground began to shake in earnest as we stumbled into the waterfall chamber. The pavilion was a rotting hulk and the pond was choked with slime and weeds. We scrambled over the rocks and out the door, then raced down collapsing corridors and through crumbling antechambers as we dodged falling masonry and leapt over widening crevices caused by the shifting earth.

As we stumbled into the formal atrium at the palace entrance, I saw the warm glow of morning sunlight streaming through the colored glass of the ceiling dome. It was broken in places, but stood amazingly intact given the state of the rest of the palace. Which meant there was plenty of glass to rain down on our heads as the shaking dome began to collapse in on itself.

"Go!" I screamed as I leaped forward. The iridescent storm of shattering glass might have been beautiful if it hadn't been so deadly. I crossed my arms above my head as I ran, ignoring the sharp stabs of pain. Then the stabbing and slicing stopped. I glanced up as I kept running to see Cael matching my stride, his shield arm over my head. I didn't have enough breath for a thank you, and he didn't wait for one as we ran together down the cracked and dusty corridor that led to the entrance.

The beautiful paintings had long-since rotted away, and thankfully most of the chandeliers had already fallen from the ceiling. Everyone was so focused on scrambling over and around the debris that it wasn't hard to make sure I'd fallen to the back of the group by the time we'd reached the door. I ducked aside to retrieve my treasure sack from beneath the bench where I'd stashed it, then ran to catch up with the others as we burst out onto the steps of the palace courtyard.

I was amazed to see that our horses were still where we'd left them. They bucked and tugged at their leads in panic as the ground shuddered beneath them, but calmed down enough as we unhitched them for us to mount up. I stuffed Tyrial's crown and the bulging pillowcase I carried into the top of my travel pack, then pulled Alleron up behind me. Together we all turned our horses and galloped through the warped and rusted gates.

If the palace had been chaos, then the city outside was a view of the eight hells. Buildings that had stood as clean and perfect as the day they'd been built when we rode in were now choked with trees and underbrush. They toppled together and crashed to the ground as though smashed by an invisible hand. I saw no sign of the thousands of stone elf statues we'd passed on our way in, but more than enough piles of crushed granite to guess what had become of them. The name hadn't made much sense to me before, but it truly was a shattered city now.

The cliffs of the mountain pass we'd used to enter the caldera looked very far away, but I aimed Shanti in the right direction and got ready to dig in my heels.

"Wait!" Cael's voice rose above the roar of the dying city and caught me up short. He pointed further into the city. Entire buildings were disappearing one after the other, and the line of destruction was moving towards us. "We'll never make it."

"You have a better idea?" I yelled back. He looked around, searching for a way through the chaos. Then Alleron tapped me on the shoulder and pointed to a wide street that lead north.

"That way!" He screamed in my ear loud enough to leave it ringing. I shot an elbow into his stomach to quiet him down a bit, but turned Shanti in the direction he'd indicated and drove her forward.

The others formed up behind me as we raced through the crumbling city. The street Alleron chose had once been a wide avenue, which left us just enough room to weave between piles of rubble and dodge away from falling walls. Shanti was as frightened as I was, so it didn't take any prompting to keep her racing forward as fast as she could manage.

The avenue charted a straight course from the palace to wherever it led, never turning or branching off. Soon enough I caught sight of a huge stone gatehouse above the rooftops ahead of us. The structure of the building was flanked on either side by the two giant statues I'd seen when we first entered the valley. They faced away from the city; their stone weapons raised to threaten any who meant it harm. The rumbling and shaking had grown worse. I saw the arm of one of the statues break free and crash to the ground, its marble sword skewering through the roof of a house that stood against the city's wall.

We rode into a wide open plaza that looked like it might once have housed a large market. Or a small army. Alleron pointed towards the gatehouse with one hand as he squeezed my waist like a python with the other. The head of the other statue broke loose and crushed a bouncing path of destruction across the plaza.

"Are you crazy?"

"It's the only way out!"

I leaned forward and willed Shanti to give it everything she had. To my surprise the marvelous old *bruta* put on one last inch of speed.

As we galloped across the courtyard the statue on the right broke away from the ground, ripping out a huge chunk of masonry as it toppled forward. Massive fortress stones and crenelations crashed down all around us. There was no point in trying to dodge them. All we could do was ride hard and pray.

Shanti thundered into the vaulted passage of the gatehouse with the rest of the group hot on our heels. The drumming of a score of hooves against the paving stones echoed the death cry of the city behind us. The gatehouse was coming apart all around us. We weren't going to make it.

Then a blast of fresh air and sunshine swept over me, and we were clear. A deafening roar shook the ground as a cloud of dirt and chips of stone swirled around us. The road from the gatehouse wound up into the hills, and I kept riding hard for another hundred yards before I gradually drew Shanti down to a walk. Her chest heaved and her legs shook as I leaned down to pat her neck.

"I'll stuff your feedbag with all the fresh grass you can eat as soon as we make camp," I promised.

Alleron slid to the ground to give the poor girl a proper rest, and I followed after him. A quick head count confirmed that everyone had made it through safely. Dirt-smeared and exhausted, perhaps, but alive. I shook my head at our crazy luck, and looked back at the city that had nearly added us to its tally of victims more times in the past two days than I cared to count.

The Shattered City was gone. All that remained was an endless field of wreckage and ruin scattered throughout an enormous crater. I doubted I could have found one stone standing atop another if I'd gone back in to look, and I also doubted that there was enough gold in the world to compel me to try.

"A fitting tomb for the fallen," Nataka said as she bowed her head to the earth. "May they find the rest they deserve."

I thought of the elven girl, and Garradin the guard captain, and bowed my head along with her. I hoped they would find more peace tomorrow than they'd known in a long while. Then I raised my head and found Sheska grinning at me like a fool. I grinned right back.

We'd actually done it. We'd entered the Shattered City and escaped with our lives and the crown. Somehow a few weeks of trail rations and sleeping under the stars didn't seem quite so bad anymore.

"Damn it all to Scarrag's gaping maw," Magnus swore as he spat on the ground.

"What now?"

He raised a hand and pointed to the mountain peaks in answer. It took me a moment to understand what he was getting at. Then it hit me. The horizon was filled with a dense tangle of peaks, valleys, sheer cliffs and ridge lines. There were no obvious paths or valleys as far as I could see in either direction, and the tangled wreckage of the city was just as bad.

"It will take us weeks to make our way through that," Sheska said. Her grin had faded into a cold and weary frown.

"But it already took us a full five weeks just to ride from Farshore to the southern edge of the range," I said.

"Aye," Magnus sighed, "that it did."

The reality of our situation punched me in the gut. We had the crown and we'd escaped with our lives, but there was no way on earth or in the hells below that we would make it back to Farshore in time to meet Trebonious' damned deadline. Which meant that even after all we'd been through, we had just died.

"I'll see about getting a fire started," Magnus said as he headed towards a clearing in the trees.

"You're pitching camp?" I asked in disbelief.

"Aye lass, I'm pitching camp," he called over his shoulder. "I'm tired, I'm sore, I'm hungry, and no amount of wailing and crying is going to carry us over those peaks today. Now make your skinny ass useful and pitch the tents."

Cael gathered our half-empty water skins and went in search of place to refill them while Nataka unsaddled the horses, Alleron unpacked some dry rations, and Sheska slung her bow over her shoulder to slip off into the woods. Everyone dragged their feet as they went about their tasks. I shook my head, then went to unpack the tents and bedrolls for lack of anything better to do.

As I rummaged through my pack the peak of Tyrial's crown glinted in the morning light, and for a moment I thought I heard an echo of the mad king's laughter in the mountain air.

The adventure continues in *Crown Of The Mad King*,
the next installment in the Farshore Chronicles

CROWN OF THE MAD KING

FARSHORE CHRONICLES BOOK 3

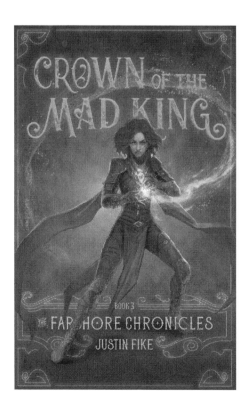

JOURNAL ENTRY

The Farshore Chronicles
From the quill of Charity The Godslayer
Penned by her own hand this 1576th year of Jovian's Wise Rule

We had won.

Against all odds, my friends and I had made our way to the heart of the Shattered City and undone the lingering effects of Tyrial's folly, saving the tortured souls of its lost citizens and escaping with our lives and our shining prize in hand. Three cheers and victory toasts all around.

Or so we thought…

Turns out our narrow escape from the city's destruction had left us on the wrong side of some very imposing mountains with no way of crossing them and returning home in time to meet Trebonious' impending deadline. With no way to get a message to him, it was only a matter of time before the skinny bastard decided we'd cut out on him and used our effigies to send a swift and gruesome death our way.

I'm not big on just lying down to wait for impending doom to catch up with me, but sometimes I wonder if it might have been better for everyone if we'd done exactly that. Because we weren't the only ones who'd just escaped from the Shattered City, and as I would soon learn, evil doesn't like to go back into its cage once you let the latch slip...

1

"It cannot be done!" Nataka shouted at Alleron's back as she pushed her way through the clinging underbrush.

"Of course it can."

The elven wizard didn't bother turning around as he argued. He slipped between clusters of alder bushes, ducked under white pine boughs, and stepped over tangled tree roots like they weren't even there, forcing the rest of us to swear, swipe, and struggle in his wake.

"You ought to have said that it *shouldn't* be done. Then I might have agreed with you, even though we have no real choice in the matter."

They'd been having the same argument for three days. I'd grown tired of it on the second. Now I was ready to murder them both with my boot knife.

"Will you two please shut it?" A branch that Magnus had pushed aside whipped back into my face. I clawed my way past it in a fit of rage, then spat out a leaf as I tried to regain some measure of calm.

"You've been talking in circles all morning. Give it a rest until we see if we can even find the damned thing, and then you can shout yourselves blue in the face."

I thought I had walked through forests back in Byzantia. I thought we had ridden through several forests on our way to the Shattered City. I was wrong on both counts. This was a forest. Everything else I'd ever seen had just been trees putting on a show.

We wove around tree trunks wider than a country cottage, each one surrounded by an army of clinging brambles, twisted vines, and clusters of ferns that tangled your ankles and tried to drag you to the ground with each step. What little light managed to filter down through the upper foliage was thin and timid, as though it knew that it had only been allowed into the lower reaches of the forest by the will of the great trees, and didn't want to give offense.

I'd never seen anything like it, never imagined that such a dense explosion of vegetation even existed in the world. And the plants weren't its only inhabitants. Birds trilled and called, small shapes darted through the shadows, and more than once I'd heard something large pushing its way through the underbrush just out of sight. I kept my eyes moving, my ears sharp, and my hand on my sword hilt. In my experience there were only two kinds of animals in the world; the ones you can eat, and the ones that can eat you.

Our first morning in the mountains outside the ruins of the Shattered City had been more than a little miserable. Whispers and strange images filled my dreams once I'd finally managed to get some sleep, and I was up before the sun feeling worse than when I'd lain down. I wasn't alone.

Turned out everyone had slept poorly, if at all. Nataka said it was an aftereffect of so many tortured souls being released to the beyond at once. Magnus said it was a gods damned nuisance, and for once I found myself in complete agreement with the surly dwarf. We shared a breakfast of thin porridge and stared at each other over our bowls until Cael finally voiced the question that had been on all of our minds all morning. What in the hells were we going to do now?

Our narrow escape from the Shattered City's death throes had placed us on the wrong side of some very imposing mountains. We were already five weeks into the two month deadline Trebonious had given us before he decided we'd cut out on him and magicked us to death from a thousand miles away. And yes, I checked with Alleron and confirmed that he could absolutely do that if he chose to.

If we'd left the Shattered City's caldera the way we'd gone in, followed the route we'd already plotted to get there, and ridden our horses hard the whole way home we could have made it. Probably. But adding on a week or more to scrabble our way over sheer cliffs and jagged mountain peaks, or through the ruined crater that remained of the Shattered City itself, had made a timely return completely impossible.

I'd begun to think that the only option we had left was to pitch the most comfortable camp we could manage and wait for death when Alleron first suggested we use the city's lost waygate. From the way the others reacted you might have thought he'd suggested we slather ourselves with honey and go running through a den of bears.

Nataka had seemed especially unhappy with the idea of dusting off some ancient elven artifacts, but he'd eventually managed to convince her and the others that searching for the waygate was a better way to spend our time than sitting around waiting for a horrible death. After another round of grumbling, we set off into the forest.

From the answers I managed to pick out of their constant bickering I gathered that the elves had once maintained a sort of arcane travel network that could move men and material across huge distances in an instant. I thought it sounded like exactly the sort of solution we needed, but Nataka and the others kept trying and failing to think of some alternative.

"If we work together we might be able to send the human a message," the orc shaman rumbled as she ducked beneath a thick branch. "Tell him we have the crown and just need more time to return."

"We couldn't manage a sending across that distance if there were ten of us, and you know it."

"What's so bad about giving this waygate a try?" I asked as I squeezed beneath two moss covered logs that had fallen one atop the other. "If it doesn't work we can keep looking for other options, but I certainly don't mind the thought of saving my ass another month in the saddle."

Nataka stopped in front of me and turned around as I clambered to my feet.

"Do you like your arms?" she asked.

"What?" I wondered if perhaps she'd cracked her head on the logs.

"Your arms," she pointed to each one in turn. "Are you fond of them?"

"I...guess so?"

"Perhaps you would prefer them arranged differently? One growing from your head, the other lodged in your stomach? Or perhaps you'd prefer they be removed entirely? Have them carved off and flung to some distant corner of the world? Because those things are entirely possible if we entered that elven death gate, and even worse besides."

"You ever seen a creature turned inside out?" Magnus asked as he squeezed beneath the logs to join us. "I once found a deer back on Skalling that had stumbled through a waygate. Least I think it was a deer. Mostly just a twitching mass of guts and muscle, but it had the right sort of hooves."

I paled a little at the thought.

"Thankfully, we are at least somewhat more capable than woodland fauna." Alleron had stopped his forced march and returned to join the conversation. I hadn't even heard him approach until he started speaking.

"I don't deny that the magic of the waygates became rather…unstable after the Sundering."

Nataka snorted, but Alleron ignored her.

"A good deal of their function was based on chronomancy. Shortening time over distance, that sort of thing. I've always been fascinated by waygates. They were one of the greatest achievements of my people, and I've studied them for decades."

He turned and stared up into Nataka's frown.

"Which is why you should believe me when I say that I can stabilize the gate enough to see us safely to our destination. I just need some time to study its runes first."

"You are all very loud."

Nataka had already opened her mouth to snap a retort, but we all stopped and looked up towards the voice. Sheska was perched on a branch overhead, frowning down at us like a mother owl whose chicks had just scared away dinner.

"I have found the stone arch you described. It is not far, but it is guarded." She directed an accusing glance at Alleron. The rest of us followed her example.

"Ah yes," he cleared his throat as he picked at a bramble that had caught in his sleeve. "There is another reason folk tend to avoid the waygates. Their guardians have all gone a bit…feral over the years."

"And just when did you plan on telling the rest of us?" Cael did not look amused.

"Once we'd found the waygate, of course. I'm sure it won't present too much of a problem. We don't even need to defeat it after all. You lot can just keep it busy until I've prepared the gate, and then we'll be off."

I was about to ask for a few more details about this guardian we would be 'keeping busy', but Alleron had already resumed his trek through the forest, following Sheska's guidance as she leapt from branch to branch overhead.

"The sooner we begin the sooner we're finished," he called cheerily over his shoulder.

"Oh, someone will be finished, all right," Magnus grumbled as he smacked fist to palm. I sighed, enjoying one last breath while standing still for a change, and we were off.

After several long minutes of slow and sweaty struggling through the foliage, I had grown so focused on planting one foot in front of the other that I almost stumbled right into the clearing. Nataka caught my shoulder before I broke through the treeline and pointed ahead of us.

The forest just stopped. We stood within the same impossible tangle of greenery that we'd been forging through all day, but an arm's length in front of me was a perfect circle of grass and glowing afternoon sunlight. The only things within the clearing were a slender stone archway and a single, massive oak tree looming over it. Alleron was already walking towards the stone arch.

The rest of us followed after him, though I'll admit I would have preferred to keep to the shadows until I'd spotted the guardian Sheska mentioned. I still didn't see anything other than the tree and the arch. The waygate was an interesting sight, at least. Two slender columns of white marble rose to a pointed arch, and both were covered in spiraling patterns of gold embossed into the stone. You could see through and around it quite easily, just more grass and a bloody great tree trunk on the other side, yet as we walked closer I felt the small hairs on my neck and arms begin to prickle.

Alleron knelt in the grass beside the right hand column and began to trace his fingers over the runes.

"When the guardian awakens just keep it occupied until I'm finished. Shouldn't take long."

"You keep talking about a guardian." Magnus had carried Hilda at the ready when we entered the clearing, but now he rested the axe blade on the ground and leaned on the shaft. "But all I see is you and that big tr—"

A branch swept down and swatted Magnus into the air. He crashed back to earth several yards away, bounced a few times, and lay still. I turned and looked up along the branch that had struck him to find two enormous eyes staring down at me. I blinked, and the tree blinked back. Then a ragged crack spread across the trunk. The crack widened into a yawning mouth, then the tree let out a booming roar that shook the forest and rattled the teeth in my skull.

"The guardian is a *treant!?*" Nataka sounded more offended than angry as she ran towards our fallen dwarf. Motes of golden light began to flicker in the air around her, growing brighter with each step. As she reached Magnus and placed a hand on his back all the light flowed down into him, turning him into a dwarf-shaped lantern for a brief moment before fading away.

Nothing happened. Then Magnus bolted upright and shook his head like a dog climbing out of a lake. The dwarf's mood only seemed to vary between annoyed and enraged, but I breathed a small sigh of relief to see him moving again all the same, then turned back to the tree. Cael stood over Alleron, turning aside sweeping branches with his shield as the elf continued to study the runes.

"Don't worry," Cael yelled over his shoulder at the rest of us, "I can hold back an enormous tree all by myself. Oof!" A heavy blow battered him down on one knee. "But I wouldn't mind some help all the same."

"Hey!" I screamed at the oak as I charged forward to lend a hand. How did one distract a living tree?

"I'll bet your mother never even knew your father, you big leafy bastard."

The tree turned towards me. Well, it didn't actually turn, as such, but the eyes and mouth slid around the trunk to look at me. And yes, it was exactly as disturbing as it sounds. I had no idea if it was the sound of my voice or the sting of my insult that had caught it's attention, but it wasn't beating on Cael anymore, so I decided to keep at it.

"That's right, she pollinated with every pine shrub and scrap of ragweed within a hundred miles before you dropped out of her branches, you sorry stack of kindling."

Tree limbs began to smash the ground all around me. I leapt to the right, then rolled to the left, barely managing to keep one step ahead of the assault. Then two leafy branches slammed down on either side of me, trapping me between them. I looked up into the treant's angry eyes, then up further still to see a third branch rising into the air above my head.

An arrow zipped past my ear just before the tree crushed me into a bloody smear on the grass. It struck the center of one of the treant's eyes, followed a split second later by a second shaft that buried itself in the other one. The creature roared and covered its face with its branches, leaving an opening for me to run clear. As I scrambled back out of the treant's reach I saw Sheska running towards me with another arrow already nocked on her bowstring.

I gave her a grateful nod, then turned back to face the tree. As its branches parted I saw that its eyes had shifted further up the trunk, but that otherwise it appeared unharmed. I sighed and took a few more quick breaths as I readied myself to draw its attention again. Then I noticed my shadow grow long across the ground as an orange light flared behind me. I turned and saw Nataka wreathed in flames. I started to run towards her to try and help, then saw that she stood calm and unconcerned within the fire.

"Keski of the Burning Hunger, wreathe our blades!" She shouted as she flung her arms out wide. A ball of fire flew towards each of us.

I yelped and dove to the ground, but the fire tracked my movements. I squeezed my eyes shut as it swept down on me, then peeked one eye open a moment later when I realized that I wasn't actually being consumed by horrible, burning death. I looked up and saw that the tip of Sheska's arrow danced with angry flames. Nataka's spear and Magnus' axe both blazed like logs in a winter hearth. I stood to my feet and drew my twin sabers to find fire racing along both blades.

Now we're getting somewhere. I couldn't stop a wicked grin from spreading across my face. Sheska's smile matched mine as she drew back her bowstring and loosed a burning arrow at the tree.

"No!"

I spun round at the panicked shout to see Alleron waving his arms as he stared in horror at the fiery missile. The shaft struck the treant with a burst of fire that left a long black scorch mark on its trunk. The tree screamed. It was a scream of pain at first, the cry of a dry pine log tossed onto a bonfire. Then the scream turned angry. The ground began to shake as the treant raged, then thick and tangled roots began to tear themselves from the earth. The treant gave one final heave, then its newly-freed roots snaked across the grass as it began to lumber towards us.

"What were you thinking? You just woke it up!" Alleron screamed.

I stared in horror at the enormous and very angry tree bearing down on me. I thought I'd grown more accustomed to the wild and impossible sights that filled an ordinary day here in Danan, but there were apparently some things that my brain still struggled to accept. My jaw dropped open and my legs froze solid. Then something slammed into me from behind, knocking me into a tumbling sprawl just as the tree crashed through the space where I'd stood gaping like an idiot a moment before.

"Stop gawking and run!" Sheska climbed off of me and took off at a sprint. Thankfully, she'd managed to knock some sense back into me, and I scrambled to my feet to chase after her just as a tree branch smashed the ground behind me.

I risked a glance over my shoulder. The whole clearing was in chaos. The treant charged about like an angry bull, its limbs whipping the air and smashing the earth in a storm of leafy death. Cael, Magnus, and Nataka were doing an excellent job of dividing its attention, but the smallest mistake would leave one of them a broken corpse on the forest floor faster than you could blink.

I skidded to a halt next to Alleron. The elf muttered to himself as he studied the runes on the left hand column of the stone arch.

"Any chance you could get this thing working before nightfall?"

"I'm trying," he said without turning around, "but your not-so-bright human colonist ancestors built their city directly over the region's waygate."

I was in no mood for arcane nuance.

"What does that mean in plain speak, Alleron?"

"It means that if I activate the portal without adjusting the terminal point first it will tear whatever is nearby into tiny pieces. Oh, and our oaken friend over there might step through and rampage through the ruins a bit. But if you'd rather I cut a few corners…" His voice strained as though he struggled to lift a heavy weight, and I noticed sweat trickling down his forehead. I sighed, and gave his shoulder a reassuring squeeze.

"No, you're doing great. Just try to hurry."

I tightened my grip on my swords, then ran to help my friends.

I dove over a tangle of roots and slashed down at them as I flew through the air. The treant had been about to crush Nataka like an insect, but my stinging cut drew its attention. As I landed in a crouch its roots lashed around my ankles and held me in place as it turned its rage and its very heavy branches on me. I tried to pivot around to cut through the tangle that held me in place, but the angle sapped all the force from my blow. Then a flaming axe blade scythed through the air an inch from my nose and severed the roots in a single chop. I dove clear just as a branch left a dent in the ground where I'd stood, then looked up to see that Magnus had done the same.

We harried the huge tree like pups nipping at a mastiff's heels. Arrows, spear, greateaxe, longsword, and sabers all nicked and teased at it, dividing its attention just enough to keep it from ripping any of us into pieces, but we were playing a dangerous game. Seconds dragged into minutes, then minutes became a whole lifetime. Sweat ran down my neck and stung at my eyes, and my limbs felt like I'd just run ten miles through mud.

You want to lend a hand here? I asked Sapphery. Or I tried to anyway. The elven queen whose spirit had claimed a corner of my mind as her own back in the Shattered City had been silent ever since she'd saved my life and helped me defeat Tyrial. I'd been more than happy to leave it that way until now, but the looming possibility of death left me desperate enough to ask for her help. She didn't answer me, but I got the very distinct impression that the grand and glorious queen was sulking like a five year old girl.

What ever happened to "if you die, I die with you?"

I had never heard an exasperated sigh in my mind before, but I recognized the sound immediately.

Now that we're out of the mirror realm I'll simply return to my prison within the necklace if you die.

How nice for you.

You could still run. The guardian will not follow you beyond the clearing.

I clenched my jaw and shook my head as I leaped over a swiping tree branch.

I won't just abandon my friends.

Then Sorellian save you, for I will not. I may be trapped in the mind of a fool, but I'll not be used by one.

She said nothing more. I was on my own. I was amazed we'd managed to survive as long as we had, but I knew we couldn't keep it up much longer.

"I've got it!"

Alleron's excited voice rang through the clearing. I turned and saw that the stone arch now cracked and snapped with sparks of energy, and the space within the arch shimmered with the image of somewhere else all together. I started running, then my thoughts caught up with me and I glanced back to make sure my friends had heard Alleron's call. They were right on my heels.

Cael batted smaller branches away with his shield while Magnus swept the larger roots aside with huge swipes of his axe. Sheska bounded through the air like an addict who'd just eaten an entire bag of Crimson Snow, leaping and twirling over anything in her path, while Nataka gestured with her spear to raise great blasts of earth and rock into the air to block the treant's attacks.

We all ran as though Magren's own horde was at our backs. The enraged wooden monstrosity trying its best to turn us all into fertilizer made for rather effective motivation. I turned, put my head down, and focused on forcing my exhausted body to put one foot in front of the other.

Cael charged past me as we closed in on the portal. I had no idea how the big man moved so fast given that he'd been fighting just as long and hard as I had wearing thirty pounds more gear. I kind of hated him for it.

"It was Callendin's Fourth Precept!" Alleron shouted with delight as we charged down on him. "Terribly clever of me, if I do say so. Once I applied that to the vector path I was able to shift the terminus without—" His words trailed off in a yelp of surprise as Cael grabbed the elf in a bear hug and dove through the portal without missing a step. Sheska passed me on my left and leapt in after them, disappearing in a flash of light. As I closed in on the waygate I saw the red and gold flags of Farshore city waving above tall wooden walls and clustered rooftops.

The portal seemed to look down on the city from some distance away. The scene warped and rippled like agitated water, and something about the cracking bolts of energy that leapt off the archway gave me pause, but I didn't have time to think about it. I covered the last few steps in an exhausted stumble and flung myself into the waygate.

2

I've long since lost count of all the strange and unusual things I've seen in Danan over the years, but to this day I still don't think anything quite compares to traveling through a waygate.

We made the entire trip back to Farshore on foot. We scaled sheer mountain cliffs, forded rivers, and camped without fires to stay hidden from the dangers of the open wilderness. We stared up at the endless expanse of the stars each night, and filled the silence of long days with small truths and stories from our pasts. We fought off a pack of wolves the size of horses whose eyes glowed green in the firelight. We crouched in the shelter of a fallen log as a pair of enormous rock trolls lumbered past.

We grew closer. Magnus even started calling me Charity when he wasn't paying attention, instead of "the human girl" or "stick legs". After weeks of weary hiking and countless footsore miles we crested the rise of a hill and saw Farshore filling up the valley below us as a fresh ocean breeze cooled our skin.

And at the same time we were swept away by a raging river of white light. We spun, tumbled, and floundered at impossible speeds through air and between trees, until I lost all sense of orientation or direction. There was no up or down, only the endless rush of speed that carried us forward.

Both experiences were true, just as neither one was real. Have you ever stood with something just at the edge of your vision, so that even after you turn your head its blurry outline still makes itself known? Now imagine if that sensation assaulted you from both sides so that no matter which one you looked at you were still half-seeing the other. Traveling through the waygate was something like that, and also nothing like that, but it's the closest I can get to a proper description.

I soon gave up trying to observe both realities and just focused my attention on our careening trip down the river of light. Of the two realities it was by far the most dangerous. Sure, our slow journey had trolls and such to contend with, but the force and speed that bore me forward without pause threatened to undo me at every turn. Every time we were jolted into the sky or flung round a bend I came out the other side a little bit wrong. Fingers in the wrong place, head facing backwards, and much, much worse. It took all of my focus and concentration to will myself back into the proper configuration. Reminding myself of who I was and what I looked like grew harder each time.

Keeping myself together was difficult enough, but we also had to fight to keep the group together at the same time. It felt like the racing light never slowed or wavered, but we all seemed to move at different speeds none the less. We swept down a cliff, and by the time we reached the bottom Nataka was a mile ahead of us. She strained backwards, and managed to slow herself just enough for Magnus to reach her with Hilda's axe shaft and pull her back to the group. We sped through a pine forest, the light tossing us about like a dog with a scrap of meat as it threaded us between the trees. Alleron was flung out around a large boulder and would have continued sailing away from us if Cael hadn't lunged forward and caught him by the ankle.

The worst moments came when we reached branches in the river. Every so often the flow would split in several directions, with other ribbons of light stretching off towards distant horizons. The momentum that carried us forward seemed to know which course to set us on, but there was always an undercurrent of force pulling us towards those other branches. Thankfully, those nexus points were bright enough that we could usually see them coming and cling to one other as we passed through.

For all of our speed I felt as though ten lifetimes had passed since I stepped through the waygate, and I hated every one of them. I was sick to my stomach the entire time, but every time I thought I might empty my guts they shifted to a new place in or on my body. Nothing about our passage through this split reality made any sense, and I felt the fabric of my mind fray a little more with each passing second.

In the few stretches of relative calm I was able to shift my awareness back to the long journey we were also undertaking to try to stay grounded in something I could understand. Cael made the mistake of mentioning that their clan bard had chosen him to receive vocal training as a boy. After two days of heckling he finally agreed to sing a song of his homeland for us. I didn't understand the words, but the haunting sorrow in his voice squeezed water from more eyes than mine.

One night when everyone else lay sleeping Sheska told me a secret she'd never shared with another soul before, but to this day I still can't remember what it was.

Then I caught sight of the endless ocean in the distance. At first it was little more than a strip of blue peeking over the blurred green of grass, trees, and hills, but it spread larger and wider as we rushed towards it, and I knew that Farshore itself must be growing closer too. I took comfort in the knowledge that the hellish journey would soon be over.

We swept over a hill, swirled through a dry riverbed, and struck another waygate nexus without warning. A stream of light swept off to the north towards a range of distant snow-capped mountains. As we tumbled into the divided current Sheska spun ears over toes into the other stream. In the chaos no one else saw her being pulled away. I dove forward, ignoring everything as I reached for her. My fingers brushed against hers. I grabbed her hand. Then something yanked back hard on my leg and broke my grip. I tried to throw myself forward again, but she was already gone.

I turned to find Alleron's hand clamped round my ankle, and his grinning face not far behind. Then we arrived at our destination.

Whenever I try to think back on our trip through the waygate I end up with a headache and a tangle of vague memories. I remember running towards the stone arch with an angry treant smashing the ground to bits behind me. Then I remember standing on a quiet hill looking down on Farshore as birds sang in the trees and sunlight warmed the grass at my feet. Everything in between is nothing but a crash of moments jumbled too close together, with none of the usual space of small daily life to soften and separate them.

I stood dazed and shivering as the ocean breeze toyed with my hair, overwhelmed by an onslaught of memories that were both real and insubstantial in equal measure. Except for one.

"She's gone!" I screamed as I regained command of my voice. Birds took flight and the rest of the group startled at the sudden noise.

"What's…who's gone?" Magnus ground his palms into his eyes like a drunk rousing from a two-day stupor.

"Sheska is gone." My feet must have sorted themselves out before my brain, because I was already walking north. Cael caught me by the shoulders.

"Hold on. Dammit Charity, just wait. What happened?"

"She was carried off just before we arrived." I fought to break free, but he held firm. Tears filled my eyes as I shoved at him without much effect.

She'd been afraid. In all the dangers we'd faced so far I'd never seen Sheska anything but grim and resolute, but I'd seen the terror in her eyes in that awful moment when her hand was torn free of mine. She'd needed me, and I'd failed her.

"Don't lose heart," Alleron said as he placed a comforting hand on my shoulder. I swatted it away and turned on him.

"I almost had her! I could have saved her if you hadn't stopped me." All the stomach-churning fear and confusion that had built up inside me during that damned portal ride came pouring out in a fit of shaking rage. "You laugh and smile like nothing matters but Sheska's *gone* and it's your fault!"

Alleron stumbled backward, his eyes wide with shock as I swiped a fist at his face. Nataka grabbed my other arm before I could throw another punch.

"And if he hadn't caught you then you'd both be lost. What good would that have done?"

I strained against her grip with everything I had, though I doubt she even noticed. Then I sagged against her sturdy frame as all the wild strength and fury drained away from me in a sudden rush.

"She's gone," I whispered, my voice a ragged mess. I'd always been alone. I'd worked with partners on occasion, until one of us betrayed the other. I'd found a few handsome faces to warm my bed, until one of us grew tired of the arrangement. The few souls I'd once called friend were long since dead, and I'd never had a face to place beside the word 'family'. Not until a crazy halfling from the far side of the world had called me Ko'koan, "one who shares my breath", and proved that she meant it every day after that in large ways and small. She'd claimed me without warning, and I'd lost her just as suddenly.

"You are too quick to despair." Nataka smoothed my hair as she spoke in the calm, steady tone I'd heard her use when calming a spooked horse. "We know only that she arrived in a different place than we did."

"But you said the waygate could break us." I couldn't help but think of all the dire warnings she'd pronounced as we'd searched for the damned gate in the first place.

"It is possible. But possible does not mean certain. We are whole and well, after all."

"She's right, lass." Magnus said as he patted my knee. The dwarf actually patted my gods' damned knee. It was without a doubt the most tense and awkward thing I'd ever seen him do, but he did it none the less. I couldn't help but smile through my tears.

"The tree rat is made of stronger stuff than you credit her for. She's safe and hale, or I'll eat my own beard."

"I'll get her back, Charity." It took me a moment to recognize Alleron's voice. There was no jest in his words or his eyes. "I swear by Sorellian's summer breath I'll do everything in my power to return her to us safely."

I swallowed hard, rubbed the water from my eyes, and nodded.

"Ok. Let's go find her."

He blinked.

"Well…I didn't mean right this very moment."

"What?"

He scuffed the toe of his boot in the dirt, looking for all the world like a boy who'd just been caught stealing sweets.

"I can divine her location, but it will require time and several components that I don't have with me. And I've no doubt she's farther afield than our remaining supplies will carry us, especially on foot."

"So we just leave her out there on her own in Vesta only knows what condition?" The thought of Sheska lying in the snow with a leg where her head should be was twisting my guts into knots.

"We finish our mission," Cael said as he turned towards Farshore.

"Once we've delivered the crown and you've caught a night's sleep you can buy a whole squadron of horses with your promised reward and ride back out in the morning."

The note of bitterness in his voice caught me up short, until I remembered that while the rest of us had been both bribed and blackmailed into this quest, Cael had simply been ordered to it by his master. We might be returning to a bright future, but he made his way back toward a cage of duty and obligation.

Most men would have wished us well and headed for the hills rather than return to servitude. Cael had revealed next to nothing about himself or his past on our journey together, but I'd come to know him well enough to realize that he valued his honor more than life itself. Which meant that once we marched through Farshore's gates I'd likely never see him again. Now that I thought about it, I didn't know what the others planned to do once we were no longer bound together by the looming threat of death. Somehow I doubted that their plans involved splitting the tab on a house and starting up a six-piece band.

Things were changing, and far too quickly. Just this morning we'd been scrambling and swearing our way through an ancient forest thousands of miles from here. Now we stood just a short walk away from my freedom and the biggest payday I'd ever seen. I should have been ecstatic. Five weeks ago I would have been. Now I just felt tired and empty.

Still, I couldn't argue with Cael's logic. As much as I wanted to race off to Sheska's rescue I knew I wouldn't get far on my own. Once we'd handed Trebonious the crown and collected our reward I'd badger Alleron into finding her for me and then set out before the sun rose. Maybe one of them would even offer to come with me, though I was growing less confident of that by the minute. I nodded, feeling every inch a traitor, and together we started walking towards the city walls.

3

———

"One more step and I pin you to the ground."

A gruff voice broke the morning quiet as we approached Farshore's northern gate. I looked up and saw the grizzled face of a legion veteran wearing a purple-crested centurion's helmet. He was flanked by a dozen men on either side, each one pointing a crossbow down at us.

"Come off it, Callix," Cael called up at him as he shaded his eyes against the sun. "We've dealt with enough shit today, and I'm in no mood to take more of it from you."

"Cael?"

The centurion leaned out over the gate for a better look.

"Magren's tits, it is you! Look at the man come marching out of the woods as bold as Balthas."

"Who did you think it was? Now crack this gate open before I grow a beard."

The centurion shook his head.

"You I know, but you're keeping some strange company. Their kind aren't allowed to walk free outside the mythic quarter right now. There's been some trouble with the locals lately."

I glanced at the others. Magnus scowled and squeezed a fist tight round Hilda's shaft, Nataka stared off towards the trees, and Alleron grinned to himself as always, but they all seemed content to let Cael do the talking for now. The tall warrior sighed and rubbed his temple.

"Look Callix, we're tired, we're hungry, and we've just crossed the continent twice over on a mission for Trebonious. I'll walk them to the arena myself every step of the way, but if you don't open the damned gate you and your men will find yourself without a seat at the games for the next year once I tell the arena master who it was that held us up over a pointless technicality."

Callix opened his mouth to snap a reply, then seemed to think better of it. He frowned, then nodded to the soldier standing next to him. The man disappeared, and a moment later the heavy gate rolled open with a clatter of iron chains and heavy hinges. We walked inside and the gate slammed shut behind us a moment later. Callix emerged from a door in the wall and clasped arms with Cael.

"I'll let you buy me a drink and tell me of your adventures sometime soon."

"It'll take more than one drink, I suspect."

"Fine by me. Just keep a leash on the mythics. Anything happens while they're walking the city and it'll be on both our heads."

Cael frowned beneath his mustache, but nodded once before turning to lead us into the city.

I took in my first good look at Farshore as we walked. When I'd first arrived my only view of the city had been what the prison wagon's route to the temple had allowed for. I realized now that it was both larger and more populated than I'd initially given it credit for. We skirted around a market square so full of shoppers, hawkers, jugglers, and criers that I doubted we could have squeezed in among them even if we had been welcomed with open arms. We clearly were not. Everyone we passed shot wary or disapproving glances our way, and I saw more than a few hands drop protectively over a coin purse as we walked past.

Farshore's main streets were well paved with cobblestone, and some even boasted of stone gutters to carry the waste off to neighborhood cisterns. Houses and shops of three and even four stories lined the narrow lanes, offering shade from the sun and colorful signs to divert the eye and lure prospective buyers through their open doors. Most were set with windows of real glass that sparkled in the sunlight. Mothers hung laundry from windows and balconies, fathers stood on street corners exchanging gossip disguised as news of importance, and children chased balls, stray dogs, and one another through horses' legs and dirt alleyways.

It was strange to walk through a city after so many days and nights spent in the empty wilderness. I'd never noticed the constant rush, crash, and jostle of city life before. The cries and clamor of a city's streets had filled my ears every waking moment of my life until the day I'd ridden out through Farshore's gates to spend a month and more beneath the open sky. Now I found myself flinching at each shriek and startling back from every new shape that loomed up at the edge of my vision.

The streets and buildings we passed were in far better repair than I was used to. Then I remembered that they had all been recently built, at least by Byzantian standards. Back home every wall and paving stone rested atop the ruins of whatever had come before it. Buildings endured the wear of centuries until they finally collapsed or burned down, making way for new construction like old growth in a forest. But everything in Farshore had been built to plan at once, and the result was a city marked more by the scent of fresh mortar and uncured wood than the cracks and dust of neglect.

The streets Cael chose followed a gentle downward slope towards the sea. After almost thirty minutes of walking I noticed that the condition of the surrounding buildings had begun to decline along with the hill. These streets had no gutters, leaving their houses' waste to make its own way downhill. Glass windows had long since given way to wooden lattice and heavy shutters with iron bolts on the inside to lock them tight for the night. Shop signs were faded where they hung at all, and most of those who lingered on street corners held out a cup as we passed by. I didn't need two eyes to see that we had entered the outskirts of Farshore's slums.

I was a bit surprised to find the familiar sights and smells of a rougher part of town here in a colonial city, but I realized that I shouldn't have expected anything less. Every city has one, just like every body has an ass crack, no matter how beautiful the rest of it might be. Put enough people together and the ones who made the rules would always find ways to crowd those who were too poor to protest into the smallest possible space to keep their noise, stink, and problems contained and out of sight.

Then the street we followed ended in a brick wall.

Not the pleasant, red brick and white mortar kind either. These bricks were the dull brown of baked mud left slick by rain and wind. It rose high enough in the air that I could barely make out the gray shingles of the houses on the far side. Our street took a sharp dog leg to the left to travel along the wall. After a few blocks we came to the narrow gate that marked the entrance to the mythic quarter.

Now that I saw it again I remembered the place from my first ride through Farshore's streets. Not much had changed. Four guards sat together by the gate, lounging on folding stools as they passed a bottle idly between them. Just inside the gate the rough cobblestones gave way to hard-packed dirt lanes marked with holes and puddles of standing water. The buildings within were different as well. While the rest of Farshore could easily have passed for a Byzantian neighborhood, the structures of the mythic quarter were about as different from one another as buildings could be.

Some were rough domes of mud and straw with feathers, painted stones, and sun-bleached bones set into the walls in intricate patterns. Others were graceful homes crafted from smooth-planed wood and decorated with trellises for climbing ivy and morning bell. Still more were sturdy cottages of stone and heavy timber, and so on. Small clusters of similar buildings huddled together all along the street, marking each block as the domain of one race or another, and I imagined the same was true further in.

Mythics walked the streets, of course. I didn't see a single human amongst them, but I recognized far more of the creatures than I had the first time I'd glanced inside. Orcs and elves were the most common, but I saw a fair number of dwarves walking in groups of three or four. Halflings too, staring with wide eyes at the stone buildings as the rest of the passers by took a few extra steps to give them a wide berth.

There were other creatures as well. A few short folk who looked somewhat like halflings, if halflings stood even shorter, wore fine clothes, and cast nervous glances all around them as they walked. There were birds, too. Not the normal kind. These stood well over six feet tall and walked on two legs with their colorful feathers draped around them like cloaks. I saw a man-sized black cat haggling with a creature that could only be described as a fish out of water over the price of his mackerel. I saw a group of brawny lizards squatting by a wall, tossing dice and hissing at one another as they basked in the afternoon sun.

And the strangest part of all was that none of it seemed all that strange to me anymore. My whole life I'd seen nothing but human faces in the streets and heard nothing but human voices in my ears. Staring into the mythic quarter was like gazing into a dream, but where it had once been little more than a horrible nightmare, I now felt a small thrill of delight and surprise at each new discovery. The ancient heroes, Caius, Quintus, Aelia and the rest, had channeled the divines' might in a great war to rid our land of magic and monsters. The legends said they had saved us all. Now I was beginning to wonder.

"Like watching sheep in a pen." Magnus spat on the ground and stormed off down the street without waiting to see if we followed.

"The centurion said that the other races aren't allowed to walk free in the city anymore," I huffed as I pushed to catch up with him. "Something about trouble with the locals?"

"Bah! You humans always find a way to blame your troubles on the rest of us."

"It's not as though some of us haven't given them reason to be cautious," Nataka said as she cast a sideways glance at the angry dwarf.

"You bust up one flimsy tavern hall and they treat you like a damned criminal," Magnus grumbled into his beard. "In Joskavar it's not breakfast time until someone smashes a few tables first."

"And that's the problem, isn't it?" Nataka stared at the ground as she walked, her voice thoughtful. "We all come here with our own laws and customs, and every one of them is new and frightening for the humans. Perhaps locking the problem away behind a wall is an understandable way of dealing with that fear, in the end."

Magnus turned on her, his cheeks growing hot and his hands clenched into fists.

"You approve of them caging us like animals in the mud? You enjoy it when those pale-skinned twigs point and stare and shut their doors as soon as they catch sight of you?"

Nataka's stared down at him in silence for a moment before answering.

"I can seek to understand a thing without approving of it. You should try it sometime."

"Why do you all come here?" I asked, seeking to redirect the conversation before it ran any further into rough waters. Cael caught my intent and offered an answer as he started us walking again.

"At first most came to trade. You might have noticed that the natives of Danan don't always get on so well together."

"So I've gathered," I said while keeping my eyes fixed straight ahead.

"The Imperial Consortium is always hungry for goods of all kinds, and doesn't much care who provides them so long as the price is right. Before long the native races figured out that Farshore makes for rather good neutral ground. They can meet here to exchange news, mend fences, and secure new arrangements more easily than if one group had to go into the other's land. Puts everyone on equal footing."

"That's how it began, but your city has become more than just a place of meeting," Nataka said behind me.

"How so?"

"Among my people the signs on the day of your birth set your life path before your first night has fallen." She pointed at Alleron walking beside her.

"The elves care only for how far back you can prove your family's blood flows, and who it flows from."

"It's really quite tedious, but what can one do?" Alleron said with a shrug.

"In Magnus' beloved Joskavar those who are not born to the warrior caste do little more than serve, farm, or craft for their betters, and those who are must prove their worth anew in blood and plunder every year or be forever shamed."

"You say that like it's a bad thing," Magnus sniffed. Nataka ignored him as she looked up at the houses all around us and shook her head.

"But here in this place a person's future is what they make of it, no more and no less. It is a strange truth, but it holds appeal for those who find the expectations and traditions of their homeland too…confining."

Something in her voice told me that she spoke from experience.

"In the colony's early years the governor offered free land to anyone who wanted to build on it, human or not," Cael said, picking up where Nataka had trailed off as we turned up a new street that led back uphill and away from the mythic quarter's walls.

"Aye, except he forgot to mention how that wonderful free land sat in your city's armpit and we'd not be allowed to leave it. Understandable or not, it won't be long until that wall brews up some real trouble, mark my words."

We walked on for several more blocks. Then I spotted the familiar sight of the arena's wall peeking up behind the rooftops ahead of us. We turned a corner, and found ourselves in the plaza that ringed the building. Cael led us around the curve of the wall, and I soon found myself standing before the entrance to the arena pits once again.

The face of the man who stood guard by the door lit with surprise as he caught sight of our group marching towards him.

"Cael! Damn, man, but it's good to see you in one piece. And I'm not just saying that because now Davin owes me two silvers."

"That much? I'm hurt that he had so little faith in me," Cael chuckled as they clasped hands.

"Master Trebonious told us to expect you back, but not for another three weeks at least."

"We made good time. Is he here? He'll want to see us right away."

"Course he is. He's barely left his office since you set off."

The man unlocked the door, swung it open, and gestured us inside. The sloping ramp was just as dark and ominous as last time. I may have been on my way to a full pardon, but I couldn't help but feel as if the freedom I'd come to enjoy since we'd first set out slipped away as the heavy door closed behind us.

4

"Enter."

Trebonious' thin voice beckoned us into his office. Cael pushed the door open and led us inside. Little had changed. The shelves were still stuffed with trinkets and oddities, logs still blazed in the hearth, and Trebonious himself still sat in the large chair behind his desk, looking for all the world like a very small spider in an oversized web.

This time, however, I realized how much the room resembled Tyrial's *alteriam* in miniature now that I'd seen the original in person. The bookshelves spaced along the wall mirrored the stone pillars in the elven king's sanctum, and the table covered in ritual components provided the same focal point.

"Ah, my champions have returned." The arena master beamed at us from behind his desk. "And in far less time than expected, no less. Your efficiency is most commendable."

As my eyes fully adjusted to the light I realized that one thing had indeed changed in the office since I'd stood there last. It was filthy. Dirty plates with moldy crusts and scraps were stacked in the corners next to rumpled piles of discarded clothing, and the faint scent of unwashed crazy lingered in the air. Trebonious frowned as he looked over our group a second time.

"But were there not six of you when you set out?"

"Sheska was...lost," I said around a sudden squeeze in my throat. No need to give him any more details than necessary, especially as I caught sight of the box that still held our effigies resting on the desk beside his hand. The less he knew of us, and the sooner we were free of this room, the better.

"I am saddened to hear it. But I assume her sacrifice was not in vain?"

I caught his meaning and slipped my pack to the floor to open it.

"Yeah, we have the crown. It's right…"

Tyrial's crown was gone.

I'd secured it on the top of my pack this morning. Had it fallen out somehow during our trip through the waygate?

"It's right here."

I looked up to see Alleron place Tyrial's crown on the desk in front of Trebonious. The man's eyes shone with a fierce and eager delight.

"It's more beautiful than I'd imagined," he whispered, then smiled up at Alleron.

"My friend, I confess I've had my doubts about you ever since you approached me with your proposal. Clearly I owe you an apology."

"Alleron, what is he talking about?" I asked, my heart in my throat. Alleron didn't answer. He didn't even turn around to look at me. Everything about this felt wrong.

"Hasn't he told you?" Trebonious turned his smile on me, clearly enjoying the moment. "How do you think I knew of Tyrial's crown in the first place?"

Alleron finally turned around. I saw pain in his eyes, but his face was grim and set.

"I'm sorry, Charity. Truly. But I knew I couldn't retrieve the crown on my own. My people need a—" he caught himself short, swallowed, then continued. "A reminder of their past if they're to have any hope of a future. Their need is greater than any one of us alone."

"Whatever helps you sleep." I stood to my feet, feeling a sudden chill despite the clinging heat of the fireplace, and began to back towards the door.

"But since you've got your treasure I think the rest of us will just be going now."

"Oh, I'm afraid not."

Trebonious stood to his feet and rang a small silver bell on his desk. Four arena guards carrying iron-banded clubs swept into the room and blocked the door.

"It will take me some time to fully unlock the power of this artifact, and I can't risk word of it reaching the wrong ears before I do. Restrain them."

The guards moved in pairs to flank Magnus and Nataka. The dwarf snarled and reached for his axe, but one club bashed his arm aside as another bounced off his skull, leaving him dazed but still standing. Nataka growled, but didn't fight back as the guards closed in on her.

"Cael, lend a hand, would you?" Trebonious said without looking up from the crown. Cael didn't move, his face filled with surprise and dismay. When he realized that his command had no effect Trebonious looked up and frowned.

"I meant now, fool, not next week."

"Master, I...this is wrong." Cael said through clenched teeth. Trebonious' frown deepened into a full scowl.

"You would defy me in this? Now, of all times? Need I remind you of your oath?"

All the color drained from Cael's cheeks, but he turned and gripped my arm without further protest, his eyes on the floor.

"Better," Trebonious said as his smile returned. "However, I suppose I am being rather unfair. I should at least allow you to stay and witness the fruits of your efforts."

He turned to Alleron and nodded.

"I have studied and practiced as you instructed since the moment you left the city, but I had expected several more weeks to prepare."

"I'm certain you are more than ready. Place Tyrial's crown upon your head and all of his considerable power will be yours to command."

Stop him!

Sapphery's voice rang in my mind as Trebonious lifted the crown over-head. I remembered what had happened to me when I first put on her neck-lace, and everything fell into place.

"Wait!"

"I've waited long enough."

The arena master placed the crown on his head.

Trebonious' eyes went wide. Then they went white. His pupils disap-peared as an emerald green light beamed from his nose, ears, and mouth. He stood frozen in a silent scream for a long moment. Then the light faded away and he blinked like a newborn babe. His eyes were a cruel and piercing green. They had been brown a moment before.

Alleron dropped to one knee.

"*Sa sanien lores, Tyrial'tai.*"

Trebonious stretched like a cat rousing from a long nap, then looked at me and bared his teeth in a wicked grin.

"Why hello again, little girl. How nice to see you in the flesh this time."

We have to go! I'd never heard Sapphery's voice so full of panic. *He'll sense my presence any moment now.*

Cael stood frozen with shock, and I had no doubt that the other guards were even more surprised, offering us a brief moment of distraction. It was a slim chance, but I knew I wouldn't get a better one. There was just one thing that needed doing before we ran.

I drove my fist into Cael's stomach, pivoting all my weight on my hips just like he'd taught me. The breath flew from his lungs and he dropped to his hands and knees, leaving me a clear path. I jumped over Alleron where he still knelt on the floor, grabbed the box of effigies off the desk, and hurled it into the fireplace.

I'd been thinking that escape would prove rather pointless if we left behind the means for Tyrial to just reach out and murder us whenever he chose. I didn't even know if tossing them in the fire would work, but it was the best I could come up with on short notice. It turns out that a box full of enchanted whatevers does not appreciate being burned to ash.

The hearth exploded in a rolling ball of fire and smoke, slamming Tyrial into the desk and throwing the rest of us to the ground. I rolled to my feet, shook my head to clear the ringing from my ears, and turned for the door.

"Run!" I yelled as I hauled Magnus to his feet and shoved him forward. Nataka was already rising. I helped her up and together we stumbled out into the hall.

I heard Tyrial screaming in Trebonious' shrill voice for the idiots to get up and go after us, but I wasn't waiting around to find out how long that would take. We charged up the sloping ramp towards the surface, then skidded to a halt in front of the locked door. I held up a hand for silence, then rapped my knuckles on the heavy door a few times. I waited until I heard the heavy bolt scrape back, then nodded to Magnus. He threw his considerable weight against the door and smashed it open. A muffled yelp of surprise was cut off with a crunch as the door slammed the guard into the stone wall, and we ran out into the open air.

The sun was down, leaving only a dim orange glow in the sky. Lanterns and firelight shone from windows and spilled from open doors into the darkening street that Nataka and Magnus were already running towards, but the plaza itself was empty. I set off after them.

"Stop!"

I'd only made it a dozen steps when I heard a familiar voice behind me. I kept running. A crossbow bolt ricocheted off the stone in front of me, forcing me to a stumbling halt. I turned around just as Cael finished loading another bolt and aimed it at my chest.

"You missed."

Cael frowned and shook his head.

"Please don't make me do it."

"From where I'm standing no one is making you do a damned thing, Cael."

"You don't understand." He sounded like someone was digging a knife into his heart as he spoke. I knew the feeling.

"You're gods' damned right I don't understand! We traveled together. Fought together. I was starting to think that meant something."

"Of course it does. But—"

"No!" I screamed across the space between us. "You don't get to make excuses. You can either let me go or shoot me where I'm standing, but don't you dare pretend the choice is anything but yours to make."

He didn't move, but I saw that his hands shook on the crossbow's stock. Then he sighed and lowered the weapon.

"They'll come after you. I can't stop that."

"Then come with me," I said as I pointed to the empty street just a few steps away. He took a step forward, then stopped and shook his head.

"I can't."

I couldn't see his face, but his voice was as ragged as broken glass.

"Trebonious is gone, Cael."

"You don't know that. If there's even a slim chance I can help him then I have to try."

I opened my mouth to argue. I'd fought Sapphery off twice, so I knew the stakes of that battle better than anyone. I would have told him every detail if it would have changed his mind, but cries of alarm and the clatter of boots echoed through the door behind him. He spun around to look down the passage, then turned back to me.

"I want to help you Charity, but I can't protect you if you run."

I shook my head, glad that the growing dark hid my face as I fought back tears.

"I don't need a savior, Cael. But I could have used a friend."

I turned and ran before he could respond. I pumped all my pain and anger down into my legs, grateful for something to focus on other than the dull ache in my chest. Cael refused to break free of a dead man's leash, and it seemed that Alleron had never been what I thought he was. Sheska was lost and alone, Magnus and Nataka were nowhere in sight, and the growing cries of "stop her!" and "there she goes!" behind me left me no time to look for them.

I was on my own and on the run, but for the first time since I stepped off the prison ship and into Farshore I finally knew exactly what I was doing.

There's a certain art to a foot chase. It's your wits and speed set against as many guardsmen as they can muster. You set the pace, but if all you do is run they're bound to cut you off or catch you up sooner or later. You have to think faster than your feet and find a way to get out of sight until the heat dies down. Farshore's streets may not have been familiar, but every city follows the same kind of logic in the end.

It was evening now. Most folk would be in their homes, but those without much of a home to go to would be headed to a tavern. I passed up two narrow alleys that felt like dead ends until I found one that felt right. I cut between two houses and out onto another street, and there I saw what I was looking for. A small crowd of young laborers, unwed craftsmen, and the unhappily married shared lit pipes and the day's news on a tavern's covered porch. Its glowing windows framed their silhouettes as they waited for the dinner bell to sound.

Shouts rang in the alley behind me as three men ran into the street further ahead. I raced towards the tavern without looking back, leapt up the porch steps and ignored the chorus of protests as I shoved my way through the crowd and tumbled into the common room. It was warm, well lit, and smaller than I was used to, which meant that even though many of the patrons still waited outside the room was busier than I had expected.

I spotted the door to the kitchens on the other side of the bar, but all the bodies in my path would slow me down too much. Thankfully, however, the serving girl had only just begun to set the tables. I jumped up onto the nearest one, ran down the length of it as men shouted and the poor girl at the other end screamed and dropped the plates she carried with a crash. As I reached the end I jumped over her head, rolled over the bar, and crashed to the floor. The impact knocked the wind out of me, but I gritted my teeth and forced myself to scramble up and into the kitchen.

The room was a mess of shocked faces, woodsmoke, and vegetable peels. I dashed between two women and slid beneath their prepping table as I made for the back door, then burst out into the chill night air again. The tavern backed onto a small yard formed by the tall walls of the adjacent buildings. There was a trash heap in one corner, an outhouse in the other, and no way out.

In short, it was perfect.

I ran across the yard towards the outhouse. I was relieved to see that Farshore's citizens still built their outhouses in Byzantian style, a small wooden structure raised a short distance off the ground on stilts so that some unfortunate soul could muck out the pit when it got too full.

Please don't tell me you're thinking of hiding inside that cesspool.

Better. I'm thinking of hiding underneath it.

I dropped into a slide that carried me boot-first into the shit hole.

I choked, gagged, and forced myself deeper into the filth.

Oh gods, I can smell it! I don't even have a nose and I can smell it! Are you an animal?

Sometimes you just have to be willing to get a little dirtier than the other guy is willing to.

Unacceptable!

I felt my arms move on their own, reaching for solid ground.

What are you doing?

I yanked back my hands as if they'd just touched a hot oven, but my feet began to push me up out of the filth of their own accord.

I'm putting an end to this interminable prison.

You're going to get us both killed!

No, I'm going to get you killed. My necklace will be claimed by someone else, and I'm certain that absolutely anyone would make for a more tolerable vessel than you.

I fought to regain control of my limbs, standing half out of the cesspool as I twitched and jerked like a madman. Then I got smart and forgot about my body to focus on the source of the problem.

The first two times Sapphery had come after me had been focused and vicious. This was different. She was distracted, agitated, and just trying to move my body somewhere more to her liking rather than shredding my soul so she could take over. That left me with a lot more space to think and respond, and in that space I began to wonder if what I was facing now was really all that different from the challenges that Mother Shanti and the other Vestan Sisters used to set in front of me.

To the Vestans knowledge was a weapon, and logic was the hand that wielded it. Cold logic in the face of emotion required strict mental discipline, which they honed through countless hours of meditation and stoic detachment in the face of physical discomfort, or even pain. Mother Shanti once made me hold my hand scant inches above a candle's flame with only the knowledge that the fire would not kill me to shield me from the pain. She switched my back every time I flinched, until I learned to separate myself from the reality of the moment.

As Sapphery tried to push me onto the eager blades of the guardsmen who fought their way through the crowded tavern I closed my eyes and began to wield the lessons I'd sweat and bled for against her. I pictured a thick wall of stone soaring up into the clouds, then placed a small door at its center. I opened the door and focused all my energy on shoving her through it.

What are you doing?

I think you and I could use some time apart.

But you can't just—

I slammed the door shut and locked it tight. The silence that followed was the best sound I'd heard in days. I knew that Sapphery was still there, and would likely find her own way through my mental barrier in time, but at least now I could focus on keeping myself alive. I took a deep breath and pressed myself back down into the muck.

By the time the pursuing guards poured into the yard I was just one more disgusting lump that no one would hazard a first look at, let along a second.

All that was left was to hold very still and breathe as little as possible while I waited to see if Farshore's guards were as lazy as the ones back home.

"Shit," panted a short, thick-set man who was very badly out of breath. "Where'd she go?"

"I saw her run through here, I tell you," said another. "Just spread out and search. She must be hiding somewhere."

The men fanned out across the yard, searched the dark corners, poked at the trash heap, and badgered the fat one into climbing up to look inside the outhouse.

"Not there either," he said around a coughing fit. He moved as far away from the stench as he could get. I might have heaved a sigh of relief if I hadn't been so sure it would kill me on the spot.

"And I don't blame her. Must have gone over the wall somehow."

"Not unless she grew wings."

"Well, she's not here. Come on, let's get back and tell the master we lost them."

"I'll leave that to you. Did you see the look in his eyes? I think he's finally snapped..."

Their bickering voices blended into the general din of the tavern, but I waited another minute to be sure. Once I was confident that they weren't coming back I hauled myself out of the muck and lay gasping on the grass like the most vile and disgusting fish ever caught. I rolled around in the grass to try and clean myself off a little. It didn't help. Finally, I stood to my feet and thought about what to do next.

A few hours ago we'd been on our way to freedom and the biggest payday of my life. Now I was a shit-covered fugitive with no friends, no money, and nowhere to hide. Now that the immediate danger had passed all I wanted to do was sit down on the grass and cry. Well, first bathe for a week, then sit down on the grass and cry. Then my jaw tightened as I remembered the sight of Tyrial's smug smile on Trebonious' face. I didn't care if I had to fight through a hundred guards and flee into the woods naked, there was no way I would give him the satisfaction of seeing me in chains.

I took a careful breath and got my thoughts in order. I needed clean clothes, shelter, and food in that order. Clothes and food I could steal, but finding a place to lay low was more of a challenge. I knew Byzantia's streets from a lifetime of running them, but Farshore was a stranger, and I couldn't afford the time to get to know her better.

Still, as a general rule when you needed to hide from the law the safest bet was to dig yourself a hole in the roughest neighborhood you could find and stay there till they grew tired of looking. Thankfully, I already knew where to find Farshore's local slum. As an added bonus I knew that Magnus and Nataka would be headed there as well. Where else could an orc and a dwarf lay low in the only human city in Danan?

I squared my shoulders and headed for the mythic quarter.

5

I landed on the far side of the wall, slipped, and sprawled face first in a mud puddle the size of a Drangian elephant.

I'd come over the wall in the narrow space between its imposing bulk and a log and mortar building that sat just on the other side. Perfect for keeping out of sight, but the building's shadow had apparently kept the sun from drying out the waterlogged ground for the past fifty years or so, judging by the three-inch deep mess that was currently trying to suck me under.

I pushed up to my knees as I tried to scrape the muck from my eyes. Then I thought about it for a moment, grabbed two big handfuls of the stuff, and smeared it onto the rest of my skin and clothes. I was already a filthy brown mess from head to toe, but at least the mud helped to cover up the stench somewhat. Taking a breath without having to fight off a wave of nausea was a nice change, at least.

You know you're having the wrong kind of day when having mud squelched into your boots, nose, mouth, and hair actually counts as an improvement on your situation. I tried not to think about it too much as I stood to my feet and took a look around.

It hadn't been too hard to find a house built close enough to the wall to provide a makeshift ladder into the mythic quarter while avoiding the gate.

Somehow I didn't think the guards would just bid me a good evening if I tried to walk past them in the state I'd been in. But that meant I'd dropped down in some out of the way corner of an unfamiliar neighborhood, and if the mythic quarter was anything like Byzantia's East End then its residents were more likely to swing first and ask questions later if they caught a mud-caked stranger skulking around their back windows.

It was full dark by now. I didn't see any sign of movement, which meant I could finally stop long enough to catch my breath and think things through. As soon as I did a wave of panic and choking tears threatened to sweep me away.

The day had moved too fast and hit far too hard.

That morning I'd awoken to the smell of Magnus' cooking and a fresh mountain breeze. Alleron and Nataka had starting arguing about searching for the waygate before the porridge cooled. At the time I'd wanted to dump my bowl over their heads. Now I would have gladly turned all the treasure I'd looted from Queen Sapphery's chamber over to the proper authorities to hear their bickering again. If I hadn't been forced to leave it behind when we escaped Trebonious' study, that is.

I growled, shook my head to keep the breakdown at bay, chose a direction at random, and started walking.

Losing five friends in one day had to be some sort of record, even for me. Even as I wove through one narrow alleyway after another I could feel the tight knot of pain and helpless anger twisting in my chest as it waited for a chance to break free. All I wanted was to crawl into a hole and sob for a bit, but I was tired, cold, hungry, and lost in unfamiliar and dangerous territory.

I couldn't afford to slow down until I'd addressed at least three out of those four problems. I locked my feelings and fears about tomorrow away like Mother Shanti had taught me, and focused all my attention on the here and now.

Now that the sun had left the sky the night air had grown chill, and I had a feeling it was going to get colder still. I needed a safe place to get some sleep. Food wouldn't hurt either. All of which meant that first I needed to find some way to clean up a bit, or else I'd just be tossed out of every tavern or hostelry in sight before I took two steps through the front door. I wove my way through back alleys and narrow side lanes until I found what I was looking for.

Every Byzantian city planner worth his salary knows that their first task is to plan an adequate number of well sites within their city's walls. Food could be imported, buildings could be demolished and relocated, but a city without water was worse than useless. Sure enough, after three or four random turnings I found a small plaza with a stone well to one side. It was enclosed on all sides by rear walls of wood and stone.

Two sandstone benches sat beneath the windows of the largest building, a ramshackle three-story with wide eaves and climbing ivy that traced thick patterns up its gray stone walls. Light and raucous tavern noise spilled out of the windows in equal measure. Best of all, a clothes line ran from one of the window sills to a nearby tree, and a few stray garments still hung uncollected. The only other entrance to the square was a short alley on one side of the tavern that led out to a wide street beyond. I waited another minute just to make sure the way was clear, then slipped across the square to the well.

I drew up a bucket, held my breath, and dumped it over my head. I nearly screamed. The water was the kind of angry cold that one usually finds in mountain streams or the deepest pits of the eight hells. I braced myself, then drew up another and scrubbed at the clinging filth as the freezing water dug its fingers into every inch of me. A thousand needles stabbed at my skin, but the mud and shit gave way before the onslaught, leaving me shivering and miserable, but relatively clean. I dropped the bucket back into the well and went in search of drier clothes.

The clothes line held a white cotton shirt, brown trousers, a faded gray scarf, and a pair of socks that would have hung loose even on Magnus' feet. Everything was three sizes too large, but they were also dry, and just then I would have kissed a camel to be dry again. I peeled off everything other than my boots and the enchanted necklace that I couldn't have pried off my neck with a crowbar. I tossed the sodden mess into the bushes, used the enormous socks to towel off, then slipped on the shirt and pants.

I felt like a child playing dress up, but a few quick knots at my sleeves and ankles ensured that everything stayed more or less in place. Then I glanced down and noticed one glaring problem.

Sapphery's necklace glowed in the moonlight, sending wisps of brilliant energy spiraling out from the gemstone. I tried again to lift it over my head, but didn't hold out much hope. Sure enough, every time I thought about removing the damned thing my arms froze in place. It seemed that even from within the mental prison I'd created Sapphery's interference ran deep enough to stop me from getting rid of her that easily.

I sighed, then grabbed the scarf from the line and tied it around my neck. The spring chill wasn't really cold enough to warrant it, but the strange looks I might draw for wearing unseasonable clothing were nothing compared to the ones I'd attract if someone spotted the priceless hunk of white gold and gemstones I was sporting. Given the circumstances keeping the necklace hidden was about the best I could hope for.

Still, some clean clothes did wonders for my disposition, and I crept up to look in the windows feeling almost human again.

The tavern's shutters were closed and bolted against the chill spring air, but I jumped up on one of the benches and found a crack wide enough to peak through. The mess hall glowed with a warm and welcoming light from a fire that blazed away in the large hearth on the far side of the room. The walls were hung with colorful weavings and bunches of dried herbs and flowers, and I could just see the corner of a well-stocked bar to my left.

If the food they served tasted half as good as the scents I smelled then I had no doubt that the place would have become the most popular drink house in the East End within a fortnight if the owners had set up shop in Byzantia. But while the tavern's offerings would no doubt have drawn every dockhand, peddler, and cutpurse within a dozen blocks, its patrons would have sent them screaming back out into the night just as fast.

A trio of orcs slammed fists and mugs on their table in time with the rhythm of the gravel-pitched song they belted out. A half dozen dwarves shouted wagers and insults as two of their number strained and heaved in the throes of an arm-wrestling contest that seemed primed to break into a full-on brawl at any moment. Elves in brown leathers, white linen, and green capes lounged gracefully in chairs about the room as they sipped their drinks, and any number of those small not-quite-halflings I'd spotted earlier sat on benches or stood against the wall as they downed huge mugs of something or other and gestured wildly in a heated debate.

An orc woman in a blue dress came bustling into view carrying a tray of plates and bowls. She deposited them on various tables with practiced efficiency, then turned and marched back towards the kitchen, ignoring the good-natured protests of those who hadn't been served yet. The place was a riot of color, sound, and energy, but I sensed the undercurrent of contained chaos that a born barman always maintained over his common room. In short, the place was everything you wanted a good tavern to be.

The sight of plates loaded with sausage, grilled vegetables, and fresh-baked bread swept away any lingering hesitation that might have kept me from trying my luck inside. I hopped down to the ground and made my way around towards the front of the building. I paused in the shadows and surveyed the street. The same mismatched assortment of buildings lined both sides, but aside from a few dark shapes in the distance the road was empty. A sign hung over the tavern's front door. The ornate brass mug spilling over with white foam made sense, but it sat next to a plate piled high with some kind of lumpy green vegetable that I didn't recognize.

The tavern door stood open and inviting. There was a good chance that walking through it would be the first step to landing my ass back in the arena cells. No doubt the owners would receive some kind of reward for turning me in if they found out I was a fugitive, but after the night I'd been having so far I was ready to take that chance if there was even the slightest hope of a decent meal and a bed to sleep in. The day had been one long string of disasters from the moment we'd stepped through Alleron's damned waygate, but surely that meant I was due for a spot of luck by now. I took a deep breath, then stepped out into the street and headed for the door.

I marched inside and wove through the crowded room as I headed towards the bar. No one noticed me at first. Then I heard the hall behind me grow suddenly quiet as everyone caught sight of the bedraggled human girl pushing through their midst with wet hair, muddy boots, and clothing loose enough to cover two of her. I didn't slow down or look around me as I pressed forward. The only cards I had left in my hand were surprise, confusion, and the lingering stench of the outhouse keeping them at bay, and I played each one to win.

Whoever owned this place was the only one in the room that really mattered. If I could look him in the eye and talk really damned fast I might be able to make a deal before the tavern patrons gathered their wits and tossed me back into the street, or worse. I slipped between two startled elves to claim a space at the bar, then knocked twice on the polished oak to call for service.

The barman came out through the kitchen door. I had to tilt my head back to look up into his face.

I stared up at him in shock as my brain processed what my eyes were seeing. Eventually it decided that I was probably looking at a human man. He stood closer to seven feet than six, his face was hidden beneath a black beard thicker than a dog's winter coat, and his broad chest and shoulders would have put a draft ox to shame, but he seemed to be human all the same. I gaped up at him, my mind blank and my tongue tied in a knot as his bushy eyebrows drew together like twin storm clouds.

"Why you are wearing my shirt?"

His voice was the rumble of distant thunder, but the shock of recognition I felt as I heard his accent jolted me back to the moment. The man was Novari, and suddenly I felt right at home.

"I offer greeting beneath the All-Sky," I said as I reached down and started pulling off my left boot. His eyes went wide as he heard the formal greeting of his people for what I guessed was the first time in years. I'd worked a job with a Novari once. The rest of the crew cut and ran when the watch patrol came back early, but he stayed with me till we were both in the clear. There weren't many of their folk who made the long journey from the frozen north down to Byzantia's sun-drenched streets, but I hadn't met one yet that I didn't end up liking at least a little bit.

The boot clung to my foot with mud-caked determination, but I finally yanked it loose and gave it a good shake. Its contents tumbled out onto the bar. The barman's eyes grew wider still as the gem-studded ring caught the firelight and sent it dancing across the ceiling.

It had raised one hell of a blister on my big toe since I'd stuffed it there back in the elven palace, but it had been well worth it. In the right hands that ring was worth more than enough to buy a round of drinks for the whole room with a bottle of their best booze left over. I looked the Novari straight in his still-startled eyes and gave him my best smile.

"It's yours if you bring me a plate of food, a mug of your best brew, give me a room for the night, and don't ask too many questions."

The man's frown turned into a full-fledged scowl.

"You think to bargain at me with a stolen thing?"

Damn. I'd forgotten that the reason the Novari I'd worked with had been running the streets in the first place was that he'd been cast out by his people for stealing. They have a thing about theft, something about it being worse than a murder because of some twisted bit of logic that only someone who'd never been one crust away from starvation could think up. In my current state even an infant could have told you that the ring wasn't mine.

I shook my head, careful to keep my eyes fixed on his and my voice calm and casual as I answered.

"Not stolen. Recovered. I found it in a ruined city, and believe me I earned every ounce of it coming and going."

The big man's scowl didn't break. I swallowed hard, but held my ground. Then the storm clouds parted as suddenly as they'd appeared, and he beamed an enormous smile down on me.

"Oh. That is alright then." His hand moved and the ring was gone. He moved fast for such a big ox.

"Anja!" he bellowed towards the kitchen, then turned back to study me with keen interest.

"You are adventurer, yes? I have the adventure dream, too, but Anja has said no. Too much business, you see?"

I followed his gesture around the room, and nodded, then turned back to the bar in time to see a she-bear in an apron emerge from the kitchen with murder in her eyes.

"Alexi Gregorovich, what I have told you about shouting to me? Your leg is broken now? You can't walk five feet?" the woman asked as she slapped the back of the barman's head to emphasize her point. From the way the big man flinched I was fairly certain that slap would have knocked me unconscious.

"Sorry, Morning Dove, I forget." Alexi rubbed the back of his head as he pointed down at me. "But look, we have new guest."

The woman was every inch Alexi's equal. She could have eaten me whole and asked for seconds. I had to fight the urge to tuck a stray curl of hair behind my ear as Anja glared down at me. I hadn't felt like such a fidget of a girl since the last time I stood on the receiving end of one of Mother Shanti's lectures.

"Why she is wearing your shirt?"

"Oh, right." I looked down at the bedsheet that they kept calling a shirt. "Mine was ruined, you see, so I…borrowed this one. I promise I'll return it in the morning."

Anja looked at Alexi, doubt plain on her face.

"She has paid up front?"

Alexi nodded and retrieved the ring from his pocket. Anja's smile could have caused flowers to bloom early. She stepped around the bar and swept me along towards a corner table.

"For this I think you may keep shirt. Come, you look like you have been hungry for ten years. Sit."

She plopped me onto a bench in the middle of a pack of the little not-halfling creatures.

"Talk with gnomes while Goruda brings food to you. They will like you."

Her glare made it clear that her words were a command, not a guess. The little gnomes gulped and bobbed their heads as Anja marched back to the kitchen, then stared at me like a flock of startled sparrows.

"Um. Hello," I said in a poor attempt to break the awkward silence. They looked like a set of dolls brought to life, all nervous twitching and large, bright eyes. The one to my left reached a small hand towards my shoulder as though I were a stray dog he wanted to pet.

"Don't touch it, Bodo!" snapped a lady gnome across the table. "You'll catch an illness."

The little thing snatched his hand back, then turned and stuck his tongue out at her.

"Come off it, Moki. You've not one scrap of evidence to support your theory. Why it doesn't even deserve to be called a theory. It's just a *guess*."

"How dare you!" Moki gasped and covered her mouth as though Bodo had just hit her with the foulest obscenity known to gnomes. For all I knew, maybe he had.

"I'll have you know that I shook hands with a human just last week and I've had the sniffles ever since."

Something poked my ribs. I turned to find a wizened old gnome with a bulbous nose and wispy white hair grinning up at me.

"How bout it, human? Got any diseases in you?"

"None that I know about."

I was rather proud that I managed to answer without laughing.

"Ha! You see, Moki? Nothing to fear."

Moki scowled at me and shook her head.

"That only proves that *this* human is healthy. We can't know about the species as a whole until we conduct a triple blind study. I keep telling you that we need to…"

They broke into a rousing argument, and soon forgot all about me as they shouted about procedures and methodologies. Which was fine by me, because just then the orc woman I'd seen before arrived with the most beautiful plate of food I'd ever laid eyes on.

"Anja has your room ready. She said to let her know when you're ready to turn in."

I nodded as I tried to keep from drooling, then dove on the food as soon as she'd set it down. By the time she returned with a mug of ale I'd already scraped the plate clean. I looked up to find the gnomes staring at me in slack-jawed wonder. As I swallowed my last bite they broke into a chorus of wild cheering.

"Marvelous!"

"Well done, indeed! Such vigor."

"A true patron of the culinary arts."

"Can she do it again, do you think? Or was it luck?"

"Probably need to wait five minutes or so to find out."

Goruda set a plate of the strange green vegetables I'd seen on the sign next to my mug. I picked one up and sniffed it as the gnomes watched eagerly.

"Go on then, two bites or less!"

"What are they?"

"Never seen a pickle before?"

I shook my head.

"Don't feel bad, we hadn't either until Alexi and Anja showed up and started serving them with every mug of ale. Now we can't live without them!"

The pickle had a kind of sour-sweet smell to it. I put it back on the plate and pushed it away.

"I think I'll pass."

A dozen gnomes all gasped and covered their mouths in unison.

"But...but...you *have* to eat them. You're in The Ale and Pickle, after all."

"The Ale and Pickle? Seriously?"

The gnomes all nodded enthusiastically as Moki slid the plate back to me. I sighed, retrieved a pickle, and crunched into it. Despite my misgivings it wasn't half bad, and I earned another round of gnome cheers for my bravery.

"Excellent, now this time dip it in your ale and get some foam on it first."

I allowed my strange flock of dinner companions to instruct me on the finer points of pickle eating. I let their antics pull a laugh or two out of me and focused on enjoying the first good drink I'd had in weeks. Anything to keep the looming question of what in the hells I was going to do next at bay for just a little longer.

6

The sound of boots striking smooth cobblestone broke the night's quiet as Cael and Alleron followed Tyrial up the road to the governor's villa. The building occupied the heights of the only hill enclosed within Farshore's walls, offering the finest views and freshest breezes the city had to offer. The rest of the Scoli Primaris spread out across the slope of the hill.

The First District technically drew its name from the fact that its foundations had been the first laid within the city, but the wide lanes, cypress groves, spacious homes, and elegant statuary made it plain that the wealthy and powerful who lived there felt it deserved its name for more immediate reasons.

"Did you know this would happen when you gave him the crown?" Cael whispered. The light from their torches illuminated the frown that hadn't left his face since Charity and the others disappeared into the city with a dozen arena guards on their heels.

"Of course I did," Alleron snapped with no trace of his usual good humor. "Your odious little master planned to use the crown to lay claim to the city. The rituals I taught him to practice made him more susceptible to Tyrial's influence, but he was so greedy for power that I'm certain he would have done himself in soon enough without my help. I'd planned on taking

258

him back to Shirael Caredis. In truth, I thought we'd be well outside the city walls by now."

Cael clenched his teeth, but said nothing. The elf had given a flowery speech about the plight of their people and the impending doom they couldn't survive without Tyrial's strength and guidance, but the elven ghost inside Trebonious' head had simply waved him off. He'd called for the finest food and wine available, then savored each bite with such utter delight you'd have thought he had never tasted food before. Cael hadn't taken his eyes off of him the entire time, searching in vain for some sign that even a small part of the man who held his blood oath was still there.

He'd expected the elven king to be angry when a messenger interrupted his feast with a summons to an immediate audience with the governor, but Tyrial had been delighted, and they'd set off immediately.

"If the others have come to harm because of your treachery I will kill you myself."

"Bah," Alleron said with a wave of his hand. "I'm sure they're all just fine. Honestly, I don't know why they made such a fuss about bolting off like that in the first place."

"Probably because they were smart enough to realize what an incredibly bad idea this was."

Cael still had no clear memories of their final confrontation with Tyrial in the strange mirror realm of the Shattered City. The only thing his mind found when he tried to recall those events were screams, blood, pain, and the strains of a shrill and mocking laughter.

"Then why didn't you scamper off with them?"

Cael shook his head. "You may have shoved your precious king inside his head, but Trebonious still holds my oath."

He thought back to the slave block, to the cold winter wind and the bitter shame that filled his heart. He remembered the thin-faced man in the black tunic who had made the final bid, and the shock of their first and last conversation as master and slave. He owed the Byzantian more than he could repay in his lifetime. Cael's fist clenched tighter on the torch he carried. He would free Trebonious from Tyrial's control if he had to reach into the man's skull and drag the damned ghost out with his bare hands.

Those dark thoughts carried him to the villa's grand entrance. The road ended in an open circle where carriages could discharge guests and horses could be passed on to waiting stable hands. White marble statues of the five Divines in classical poses lined the circle, guiding the eye towards the villa's facade. Columns of polished gray marble divided the wall into even sections, while carvings of antique scenes filled the frieze above them.

The villa was actually a collection of buildings. A grand dining hall for entertaining, private baths to escape summer's heat and winter's chill, and the private residences that would have supported the governors' family if he'd had one.

Two legion soldiers in full armor flanked the villa's door. They gave no indication that they noticed the approaching strangers, but the door swung open as they stepped into the lantern light to reveal an elderly man in the white tunic and red sash of a house servant. He offered a very slight bow, then gestured inside.

"Master Trebonious. Governor Calligus is expecting you."

"Delightful!" Tyrial stepped past the man without looking at him and continued on down the hallway with Cael and Alleron at his heels. The servant hurried to catch up with them, then proceeded to guide them through the maze of hallways and gardens with the ruffled dignity of an owl roused from slumber. Soon they came to a halt before a thick oak door. The servant knocked twice, then turned on his heels and marched away without a backward glance.

"Come in."

Tyrial pushed the door open and stepped inside.

The governor's stateroom was lavishly furnished. Paintings and polished silver mirrors covered the walls. Busts and demi-sculptures stood on pedestals while rich carpets cushioned their steps. Calligus stood behind a large mahogany desk covered with quill pots, stacks of paper, and a small bronze globe which showed Byzantia and its surrounding kingdoms in sharp detail, with Danan's hazy outlines on the far side. He stood with his back to them as he looked out through a large pair of windows at the twinkling lights of Farshore spread out below them.

"Marvelous, is it not?" Calligus drank in the sight for a moment more, then turned towards them.

"Did you know that when I first arrived this city was little more than a plague-infested hovel? Now it stands as equal to any city in the empire save Byzantia herself."

"It's rather quaint, but I suppose compared to the warrens that the orcs call home it's impressive enough."

Tyrial moved about the room as he examined its contents with a discerning eye. Calligus watched him with a deepening frown.

"There's much more to come. Next year we'll dismantle the walls and rebuild them with stone further afield. More space for homes and markets, temples and businesses, all paying their taxes and proper respects to the governor. On behalf of his imperial majesty, of course. But all of that depends on one thing above all: immigration. The city needs new blood. Not just convicts, but honest Byzantian citizens who will work and thrive and raise their families here."

Calligus moved around the desk and stood to block Tyrial's errant path, forcing the smaller man to finally stop and look at him.

"But that won't happen unless the citizens who live here remain happy enough to write glowing letters to their friends and families back home, happy enough to entice others to overcome their foolish superstitions and accept the offers of free land and fortune that have so far born too little fruit. And do you know the surest way to keep a population happy?"

"Public execution of dissidents?"

Calligus blinked, then shook his head.

"Games! Entertainment! Diversions so marvelous and astounding that they drive all thought of trouble and strife from a man's mind. Or, at least they should be."

The governor placed a heavy hand on Trebonious' thin shoulder.

"Your attendance to your duties as arena master has been woefully lax of late. The games you've prepared have been dismal affairs, and I've begun to hear disturbing reports. Talk of late nights, strange lights and sounds, and requisitioning of supplies said to be used in the foul magics of the native populations. Spurious rumors, no doubt, but if you continue to disappoint I will be forced to replace you with someone more eager for your office. Do we have an understanding?"

Tyrial picked up Calligus' thumb in two fingers as though it were poisonous, and slid the governor's hand from his shoulder.

"I'm afraid not."

"What?" Calligus seemed more startled than upset. Cael and Alleron exchanged a nervous glance.

"I'll be far too busy with more important matters."

"Such as?"

"Oh, ruling this city, for a start. A few wars in the near future, I'm sure, but first I'll need to see to some redecorating."

Tyrial stepped around the man and moved to take his place at the window.

"It's no Shirael Toris, but it seems as good a place as any from which to reclaim my rightful rule of all of Danan."

"So you have gone mad."

Calligus marched around the desk and spun the smaller man around to face him.

"This cursed land has broken your mind."

"You're more right than you know, peasant."

Tyrial placed a hand on Calligus' chest.

Inky black tendrils coiled up around his fingers, then disappeared through the governor's tunic. Calligus opened his mouth to shout, but no sound came out. His eyes went wide as black veins appeared at his collar and traced coiling paths up his cheeks. He stumbled backwards, clawing at his throat. His eyes turned blacker than fresh-mined coal, then he crumpled to the floor.

"What have you done?" Alleron stared at the governor's corpse in shock as the blackness faded away, leaving only surprise and terror on the dead man's face.

Tyrial ignored him as he began searching through the papers on Calligus' cluttered desk.

"Surely one of these will…ah! Perfect."

He removed a piece of paper from a stack. It was covered in bold, looping strokes and bore the governor's signature at the bottom. He laid it out on the desk, placed a clean sheet beside it, and touched a finger to each one as he muttered a few arcane phrases. Cael knelt by the governor's body and felt for a pulse as both pieces of paper began to glow with a faint blue light.

"Now let's see," Tyrial said to himself as he looked up at the ceiling in thought. Then he nodded, cleared his throat, and spoke to the glowing paper in Trebonious' thin, reedy voice.

"In the event of my untimely death, in the interest of maintaining order and for the good of the colony, I hearby invest all the power and authority of my office in the person of Trebonious Leucator until such time as the emperor sees fit to appoint my replacement. He is to be obeyed in all things and without question or hesitation. By the grace of the Divines and signed by my hand…"

Tyrial paused, furrowed his eyebrows, and turned to Alleron.

"What was this man's name again?"

7

I slept like shit that night.

The room was wonderful. Far more space than I was used to, with a standing dresser where I could store the clothes I didn't have and a bed big enough to hold three. Anja and Alexi more than kept their side of our bargain, but my restless mind wouldn't quiet down long enough for me to enjoy it. Just when I began to drift off to sleep one of yesterday's memories would slap me awake.

Sheska's eyes as the waygate current ripped her away. Alleron looking at anything but me as he handed the crown to Trebonious and tricked him into putting it on. The pain in Cael's voice as he refused to join our escape.

Eventually I gave up on sleep and settled for pacing and planning instead. I'd almost succeeded in wearing a hole in the rug by the time the sun dragged itself into the sky, but I was no closer to a plan. If we'd been in Byzantia I would have known what to do, where to hide, or who I had to bribe to get out of this mess. Hell, I probably would have left the city by now and been on my way to Cordis or Antiam to lie low for a few months. Or years.

But all my thoughts of running or hiding ran aground on the same rock; I didn't know anyone in Farshore, and the lands beyond remained little more than a dangerous mystery unless I felt like retracing our steps to the Shattered City, assuming I could even manage that much on my own. All I really wanted was to stay tucked away in that room forever, but that wasn't an option either.

At least Anja had promised me breakfast as part of our bargain. When my stomach growled at me for the third time I finally gave in, pulled Alexi's curtain disguised as a shirt back on, retied the scarf over Sapphery's necklace, and went downstairs to take her up on it.

The common room was a different place in the morning light. The jostling, shouting, spilling, swilling, and laughing of the night before had given way to the soft glow of morning sun and a faint but pleasant humming from the kitchen. There were no patrons yet, so I had my choice of seats, but I made my way back to the same corner table where I'd shared supper with a gaggle of gnomes the night before. I would have welcomed their non-stop chatter, if only to break the silence and distract me from my dreary thoughts.

Anja slid a plate of food under my nose. I'd been so distracted that I hadn't even heard her coming.

"You look troubled."

"That's because I am troubled."

Anja considered my words for a moment, then patted me on the head.

"Eat first, then think. Anja's mother tells her many times 'never think of trouble with an empty stomach', and she live through eighty winters."

"I can't argue with that."

Breakfast was as excellent as supper. Fried egg, ham, grilled vegetables, and mushrooms stewed in a brown sauce that had a surprising hit of spice to it. I worked on the food for a while, but my heart wasn't really in it. I didn't understand what was wrong with me. It was the first quiet meal I'd enjoyed by myself in what felt like a lifetime, yet there I sat moping like a wet dog.

Then it hit me; I was moping *because* this was the first meal I'd eaten alone in ages. I'd risen alone, eaten alone, and gone to bed alone for the better part of a decade. It had been all I'd known for so long that I'd come to assume it was the way I always wanted things to be. Three months packed in beside a horde of strangers on the prison ship had nearly killed me, and every meal I'd eaten in the arena pits had been nothing but a nervous rush to finish my food before someone started some trouble.

But the journey to the Shattered City had been different. Within the first week we'd fallen into a morning routine that became so familiar we didn't even discuss it. Sheska foraged, Magnus cooked, Cael and Nataka tended to the horses, Alleron and I packed camp. Every morning for a month and more was spent in simple conversation or companionable silence, and every evening had been the same.

It had happened so gradually that I didn't even realize how much I'd come to enjoy those moments until I sat in front of an excellent meal and realized that I couldn't truly enjoy it alone.

The realization that I had somehow become dependent on others without even noticing the change left me a little dizzy, especially after two of the very short list of people I called friend had betrayed me in one night. But at least the insight cleared away the fog and gave me a goal to focus on.

I was going to find my friends. My real friends, anyway. Cael and Alleron could both suck a lemon, but I would find Nataka and that grumpy ass dwarf and drag them along with me to go save Sheska if I had to knock them unconscious and tie them to their horses. We could decide on what came next once we'd found my Ko'koan, but whatever it was would be a damned sight better than cowering alone in a strange city while I waited for Tyrial to find me.

That meant I needed to get my hands on a week's worth of food and provisions along with a few horses. I had no idea where I was going to scrounge all that, but working through a challenge I could actually do something about came as a relief after the night I'd just had.

I nodded to myself, then set about showing my breakfast the respect it deserved.

The first patrons walked into the room just as I finished scraping the last bits of egg from the plate. At least I assumed they were patrons when I heard their boots drumming on the tavern floor. As soon as I took one look at them I knew I'd been wrong.

Three human men strode towards the bar, one in the lead with two to back him up. They wore a mismatched assortment of brown, black, green, and gray that somehow managed the feel of a uniform when you looked at them all together. Each one wore a dagger on his belt and a simple gold hoop in their nose or ear. Even without the bit of flash I would have known them for Ghazi thugs anytime of the day or night. They had the walk, moving like a school of ripper fish, cruel and confident as they dared the world to tell them 'no' one more time.

The lead basher leaned against the bar and rapped a knuckle on the counter. His head was shaved down to his sun-browned skin, his nose bore a lump where it had been broken once before, and a thin white scar traced its way from cheek to chin. His kind were as common as fleas back on Byzantia's streets, but that didn't make them any less dangerous.

Alexi came out of the kitchen with a wet mug in one hand and a drying cloth in the other. The sour frown that spread across his face as he caught sight of the thugs confirmed my guess.

"Tarim. I have seen too much of you this week, I think."

"Now, now, Alexi, is that any way to greet a friend?"

Alexi set down the mug and towel and placed his large hands flat on the bar as though he braced against a storm.

"We are not friends."

Tarim just smirked.

"Well, business associates then, and it's business that I'm about anyways. Your tax is come due."

"No. I pay you leeches last week already."

"Sansa changed the schedule. Now it's every week for those that want to stay on good terms, and we both know you're smart enough to want that."

Alexi clenched his hands to fists.

"I show you what I want you thieving—"

A cough from the doorway caught him up short, and we both turned to see Anja shaking her head. Alexi sighed, then turned back to the Ghazi.

"How much?"

I slid off the bench and stepped up next to Anja as the two men argued over a number.

"How long have they been squeezing you?"

"Two months," she whispered. Her frown could have curdled milk. "At first it was not so much, then it goes up."

"It always goes up."

My wheels were spinning now. If the Ghazi had been running protection that long then they must have dug their toes pretty deep into the local sand, which meant I had a solid guess about the source of that trouble the centurion had mentioned when we'd arrived yesterday. The pieces began to fit themselves together, and I saw a way to get what I needed out of the mess. Or get myself killed. But what else was new?

"What is it worth to you for me to take care of this?"

"You say what?"

I took one more minute to size up the thugs. The thug that Alexi had called Tarim was focused on squeezing as much out of the day as possible. One of his bruisers walked with a limp, and the other one stared out the window with obvious boredom. I nodded.

"If I get them out of here and off your back for good then you'll pack three bags with travel provisions and the coin you would have given them today."

Anja looked down at me with undisguised doubt and more than a little concern.

"What can you do to them that we cannot?"

"Let's just say I know how to speak their language, but does it really matter? If I pull this off you won't have to pay them another copper. If I'm wrong then I'll be dead and you'll be no worse off than before. Deal?"

Her expression didn't change as she thought my offer through. Then she slowly held out her hand.

"I—"

I shook it before she could change her mind, grabbed a wine bottle, then got moving before I could change my mind either. I circled around the bar and walked towards the thugs with what I hoped was one of those "come hither" smiles I'd heard of plastered across my face.

"That's an awful lot of shouting for so early in the morning."

I let Alexi's shirt slip down off one shoulder as three pairs of eyes turned towards me. The bored thug's face lit up as I waggled the wine bottle at him.

"Why don't we share a drink instead?"

"You can quote us your price later, honey," Tarim growled, clearly annoyed at the interruption. "Right now we have a different kind of business to take care of."

"What's a quick drink among friends?" I pushed my smile even wider. Three more steps. Two more steps.

"Come on, boss, how can you say no to such a beautiful—"

Close enough. I jumped forward and drove my boot heel into the limper's kneecap as I smashed the bottle into the smiling thug's face. They went down in a heap of shrieks, flailing limbs, and Drangian Red. Tarim reached for his knife. He was damned fast, but I was faster. I pressed the jagged edge of the broken bottle against his throat and shook my head. He let his hand fall back to his side as he stared at me with murder in his eyes.

"Who are you, *bruta*?"

"Just someone that wants to have a chat with your boss."

He blinked.

"If you're that keen on dying you should have just let me gut you. Would have been a lot quicker."

"True, but my way is more fun."

"You think I'm just gonna walk you back to our base like a—" Whatever he'd been about to say cut off in a gurgle as I dug the glass in a little deeper.

"That's exactly what you're going to do, because we both know that you've got orders to report back anytime one of your marks causes trouble, no?"

He clenched his jaw, but nodded. I looked down at the two bruisers who lay moaning and clutching their injuries.

"Well, consider me trouble. Now be a good little doggy and run me back to whoever is holding the other end of your leash."

For a second I thought I might have pushed him hard enough to reach for his knife despite the razor edge of glass I held to his throat. If he'd been independent he might have done just that. But the first thing every Ghazi learned after they joined up was that wearing their gold meant following their orders, no questions and no second chances. It was their one iron-clad rule, and it was also the reason I never joined up myself. We glared at each other for a long minute. Then he spat on the floor and shrugged me off of him.

"Fine. I'll enjoy watching Sansa flay you like a carp. Come on, move it you useless lumps." He kicked at his miserable companions until they managed to drag themselves to their feet and shuffle toward the door. "Call yourself Ghazi then get taken down by a slip of a girl in a nightgown. Honestly…"

I followed them, but paused at the door and turned back to Anja and Alexi. They both stood with their mouths hanging open.

"Remember our deal," I said. "Three packs by tomorrow morning, and don't skimp on the good stuff."

I turned and stepped out into the street to go and meet with the Ghazi.

8

Tarim and his battered minions set a straight course for the mythic quarter gate, then marched past the guardsmen without breaking stride. I gathered from the way the soldiers focused on looking at anything except the troop of dangerous looking thugs walking by them that the Ghazi had already secured their usual arrangement with the rank and file who enforced the city's laws. These soldiers wouldn't pay any attention to a man wearing Ghazi gold unless they saw him committing a crime in broad daylight, and even then they'd give chase a little slower than usual.

I almost lost sight of my guides twice as we wound through Farshore's streets. They clearly knew their way around, choosing their turns with confidence and even cutting through some storefronts along the way, which only served to underscore how lost I still was here. Moving through an unfamiliar city was a strange feeling. Every new twist and turn offered some fresh discovery, and I hated every bit of it. Traveling in Byzantia had become so familiar that I could have gone sleepwalking and still wound up where I wanted to go, but here every new intersection only offered more uncertainty.

We moved east through the city. As near as I could tell we were more or less retracing the route my wagon had taken to ferry me from the south gate to the Divine's temple when I'd first arrived, so by my guess we were headed for the Scoli Agricarum. I hustled to catch up with Tarim as he rounded a corner. As I stepped from the narrow street into an open square I saw that I'd been right about our destination.

The Agricarum was a breath of fresh air. Well, metaphorically speaking. The familiarity of a Byzantian trade yard was a welcome sight, but in practical terms it smelled terrible. Horses, oxen, and all manner of strange and unfamiliar draft beasts milled around its edges, munching, crunching, or slurping down a meal as they waited for their handlers to offload the cargo they carried. The Agricarum was less a market square and more an enormous holding pen for the trade wagons and caravans that came and went through Farshore's gates, since nothing larger than a carriage was allowed further inside the city.

I caught glimpses of all the common races of Danan maneuvering through the crowds or loading newly-purchased goods into crates. The buildings which lined the length of the Agricarum were multi-floored monstrosities with large bays for loading and unloading, and it seemed that each race had claimed one or more of the warehouses as their own. Judging by the number of windows in the buildings' upper facade I guessed that the teamsters and merchants spent their nights in the city there as well. Legionaires stood watch at every entrance into the city proper. It wasn't as pronounced as a stone wall, but the message was clear; we might want your money, but we don't want you.

Tarim and his thugs cut straight through the center of the yard, dodging wagons and foot traffic as they made their way towards the far side. I stopped gawking and hurried to keep pace. Soon enough we came to a stop next to an enormous covered wagon that was drawn up in the shade of a warehouse dock. It had six wheels and an ox haft the size of an oak tree that currently rested on the ground. I didn't even want to think about what manner of beast you'd need to pull it.

Tarim cast a quick glance around to make sure no one was paying us any attention, then jumped up into the back of the wagon. I waited for the others to follow him, then climbed in after.

The inside of the wagon was cool, dark, and loaded with stacks of empty crates, sacks, coils of rope, and other debris left behind after whatever it had carried had been unloaded. From the dust and faint smell of mold I guessed that the wagon hadn't seen use in a long time. Tarim picked his way through the clutter, shouldered a stack of crates to one side, and ducked down to climb through the hole in the wall that had been concealed behind them.

The hole led from the wagon down into a hollow space behind the wall of the warehouse. It was an artifact of the building's architecture, a small crawl-space that led nowhere. Or, it had led nowhere until the Ghazi found it and started digging.

A set of rough dirt stairs had been carved into the earth. The only light to see by was the little bit that filtered down through a break in the eaves overhead, but that disappeared as soon as we began to make our way down. Tarim didn't bother with a light. Soon all I heard was the scuffle of boots in the dirt, and the steady breathing of three men whose only incentive not to kill me on the spot was that their boss might find out and take issue with it.

I took advantage of the pitch black to check and make sure my scarf was still tied securely in place. I wasn't stupid enough to think that even the threat of Ghazi discipline would save me if Tarim or his mates caught sight of the enormous fortune draped across the neck of the girl shuffling along beside them.

Soon a light began to illuminate the tunnel ahead as we followed its curve around to the left. After another dozen steps I saw that it spilled out from beneath a heavy, iron-banded door. Tarim stepped up and banged on it three times. A narrow iron plate slid to one side, revealing more light and a pair of eyes for a moment before it closed again. I heard the clatter of iron bolts being drawn back on the far side, then the door swung open and we walked into the Ghazi's secret base beneath the city.

The hideout filled most of a large natural cavern formed by centuries of water finding its way down to the sea through the rock. Lanterns hung from the stalactites overhead, while the ground had been smoothed, leveled, and set with tables, cots, faded rugs, chests, and all manner of mismatched furniture lifted from here and there. A small kitchen with cooking fires built into natural chimneys stood against one wall. I spotted a half dozen people lounging on cots or finishing their morning meal, but there was enough space for a score or more to gather at once without stepping on anyones toes.

The two thugs greeted friends as they walked over to display their bruises and share their woes, but Tarim was already walking towards two figures who stood over a well-lit table covered in scrolls, quills, and copious stacks of paper. I hurried to catch up, and took stock of the two strangers as I got closer.

The first was a blonde girl even shorter than me, dressed in a Byzantine tunic despite the spring chill that still lingered in the city overhead. She used the tip of a dagger to count down the items on a list, and she didn't seem happy about the result. The other was a giant black man dressed in Sahkri robes. He wore a saber strapped to his side, and a frown on his face that could have split stone.

"...grown tighter than Jovian's asshole," I heard him mutter as we approached. "We'll never make it at this rate."

"Boss, got someone here who went through a whole lot of trouble to talk to you."

I smiled up at the Sahkri and was just about to introduce myself, but the blonde girl slammed her dagger into the table and left it quivering in the wood before I could speak.

"Dammit, Tarim! I gave you the easiest job on my list, so why don't I see fresh coin in your hands?"

"You told us to let you know if anyone caused a fuss during a collection."

"And?"

Tarim scowled and hooked a thumb over his shoulder at me before storming off to join his friends. The girl, who I now realized was the Sansa he'd spoken of earlier, watched him walk away, noticed the bruises on two of her men, then turned back to me.

Now that we stood closer I realized that she was older than she'd first appeared. Unless I missed my guess she couldn't have been more than a year or two younger than me, which probably meant we'd run the streets at the same time growing up, though I didn't think we'd ever crossed paths before. She eyed me up and down, then sniffed.

"You tired of breathing?"

This might be harder than I'd thought.

She was angry and on edge, and even with the Princeps' backing she obviously knew better than to show even the slightest hint of weakness in front of her thugs. I raised my hands and smiled.

"I'm just here to talk."

Sansa scowled.

"You picked a bad day for a social call. Adan, cut off her head and toss her in the trash heap."

The Sahkri had his sword half-drawn before I'd blinked twice.

"If you kill me your payday dies too."

She narrowed her eyes and dropped a hand on the giant's arm.

"You've got two minutes."

I let go of the breath I'd been holding in, then took one more quick glance around the room. Crates, bags, small chests, sculptures, paintings, bolts of cloth, and other assorted valuables were stacked together on a wooden platform in the back of the cavern. It would have been a windfall for a private thief, but for an organization like the Ghazi it was modest at best. The crew I could see did their best to appear relaxed and disinterested, but the nervous tension in the room was unmistakable. Most of the beds looked like they hadn't been used in a long time, if ever.

It all fit. If I was wrong I'd be dead wrong, but it was a little late too worry about that now. I nodded, and turned back to Sansa.

"The Princeps sent you over here with little more than a kiss for good luck and expected you to turn this place into the next Sha'lai in just a few months. You've had a harder time finding fresh recruits than you expected, the legion has been out in force lately, and now the ship that's supposed to carry your first quota is leaving soon and you're short by more than a few coppers. Sound about right?"

Sansa shrugged. She was trying hard to look bored, but I noticed that she toyed with the end of her braid without realizing it.

"All I'm hearing from you so far are things I already know. One minute."

"Hear me out and I promise I'll solve all those problems and tell you how to rake in ten times that haul at the same time."

"Let me guess, you're selling the map to Altrin's treasure?"

"Better," I said with my best smile. "I'm selling knowledge."

"You think it's worth your life?"

"And then some."

"Then what do you want in exchange?"

I shook my head. No need to get ahead of ourselves.

"We can talk about that once you know what I'm worth, but I promise you'll be getting the better end of the bargain."

She thought over my words for a minute, then nodded and let her hand slip from the Sahkri's arm.

"Alright then, you've got yourself a meeting."

"Excellent," I said, trying not to show my relief. "But not here. Too many ears."

She glared around the room. Everyone suddenly remembered a task they needed to be about. Then she nodded and turned to walk further back into the cavern. I followed her as she led the way to a small door tucked out of sight behind a spur of rock. She pulled a brass key from around her neck, unlocked the door, and stepped through into a small bedroom.

The room was surprisingly comfortable considering it began its life as a hole in the ground. A bed with a stuffed mattress and thick covers occupied one corner, a small table with two chairs filled the other, and several sheep-skins softened the floor in between. Oil lamps rested on plinths carved out of the rock, and a walnut cabinet stood by the table with stacks of dirty dishes spilling out of its drawers. But the pride of the room was a rosewood vanity with a real glass mirror that occupied the far wall. The vanity held an assortment of glass bottles, rouge boxes, and colored ribbons, though I hadn't noticed any makeup or perfume on her.

She was already halfway to the bed by the time I stepped into the room. I caught a brief glimpse of a doll in a pale blue dress before she shoved it under her pillow. By the time she turned around I was busy studying the rest of the room.

"Nice place."

"It's home," she shrugged as she waved me towards one of the chairs. "Can I pour you a drink?"

"Gods, yes." I took a seat as she retrieved a bottle and two mugs from the dresser. She filled both mugs, slid one across the table, then raised hers into the air.

"Quick hands."

"Quick feet," I replied as I touched my cup to hers and took a sip. It wasn't wine. I barely managed to hold back a cough as a line of liquid fire tore down my throat.

"Smooth stuff."

She grinned, took another drink, then set her mug on the table. She placed her dagger in plain view beside it and leaned back in her chair.

"So, we were discussing how you were going to solve all my problems and make me rich."

She was noticeably more relaxed now that we were out of the common room, but I didn't miss her message. I had no doubt the big man with the wicked sword was waiting within earshot. I took a careful second sip as I collected my thoughts.

"Some questions first?"

Sansa nodded.

"How many hands do you have on your crew?"

"Eight that I can count on. You weren't wrong about recruitment proving more difficult than I'd expected."

It made sense. Byzantia's street were lousy with orphans, runaways, gamblers, and more all desperate for a better life. The Ghazi had always had their pick of talent, but everyone in Farshore was either a proper citizen who'd chosen to travel half-way across the world to start up a new life here, or a prisoner already in irons.

"And how much are the Princeps expecting you to load on that ship?"

"Two hundred gold drachins in comparable value."

I whistled. She nodded, and took another drink. That was "buy a villa and retire in comfort" money. It made sense though. The Princeps sent a promising kid who was probably causing more trouble than she was worth back home to get things up and running in the new world, and set the bar so high she'd have to jump twice to clear it.

If she actually succeeded, then they got paid. If not, they'd send someone to replace her, and then they'd get paid. She was in over her head, and trying everything she could think of just to keep from going under.

"So you've had your crew pin their jobs on the mythics?"

"Of course. It's the easiest frame I've ever pulled. Every shop owner and housewife is so terrified of the monsters next door they don't bother to look twice."

"And that was your first mistake."

Her eyes narrowed as she drummed her fingers on the hilt of her dagger, but she waited for me to continue.

"What's the biggest threat we face in our line of work?" I asked. She considered my question for a moment.

"The city watch, I suppose."

I shook my head.

"They're just the stick that delivers the beating. Our biggest threat is the hand that wields them, specifically a merchant who's been pinched hard enough to finally get off of his lazy ass and complain to the governor. Have the watch patrols increased this month?"

"Nearly doubled," she said with a frown.

"That's because you've given them something to be afraid of. They've lived with thieves since time began, but mythic thieves? Divines preserve us. Watch out, those horrible monsters who live behind the wall will come for you in the night! And now that the watch is on alert in the city proper you've turned to squeezing shops in the one place they don't bother with, but there's not enough juice in that grape."

"You're very good at naming other people's problems, but so far I'm not hearing any solutions." She leaned forward and fixed me with a cold stare. "I'm well aware of the hole I'm in, now how do I climb out of it?"

"I'm getting to that. Just one more question."

"Make it count."

"How many goods from the kingdoms of Danan does the Consortium officially trade in?"

She blinked, then thought for a moment.

"Twenty three."

"Mostly raw materials and resources, yes?"

She nodded. "So?"

"So, do you honestly think that in all of Danan there are only twenty three things worth a stack of coin? Did you know the elves can brew potions that will add ten years to your life? The dwarves carve runes into their steel to make it harder and sharper than anything you've ever seen, or burn with fire that will melt through a breastplate like butter. Rings that can turn you invisible, cloaks that will carry you through the air like a bird, philters that can cure any ailment; a whole world filled with possibilities, and not one of them being bought or sold in Farshore's markets."

"Because the temple priests declared all magic illegal when…" her words trailed off as her thoughts caught up with them. I asked the question that I could already see in her eyes.

"How much do you think a man would pay for something like that?"

She thumped back in her seat with a little whuff as the thought of all that coin hit her in the gut. Then she looked up as her racing thoughts hit a snag.

"Hold on. How are we supposed to steal something that isn't allowed inside the city in the first place?"

"Who said anything about stealing?"

She furrowed her brow. I pointed a finger at the ceiling.

"There's a whole neighborhood full of mythics up there that no one in this city wants to talk to. A neighborhood full of people who still have family and connections back home. Start making friends."

"You're talking about setting up a black market for magic."

"Why not? It'll be a damned sight easier than pinching silverware or trying to squeeze the last copper from an orc. Safer too."

"But what do we use to pay all our new friends for their shiny magical trinkets so that we can go out and sell them?"

I looked over my shoulder towards the door.

"Maybe it was the dim light, but I could have sworn I saw a tidy little pile of treasure out there when I walked in."

I heard her chair scrape back and hit the floor. When I turned around she was staring at me as though I'd just grown a second head.

"You want me to play games with the Princeps' money. The fucking Princeps."

"Not play games. Invest. If there's one thing I know about those smug bastards it's that they never argue with results. Play this right and you'll be able to double their cut without breaking a sweat."

"Then what do I put on the ship that leaves next week?"

"Nothing."

She stared at me, then picked up her chair and fell into it. I slid her mug towards her. She grabbed it and drained the whole thing in one long swallow.

"It's a three month voyage back to Byzantia," I leaned forward, tapping the table to emphasize my words. This was the tough sell, but if I could convince her then I'd be in the clear. I didn't bother thinking about what would happen if I couldn't.

"That's six months before your masters send a response, more if the winds are bad. If you send them half their quota now then they'll brand you a failure, and you can be damned sure they'll do something about it. But if all you send them is a nice note explaining that you invested their cut into an even bigger payout then they won't know what to think. They'll send agents to investigate, and by the time they arrive you'll have such a shiny operation running that all they'll be able to do is beg you to go right on running it."

She stared at her hands for a long time. To her credit, they weren't shaking nearly as bad as mine would have been. Then she looked up and locked eyes with me.

"What if this doesn't work?"

She spoke it like a question, but from her tone I knew she'd made up her mind. I leaned back in my chair and truly relaxed for the first time since Tarim and his bashers had walked through the door of the Ale and Pickle.

"Then you'll be out of a job. And probably dead. But that's already the port you're sailing toward, isn't it?"

She nodded, then grabbed my mug and drained that one too.

"Oh hells, why not? It's the first decent idea I've heard in a fortnight. We'll probably all die horribly, you know."

"Probably."

"But at least I'll go down doing something interesting. So, what do I owe you for this timely bit of wisdom?"

"Three horses."

"That's it?"

"That's all I need. Well, that and you have your crew track down some friends of mine."

I gave her Magnus and Nataka's description.

"They don't sound like they'll be too hard to find."

"Just tell them to follow the trail of broken bar tables and black eyes."

She grinned and reached a hand across the table. I shook it, and found myself grinning back.

"I'm Charity, by the way."

Her grin took on a devilish gleam.

"Oh, I know who you are."

"What?"

"Princeps Derin sent a letter months ago. Told me you'd been pinched and were tucked away in the hold of a prison ship headed to Farshore. 'That *bruta* is the sharpest alleycat I've ever seen, and I'm damned glad she's about to be your problem instead of mine.' His words, of course."

I sat in stunned silence for a minute. The Ghazi had offered me an earring once or twice. Sooner or later they made the offer to anyone who was good enough to make their own way for a while. Most thieves were smart enough to say yes, but I'd always kept my distance. Running with the same crew, taking the jobs you were handed, and passing on half of the profits felt too much like slavery for my tastes, even if it came with square meals and a steady bed. The fact that one of the Princeps even knew my name, let alone cared what I did with my time, came as a bit of a shock.

Then the obvious question hit me.

"Wait…if you knew who I was then what was all that 'cut her up and throw her in the trash heap' business?"

She laughed. It was a genuine laugh, full of mischief and from the gut, and damn if it didn't make me like her a little more despite my better judgment.

"I wanted to see if you were as good as I'd heard," she said as she caught her breath.

"Was I?"

"You're still breathing, aren't you?"

I decided she'd meant that as a joke. Probably.

"You'll have your horses by tomorrow. Where should I send your friends once we find them?"

"Same place I had the pleasure of meeting Tarim and his mates."

Another night's stay hadn't been part of my deal with Anja, but I had a guess I could sweet talk her into it. Sansa nodded.

"Anything else?"

I shook my head and started to stand up, then stopped and looked down.

"Actually…I could really use another shirt."

9

I only lost my way twice as I retraced my steps to the mythic quarter. At least that gave me more time to think things through on the way back.

My meeting with the Ghazi had gone even better than I'd hoped, at least in the short term. I'd started the day with little more than desperation and bad dreams. Now I had a plan, resources, and contacts. Part of me wondered how good of an idea it had really been to set a ruthless criminal organization on the path to cornering the market for magical artifacts, but the idea had been growing in the back of my mind all throughout the long journey to the Shattered City, and it was just about the only thing of value I had left to bargain with. I had more immediate problems to deal with anyway, like evading the watch long enough to gather my friends and slip out of the city before Tyrial caught up with us.

The guards at the gate didn't give me any trouble. I guess passing them once before in Tarim's company had been enough to place me in the "we never saw you" camp. It was a short walk from there to the Ale and Pickle.

Keeping a low profile usually requires doing your best not to be seen in one place too often. The more folk see your face, the easier it is for them to recognize it on a wanted poster and report you to a watch patrol, but I'd already gotten the sense that the inhabitants of the mythic quarter weren't overly eager to speak to human soldiers.

Besides, if Anja kept to her word then the packs of provisions that were waiting for me at the tavern would carry us far and fast on our rescue mission, and right now every hour counted. I needed Anja's food, Sansa's horses, and my friends to all end up in the same place if I wanted to set out to find Sheska. With any luck the three of us would be well provisioned and riding north through the Wildlands before the sun had crested the city walls.

I made it back before the lunch crowd really filled in, so the common room was empty aside from a few customers who'd come in early to claim a good seat. I walked inside and waved as I caught sight of Anja behind the bar. She welcomed me with a smile of genuine delight and more than a little relief as she wiped her hands clean on her apron and came around to greet me.

"Little Charity, you are not dead!"

I'd expected a handshake or a pat on the shoulder, but got a rib-cracking hug instead.

"Not yet, anyways," I said, my voice muffled by the folds of her apron, "but I will be if you keep squeezing like that."

"Ach, sorry, sorry, I just am pleased to see you breathing. The thought of you coming to hurt for us was making my stomach *druzachnik.*"

"You didn't need to worry. I can take care of myself."

In truth, I was touched that she had, but I managed to keep a lid on it fairly well.

"Besides, it was worth the risk. You won't need to worry about the Ghazi anymore."

"Truly?"

"Truly."

She started to go for another hug, but I managed to dodge out of the way just in time. She grinned, and held out a hand instead, which I shook with relief.

"I have the bags you ask for. It felt like good luck to pack them for you to come back for, and it was! But why three? I not think you can even carry one of them, so small you are."

"I'll manage somehow, but the other two are for my friends."

"Ach, Anja so excited to see you she forget, you have a friend here already!" She pointed towards a table behind me.

"Wow, the Ghazi really don't waste time when they—"

I turned around to see Cael rise from the table and move to block the door.

"I'll give you credit for being damned hard to find when you don't want to be."

It had only been one long day, but he already looked like a different person. Judging by the dark circles under his eyes he hadn't slept any better than I had, but it was more than that. The last time I'd seen him he'd been a friend, someone I'd come to know, to trust even, after weeks of meals shared and dangers narrowly escaped. Now all I saw was another soldier come to do his master's bidding.

I charged forward, punched him in the gut, and slipped past him to escape out into the street.

Or that's what I attempted to do, anyway. He jumped back in surprise as I rushed at him, then blocked my punch, spun me around, and locked his arms around me like a vise clamp.

"Dammit, Cael!"

I kicked at his legs.

"I trusted you!"

I scratched at his arms.

"Don't do this. I have to go find Sheska!"

I'd come so close to salvaging something from the smoking wreckage of yesterday. To have Cael, of all people, be the one to kick the legs out from beneath my plans hurt more than I could bear.

"Well stop biting me and go find her then."

I froze, unclamped my teeth from his fist, and swiveled around to look up at his face.

"What?"

His eyes were sunken and lined with dark circles, but they still sparkled with a little mischief as I stared up at him.

"Did you really think I came here to march you off to a jail cell?"

"I...that is..." Now that my initial fight or flight instinct had begun to settle I realized that if he'd meant to bring me in he wouldn't have bothered to come alone and wait quietly by the door.

"I thought Trebonious held the other end of your leash."

I cursed my stupid mouth as I saw my words drive the spark from his eyes. He frowned and shook his head.

"He holds my oath, and that is a very different thing."

They certainly seemed the same from where I was standing, but that time I had enough sense to keep the thought to myself.

"Besides, it was Tyrial who ordered you captured, and I owe him less than pig shit. As long as there's even the slightest chance that I can free Trebonious from his control then I have to stay and try, but I'll do whatever I can to see you to safety before I do."

I wasn't fighting him anymore, but he hadn't let go of me. To tell you the truth, I didn't really mind.

"Cael, did you come to rescue me?"

I offered him a slow, uncertain smile. To my great relief, he smiled right back.

"You don't need rescuing, remember? But I thought you could use a friend."

I tried to find something to say that wouldn't tip me over into tears of relief and leave us both feeling awkward, but he released his hold and held up a hand to save me the trouble.

"We need to get moving. Tyrial sent a full squad of legionaires to grab you. I came as soon as I could slip away, but I don't know how far they are behind me."

I nodded, not trusting my voice just then, then froze as my brain finally turned its attention to the rather important question I'd missed until then.

"Wait..how did he know where to find me?"

"A stranger showed up just a few hours ago and sold him your location."

"Let me guess; shaved head, gold earring, and a nasty scar on his cheek?"

"How did you know?"

"Lucky guess," I sighed.

It seemed that Sansa had a bit of a loyalty problem on her hands, which I'd be quite happy to tell her about assuming I survived long enough to do so. I had no idea how we'd meet up with Magnus and Nataka now that the location I'd named as our meeting place was about to be overrun with soldiers, but we'd just have to tackle one problem at a time.

"Right, let's get gone."

"I think is already too late for this," Anja said as she nodded towards the street. I looked out the window and saw a dozen steel helmets reflecting the midday sun as they moved up the street. Then a dozen more came into view from the other direction.

"Is there another way out of here?"

"Yes, through the kitchen, but hurry!"

I grabbed Cael's hand and ran around the bar. The kitchen was a jumble of steaming pots and simmering pans as Alexi chopped vegetables for the lunch crowd. We dodged through the clutter and ran past him.

"We have your packs, and...where you are going?"

"Thanks for everything!" I called over my shoulder as we burst through the door and out into the small courtyard I'd stumbled into the night before. I ran towards the closest alley, only to stumble to a halt as two soldiers stepped into view. I spun around to see three more entering the square from the other side. In the span of two breaths a score of legionaires had formed a circle around the yard from shield to heavy, red shield.

"Good job getting here before us to apprehend the fugitive."

The centurion who'd greeted us at the gate the day before stepped through the circle and walked towards us.

"That's what we all saw here, Cael. Just a good man come to fulfill his duty."

Cael stepped in between me and the soldiers.

"Trebonious isn't who you think, Callix. He's not *what* you think. If you arrest us now then Farshore is headed for some very dark days."

Callix frowned, then shook his head.

"I have my orders, and with the governor dead we need to follow the law now more than ever."

"Calligus is dead?" I gasped. Callix turned his frown on me.

"You should know. You and your accomplices killed him."

"What? That's crazy!"

"Is it? The Praetor determined that the murder was accomplished through foul magic, on the very eve that you all returned from an expedition to retrieve a powerful artifact. Master Trebonious has been appointed Farshore's governor until the emperor names a successor. He told us of the mission he gave you, and how you could have used this crown as a weapon."

"Tyri...Trebonious is the one with the crown! We gave it to him right after we returned to Farshore."

Callix looked thoughtful for a moment, then shook his head.

"We can sort out who did what from the comfort of the legion barracks."

He held out a hand to Cael.

"Now, can I congratulate you on a job well done, or are you going to force me to make two arrests today?"

Cael sighed as his shoulders sagged in defeat. Then he reached out and shook Callix's hand. The centurion had offered him a way out, and even as my heart dropped down into my stomach I couldn't say I blamed him for taking it.

Then Cael slammed his other fist into the centurion's face. Callix dropped like a sack of flour. His soldiers stared at their fallen commander, only slightly more stunned than I was.

"Get out of here!" he yelled over his shoulder. His voice shattered the moment, and the soldiers rushed forward with shouts of rage on their lips and fire in their eyes. The closest one swung the butt end of his spear at Cael's head. I jumped in, caught the swing before it had time to develop much force, and pivoted with the momentum to send the soldier into his neighbor. Their steps tangled together and they crashed to the ground in a heap.

"Idiot! You think I'd cut out on you after all that?"

At first their initial rush turned their numbers into a disadvantage as they bumped together and got in each others' way. I snatched up the fallen soldier's spear and tossed it to Cael just in time for him to use it to sweep the legs out from under a man who seemed very intent on caving in his skull. He tucked the toe of his boot under the lip of the soldier's fallen shield and kicked it up into his hand, then flung it like a discus. It whooshed past my ear and caught the man behind me in the teeth. The yard devolved into a mad tangle of punches, kicks, swinging clubs, and cries of pain as we fought to hold our ground.

If they had been street thugs or even Ghazi bashers we might have been able to beat ourselves a path and get clear, but these were Byzantine legionaires. Soon their blind rage gave way to the years of training that had been drilled into them. They formed three man teams, shields raised and ready, and pressed forward in a relentless march of steel. I ducked under a spear shaft, then stood up straight into an oncoming shield bash that knocked the wind out of me and sent me reeling backwards.

Then something hard and heavy cracked across the back of my skull, and I was out before I hit the dirt.

10

I didn't want to wake up, but soon the screaming pain in my head left me no choice.

I opened my eyes, regretted it, and squeezed them shut again. That brief glimpse had been more than enough to take in the whole room. Rough stone walls, cracked stone floor, heavy wooden door, and a pathetic excuse for a window up by the ceiling to allow the barest flow of air and sunlight to trickle down into the cell.

I gave myself a quick once-over to make sure everything was still in one place. My fingers triggered a spike of pain when I sent them searching over my skull. They came away sticky with blood, but after a bit more gentle probing I decided that the damage wasn't too serious. The rest of me seemed to be in surprisingly good shape considering I'd just scrapped it out with a squad of legion soldiers. Even my scarf was still tied in place, and since I still felt the weight of Sapphery's necklace beneath it I figured they hadn't bothered to search me before they dumped me in a cell.

The only prison I'd spent time in before had been the shitbox where I'd waited for a ship to carry me to Farshore. The two cells were separated by a vast ocean, but in terms of their design they might as well have occupied the same building.

I suppose there wasn't a lot of need for variation when your entire purpose was to keep someone from going anywhere, but I still thought they could have put in a little more effort than four rough walls and a cracked stone floor. A bench where the cell's weary occupant could sit and contemplate their poor life choices, or maybe a nice noose in the corner for those who preferred not to spend weeks waiting for the end. A little touch like that would go a long way towards breaking up the endless monotony of sitting in a stone box day in and day out.

The only upside to jail time is that no one bothers to tell you what to do. I lay on the floor and counted my breaths as I waited for the aching in my skull to quiet down. It didn't, but at least the pain gave me something to focus on.

Of course, even your captors' apathy becomes another form of punishment after a while. After a few hours of laying on the hard ground full to bursting with boredom and misery I would have paid two silvers for a guard to come in and tell me to look sharp as he prodded me with his boot.

The minutes stacked themselves one atop the other until they began to spill over and run across the floor. I finally pushed myself up to my feet just to avoid drowning in them.

I moved to the door and stood up onto my toes to peak out through the iron grill of the thick wooden door. What little I could see of the hallway outside mirrored my cell. I stood at the end of the hall, with four more doors on either side of a corridor that ended in a flight of stairs not far from where I stood. Cael was probably behind one of them. From what Callix had said I gathered we were underneath the legion barracks, which meant that even if I managed to somehow escape my cell and reach those stairs I would just be walking into a nest of angry soldiers. I sighed and dropped back down to the floor.

I don't know how long I waited there. I paced, traced the mortar between the stones with my fingertips, counted chips and cracks in the wall, and imagined the wild and desperate men who might have stood here before me. Finally, I gave up, marched to one corner of the room, and sat myself down on the floor.

The flagstone shifted beneath me.

I jumped up, then knelt to examine the floor. I hadn't noticed it before, but the dirt around the stone was loose. It had been scraped away and then replaced. I dug my fingers in around the stone, and after a few minutes of digging and clawing it came loose. A linen pouch lay at the bottom of a small hole that had been hollowed out beneath the stone. The cloth was still white and sturdy, which meant that it was more recent than a long-lost secret hidden there by a former prisoner.

I picked up the bag. It was heavier than I'd expected, weighed down by a lump of something at the bottom. I loosened the drawstring and shook the contents out onto the floor. A small brass key clattered onto the stone, ringing like a tiny bell in the silence. I scooped it up and stuffed it in my boot on the off chance that someone might have heard the sound and come to investigate, then took another look inside the bag. I saw the corner of a folded piece of paper, reached in and pulled it out. Both sides were covered in writing. I read the first line.

Please allow me to begin with an apology.

It was Alleron's handwriting.

My first instinct was to rip the damned thing into pieces. What right did he have to apologize after what he'd done? Did he think a few words scratched out on a piece of paper would put everything right? Thankfully, I am occasionally capable of behaving like something more than a stubborn toddler. He'd obviously gone to a lot of trouble to place this letter in my cell, and given that I was currently the very definition of a captive audience, I decided that I might as well read it over. I took a deep breath and continued reading.

I know you have little patience for repentance or explanations, but given that you currently have nowhere else you need to be, I do hope that you'll indulge me. I also know that your own personal history will make it more difficult for you to understand, but I'm asking you to try. Pretend for a moment that you were raised by good parents in the heart of a city whose cracks and flaws you only came to understand long after you'd left your childhood behind. Pretend that you discovered at great cost that everyone and everything you love, every noble thing you admire, every beautiful thing you treasure, would soon be swept away in a tide of fire, blood, and darkness. Imagine that you were the only one among your whole stubborn race who could hear the steady footfalls of the end of days.

What price would you pay then to purchase even a small hope for a better future?

I have believed in Tyrial's story for three hundred years. He was misguided, perhaps, but he was also the last elf in Danan to dream a great dream and dare to pursue it. I feasted on his legend as a boy, so when my research revealed the possi-

bility that he might yet be reclaimed from the ruins of our past I felt I had finally found my purpose.

I was wrong.

He is mad, Charity. Broken beyond repair. If there ever was a noble instinct or higher purpose within him it drained away through the cracks long ago. I had thought that once I freed him from his crown he would return with me to Shirael Caredis to begin the long and uncertain work of uniting my kin behind a common purpose once again, but he speaks only of power, privilege, and a return to all that he feels is his by right.

Which is more or less everything. He dreams of war and conquest the way a man long lost in the desert dreams of water. I've listened as he speaks of uniting Danan beneath his crown, of sailing at the head of a great war fleet to Byzantia's shores. My greatest fear is that he is actually capable of turning his mad dreams into terrible reality.

And I don't know how to stop him. I'm going to try, but I hold little hope of success.

I may not be able to undo my mistake, but I can at least set some things right before the end, and that starts with getting you and our friends out of the city.

I've spent all night divining the threads of possibility and probability, and I have to say you are in some seriously deep shit.

I won't lie to you, because I need you to take my instructions very seriously: odds are, you die today. I've watched your life end so many times that I'd almost given up hope of finding a path that leads to tomorrow's sunrise. Thankfully, I have, though it's narrow enough to thread through a needle without touching the sides.

I know you have little reason to trust me right now. In the next few hours you're going to be tempted to ignore my instructions.

Don't.

Not even for the best of reasons. My blindness may have doomed the world, so please help me save at least one good thing before the end.

You've already found the key I included. It unlocks Cael's cell, second door on your right. As you finish reading this letter a guard will bring your meal. Ask him for a spoon and you'll have your opening to escape. Take Cael with you, and when he tries to argue tell him that the White Stag holds to his honor even as he roams free in the Ordenfrage, and it's time he did too. Wait at the top of the stairs until the fat one chases the dog, then take their cloaks. Follow the east wall, but stop to stir the soup five times. Wait beneath the eagle until the jackdaw sounds the all clear. Then find *the locked door, but don't open it until you hear the knock. A friend will be waiting on the other side.*

Live well, Charity, and remember me as you do.
Alleron Telvarian

I scanned the letter again, struggling to make sense of it all. It was a lot to take in, it hardly made any sense, and the loud echo of boots on stone that I suddenly noticed outside my door told me I had just run out of time to think about it.

I heard the click of a key turning in the lock, then the protest of rusty iron as the bolt was drawn back. I stuffed the pouch and the letter behind my back just as the door swung open and a sour-faced legionnaire with a livid purple bruise on his cheek and black swelling around one eye stepped into the room. He set a clay bowl filled with stew on the floor, then turned to leave without saying a word. I remembered Alleron's letter just in time.

"Hey, don't I get a spoon?"

The soldier froze, then slowly turned around. The ugly in his eyes matched his injuries.

"You bust up my face, and then you have the nerve to ask for a spoon?"

He kicked the bowl. It flew across the room and shattered against the wall in a spray of steaming vegetables and broken pottery.

"I think it's time someone beat a lesson or three into your hide."

His cheeks were flush, his knuckles clenched white, and there was nowhere to run. He rushed at me and aimed a vicious kick at my ribs. I couldn't have asked for a better opening if I'd said please.

I dove forward. His foot struck the wall behind me with a nasty crunch. His snarl of rage turned to a scream of pain as he reeled backwards. I grabbed his other foot and wrenched it off the floor. He hung suspended in the air for a moment, then crashed to the ground. It looked like the kind of fall that would have really hurt if the back of his skull hadn't struck stone first and snuffed out his candle before the rest of his body caught up to it.

I crawled over and held a finger under his nose. He was still breathing, but I had a feeling he wouldn't be too happy about that fact when he woke up. I stepped over him, slipped out into the hall, and made my way to the second door on the right. Cael stared through the grill in surprise as I retrieved the key from my boot, unlocked the door, and pushed it open.

"Charity?"

"Were you expecting someone else?"

"No, but…how did you…"

"Tell you later," I said as I grabbed his wrist to pull him forward. "Right now we need to get moving."

He didn't budge. I turned to find him chewing his lower lip as he stared at the floor.

"You know I can't go with you. I can talk my way out of that fistfight, but fleeing prison will have every soldier in Farshore out for my blood. I have to stay close to Trebonious until I find a way to free him."

Anger curled in my stomach like a slow fire. I was getting really damned tired of watching Cael tear himself apart over some vow he'd made when he was just a child. I wanted to slap some sense into him, but I knew the man well enough by now to realize how trying to argue would only drive him to dig in his heels even more. I had no idea what Alleron's cryptic words actually meant, but I figured it couldn't hurt to try them.

I took a step towards Cael and looked up into his eyes.

"The White Stag holds to his honor even as he roams the Ordenfrage. It's time you did too."

Cael turned white and jolted back as though he'd just seen a ghost, and then that ghost had punched him in the gut.

"What do you know of the White Stag?"

"Honestly? Not much beyond the story."

The Gallean hero Cuernos had featured heavily in Sister Gizella's lectures. His story ended when he broke his solemn oath for love. Kressida took pity on him and turned him into a great white deer to roam the forests of his homeland to spare him the shame of an oathbreaker's death, or some nonsense like that. She'd made me write an essay on the moral within the tale. I worked up a lot of nice words, but all I really learned from it was never to make a promise to a Gallean, and that those who drew the gods' attention were rarely glad of it in the end.

The story clearly meant something to Cael, though. A faint sheen of sweat had broken out across his forehead, and his eyes darted left and right as if searching for a place to hide. I took another step forward and aimed my words at the gap that had finally opened in his armor of honor and blind loyalty.

"If Tyrial had driven a blade through Trebonious' heart instead of taking over his mind, would you still be bound by your oath?"

"Well...no. When he gave me my freedom I swore that I would obey him as a father and serve him all my days. If he had died there would no longer be a man to serve, but—"

"Trust me, Cael, he's dead."

I thought of Sapphery's wild fury as she tore at my soul, and the feeling of forgetting myself as I faded beneath her onslaught. If I hadn't found a way to hold my ground against her I was certain there would have been nothing left of me. I placed a hand on his arm.

"I'm sorry, but it's the truth."

"You're certain?"

I nodded. He held my gaze for a moment, then sighed and nodded in return.

"Then let us put this damned city behind us."

"Sounds like my kind of plan."

Of course, to do that we first needed to make our way past an entire legion of armed soldiers and over the barracks' wall somehow, but at least now we'd face that challenge together.

We ran down the corridor and took the stairs two at a time until our flight ended in front of an iron-banded door. Thankfully, no one had bothered to lock it behind the guard who'd brought my food. I pushed it open far enough to peak out through the crack and see just how deep in the shit we really were. The answer was "really damned deep," in case you were wondering.

The door to the cells stood on one wall of a large rectangular building that enclosed an open yard at its center. This was the heart of the barracks, with dormitories, kitchens, supply rooms, and an armory through the various doors that lined the walls, and officers' quarters in the tower that rose above the east wall. The drill yard was a bustle of activity. A score of soldiers in training gear sparred under the sharp eyes of a centurion who barked insults and drove home his instructions with sharp raps of his parade stick.

A dozen more worked to unload two supply wagons into the larder across the yard by the main gate. Soldiers, staff, and servants came and went, stepping in and out of doors in a flurry of efficient activity that would have put an anthill to shame. Everyone had a job. Standard issue legion cloaks and insignias of rank were visible everywhere. I shook my head. We could try to leg it, but we'd be spotted before we took two steps through the door.

It didn't help that three legionaires sat on camp stools just outside the door as they ate their midday meal. They sat just beyond the shade of the portico roof with their cloaks draped over the railing, enjoying the spring sunshine. Two of them had the compact, wiry build of the Byzantian farmboy who had formed the legion core for centuries, but the third must have been a quartermaster or scribe, since I didn't see how a rank and file soldier could ever get away with packing on that many pounds. His stool creaked and groaned with the slightest shift of weight. His companions each ate from a single clay bowl, but he held a loaf of bread and a second helping of stew balanced in his lap as he worked on scraping his first bowl clean.

He was so focused on his food that he didn't notice the small terrier sneaking up behind him. It looked more like an officer's pet than a stray mongrel. It's white and black coat was washed and brushed, and it wore a leather cord around its neck, but I knew a born-and-bred thief when I saw one. The dog eased around the man's leg, checked once to make sure the coast was clear, then darted up to snatch the loaf of bread from his lap. The fat man jolted back in surprise, which was more than the poor stool could handle. The back leg snapped in half, dumping him on the ground with a face full of stew as the little dog leaped over him and raced for safety with a loaf twice its size in its jaws.

The fat man came to his feet in a rage, sputtering and swearing as he set off after his attacker. His friends didn't seem inclined to join in, but they were more than happy to shout advice, cheers, and insults as their friend chased the dog around the yard. The scene quickly drew more attention, and soon even the stone-faced centurion laughed and pointed his stick at the show. I motioned for Cael to wait for me, then slipped out and moved to the rail in a low crouch to grab two red cloaks. I passed one to Cael, wrapped the other around my shoulders, and together we turned left and followed the portico along the east wall as fast as we could manage without actually running.

The muscles in my back and shoulders held a contest to see which one could clench the tightest as I braced for a shout of alarm. Walking with legion red on our backs might keep a casual glance from picking us out of the crowd, but one good look was all it would take for someone to notice that I had breasts and Cael had hair grown out to his shoulders.

We made our way along the covered walk, passing dark rooms lined with cots and a large kitchen whose wonderful smells reminded me that I hadn't had a bite to eat since breakfast. I began to think we might actually make it to the gate. Then two soldiers stepped out of a door further down and began walking right towards us.

I grabbed Cael's arm and pulled him into the kitchen on instinct. A table covered with chopped vegetables and cuts of meat stood in the center of the room, while two large cauldrons simmered over the open hearth on a wall lined with hanging pots, pans, and utensils. A hallway led further into the building, and I saw a man in a white apron at the far end walking back towards the kitchen with a loaded basket in his arms.

"We have to go," Cael whispered, but I caught his arm as he turned for the door, put a finger to my lips, and pulled him over to the cauldrons. I grabbed a spoon off the wall and began to stir the pot.

One. Two.

"What in the hells are you doing?"

"Just trust me."

Three. Four.

"Charity…"

Five.

"Hey, get your dirty paws away from the soup, you damned—"

I turned and shoved Cael out the door without looking back. The two soldiers had just walked past the door a split second before we stepped through it. We continued down the portico before they had a chance to turn around.

We reached the end of the covered walkway without incident. All that stood between us and freedom was a strip of grass and the gatehouse itself. The heavy gates still stood open from letting the supply wagons in, but I didn't know how long that would last. The soldiers had nearly emptied the wagons. Their work kept them closer to the gate than I would have liked, but I figured if we ran fast enough we could dash through and disappear into the city before they caught on.

I stepped down onto the grass and froze in my tracks. A black shadow lay at my feet, wings outstretched in flight. I looked up and saw that it was cast by the legion's eagle standard that stood watch above the gatehouse.

"What's wrong?" Cael asked as he glanced back over his shoulder.

"We have to wait."

"Here? Are you crazy?"

He was right. There was no cover, and nothing to explain our presence. All my instincts screamed at me to get moving, but Alleron's letter hadn't steered us wrong yet. I stared at the eagle's shadow, torn between the elf's instructions and my better judgment.

Then a man stepped out of the gatehouse door. I recognized his grim face and purple-crested helmet. It was Callix, and he was walking straight towards us. If we'd been running across the grass he would have seen us immediately, but waiting beneath the roof had only bought us a second more. He seemed distracted, frowning as he worried at a thought like the little terrier who now lounged nearby tore into his loaf of bread, but I knew that wouldn't last much longer. I gathered myself to run. I knew it wouldn't save us, but anything was better than standing like a frightened mouse waiting for a snake to swallow it whole.

A crash rang out from across the yard. I looked and saw that a crate had fallen from the wagon and broken open on the ground, spilling rice grains across the clipped grass. A jackdaw who'd sat perched on the wagon leaped into the air and screeched a startled protest as it flew off.

"Damn your useless hides to Magren's halls!" Callix shouted as he spun and marched towards the offenders. "Shift that crate, and I want to see every gods damned grain accounted for, or you'll be scrubbing pots for a month."

"Go!"

We stepped off the portico, but by now I knew better than to second guess Alleron's letter by heading for the gate. I looked to my left as we stepped away from the main building and spotted a small postern gate tucked away in the corner of the barrack's outer wall. We hurried towards it, slipped into the cool shadow of the mortared stone, and waited for a knock. Thankfully, we didn't have to wait long. I'd only taken two breaths when I heard a faint tap tap coming from the other side of the door. I drew back the heavy bolt and pushed the door open.

"Right on time, Ko'koan."

I stared at Sheska in stunned silence, then leaped forward and lifted the little halfling off the ground in the biggest hug I could manage.

"You're safe!" My heart was hammering in my chest, I was smiling like a lunatic, and I didn't care one bit. After losing so much so fast the sudden shock of seeing Sheska whole and healthy was like a glass of cold water on the hottest day of summer.

"Ack!" she spluttered as she fought to break free. "If I'd known you'd grown so soft I would have stayed lost in the mountains."

She finally wrestled free and took a moment to smooth her rumpled shirt with offended dignity, but I caught the hint of a smile tugging at the corners of her mouth.

"Good to see you well, Sheska," Cael said as he glanced back towards the drill yard, "but could we save the rest of the happy reunion for when we're free and clear?"

"The big man has twice your sense," she sniffed as she punched my thigh. "Come, we have no time to lose if we are to escape the city before nightfall."

She set off down the narrow street beyond the door as Cael and I chased after her, and together we ran towards freedom.

11

Sheska led us back to the mythic quarter and straight to the front door of
the Ale and Pickle. Once I realized where we were headed I tried to
warn her that soldiers might still be in the area, but she didn't even break
stride and just said that it wasn't a problem. She ran all the way across the
city, so I had to focus on steady breathing and quick footwork rather than
asking questions.

We stepped through the door to find Magnus and Nataka seated at one of
the tables. They were finishing their ales and arguing over the best method of
eating pickles as if nothing had happened since I saw them last. Sansa leaned
on the bar with a drink in her hand and a thoughtful look in her eye, while
her giant Sahkri bodyguard and a half-dozen Ghazi scraped their plates
clean at a corner table. Anja was wiping mugs behind the bar, but she didn't
look like she wanted to murder anyone with them, so I guessed that the
Ghazi had paid for their fare this time.

Nataka was on her feet before we'd taken two steps inside.

"My friends! It is a joy to see you all well." Nataka's face was one big
toothy grin. Magnus nodded and raised a hand in greeting without swearing
or even scowling, which made that the most surprising moment in an
already eventful day.

"Especially you, fierce one," Nataka said as she gave Sheska a small bow of greeting. "How did you survive the waygate?"

I'd been wondering the same thing as I chased Sheska across the city. I turned to hear her story and found her staring out the window with a far-off look in her eye.

"I almost didn't. The portal deposited me high in the Frostspire range. I tried my best to find shelter, but it was very cold."

Given Sheska's talent for understatement I could only imagine the frozen hell she had endured. The memory of Sapphery's ice-cold rage tearing at my soul sent a shiver of sympathy down my spine. Then Sheska looked up at me.

"I do not think I would have survived the night if Alleron hadn't found me before the sun set."

"He what?" My shiver turned into a shock of surprise. Sheska shook her head as though she didn't believe her own memory.

"He appeared from nowhere to dig me out of the snowdrift I'd fallen into, then carried me back through the waygate." She turned her eyes to the rest of the group in turn.

"He asked me to tell you all that he always keeps his promises, even if he doesn't always tell the truth."

I remembered his words when we'd lost Sheska. He'd promised to do everything in his power to bring her back. After learning that he'd used us all just to get what he wanted I had assumed he'd just said that to convince us to continue on to the city. Clearly I'd been wrong about that, which left me wondering what else I'd been wrong about.

Sansa finished her drink and walked over to join us before I'd arrived at an answer.

"Didn't think I'd be seeing you again after I heard the legion grabbed you," she said as she held out a hand. "I'm not sure if you've got the worst luck in the world for walking into a trap, or the Divine's own grace on you for walking out of a jail cell like it was the Plaza Novi."

"A bit of both, I think," I said as I clasped her arm. "Although I have to admit that we had a little help."

I showed them Alleron's letter and explained everything that had happened since I woke up in the jail cell. I expected questions, but Magnus,

Nataka, and Sansa all produced a letter of their own, each displaying the same looping script on fine white paper.

"I found it on my desk this morning," Sansa said. "He knew things that no one could know. He offered me something that I didn't even know I wanted in exchange for helping you past the walls. How is that even possible?"

"Magic," I shrugged.

She held the paper between two fingers and eyed it as though it might decide to wake up and bite her at any moment. Just a few weeks ago I would have stood flinching right along with her.

"You get used to it, eventually." I looked down at Sheska.

"Is that what I looked like when I first got here?"

"Oh, she is handling things far better than you did. Her eyes don't seem to be in danger of popping out of her skull."

"We both found our letters this morning as well," Nataka explained. "They told us to meet with you here."

"Almost tossed mine in the fire," Magnus grumbled. "That damned elf has a lot of nerve giving us orders after what he's done."

"He's trying to put things right, Magnus. That ought to count for something."

I realized it was true as I said it. I was still furious with the idiot for keeping his plans a secret and nearly getting us all killed, but it's not as though I hadn't made my share of mistakes over the years. If I'm being honest I tended to solve my problems by just leaving them behind me rather than trying to clean them up.

"Hmph. At least he chose a spot with good drinks."

"I hope you had one for the road," Sansa said as she nodded towards the door, "because we need to get moving if we're going to keep to the schedule your friend laid out. The execution will start in a few hours, and we need to get you lot in position before then or we'll miss our window."

"Right, then—" I paused in mid sentence.

"Wait, what execution?"

"You didn't know?"

"If I already knew then I wouldn't have asked."

Sansa stared at her boots for a moment, then sighed and looked at each of us in turn.

"Your friend has been accused of the murder of Governor Calligus, and the attempted murder of the governor elect. He'll be executed at sundown."

Everyone started talking at once, but I didn't really hear them as the pieces all came together in my head. Now I understood what Alleron had been trying to say. If he'd been divining the future then he already knew that his attempt to take out Tyrial would fail, but for some reason he tried anyway. Maybe he couldn't stand the thought of watching as the tyrant he'd unleashed drowned the world in war, or maybe he really did just want to make things right with us, but whatever the reason he was sacrificing himself as a distraction to get us out of the city.

"…why you need to get moving," Sansa argued as she pointed out the door. "He's as good as dead, but if you stay and die with him it will have been for nothing."

"No."

Everyone looked at me. I clenched my hands to fists and glared back at them.

"Alleron may have been the one who handed Trebonious the crown, but we all traveled to that damned city and brought it back here together."

This was what Alleron had tried to warn me about. He knew I'd want to stay and try to save him. According to his visions that didn't end too well for me, but to my surprise I found I no longer cared. Running now might get me to tomorrow in one piece, but then I'd have to face it knowing I'd let a friend pay one hell of a price for my freedom, and I just didn't have the stomach for that anymore. If I had needed any final evidence of how much I'd changed since I came here, this was sure it.

"Let's say we escape Farshore. What then? Tyrial will still be here, and it sounds like it'll only be a matter of time before that ends up becoming our problem again. Only he'll be far harder to deal with if he has an army at his back. Besides, even if we ran far enough that we never had to think about any of this again, I don't think I can live with the—"

Magnus put a hand on my arm.

"No one is arguing with you, lass."

"What?" I'd been ready to cajole, shame, and badger until they agreed to help me rescue Alleron, but the grim looks on their faces told me none of that was necessary.

"I might still kill the bastard after we free him, but if you think I'm going

302

to run for the hills and let a mangy pack of humans string him up like a plucked goose, then you don't know shit about Magnus Ironprow."

"We're all with you," Cael said as he squeezed my shoulder. "Tyrial has a lot to answer for."

"The wizard saved my life once already." Sheska's hands were clenched tight at her side. "I'll die before I let him do it again."

"You're all crazy," Sansa huffed as she eyed the door. "The legion honor guard will be on watch, and they'll be expecting trouble."

Sansa spoke as though she were explaining how rain works to a small child.

" You really think that five of you can fight through a score of soldiers, save your friend before he hangs, and then escape before they carve you into tiny pieces?"

"We faced a horde of ghosts and lived to tell of it. At least humans bleed," Sheska said with a feral gleam in her eye. She took a small step forward, and Sansa shifted backward before she could catch herself.

"That may be true," Nataka dropped a restraining hand on Sheska arm, "but some sort of plan is probably in order."

"I'm working on that."

Everyone turned to look at me. My mind raced along at double speed, and the outlines of an idea were beginning to take shape.

"The legion is only following his orders because they think he's the duly appointed governor. Once they see what he really is they'll stand down at the very least. If they see him tossing enough magic around they might even help us take him out."

"You're assuming they'll hold their swords long enough to stop and think," Cael pointed out. "They won't."

"I know. That's why we'll need to stop them ourselves until they've had a chance to reconsider who they want to stab first."

"I hate to admit it, but the pale human girl is right about the odds," Magnus grumbled. Sansa glared at him, but I doubt he even noticed. "Taking on that many soldiers at once would be a tall order. One of them is bound to get lucky sooner or later."

"Right you are, master dwarf," I said, but I kept my eyes fixed on Sansa as I spoke. "That's why my plan needs a lot more than five people to pull off."

"Oh no," she said, raising her hands and backing away as she caught the way my words were drifting. "Your elven friend barely managed to convince me to help you escape the city as it is. There's not enough gold in Danan to bribe me into killing legionaires."

"Who said anything about killing? All I need is for your boys to help us keep them still for a bit. If everything goes as planned the worst they'll suffer are a few bruises."

She paused, her eyebrows crowding together as she thought it over.

"And what do we get in return?"

"You get to help us stop a mad archmage from taking over the city and turning it into his own personal plaything. I suspect that would be bad for business."

She frowned, then sighed and nodded.

"Every time we meet I end up agreeing to something against my better judgment."

"Try dividing up the dinner portion with her," Cael said under his breath.

I ignored him and turned to Nataka.

"Can your magic be used to carry something?"

"What kind of something?"

"Nets. Heavy ones. They'd need to stay hidden, then cover ground fast when it's time."

She thought for a minute, then nodded.

"Excellent. Cael, you and Magnus head out to Shoreside and bring back as many fishing nets as you can get your hands on. Beg, borrow, or steal if you have to."

I turned to Sheska before he had a chance to argue.

"The plaza will be ringed with buildings on all sides. Scout it out and find a rooftop with a clear view of the gallows. Take your time and get settled in. When it's time I'll need you to make an impossible shot from a hundred yards away on the first try."

Her eyes lit up a little.

"I thought you'd like that. Once you've picked your spot you'll need to find Cael and Magnus and show them where you'll be."

I turned back to Sansa.

"Have your boys meet up with them to stash the nets wherever Sheska tells you before the crowd starts to gather, then stand by to follow their lead once things start flying."

"I have a question." I turned to find Nataka staring thoughtfully at her boots. Then she looked up at me, and I saw concern etched on her face and a hint of fear in her eyes.

"None of us remember what happened when we faced Tyrial before, but the fragments I can recall are not pleasant. If your plan succeeds we'll be facing an angry wizard who just lost the only reason he has to avoid using his magic. What will stop him from killing us on the spot?"

"I will."

"You will?"

I took a deep breath, untied my scarf, and pulled Sapphery's necklace out from under my shirt. A round of gasps greeted its brilliant sapphire glow.

"I found it in the Shattered City, but it came with a little more baggage than I bargained for."

I told them the whole story; how Sapphery had been skilled and strong enough to bind her soul within the necklace she had loved in the heartbeat after it had been torn from her body by the Sundering, just like Tyrial was bound to his crown. I detailed how she'd tried several times to dominate me, but also how she'd lent me her magic and helped me defeat the mad king and free us all from the mirror realm. I was surprised at how good it felt to share it all with them.

"So that's it. Once we make our move I'll keep Tyrial busy while you get Alleron free, then we run like Magren herself is behind us."

"Why didn't you tell us?"

Sheska sounded genuinely hurt as she stared at the necklace I'd kept hidden.

"Well, at first I had no idea what had even happened," I stammered. My guts twisted as I looked for a way to be honest without telling the whole truth that even just a few days ago I was still planning to cut them loose and strike out on my own as soon as we got back to Farshore.

"By the time I really figured it out we were on the run, and things have been a little busy since then."

"But you knew."

Cael's voice was as cold as the look in his eyes.

"You knew about the crown and what it would do before we gave it to Trebonious, because you've been wearing that thing the whole time."

"I didn't *know* anything."

The words caught in my throat. I'd known enough to put the pieces together if I'd bothered to stop and try.

"Maybe I should have, but I didn't really stop to think about it. I just wanted to hand the damned thing over and get my life back."

"Whatever it takes to get what you want, right Charity? Words are just tools to you."

"What are you talking about?"

Then I caught up to what he was saying. I'd convinced him that Trebonious had died when he put on that crown, yet here I stood wearing an artifact just like it, or at least that's how it looked. They weren't the same though, were they? I'd assumed that when Tyrial had taken control of his body he had also destroyed Trebonious' mind. Could I have been wrong?

"You *lied* to me." Cael's face was a thunder cloud, and I had nowhere to run.

"Cael, I—"

He turned and stormed out the door before I could finish.

"I'll make sure we have those nets for you," Magnus said as he chased after him. "Just have everything else ready when we do. Slow your pace, Longshanks! Damned humans always walking like they've got coals in their boots."

His grumbling faded away as he disappeared out the door, leaving me standing in stunned silence as the others cast sidelong glances at each other. The more I thought about his words the guiltier I felt. I'd never understood his stupid oath or his fixation with something as intangible as honor. Had I been so eager to talk him out of it that I'd only seen what I'd wanted to see? Even if that were true I still didn't know what I would have said or done differently.

Whichever way I looked at it, things always led to this point. He would always turn words into a binding net, and I would always twist and turn to avoid being caught by it, which made any thoughts I'd had of a friendship between us, or even something more, seem really damned foolish in hindsight.

All in all I felt very reminded just then of why I'd made a point of living and working alone for so long. People always come with a price. The more you cared, the bigger the bill would be when it came due.

I shook my head and pushed those thoughts aside. Cael might throw a fit, but I knew he'd still follow through on his part of the plan as long as someone's life was on the line, which meant I still needed to do the same.

"Anja, could I borrow a room for a bit?"

"Of course, young one. You will feel better after good crying time."

Sheska snorted. I did my best to ignore them both as I focused on the task at hand.

"We all have a job to do, so let's get to it. They'll begin the execution at sundown, so that only leaves us a few hours to get everything ready."

"Where will you be?" Sansa asked as I started to walk towards the stairs.

"I'll make my way to the plaza before the fun begins, but there's one more person I need to recruit first."

I climbed the stairs in a hurry, partly to avoid more questions I couldn't really answer, and partly because I really wanted to be alone just then.

The second floor was quiet as I made my way back to the room I'd slept in the night before. Thinking about how much had happened since I'd walked through the door that morning made my head hurt. I pushed it open to find that Anja had already straightened up, kicked off my boots and climbed onto the bed. I sat cross-legged with my back against the headboard as I focused on slowing my breathing and quieting my mind.

It wasn't easy. My insides were churning like a tidal basin at dawn, but eventually the techniques that Mother Shanti and the Vestan Sisters had drilled into me began to take effect. When the rolling jumble of thoughts and emotions finally died away I closed my eyes and focused my attention inward.

We need to talk.

Nothing happened at first. Then I felt a wrenching pull, and suddenly I was falling down into an infinite night. I tumbled boots over ears until the sensation of falling faded away into a simple weightless drifting. Then I felt my feet touch down onto something soft, and opened my eyes to find myself surrounded once again by snow and ice as far as the eye could see.

12

The first time I'd found myself in this place I had been completely disoriented. Now I knew that it was a part of me, albeit a part I seemed to have lost control over. The snow and ice and biting wind were still there, but deciding to simply ignore them took most of their sting away. I turned in a circle until I saw the huge white tree. Last time it had stood alone in an empty field. Now it was surrounded by walls on all sides.

I got a better look as I marched closer. White marble arches and tall windows of blue crystal rose into the air, reminding me of a temple to the Five Divines. The architecture was different, but the solemn menace and arrogance was exactly the same. The walls rose some twenty feet into the air, then dissolved into tatters of mist and fog. It looked like someone had used a wet rag to smudge away the top half of an oil painting, leaving the interior exposed to the open sky.

The structure formed a long rectangle, as though a throne room had been carved out of a palace and deposited into an empty field. It made for a strange sight, and it also made one thing abundantly clear; whatever this place might once have been, it was Sapphery's home now.

The large arched doors swung open as I approached. I squared my shoulders and stepped inside to find a center aisle of glittering sapphire bricks that led from the door to the tree at the far end of the hall. Tall statues of ice flanked the aisle on either side. Each one depicted the same subject; a beautiful elven woman striking various poses in flowing robes, graceful gowns, and even a suit of stylish battle armor. It was the same woman who now observed my approach from a towering crystal throne that stood at the base of the tree.

I took my time as I walked towards her, partly to show her that I wasn't intimidated, and partly to give me time to size her up. I'd heard her voice and felt her presence, but this was the first time I'd seen Sapphery in person. She wasn't entirely what I'd been expecting.

She had the same slender build and tall pointed ears I'd come to expect of an elf, but her skin was a pure porcelain white and her eyes shone with a piercing blue that matched the gemstones beneath my feet. She wore her silver hair in an intricate coif, with twists and curls bound up behind a glittering tiara to come tumbling down her neck and back like moonlight poured out of a pitcher. When I'd first seen Alleron I'd mistaken him for a human, but no one would ever make that mistake on seeing Sapphery. She radiated an otherwordly grace that was beautiful and unsettling in equal measure.

"You are a good deal more…common than I had expected," she said as I came to a stop in front of her. Her voice was light and musical, but I sensed a cold undercurrent beneath her poise.

"Thanks. I knew you were one frosty *bruta*, I just didn't expect your looks to match your personality so well."

"Charming. I suppose I should have expected a coarse appearance from one who delights in using such coarse language."

She propped an elbow on the arm of her throne and rested her chin on her hand as she studied me.

"But what *are* you exactly? You're no elf, unless my race have suffered a truly horrific decline in my absence."

"You've never seen a human before?"

"Human?" Her eyebrows arched toward the ceiling in surprise. "And here I thought your kind were just a myth."

"Well how's that for irony," I laughed. "We've always thought the same of you. Now it's my turn to ask the same question. You don't look like the other elves I've seen."

"You mean the Meadowlanders? Sorellian's grace, I should hope not. I am a princess of the *antariel*. Pale elves, I suppose you would say in this vulgar tongue we're speaking."

"There's more than one kind of elf?"

"Of course. Does every human appear as you do in your land?"

"Well, no I guess they don't."

"Then why should my kind be any different? The *arboriel* are the most numerous of my race, tis true, and the fondest of building cities and obsessing over the tedium of statecraft and courtly ritual. My kin range free beyond the Frostspire, and live far better for it."

Her eyes narrowed and she leaned forward slightly. The air around me grew steadily colder.

"Now that we've finished sniffing one another, perhaps you'd be so kind as to tell me what you want. If you've come to settle our contest over this body I am quite ready to oblige."

"The opposite, actually," I said as I held up my hands and tried to ignore the deadly chill.

"I've come to propose a truce."

She blinked in surprise, then frowned.

"I beg your pardon?"

"A truce. A ceasefire. A spit-and-shake. Call it whatever you like, but I want us to stop fighting, and then I want your help. As far as I can see there are only three outcomes to our little stalemate. One, you catch me when my guard is down and destroy me. I've beaten you off twice now, so I don't think that's likely. I'll admit it's a possibility, though, and I can't spend the rest of my life looking over my mental shoulder all the time. Two, I kick down your front door and destroy you. By now I think I know how, but in all honesty I don't really know what that would do to me in the process."

She frowned, but didn't argue.

"And the third option?"

"We coexist."

She leaned back in her throne and steepled her fingers as she considered my words.

"I confess you've surprised me, human. I don't know if what you ask is even possible, but I'm willing to listen for the time being. What do you have in mind?"

I tried not to cough on the frigid air as I organized my thoughts one last time. Then I looked straight into her brilliant blue eyes and laid out my proposal.

"I let you out of the mental closet I've locked you in. You get to see, hear, smell, feel, and taste again, and you don't have to risk your life for it."

"Intriguing."

I held up two fingers. "I have two conditions. First, I remain in control of myself at all times. If I so much as feel the urge to put on a blue dress or roast a few peasants then our deal is over and we pick right up where we left off."

"A reasonable stipulation," she said with a twitch of her mouth that might have grown up to be a real smile one day if she hadn't smothered it so quickly. "And the second?"

"You give me your magic."

Her glare could have flash-frozen a bonfire.

"Be very careful of what you say next, human."

"What's the problem? You did it once before."

"That was different," she sniffed. "Both our lives were in danger."

"I can absolutely guarantee that won't be the last time," I said with a grin. "Think of it like a loan if you want, one with a very good return on investment. You have the kind of power that I need to survive in this crazy place. Teach me how to use your magic and we'll both stand a much better chance of making it through whatever near-death experiences I'm stupid enough to throw us into."

She sat in thought for a long moment. Then she looked up and nodded.

"I accept your offer."

I puffed out a small cloud of steam as I released the breath I'd been holding in, but she held up two dainty fingers of her own before I could speak.

"However, I have two conditions of my own."

I didn't like the sound of that, but I supposed I couldn't argue.

"I'm listening."

"First, I choose the wine we drink."

"Are you serious?"

"I am deadly serious. I absolutely refuse to sip on whatever vinegar swill you deem drinkable."

I didn't even try not to laugh.

"Whatever you say, *bruta*. Anything else."

Her eyes narrowed to a dagger's edge.

"Yes, actually. You will never use that vile word to address me again."

"What, *bruta*? It's just Byzantian slang for a female dog who—"

"I know what it means," she snapped. "Living in your head has introduced me to a whole world of new vulgarities. Every time you direct it at me, however, it takes all of my self-control to keep from forcing you to claw out your own eyes with your fingernails, so I'd appreciate a small measure of decorum on your part."

I stopped laughing. She hid it well behind the haughty mask that passed for a face, but now that I really looked for it I saw that the word genuinely bothered her.

"Fair enough. What should I call you then?"

"My subjects addressed me as *Sappheria'ten*."

The word was elven, but somehow I understood it as she spoke it: glorious Sapphery, White Queen of the North.

"How about we meet halfway and I just call you Sapphery?"

"That's still rather familiar for my tastes," she sighed, "but coming from you it's practically a high court bow, so I suppose I'll have to make the best of it."

"I suppose you will *br*...Sapphery. So what happens now?"

"Now we both keep to our bargain."

She flicked one finger towards the sky and I felt my feet wrenched out from under me as I flew upward. The white light of her winter kingdom in the deep corner of my mind faded back into infinite blackness. Then I slowly became aware of the feel of the soft mattress beneath me and the warm glow of afternoon sunlight on my skin. I opened my eyes and looked around the room in a daze.

At first everything looked blurry and indistinct, as though I was looking through the rippling surface of a pond. I shook my head, rubbed my palms into my eyes, and when I blinked them open I was relieved to see that things looked normal again. I took a few deep breaths, then focused on letting Sapphery out of her cage.

I didn't know exactly what I was doing, so I just concentrated on the image of opening a door and inviting her through it. Nothing happened.

Sapphery? I shouted in my mind.

Not so loud, child. You'll leave me deaf and senseless before sundown.

Her voice came through far louder and clearer than it ever had before.

I take it whatever I did worked, then?

So it would seem. I'd forgotten how bright the world can be.

The wave of mixed sorrow and wonder that swept through me took my breath away. Feeling someone else's emotion as if it were my own was as strange and uncomfortable as you might expect.

My apologies, it seems I've distressed you. You've held to your word, so I shall hold to mine. Let us begin.

You're going to teach me magic right now?

Why not? You have a great deal to learn and little time to learn it in. Best we get started.

I just assumed you'd need, you know, books and scrolls and such. Every lesson the Daughters of Vesta ever taught me came with hours of reading and twice that in practice.

Her laughter sparkled like sunlight on icicles.

Then you can be grateful you are not bound to a wizard who draws his magic from dusty tomes and endless repetition. My magic comes from the soul. Open your hand.

I did as she asked and stared at my empty palm.

Now call up the ice.

I stared harder as I waited for ice crystals to form and bind together. Nothing happened.

No. You cannot simply hope. You must know that it will be as you will, and then make it so.

She made it sound so easy, but how was I supposed to be certain of something that I didn't understand?

Think of it this way. The air around you is filled with water. Water freezes as easily as it boils. You're simply telling the water to do what it already wants to do, and your will is the conduit that carries that message.

That...actually makes a strange kind of sense.

I am so pleased you approve. Now do it.

I focused inward again. This time instead of watching for a sign that something was happening I looked at my hand as if the thing I expect to see was already there.

And then it was.

Vapor swirled together to form a jagged crystal of ice in my palm. I tipped my hand to let it roll off, then caught it with my left and laughed aloud in relief.

Congratulations. You've achieved a feat that every antariel child learns before they can walk. Now this time I want you to picture a shape for the ice to flow into.

I sighed, placed my little ice crystal on the nightstand, and set about learning to wield magic.

13

The Plaza Novi was already crowded by the time I arrived. Public executions were relatively rare given that most everyone in Farshore with criminal inclinations was already confined to hard labor, and most of those who did break the law were sent to fight in the arena. Word that the villain who had murdered the governor was to be hanged at sunset would have drawn out half the city on its own. The fact that he was also a mythic drew the other half.

The Plaza Novi was Farshore's central square. Its granite flagstones spread across an area the size of a shipyard, with a bronze statue of Emperor Octavian rising twenty feet into the air at its center, and the dome of the Capita rising higher than that on its north end. Byzantia's own Plaza Vitorum was larger than some towns and frequently hosted huge crowds, but from what I'd heard the Plaza Novi was something of a running joke. With no senators to give speeches or circus troupes to draw crowds the huge space usually sat empty, but tonight it lived up to its potential and then some.

Every square inch hosted a man or woman who pushed, jostled, stood on their toes, or raised children onto their shoulders for a better view. Some enterprising youngsters had even climbed Octavian's statue to perch on his arms and shoulders. The sun had already dipped below the rooftops, but hundreds of torches and lanterns had been lit around the square. The gallows platform stood tall enough to provide everyone with a decent view, but Sapphery's lessons had taken long enough that I now had no hope of moving beyond the plaza's edge. I climbed up onto a rain barrel beneath the eave of a candlemaker's shop, and settled in to wait.

I didn't have to wait long. Scarcely ten minutes had passed before a stirring in the crowd across the plaza announced the arrival of the Patriari. Farshore's nobility arrived in their finest as a squad of legion soldiers in parade kit pushed, shouted, and shoved a clear path through the crowd. They made their way to the wooden stands that had been erected on either side of the gallows and took their seats by order of rank and standing. Once the last of them had settled in the blare of trumpets announced the arrival of the main attraction.

My meager perch didn't afford the best of views, but I knew from the sudden outburst of boos, jeers, and curses that Alleron had just been led into the plaza. The shouting marked his progress through the crowd, until I finally caught sight of him as he and the imperial executioner mounted the gallows steps. His arms were bound behind him, and his shoulders stooped low. Tyrial followed behind them carrying a speaking trumpet, still hidden within Trebonious' small, black-clad frame. He turned to address the crowd as the executioner settled the noose over Alleron's neck.

"Good people of Farshore colony, I greet you in Jovian's good name on this sad day, and stand before you as governor-elect by the emperor's favor and the grace of the Five Divines."

The trumpet carried his voice across the square, and the crowd fell silent as they strained to catch his words. I had to give the bastard credit, he'd learned how to talk the talk. It seemed that the same connection that had taught Sapphery the meaning of some of the saltier Byzantian slang I spoke, and enabled me to understand ancient elven, had afforded Tyrial a thorough understanding of Byzantian speech and customs. If I hadn't known that a psychotic elven archmage lay hidden inside that thin and unassuming body I never would have guessed that anything was amiss.

"We have suffered a great tragedy. Our noble governor has been laid low by this elf's foul magic. Since we arrived on these shores we have only ever sought peace with its natives, but their treachery has made a mockery of our noble intent. Tonight we gather to see justice done, and on the morrow I will issue a formal call for all men of good faith and righteous hearts to join in the formation of a second legion corp. I will dispatch our fastest ship to petition the emperor for a third, and a fourth, and a hundred more, until the fields of Danan shake beneath the marching boots of the greatest army this world has ever seen. We will answer their violence a thousand fold, and bring the light of the Divines' truth to every corner of this dark land."

The screams and cheers that answered his words would have deafened an elephant twice over. The windows behind me shook with sound and fury for a full minute, and the roar only subsided after Tyrial waved his arms for silence. The hush that followed that outpouring of rage left me feeling very small and very afraid.

"Let this mythic's life be the first of many laid at the feet of the Divines."

He turned and nodded to the executioner. At his signal the burly man turned the spokes of the winch at his side. The rope went taut, and Alleron began to rise into the air. The crowd screamed again as he began to kick and flail, fighting for breath against the unrelenting rope. One full second passed, then another, and another. Alleron's struggles faded to a few pitiful twitches as the life drained from his body.

Sheska should have acted already. Something had gone horribly wrong.

I knew I'd never reach him in time, but I gathered myself to try anyway. Just before I started to move something blurred out of the shadows of the rooftops above the gallows.

Sheska's arrow threaded between the gallows' posts and sliced through the rope like a knife.

The shouting turned to a stunned hush as Alleron dropped to the ground. He wasn't moving, but at least he wasn't hanging anymore, and that brief moment of surprise was the best opening I was going to get.

Remember, don't hope. Know.

I took strength from Sapphery's confidence and jumped. The force of my legs carried me out over the heads of the people in front of me. As my momentum began to die away I summoned the cold wind to do the rest. Frost gathered on my skin and broke away to drift to the ground like snowflakes, but the current carried me up into the air.

It wasn't flying as a bird would understand it, but it was close enough.

As I shot forward on a stream of ice the screams of shock and alarm I heard beneath me confirmed that the crowd had taken notice of the white comet overhead. The voice in my mind that never stopped questioning still protested that this was impossible, but the rest of me surged with a fierce thrill as I flew through the air on a frozen current. Sapphery had said that magical flight was a feat that few ever managed, and those that did only achieved it after a lifetime of honing their power. Thankfully, I didn't have to wait that long, since all I'd needed to do was learn how to tap into and channel Sapphery's incredible well of arcane power into the world.

The crowd began to churn as Farshore's citizens shrank away from the strange sight, but the legion cohort raised their shields and rushed to form a ring around the gallows. From the speed and confidence of their movement I guessed that Tyrial had given them some sense of what to watch for, and instructions for how to react. Thankfully, I had too.

I filled my lungs with as much air as they could hold and screamed over the clamor as I sailed towards the gallows.

"Nataka! Now!"

A figure broke away from the front ranks of the crowd and threw back her hood to reveal gray skin, yellow tusks, and rows of tight-woven black hair.

"Taski, Steward of the High Vaults, lend me your aid!"

As her gravel voice rang out above the milling crowd the sky overhead began to churn with a sudden rush of storm clouds. Bits of gray-black vapor broke away to funnel down to earth. Each one resolved into the rough shape of a man, their arms and legs pumping furiously as they ran down from the heavens. They converged on the dome of the Capita itself, alighting for a brief moment to gather something in their arms before lifting off again, then soared out over the legionaires and dropped a half-dozen fishing nets over their heads.

The soldiers went down in a tangle of weighted hemp, fighting and thrashing to free themselves. No doubt they would have succeeded before long if Magnus, Cael, and a dozen Ghazi toughs brandishing heavy clubs hadn't forced their way through the crowd.

"Let's crack some heads!"

I had to smile at the obvious glee in Magnus' voice as he led the charge. The red-headed dwarf crashed into the soldiers like a one-man avalanche as the Ghazi followed close behind, smashing and striking with their clubs at every hand and helmet that began to break free of the nets. In an open battle they would have been cut down in a heartbeat, but this was dirty fighting, and that was a Ghazi specialty.

I touched down on the gallows platform as the thugs and soldiers scrapped it out below and drew my sabers the instant my boots hit something solid. Alleron still lay sprawled on the platform, but the executioner stood over him with his sword held high to strike. I leaped forward and raised my blade just as his own flashed in the torchlight. The clash of steel on steel rang out as I caught his strike an inch from Alleron's head.

The big man stumbled back in surprise, then gathered himself and aimed a vicious chop in my direction. I almost felt sorry for him. It was clear he was no swordsman, but his blade could still cut deep if I allowed it. I parried his swing with one of my own, twisted to wrench it away and send it spinning over my shoulder, then buried the other in his chest.

"How disappointing."

I turned to find Tyrial standing with the executioner's sword in his hands. "Does no one study the deadly arts anymore?"

I settled into a ready stance and beckoned him with the tip of my saber.

"Come and find out, if you've got the balls."

He smiled at my weak insult, then lunged forward. Tyrial slashed, parried, and cut like he wasn't human. Which was appropriate, I suppose. It was more than just speed or power, although he had both to spare. He moved with a deadly and precise grace that sent every strike to exactly the right place, and countered each of my attacks with ease. Even working with Trebonious' thin frame and untrained muscles he fought like a demon of steel and death, and he managed to look bored while doing so.

"Protect the governor!" I spared a quick glance at the plaza below to see that Callix had cut himself free of the nets and was fending off three Ghazi bashers to give his men time to do the same. "For the emperor! For the eagle!"

Things were not going well. The legion soldiers saw only a heroic man holding back another assassin. If I couldn't bait Tyrial into revealing himself we were all dead, but cold steel didn't seem to be doing the job.

You asked for my help, so why don't you use it?

Sapphery sounded like a frustrated child, but I couldn't fault her logic. I turned a parry into a quick backstep to gain a bit of space, then focused my will.

He favors his left side.
Thanks.

I conjured a veil of ice along my sword and slashed the air to send it arcing towards him. He cut upward to shatter the ice and send a shower of harmless fragments over his shoulder, which left his right flank wide open for the second ice wave I had thrown just after the first.

The blade of razor ice cut into his side, white frost mixing with a sudden spray of blood. He twisted aside on instinct, so he managed to keep his guts on the inside, but the cut was deep and from the shock in his eyes I could see that it had hurt.

"What's it going to be, Tyrial? Hide and die, or face me on equal grounds?"

He grinned at me like a jackal as he clamped a hand over his wound.

"You should be more careful of what you wish for, little girl."

Then he closed his eyes and began to change.

Trebonious' hunched and bleeding form began to warp like a candle held too close to an oven. His limbs grew longer and filled out with the muscles of a lifetime of sword drills. Trebonious' black tunic morphed into elegant robes of white and green. His ears extended to pointed ends and his short-cropped black hair faded to a golden blonde as it grew down to the small of his back. Finally, his pinched features slid aside as a regal beaked nose, pointed chin, and emerald green eyes pressed forward like a face emerging from beneath the surface of a murky pond. It was, in short, the strangest damned thing I'd ever seen.

And I wasn't the only one who found the sight disturbing. Callix, his soldiers, and the Ghazi all stood gaping up at us in stunned horror as Tyrial stood to his full height and stretched.

"So much better."

He tossed a lock of golden hair over his shoulder and smoothed down the front of his robes.

"I suppose I ought to thank you. This mask was diverting at first, but it's grown rather boring of late. You humans are far too fond of pious speeches."

"Can't say I disagree with you on that."

I lunged forward to strike him down while he fussed with his clothes. My sword struck a wall of shimmering golden light and glanced off to the side. As the light from his ward faded away he looked up and grinned at me with all the malice of a cat who looked forward to playing with his food before he ate it.

"Now where were we?"

He thrust his empty hand at my chest. Just before his palm touched me the same golden light flared for an instant. Then a force like the weight of a crashing boulder struck my chest, lifting me off my feet and flinging me backwards. I slammed into one of the gallows posts, then slid to the ground. The world spun around me, everything hurt, and as if that wasn't bad enough, I quickly discovered that I couldn't breathe.

I struggled for air, but each time I tried to fill my lungs a sharp stab of pain wracked my chest and caught me up short. Blood welled up my throat and soaked my tongue with a thick, bitter tang.

Tyrial smirked, then turned and walked towards the stairs as if I were already dead.

14

Your ribs have fractured and pierced your lungs. If you take a full breath you'll die.

Sapphery's voice was maddeningly calm as she stated the obvious.

Not breathing isn't much of an option either!

I fought to control my rising panic, but it was a losing battle.

Keep your head clear. Magic does not respond well to fear and doubt.

Easy for you to say. You're not the one bleeding out and suffocating at the same time.

I feel everything you do, remember? Now focus your mind and heal yourself while you're still conscious.

How?

None of Sapphery's lessons had mentioned any kind of healing, but then I remembered the wound I'd walked into her bedroom with back in the Shattered City, and how it had mysteriously disappeared when I woke up after putting on her necklace and accidentally letting her into my head.

Your body is mostly water. Speak to it. Make it work for you.

I kept one eye on the plaza as she walked me through the process of stitching my insides back together.

At least the crowd had the good sense to run for it. The square had already begun to empty out, but it would take some time before everyone had managed to flee to safety.

"Form up and surround him. Defend the citizens!"

Callix barked orders as Tyrial descended the steps from the gallows platform and his men rushed to obey. Tyrial watched as they formed a half-circle around him and locked shields to bar his path. Callix leveled his sword at the elf.

"Who, or what, are you?"

"I am the rightful king of all Danan, and I have returned for what is mine."

Tyrial took another step forward, ignoring the sword point as it touched his chest.

"These lands were mine long before your father's father shat his first waistcloth. You are trespassers, and so your city is forfeit. Yield and serve me, or your lives will be as well."

"We serve none but the emperor and the Divines themselves," Callix spat, then thrust his sword forward with all his strength. The metal folded like soft cheese. Tyrial winked at him, then flung his hands out to his sides. Small blue sparks danced across his fingertips, then a wave of thunder exploded out from him in all directions. The force of the shockwave struck the soldiers' shields and sent them all flying through the air.

Nataka managed to keep her feet against the onslaught. She shook her head like a dog coming out of the water, then growled and slammed the butt of her spear into the ground. The stone floor rumbled, then cracked apart in a dozen places as thick roots burst up from the earth to wrap themselves around Tyrial's legs and wrists.

The wizard shouted, then a nimbus of dancing fire burned the roots to ash in an instant. As the flames faded away Tyrial thrust out both hands, and a column of stone shot out of the ground and slammed into Nataka like an uppercut thrown by a giant to send her crashing into the pile of dazed soldiers.

"Yaaaah!" Magnus jumped over the fallen soldiers in his path with his axe already in mid-swing. Tyrial spun, deflected the strike with his sword, and launched a counter that would have taken the dwarf's head from his shoulders if it hadn't been absorbed by a shield that suddenly appeared in its path. Cael pressed forward, thrusting with his blade and shoving with his shield as he sought an opening.

Tyrial didn't give him one. The elven king countered every attack, then swept his free hand in an arc that ripped Cael's shield away with a sudden burst of wind. Tyrial seized on the opening, closed his eyes, and pointed his sword at Cael and Magnus as they gathered themselves and began to leap back into the fight. Green light rippled along its surface, then shot out in twin beams. As the light washed over the two warriors they froze in mid-step, weapons raised and faces caught in twin expressions of battle fury.

Tyrial opened his eyes and smiled as he raised his sword in mock salute, then thrust it straight at Cael's heart.

In the instant before his attack struck home he caught his momentum and jumped backward just as an arrow sliced through the air where he'd been standing. He looked over his shoulder to see Sheska running towards him from out of the shadows, another arrow already drawn and ready.

He snarled a string of syllables that sent a chill into my bones, then thrust a clawed hand towards her as his words echoed in the night air. The shadows began to move, swirling around her like sharks scenting blood as a dozen pairs of red eyes sprang to life in the darkness.

One of the forms surged towards her. Sheska dropped her bow, pulled the long knife from her belt, and slashed the creature as it dove on her. Its form dissolved in a shriek of anger and pain, but the others circled around her on all sides.

I pushed myself up from the post and crawled my way across the wooden platform towards Alleron's sprawled form. Every movement sent a hot stab of fire through my chest, but I ground my teeth together and pressed forward anyway.

Stop moving! You're not fully healed yet.

Don't care. Have to help my friends.

Tyrial spun around and pointed his sword to where Nataka, Callix, and his soldiers had just gained their feet.

"Pathareon vas toxitis."

Inky coils of green gas rose from the stones at their feet. The soldiers doubled over and began retching and gagging as they fought for breath. Even from a dozen feet away the horrible stench sent me into a coughing fit as I rolled Alleron onto his back. His chest sat terribly still as I drew my boot knife and sliced through the noose and the ropes that bound his wrist. The ugly red welt around his neck didn't look good, and his blue lips and pallid skin looked even worse.

Can that healing magic of yours work on someone else?

Yes, but it takes a great deal more energy. You're not—

I placed my hands on Alleron's chest and threw everything I had into him. A faint blue light flared on his skin for a moment, then his eyes snapped open.

"Charity?"

"Good morning, idiot." I let the magic fade away and sagged back on my heels. I felt as if I'd just run through a lake of mud with rocks in my boots.

"What in the hells are you doing here?"

"You're welcome."

He sat up, then his eyes grew wide as he took in the scene.

"Sorellian's grace, what have you done?"

Sheska fought in the shadows as she bled from a dozen cuts and gashes.

"Saved your ass, for starters. Now get up and help us deal with Tyrial."

"You don't understand! I've seen this future, and it does not end well. Not just for us, but for the whole city."

Nataka and the legionaires struggled to crawl free of the choking cloud, but it wrapped its tendrils around their faces as it sapped the breath from their lungs.

Alleron tried to stand, but his legs wobbled beneath him and he pitched forward onto his knees. He looked as though he could already see a different scene than the one in front of me, and the horror in his eyes chilled the blood in my veins.

Magnus and Cael stood as still as statues, and at the center of it all Tyrial shrieked with wild laughter as he savored the chaos he had unleashed.

"Why didn't you listen?" Alleron whispered. "He would have been content for a time, then moved on when he grew bored. A few hundred would have died, but now you've doomed them all and more."

His voice had grown so faint I had to strain forward to hear him, and his eyes swam with visions only he could see.

"So much death to come. So much pain. My life isn't worth what you've just unleashed."

He was lost within his nightmare as the line between real and foreseen blurred away. I finally understood the fear that had always hovered beneath the surface of his foolish grin and lighthearted banter. I hadn't understood how close his divinations carried him to the edge of sanity. Now that I thought about it I had never actually seen him perform any divination magic, which meant he'd been cautious enough to avoid using it until recently.

Judging from the letter he'd left in my cell he'd spent far too much time searching through the tangled paths of cause and effect for his own good in an effort to atone for his mistake in setting Tyrial free. Maybe he was right. Maybe his vision of the future really was inevitable, and I'd just doomed tens of thousands to a horrible death and an entire continent to a storm of war and blood.

But I'd spent my whole life kicking the odds in the teeth, and I had no intention of laying down to die just because some mystical forecast told me to. The only way you survive a world full of bullies and thugs is to keep scrapping as hard as you can no matter what, and that's exactly what I intended to do. But first I had to help Alleron find his way back.

"Ten silver."

He blinked back into focus and looked at me in surprise.

"What did you say?"

"Ten silver says we kick Tyrial's ass across the plaza and look damned good doing it."

I struggled to my feet and took my first good breath since Tyrial had nearly killed me. The flood of healing magic I'd used on Alleron seemed to have put the rest of me back together as well. The power I'd already thrown out had left me dizzy on my feet, but raw adrenaline had already begun to rush in to fill the void. I didn't know how long it could keep me going, but all I could do was ride the wave till it crashed and hope it was enough.

Alleron frowned and shook his head, but at least he seemed to have returned to the present.

"I only wager on outcomes I haven't foreseen. That's the whole point.

I reached down to grab his arm and pull him to his feet.

"You told me before that your visions showed you possible futures, but that nothing is ever certain. If you don't like the one you saw, then stop moaning and help me change it."

He stared at me for a moment in surprise. Then the stupid, goofy smile that I'd come to know and love spread across his face.

"Alright then, you have yourself a bet."

I grinned back at him and pointed down to the plaza where our friends fought against Tyrial's magic.

"Go help the others while I distract him. Then we take him down together."

He nodded, and I turned and threw myself into the air. I wrapped the cold wind around myself to fly out over the scene below, then sent an arctic gust down towards the ground. The blast of wind swept through the cloud of gas and scattered it into mist, leaving Nataka and the soldiers gasping like fresh-caught fish, but alive.

"Nullis an'Pariam!" Alleron's voice rang out across the empty plaza, followed closely by a ring of silver light that swept the square. The shadows that harried Sheska were swept away as Cael and Magnus stumbled forward, dazed but finally mobile again. Tyrial whirled around and leveled his sword at Alleron.

"You! You above all should see what has become of this world since it slipped from our fingers. The glories of old replaced by broken cities and pitiful creatures squabbling over the scraps of our empire. These primitive humans are so eager to be loosed like hounds scenting blood. They could have made useful tools, the first armies of conquest and restoration until they'd outlived their usefulness. Now I shall have go in search of more brutish means to my end, but I will not rest until Danan has been restored to it's rightful order. Surely you of all elves can understand what must be done?"

Alleron shook his head, his face grim.

"All I understand now is what a fool I was for ever believing in you."

The crazed hatred in Tyrial's eyes could have melted stone.

"Then die a traitor's death!"

Writhing black tendrils began to coil around his arms as he pointed them at Alleron and opened his mouth to shout whatever arcane words were needed to complete his spell.

"Up here, asshole!"

He looked up just in time to see the storm of ice shards I'd sent flying at his face. He crossed his arms and raised his golden ward again. The ice hammered at the shield, pounding and slashing with razor-edge ferocity. The ward almost held, but the last shard broke through in a frost-white streak and speared into his shoulder. Tyrial screamed in sudden pain and fell to one knee.

"For the emperor!" Callix led his rallied soldiers in a frenzied charge. Farshore's honor guard raced forward, their parade armor bent and battered but still shining the torchlight as their weapons sought blood.

Then Tyrial looked up at me. His smile was gone. In its place I saw only hatred churning within a cauldron of madness on the verge of spilling over.

"Wait!"

My warning came too late. Tyrial flung a hand towards the soldiers, and each one was impaled by a spike of stone that shot from the ground beneath their feet. They didn't even have time to scream before they died.

Tyrial stood to his feet, pulled the ice spike from his shoulder, then evaporated it as he conjured a roiling ball of fire in his hand. I dodged to the side as he flung the white-hot sphere at me, but it swerved in the air to follow after me. I threw a wall of cold in its path, and the fire exploded as the two forces collided. A wave of hot steam swept over me, disrupting the air that held me in the sky and sending my tumbling back to the ground.

I was about a dozen feet up, which gave me just enough time to recover from my surprise and summon a gust from the ground that was rapidly rising to meet me. It slowed my fall just enough to let me tuck into a roll as I landed instead of splattering into a puddle of Charity. I bounced hard, rolled across the flagstones, and skidded to a stop at the feet of Octavian's statue.

Dark clouds rolled across my vision as I swam on the edge of unconsciousness.

Get up, Charity.

Sapphery's voice broke through the fog. I shook my head and pushed up to one knee, but the spinning didn't stop. Magnus, Cael, Nataka, Sheska, and Alleron were going after Tyrial with everything they had, and he was beating them back. Lightning flashed, flames roared, steel rang out, and Tyrial was winning.

I should have listened to Alleron.

He'd warned me, everyone had warned me, but I'd been too stubborn to listen.

Maybe you still can.

What? No!

Despite everything that had happened the thought of running and leaving my friends to die still turned my stomach.

I'm not talking about running, fool. I'm talking about this.

A memory surged up out of my mind. I stood next to Alleron as he worked to alter the waygate runes while the treant raged and smashed nearby.

"Your not-so-bright human colonist ancestors built their city directly over the region's waygate…if I activate the portal without adjusting the terminal point it will tear whatever is nearby into tiny pieces. Oh, and our oaken friend over there might step through and rampage through the ruins a bit. But if you'd rather I cut a few corners…"

I snapped back to the present. With everything that had happened since then I'd forgotten all about that small comment, but Sapphery hadn't.

Do you think the original terminal point is nearby?

I can't be sure, but there's a very good chance it's right here in this square. The city's founders would have been drawn to site their new colony over the nexus of energies here even if they weren't aware of the reason, and this is the heart of the city.

That's good enough for me.

It was blind a guess, but the logic made a certain kind of sense, and it was only a matter of time before fatigue or injury slowed one of us down just enough for Tyrial to finish the job. We'd only held on as long as we had by working together and forcing him to divide his attention. If one of us fell the others wouldn't be far behind. I stood to my feet and ran to rejoin the fight.

"Alleron!" I screamed as I came closer. He ducked beneath the swipe of a spectral sword then turned in my direction.

"Open the waygate!"

"It's a twenty minute ride outside the city. What possible—" Then his eyes went wide as he realized which waygate I was talking about just as I skidded to a stop beside him.

"How hard did you hit your head when you fell?"

"Just do it."

He shook his head, but stepped away from the battle and closed his eyes. A nimbus of dancing lights began to spiral around him. A moment later a crack of thunder shook the air, and I turned to see Octavian's statue split down the center. The two halves fell away like the shell of a cracked nut, and a swirling green vortex of energy began to expand out in all directions.

Then the lights that danced around Alleron shot out to surround the pool of crackling green. They formed a loose circle, and everywhere the vortex touched a snap of white pushed it back into place.

"Whatever you're planning, you'd better do it now," Alleron gasped. "I can't hold this for long, and you don't want to know what happens if I lose control of it."

I leapt in to take Alleron's place as he concentrated on holding his spell. I'd lost my swords in the crash landing, but I didn't have time to gather them up. I spun my arms in a wide circle, gathering the chill of midwinter in front of me before flinging it at Tyrial.

A ball of ice the size of a wine barrel smashed into his shield. His wards held, shattering the missile to pieces, but the impact threw him several steps backwards.

"Drive him towards the portal!"

The others took my cue and began to press him back towards the waygate. Sheska launched a stream of arrows from his left. Nataka chanted, and the flagstones at her feet shot up to race the arrows towards their target while Cael and Magnus jumped forward to strike in unison from his right.

Tyrial launched himself into the air. Blades and missiles sailed harmlessly beneath his feet. As he soared backwards the air around him crackled with power, then six bolts of lightning shot down at each of us. I jumped in front of Alleron and threw up a wall of ice. The white-hot bolt of energy struck my shield and sent me spinning away in a cloud of steam. The shock rattled my teeth and left my head spinning, but it was better than taking a direct hit.

The others weren't so lucky. Lights flashed as they were dashed to the ground by the force of the blasts that struck them. I gasped with relief when I saw each one of them struggle to rise to their feet, armor smoking and hair stood on end. They lived, but that wouldn't last much longer seeing as they could barely walk, let alone defend themselves.

Tyrial touched down in front of the portal with the grace of a festival dancer.

"Did you fools truly think you could—"

An earth-shaking roar drowned out whatever he'd been about to say, and

Tyrial spun around to find himself staring up into the eyes of a confused and very angry treant.

The archmage shouted in surprise as the huge tree snatched him off the ground in a tangle of twisted branches. Then his shout became a scream of pain as the branches began to crush and squeeze. Tyrial tried to wrench himself free, but the treant battered his head and shoulders as it wrapped more branches around his body. With a desperate heave Tyrial pushed himself towards the treant's face. He lunged forward, straining against the unyielding branches for every last inch, then touched the tip of his sword to the rough bark.

Red light flared in the darkness, but instead of fading away it grew brighter and brighter. The treant threw back its head and screamed to the heavens as flames burst from its eyes and mouth to jet up into the night sky. Its scream was an endless wail of pain and fear that stretched on and on long after living lungs would have failed.

Tyrial dropped to the ground as the limbs that held him began to snap and break apart. The fire spread out across the whole surface of the tree, lighting the night with the brilliance of a thousand bonfires. Then the flames faded away as quickly as they'd appeared, leaving a mountain of ash in their wake.

Tyrial stood to his feet, battered, bloody, and breathing hard, but still very much alive.

Blood streamed from a cut in his scalp and his eyes shone with crazed fury as he raised both hands towards the sky. I felt the earth tilt as he began to draw power to him. The clouds split overhead, fire and death churning in the yawning void, and I knew in my bones that his terrible spell would turn every man, woman, child, and stray dog in Farshore to ash the instant it was completed.

Sorellian's grace, he's summoned void fire. I never believed he would actually do this...

"Hey asshole!"

Thankfully, I'd started running as soon as the treant had begun to burn, gathering power with every step.

"Get out of my city."

I swung my fist, and the mountain of ice and snow I had gathered around me crashed down on him in an avalanche of fury. The blast threw him into the air like a leaf caught in a summer storm. Shock and disbelief flashed across his face as he tumbled through the air. Then he plunged into the waygate portal and disappeared.

Oh my. Very well done, child. I've been dying to see that accursed smile wiped off his face for five hundred years.

Sapphery's voice was the purr of a cat who'd just savored a good meal. A moment after Tyrial plunged into the swirling green vortex the violent rumbling in the earth and sky subsided, and the flashing maelstrom that the mad king had begun to summon in the sky above Farshore began to break up and drift away, leaving a brilliant pattern of shimmering stars in its wake.

The white light of Alleron's spell grew brighter, then collapsed in on the portal. I covered my eyes to shield them from the brilliant glare. When I looked up again the waygate was gone, sealed and invisible once again. I turned around to find the others stumbling over towards me.

The plaza stood in ruins all around us. Broken flagstones, scorch marks, melted bronze, ash, and blood marked the progress of our battle. As the rush of impending death faded away I felt every bruise, scrape, and cut I'd just acquired fighting to see who could scream the loudest for my attention. I sighed, flopped down on the ground, and closed my eyes.

15

"We sail at first light. Be on board before the tide turns or you'll forfeit your berth and you can go tell that little blonde witch who lost her fee."

"A pleasure as always, captain."

I turned and walked down the gangplank back to the shore. The three days since our battle with Tyrial had passed in a haze of activity. Work crews set about repairing the plaza, Callix and his men were honored with a state funeral, and Knight-Captain Alexios had us all hauled in to explain what the hell had just happened to his city.

As the general of Farshore's legion he'd assumed temporary command of the colony until a full report could be dispatched to Byzantia. Thankfully, we managed to convince him that martial law and the expulsion of all mythics from the city wasn't necessary now that Tyrial was gone. He didn't say thank you, but he also didn't order us imprisoned and executed for more or less destroying the Plaza Novi in the process, so I called it a win and ducked out the door before he had a chance to change his mind.

Sansa had been waiting to scoop me up as soon as the legion turned us loose. We'd made a deal and she made sure I held to my end, keeping me up till the small hours going over every last detail of her new efforts to establish a clandestine market for discerning patrons in search of rare and magical goods. Three days later she had her plan, and after a beautiful display of bribery and veiled threats leveled at *The Zephyr's* captain, I had my ride home.

Home. The word sent a quiver through my knees as I walked past dock hands ferrying crates of raw ore, stacks of smooth-planed lumber, sacks of wheat, bales of barley, and numerous other trade goods onto the ship in preparation for its departure. I wove through coils of rope and bustling sailors, stepped down from the pier, and kept right on walking.

The wagon that had carried me out to Shoreside wouldn't return to Farshore for another hour, but the shouts and jostles of the busy dock had set my nerves on edge. I knew if I tried to sit still that long I'd end up pulling out my hair, picking a fight, or both long before the wagon got rolling. A walk through the woods sounded like a fair bargain in exchange for some room to breathe.

The clamor behind me soon faded away as I followed the dirt road that wove through the trees back towards the city. I set a fast pace at first, but after a while the smell of pine needles and wet earth soaked into my lungs and brought a soothing calm along with it that slowed me down to a steady walk. Cool shadows, trilling birds, and swaying branches surrounded me, and to my surprise I found that I actually welcomed their company.

When the prison wagon had first carried me up this road I'd jumped at every sound and movement in the trees. I'd heard a hundred stories of Farshore and the strange world beyond its walls, each one of them bad. Now that I'd journeyed to the heart of Danan and back again I don't know how I'd ever seen these woods as anything other than pleasant and safe.

Goblins and trolls never ranged this far south of the Frostspires. There were no caves for dire wolves to den in, no swamps for lizardfolk or naga to raid from, and the payment of regular tribute ensure that any dwarven warships that prowled these waters kept right on sailing. Whether they'd planned it this way or just gotten insanely lucky, the colony's founders had chosen the perfect place for humanity's fragile outpost here in this land of myth and monsters.

And tomorrow I would leave it behind forever.

Byzantia's glorious bustle and endless tangle of streets had always been my home. Since my first steps in Farshore I had always believed that I would find my way back somehow. Now I'd be sailing back with a proper berth, a full pardon, and more gold in my pack than a spice merchant sailing back from Drangia. True, we'd lost out on the windfall Trebonious had promised us when Tyrial had taken over his mind, assuming he'd actually intended to deliver on his word in the first place. That's why the first thing I'd done when Sansa had finally let me out of the Ghazi hideout was march straight back to the arena pits.

Knight-Captain Alexios had sent soldiers to secure the arena until a new games master could be appointed to Trebonious' post, but they were far more concerned with keeping the rowdy prisoners in line than on keeping their eyes on the shadows. It had been all too easy to slip through the door during a shift change and make my way to Trebonious' old office. Sure enough, my pack lay tucked away in the corner right where I'd dropped it.

No one had bothered to clean out the singed and jumbled mess of a room, though I doubt they would have bothered with my pack even if they had. One of the perks of growing up as a dirt-stained street rat is that the things you own end up ragged, stained, and soiled before very long. My pack had fared worse than my things usually did on the long trip out to the Shattered City. I'd slipped into the office, shouldered the ratty bundle, tightened the straps to keep the rather ludicrous amount of gemstone encrusted jewelry hidden inside it from making too much of a clatter, and dashed back out into the city before anyone knew I'd been there.

I shifted the pack on my back as I walked up the narrow road, enjoying its reassuring weight. You can be damned sure I hadn't let the thing out of my sight over the past two days. There was enough wealth clinking around in there to buy myself a house in the country, a Novari chef, and even a handsome manservant to peel me grapes if I wanted one.

Escaping the arena and making my way back to Byzantia was the goal that had kept me going these past months. Returning richer than a silk merchant's wife was more than I ever would have dreamed possible, but somehow I still felt lost and empty. Whether in Byzantia or Farshore my days had always been driven by the needs of basic survival. What was I supposed to do now that I could choose something other than steal, run, fight, or hide?

The walk back to the city ended before I'd found an answer.

The soldiers on watch offered me a quiet nod of greeting as I walked through the gate. One of their comrades in the honor guard had survived his wounds, and the story of my friends and I battling the usurper in a whirlwind of magic and steel had spread through the city like a wave at high tide. I was totally unprepared to see anything other than a suspicious glare or cold indifference on a guard's face, and I hated it. Recognition like that is a death sentence for a thief. Then again, was I even still a thief anymore?

I stood inside the gate staring up the length of the Agricarum as I tried to decide what to do next. Sansa had kept me locked up in the Ghazi cave for days, and I was in no hurry to return for more damp chills, loud snores, and bland food. The day was mine, and I had absolutely no idea what to do with it. Finally I gave up and let my feet decide for me. They led me through the Agricarum's dusty clamor and onto the Breezeway that led into the heart of the city.

Farshore's largest street was wide enough to catch the cool, clean air that blew in from the coast, hence its name. It boasted a long stretch of shops, stalls, bathhouses, and even a small public garden midway along the path it traced from the Agricarum to the Plaza Novi at the heart of the city. Aristocrats who had descended from the heights of the Scoli Primaris mingled with wealthy merchants and artisans who lived in spacious two and three story homes that rose above their shops all around me. When I'd first arrived here I never would have dared to set foot here, and no doubt the city watch would have chased me off if I tried. Now I walked amongst Farshore's citizens wearing clothes as clean and trim as theirs, and no one paid me any mind.

I wandered down the Breezeway for hours, peering through windows and poking my head into shops at random. When I grew hungry I followed my nose to a shaded stall serving spiced Sahkri dishes and ate until I couldn't manage another bite. Then I actually paid for my food. With money. The vendor thanked me and wished Kressida's blessing on my head, which left me feeling even more unsettled as I walked away and turned onto a side street.

I roamed Farshore's streets like an honest citizen for hours, feeling like a fraud the whole time. No one chased me away from their shop or dropped a wary hand to their coin purse as I passed by, but I knew I didn't really belong among the proper men and women all around me. They had homes, jobs, and families to return to. I had a cot in the corner of a damp cave, and a few inhuman friends who hadn't even bothered to come looking for me when I'd disappeared. Once I boarded my ship in the morning I'd have even less than that.

You're rather gloomy for such a pleasant day.

Sapphery had mostly kept to herself while I busied myself with keeping my part of the bargain with Sansa. She'd mostly just complained about the food, but even that had been infrequent enough that I had sometimes forgotten that I still had the disembodied soul of an ancient elven queen along for the ride.

What's so pleasant about it?

The sun is high, the air is clear, you have food in your stomach, coin in your purse, and a berth on a ship to carry you across the waves tomorrow. Take your pick.

You're not going to try and stop me from carrying you halfway around the world?

I'm rather excited about it, truth be told. I hadn't held out much hope for a city built by humans, but from your memories of the place this Byzantia of yours seems almost tolerable. I think it should hold my interest for a week or two at the very least. Are you not eager to return there?

I...

The answer should have been easy. Right now my future was brighter than it had ever been before, but that thought didn't warm me like it should have. No doubt I'd feel differently once my boots touched Byzantia's cobbled streets again, but for now all I felt was cold and dreary. I chose streets at random, lost in my clouded thoughts.

Then I looked up and found myself standing just inside the gate to the mythic quarter. Inhuman crowds, mismatched buildings, strange smells, and a riot of warring colors swirled all around me. I drew in a deep breath as my unease faded into the background. I still felt lost and alone, but it was hard to pay those feelings much notice when the impossible beckoned from every corner. I started walking, this time with a purpose.

Two lefts and a right, and I was climbing the steps of the Ale and Pickle again. As soon as I'd stepped through the mythic quarter's gate I knew there was nowhere else I'd rather spend my last night in Farshore.

I stepped inside to find my friends all waiting for me.

"Ya ha! There's not an orc alive who can best Magnus Ironprow in honest competition. Another round on my friend's tab, barkeep!"

Magnus crowed his victory as a burly orc slunk off in shame and another took his spot on the bench, slammed his elbow down on the table, and clasped hands with the dwarf. From the veins that rose on their necks as they heaved and strained I thought there was a good chance that one of them would tear the other's arm off before long.

Sheska and Nataka sat at a corner table, empty plates set to one side to make room for a game of Boggart's Delve. Swap the table for a bare patch of ground beside a campfire, and they looked just as they had on any of the dozens of nights we'd traveled the open road together. Nataka smiled and Sheska waved before turning back to their game. I got the sense that they weren't surprised to see me.

Alleron grinned over his shoulder from the bar as he offered me the empty stool beside him.

As I started walking towards him I caught sight of Cael sitting alone in the corner. He ignored me, scowling down at his mug and refusing to look up in my direction. I shook my head and headed for the bar. He'd either get over himself and forgive me, or he wouldn't. Either way it wouldn't be my problem by tomorrow morning.

"Quite a party you've got going here," I said as I slid onto the stool and waved at Alexi for a drink. "Celebrating our glorious victory?"

"Of course not. We wouldn't dream of beginning without you. I tried to convince Nataka to let me bake her into a cake so she could jump out and surprise you, but for some reason she said no. Repeatedly."

"What a poor sport." I hid my grin with a sip from the mug that Alexi placed in front of me.

"Exactly! Orcs have no sense for theatrics."

"It's a problem."

Then my smile slipped away as my brain caught up with the situation.

"Alleron…how did you even know to find me here?"

He waggled his fingers and his eyebrows at me at the same time.

"Wizard extraordinare, remember? Tremble as you behold my awesome power."

I snorted a bit of foam off the top of my drink.

"Which reminds me…" he placed a stack of ten silver coins in front of me. "I believe I owe you this, and a great deal more."

He looked at me with such sincere gratitude that I couldn't help but squirm a little on my stool.

"Thank you for coming back for me."

I shrugged. "You stuck your neck out for all of us. All I did was return the favor."

"You did a great deal more than that. I don't know how you managed it, but because of you we're sitting here in this delightful tavern instead of mouldering away as a pile of ash in a blasted ruins of the city. You found the one path I could not see. Perhaps Tyrial wasn't the only hope we had of standing against the dark tide."

His voice had begun to grow distant again.

"Alleron, in the letter you left in my cell you mentioned a horrible doom you'd foreseen. Something about the end of all things. What was all that about, anyway?"

He sighed, then took a long drink from his mug.

"Some years ago, when I was still a student at the Chromatis Arcani, I... lost someone. Someone very dear to me. She followed the twisting path of possibilities much farther than was wise, and became unable to find her way back to her body. I tried to save her. I failed. But in the attempt I saw what she saw, and managed to find my way back to the present afterward."

He looked up at me, his eyes haunted.

"A great darkness is coming to this land, Charity. I don't know when or where, but someday soon it will rise from the cold depths of the ocean itself with unrivaled fury and terrible destruction. Unless the warring races of Danan stand united against the threat, the dark tide will scour all life from the land within a year."

I sipped at my own drink as I took in his words. He'd more than proven the effectiveness of his visions, but that had been in relation to events in the near future. He'd told me himself that reality became twisted and uncertain the further you moved from the solid anchor of the present. Given every-thing we'd just been through I wanted to believe him despite how crazy his words sounded, but even if I did I wasn't sure what exactly he expected me to do about it.

"Darkness from the sea, huh? Did you see anything else on your little psychic voyage? Something we could use to get a better sense of the threat?"

"I did, actually." His eyes locked on mine with sudden warmth. "I saw the face of a young Byzantian thief standing on the shore, her face shining like the morning sun as she stood against the end of days."

Then Alleron caught himself and cleared his throat, clearly realizing he'd just said more than he'd meant to.

"But that's a subject for another time, I think. Tonight we have a celebration to attend to."

"But what did—"

He snatched the mug from my hand and drained the last of its contents in one long swallow, then waved the empty vessel at Alexi.

"Our heroine is in need of a refill, good man!"

The Novari swapped it out with a foamy replacement which Alleron pressed it into my hands before I could argue further.

"Relax and enjoy, my dear. Once the rabble clears out after dinner we'll have the place to ourselves."

I tossed him a skeptical look, which he answered by pointing at the ceiling overhead.

"I've reserved all of the rooms in this fine establishment for the next month. We can all get as drunk as a dwarf on holiday, and as long as we can manage to assist one another up the stairs we'll still spend the night in comfort. Don't know why I didn't think of it sooner."

"That sounds like more fun than I can afford," I said with a shake of my head. "I have a ship to catch before dawn."

Seeing them all again had made that thought a little harder to bear, but I found that I was glad I'd come nonetheless. A proper goodbye wouldn't kill me, after all, even if it was the first one I'd ever experienced. I took a long pull from the mug to try and clear the tight knot that had begun to form in my throat at the thought.

"Ah yes, the ship. A good thing you decided to put all that nonsense behind you and stay here."

I stared at him in confusion until he gasped and covered his mouth with one hand.

"Oh dear. Have you not arrived at that conclusion yourself yet? Terribly sorry, the perils of divination and all that. You go right ahead. I'll wait here."

At first I had no idea what he was talking about. Then it hit me.

I could stay in Farshore if I wanted to.

I'd been so set on getting home that I hadn't even stopped to consider whether Byzantia was still my home at all. There were aspects of life in the old world that I missed, but I was beginning to suspect that I'd feel the same or worse about Farshore once I got there. Danan was a strange place, full of danger, mystery, and unexpected surprises, but damned if I wasn't beginning to love it. The thought of returning to a normal human city, even one as grand as The City of a Thousand Bells, seemed a dull and dreary prospect in comparison.

"I suppose there will be other ships…"

"One a month, at the least," he said, nodding as though we were discussing the mild weather.

"I could make the trip anytime I wanted, after all."

"Of course you can, love. Anytime at all."

A slow smile crept onto my face. He smiled in return, lifted his mug, and together we toasted to my new home.

The adventure continues in Vaults of the Undergloom ,
the next installment in the Farshore Chronicles

ABOUT THE AUTHOR

I've loved stories for as long as I can remember. As a boy my grandma often told me tales of her adventures growing up on the South Dakota prairie as I drifted off to sleep, or filled my head with faerie queens, questing knights, and everything in between. Those stories shaped the way I saw the world and helped me understand my place in it. Eventually, I realized that I wanted to spin stories that would be just as important for someone else someday.

Pursuing that dream led me into a lifelong pursuit of the writer's craft, both on my own and by learning from some of the most well-regarded professionals in their spheres at the Masters in Creative Writing program at Oxford University.

I grew up in the Blue Ridge mountains of Virginia and was blessed to have a mother who didn't complain when I came home from the woods covered in mud and burs, and a father who told me the stories that sent him out there in the first place.

I live in Colorado with my amazing wife Mindy and pixie in disguise who permits me to claim her as my daughter at parties.

You can connect with me through my website: www.justinfike.com

Or through my Facebook page: www.facebook.com/JustinFikeAuthor/

BOOKS BY JUSTIN FIKE

Farshore Chronicles

Shadows of the Past: Companion novella

* * *

A Thief in Farshore
Into the Shattered City
Crown of a Mad King
Vaults of the Undergloom
Flowers of Belhame
Siege of Farshore

* * *

Farshore Chronicles Box Set: Books 1-3

Printed in Great Britain
by Amazon